PENGUIN BOOKS
SISTERS

Shobha Dé was born in Maharashtra in 1948 and was educated in Delhi and Bombay. She graduated from St. Xavier's College, Bombay, with a degree in psychology. She began a career in journalism in 1970 in the course of which she founded and edited three popular magazines—*Stardust, Society* and *Celebrity* and was Consulting Editor to *Sunday* and *Megacity*. At present, she is a free-lance writer and columnist for several newspapers and magazines. In 1988 she wrote her first novel—the best selling *Socialite Evenings* and in 1990 she published *Starry Nights*.

Shobha Dé is married, with six children. She lives in Bombay and is completing her fourth novel.

SISTERS

SHOBHA DÉ

PENGUIN BOOKS

Penguin Books India (P) Ltd., 11 Community Centre, Panchsheel Park,
New Delhi 110 017, India
Penguin Books Ltd., 80 Strand, London WC2R 0RL, UK
Penguin Putnam Inc., 375 Hudson Street, New York, NY 10014, USA
Penguin Books Australia Ltd., 250 Camberwell Road, Camberwell,
Victoria 3124, Australia
Penguin Books Canada Ltd., 10 Alcorn Avenue, Suite 300, Toronto,
Ontario M4V 3B2, Canada
Penguin Books (NZ) Ltd., Cnr Rosedale and Airborne Roads, Albany, Auckland,
New Zealand
Penguin Books (South Africa) (Pty) Ltd., 24 Sturdee Avenue, Rosebank 2196,
South Africa

First published by Penguin Books India 1992

16   15   14   13

Typeset in Palatino by I.P.P. Catalogue Publications Pvt. Ltd., New Delhi
Made and Printed in India by Swapna Printing Works Pvt. Ltd.

To my parents,
Indira and Govind Rajadhyaksha
my brother, Ashok
and my sisters,
Mandakini and Kunda
— for tolerating me

ONE

Mikki hated white. God, she hated it. Yet, all she could see around her was white this morning. She stared at her hands lying passively in her lap and suppressed a smile. She'd forgotten to remove her nail polish. Ten clots of blood stood out against her white, hand-embroidered kurta. She wiggled her bare toes and studied them. Crimson red toenails against the dead white of the marble flooring. She adjusted a toe-ring absently. Antique silver. She remembered the day she'd bought her first set. She had been fifteen. Abruptly she looked up, her eyes searching for Gangu. God! She was still crying into her crumpled *pallav*. Gangu's huge *bindi* was smeared across her dark forehead and her glass bangles made such an embarrassing jangle each time she rubbed her swollen eyes. People were staring coldly at her. Mikki scanned the assembled crowd for Dhondu. He was probably busy in the kitchen downstairs organizing tea and coffee for everyone. Special tea and coffee, excessively milky and lightly spiced with cardamom. Their home was renowned for both. Visitors often demanded a cup adding, 'How can we leave Seth Hiralal's home without tasting Maltiben's *masala chai*?' An involuntary sigh escaped Mikki. She was so exhausted, she could barely keep her eyes open. She felt like a coffee too. But not Dhondu's brew. American coffee. Strong, black and without sugar. Mikki needed to wake up and face reality.

Mikki's mind drifted back to her toe-rings. How her mother had objected to them! 'Girls in our family do not wear silver toe-rings like the *ghatis*—these are meant for servants. Take them off immediately.' Mikki had ignored her and walked off to show the toe-rings to Gangu—who would appreciate them. But Gangu had surprised Mikki by her reaction: 'Dear God! Has your mother seen these? Quick! Remove them, Sethani will get furious. Girls from good families don't wear such things. And silver! Remember, your mother is a princess. She is entitled to wear gold on her feet.' Mikki had pulled a face and asked Gangu to shut up and get her a fresh orange juice. She had loved her new acquisitions. They had made her feet look so dainty. Mikki knew she had pretty feet with graceful arches. Just like her mother's. Everybody had said she resembled her closely, in every way. Slanted sunlight had filtered in through the trellis outside the broad veranda as Mikki had kicked off her sandals and clicked her brand new toe-rings on the hard marble floor. They had made a lovely sound.

Mikki dreamed that she was dancing, her toe-rings clicking rhythmically...faster, faster, faster. She whirled through the unending corridor...the entire bungalow was beginning to spin around her head. She could hear chants. Voices all around her singing something familiar...her nostrils were filled with a heady fragrance she knew must have come from the joss-sticks in the *puja* room. She heard cymbals and her nose was filled with the slightly sickening smell of stale roses and spider lilies...Mikki awoke with a sharp start as she felt a heavy arm around her shoulders. 'It's all right...we are all here with you. It's all right. You are not alone. Cry...cry a little...it will be good for you. Once the tears come, you will feel better....' Mikki looked up into the small, mean eyes of her aunt, Anjanaben, and pulled away.

Gangu came and stood by her. As soon as she saw that Mikki was observing her, she burst into tears again. Her wails began to annoy the young girl. 'Gangubai, please stop that,' she said, 'what has happened has happened.' Gangu wiped her tears with the *pallav* of her nine-yard sari. 'Baby...God has dealt you a severe blow. You are orphaned...what worse fate can a child suffer? Listen to me, I'm only an illiterate woman, but I have raised you from the day you emerged from your mother's womb. She was too

weak to even suckle you...you are like my own child...this tragedy...' and Gangu broke down once more. Mikki raised her up
gently from the floor where she'd been sitting. 'Go and get me a
coffee,' she said and pushed her out.

The *Times of India* had had a two column photograph of her
father on the front page—the usual one that accompanied his press
releases. 'Industrialist and wife die in air mishap,' the headline had
said. The text had been brief and to the point. The standard bio-data
and the predictable messages from the presidents of various businessmen's clubs and associations. There was a line from the Chief
Minister, another from the Governor. 'A great loss', 'A severe
blow', 'His place can never be taken'. He had been in the obit
column too. And there had been a longer report on page three with
her own picture. At least they could have caught her at a better
angle, she had thought wryly. 'Survived by his only child, a daughter, Mallika, studying at present in the U.S.' The business section
had had a longer profile, tracing Seth Hiralal's rise from a small-
time merchant of scrap to his position, when he died, as the
undisputed tycoon of tycoons with a string of industries to his
name.

Her father had been quite a man, Mikki mused. Quite a bastard
too.

*

Just a few miles away from Mikki's bungalow, in a small suburb
of Bombay, another pair of young eyes was scrutinizing the same
paper. Alisha nudged her mother, 'See...see this! Just look! Nobody has thought of us.' Her mother shifted in the large double-bed
and pushed Alisha's hand away. 'Baby, you are really stupid. Did
you expect to be mentioned or what? Who are we to that family?
Nobodies. You know that. You've always known that. Let me
sleep. As it is, I'm feeling awful. And now you are pushing newspapers in my face.' Alisha continued to read, her eyes narrowing
at the references to Mikki. 'Look at this! Ha, ha! "Survived by his
only child." Mummy, wake up. You must see all this rubbish!
"Only child," she mocked. 'And what about me? What am I? A
puppy? A kitten? A pet?'

The older woman got up, her eyes still heavy with sleep. 'Why
don't you shut up? My Bachchoo is dead. Papa is dead. That is all.

We have to plan on what to do. My head is full of worries about our future. And you are talking all this nonsense. Go… get some tea.' She pushed Alisha off the bed and walked towards the bath-room.

Alisha went into the neat kitchen and woke up the servant-girl. 'Hey…Savita…get up! Memsaab wants tea. Quickly! And my milk. Lazy, lazy, lazy! Sleep all day! Come on—up!' The girl scampered to her feet and put the milk on the boil.

Alisha looked out of the kitchen window. This place was getting so crowded! She remembered growing up in the apartment when there were just four or five buildings around. Vile Parle was a quiet suburb at that time. And now it had become a slum. A filthy slum.

So…he was dead. Alisha thought that over. It was going to make a big difference to her plans. And her mother's. Would she still be able to go to America? Where would she get the money from? He had promised to send her abroad. Promised to pay for everything. She thought of him, of his last visit to their home last week. She'd been nasty. And now Alisha regretted her words. All those accus-ations and harsh words had tumbled out before she could stop them. But how could she have known then, that he would die so suddenly…so soon?

Alisha walked back into her room and started combing her long hair. Her father used to stroke it when she was younger. She used to love those occasions when he'd arrive straight from work and spend the whole evening with them. The whole night too, but that wasn't often.

Alisha looked at the collage of photographs her mother had stuck untidily on a board in her room. Papa had become quite fat during the past two years, she observed. And Mummy too. She smiled, staring at the three of them holidaying in Ooty. X'mas time, four years ago. Alisha was just fifteen then. A pretty fifteen, but nothing compared to the precious Mallika. Just the thought of her half-sister made Alisha screw up her face. Mallika, always Mallika before her. Mummy used to say that when both of them were babies, Papa often mixed them up! He'd call her, Alisha, by the other little girl's name. But she was certain Papa must've been careful enough not to call Mallika by her name—at least not in front of people. And certainly not in front of Mallika's stuck-up mother!

Alisha went to check whether her mother had finished her tea. She found her staring vacantly out of the window. 'Mummy, don't tell me you took those pills again last night,' she scolded. 'Just look at you! Look at your eyes!' Alisha turned away in disgust.

'Please, baby. Not today. As it is I'm feeling terrible. This is a woman's fate. My mother always used to tell me, "Leela, you will have everything in life, but not domestic happiness. It is written here"'… and she tapped her forehead. 'My fate is such. Even my horoscope says that.' Alisha knew she was in for another one of her mother's self-pitying lectures. She sighed and tried to change the subject. 'Mummy, don't you think we should at least go for the funeral?' Her mother stared at her with wide eyes and nearly screamed, 'Are you crazy? *Pagli!* Who will allow us to get inside? Don't you know how that family hates us? How they've insulted us? You want to go there and be thrown out like some street beggar? Never! I may have nothing left, but I still have my pride.' Leelaben reached for her silver *supari* box and started fixing a *paan*. Alisha looked distastefully at what she was doing. 'Mummy, please!' she said sharply. 'Papa used to hate your *paan*. He always fought with you over it. And that too, *tambaaku*. *Chhee!*' Leelaben pleaded with her eyes, 'Baby, I told you…not today. I promise I'll give it up soon. But leave me in peace today.'

Alisha stomped out of the room and slammed the door of her bedroom behind her. She lay down and cursed everyone, including her dead father. Life wasn't fair. Mallika had already been in America for five years. Five years! And here she was stuck in India. Stuck in Bombay. With Papa gone, she'd be stuck forever. She hated college. It was so boring. Papa had promised to send her abroad the following year. Mummy, of course, hadn't wanted her to go. Mummy didn't want her to go anywhere. Not even to her own father's funeral. Rubbish! She would go. Mummy could cry if she wished. But she was not going to hide any longer. She would go and face them all. What could they do to her? What would Mallika do? She wanted to see her face when she walked into their grand bungalow. Everybody would stare. She knew that. So what? Papa's mistress and his illegitimate daughter were known to everyone. They were an 'open secret'—as people called them. Well, she was going to make sure the 'open secret' was made official now. She was going to Shanti Kutir as Seth Hiralal's other daughter—the one he had fathered but never acknowledged.

*

The servants at Shanti Kutir had got up very early to clean the main hall downstairs on the day of the funeral. Thousands of people were expected. Important people. The garlands and flowers had arrived. Mikkiben had overseen most of the arrangements including fresh white covers for the dozens of mattresses spread out on the floor over the large carpets. A very courageous girl. Hardly any tears.

Ramanbhai had also arrived early to supervise the arrangements. Good thing he had turned up, thought Mikki, or else Anjanaben would've interfered and tried to boss everybody around.

The two bodies were laid out on an impressive carpet, under the enormous chandelier in the main hall. They were draped in priceless Jamevar shawls, and Mikki noticed her mother's face was made up and her hair coiffed. She was dressed in one of her countless French chiffon saris. Mikki also noticed that someone had got a bit carried away and applied *sindhoor* in the slight parting of her mother's stylish bouffant. Her mother never wore *sindhoor* when she was alive. Mikki wished she'd been consulted. She looked at her father's face. She hadn't realized till then what a cruel mouth he had. Or did it look like that in death? 'Bachchoobhai' as he was popularly know, lay rigid on his bier, his lips twisted into what looked like a sneer. Mikki wondered whether anybody was sorry to see him go. Was she?

Mikki knew she wouldn't be able to get out of wearing a white sari for the funeral. Anjanaben had opened her mother's huge oak-wood cupboard and pulled out two crisp organdy saris with discreet daisies embroidered all over them. 'Here, Mikki. Wear one of these. Your mother used to love them—and now they are yours.' Then, after a pause, she'd added, 'How silly of me to say that. Everything in this house is yours now. Sad. So sad. A motherless, fatherless child. But we are there, you know that. Kaka, me, your cousins, *ba*, everybody….'Mikki had looked at her, barely concealing her hatred. How she detested her aunt! Then she checked herself. Poor Anjanaben, she thought. Harmless old gossip with nothing to occupy her mundane life. Yes, she could be scheming and manipulative, but so transparently that everybody saw through her. Mikki knew she was prejudiced. Her mother had always maintained a cold distance from this pushy, bossy, loud woman. Mikki recalled her mother's conversations with Papa, complaining about Anjanaben's nosiness and interference. Mikki also remembered her own distaste for her aunt when, as a child, she'd been forced to visit their home to play with Shanay, Anjanaben's only son. Mikki wondered idly if he was still somewhere in the United States, wheeling and dealing like his mother had probably trained him to do. They'd been out of touch for so long.

She felt Anjanaben's eyes on her and forced herself to smile. She took in her embroidered nylon sari, the cheap trinkets, dishevelled hair and darting eyes. Oh well, Mikki sighed, she'd just have to tolerate her. At least for now.

Mikki had heard a few stories about Shanay's *modus operandi* from his proud mother. He had inherited his uncanny instinct for smelling out a deal from her. While Anjanaben concentrated on buying, and subsequently flogging, anything and everything from Ahmedabadi saris to silver-finish serving dishes, Shanay traded in commodities indiscriminately: oil seeds one day, waste-paper the next, chemicals, electrical components, wheat, garments, even second-hand TV sets. From all accounts he was very successful. But sleazy, Mikki shuddered, thinking of the odd call he had made to her campus enquiring solicitously about her health before going on to the real purpose behind the call—'You are knowing anybody wanting cotton bales from India? Good commission also.' Quickly, Mikki reminded herself that Shanay had his better side too. He invariably remembered her birthday and always sent her a small gift—a cheap one, no doubt. Perhaps a free sample lying around. But it touched her that he didn't fail in his duty, year after year. Stray acts of kindness came back to her and she told herself not to feel so hostile. He had his good points, and his uses.

'Remember to keep your *pallav* properly on your shoulders,' Anjanaben said suddenly, bringing Mikki back to the present. Mikki struggled into her mother's sari. She still wasn't comfortable wearing saris, even though she'd been wearing them on festive occasions from the time she was eleven or twelve. Mikki looked at herself in the mirror. She debated about whether or not to line her eyes with a kohl-stick. She didn't feel herself till she had her 'eyes on' as she put it. She created a small *bindi* with a *kaajal* pencil between her brows and adjusted her lacy bra so that the straps wouldn't show. There hadn't been sufficient time for her to get Chandu to stitch a new sari *choli* for her. The old ones were a bit too sexy for such a sombre occasion. Mikki suppressed a giggle. She thought of all the *dhotiyadaases* who'd be present, probably getting an erection at the sight of her breasts peeping out of the low-scooped neckline of her semi-transparent white blouse, through which one could see the cups of her Gossard bra clearly. Let the sex-starved old fogies get their thrills, she thought, as she pleated her sari carefully and yanked it above her navel. Another thing that used to bother her mother. 'Mikki, pull it up, your belly button is being seen.' Mikki would grin, 'That's the whole idea, Mummy,' and sashay out of the room. But today she would be the cynosure of all eyes. She had to dress appropriately for the part fate had so suddenly created for her.

Anjanaben grabbed her arm and led her to the centre of the carpet on the ladies' side of the room. Without a warning, she began to wail. Mikki, startled by the outburst, looked at her aunt sharply. Of course. Anjanaben was performing for the benefit of the assembled women. Mikki blushed with embarrassment as dozens of perfect strangers descended on her, cluck-clucking noisily and wiping away the tears she still hadn't shed with the starched ends of their *pallavs*.

Mikki sat down on a mattress and tried not to listen to the scraps of conversation around her. She was seated with the ladies on one side of the hall. It was an area of the bungalow she used to avoid even as a child. Cold, impersonal, it had been a ballroom at the time the bungalow was constructed. Her father had stripped it clean, removed all the European touches—the gilt cherubs, the elaborate corniches and the heavy velvet drapes. He'd instructed the decorators to make it look Indian. Only the enormous chandelier had been left in place. Today, it gleamed down on the Seth and Sethani, as the congregation broke into its last *bhajan* before the final journey to the simple crematorium by the sea.

It was time. A dozen men came forward and lifted her parents' bodies on to their shoulders. A firm hand helped Mikki up. Her feet felt numb. All that cross-legged sitting had given her pins and needles. Mikki stumbled and once again the same hand steadied her. Flustered, she looked up and met a pair of calm eyes. 'Oh, Ramankaka…. I'm sorry. I don't know what happened. I'm just so tired,' Mikki stammered. He patted her gently and led her out into the sunshine. Mikki caught sight of herself in the mirror-lined passage adjoining the portico, where they now stood, waiting for the bodies to be brought out. God! She looked terrible. And so completely out of place. Her hair had been recently styled. She wore it very short along the sides and at the nape of her neck, and thick on the top. A campus friend had persuaded her to streak it with blond highlights. It had looked terrific. Everybody thought so. It went well with her slightly square-jawed face and the golden strand falling over her almond-shaped, honey-brown eyes gave her a delightfully gamine appearance. She'd acquired a gorgeous tan at Cape Cod that summer, and her nose was peeling. Somehow her new look didn't work in this setting.

Mikki was famished, and thirsty, and tired. She wanted to be alone. And she knew it would be hours before all these people left. And even after that, all the senior members of the family would stay back to console her. That was the tradition. Her aunts would take over the kitchen and the uncles the running of her father's empire. Mikki would be expected to stay home for at least ten days and receive visitors. That's all she needed! Given the choice, Mikki wanted this nightmare to end now. Her parents were dead. There was nobody she cared for. And nobody who cared for her. She wanted to catch the first flight back to Boston. Back to her interrupted semester. Back to her friends. Back to Sean. She was nineteen. Her twentieth birthday was just three months away. She didn't want to be a part of any of this. Her life in India, in Bombay, off Nepean Sea Road, was over. Didn't all these people in white milling around her, know that?

Ramanbhai took Mikki's arm and whispered, 'You've been a brave young lady so far. Keep it up. And don't worry about anything. I'm here for you. We'll show everybody what you are capable of. I've already spoken to the lawyers and they're drawing up the papers. Fortunately your Papa had made a will. That is God's grace. Mallika Hiralal, I'm privileged to inform you that starting tomorrow, you—yes you—are the head of Hiralal Industries! And now, hold your head high and face the world. Let everybody here know that henceforth they will be dealing with you.' Before Mikki could recover from the impact of his words, she heard the rhythmic chanting of the priests as the two flower-bedecked bodies of her parents were brought out of the house by her uncles and male cousins. '*Ram naam satya hai, Ram naam satya hai,*' said the fat priests, and the lines were soon taken up by the others. The sun was fairly high in the sky by now. Its hot, harsh rays hit Mikki straight in the eyes, blinding her momentarily.

Suddenly there was some sort of a disturbance and everyone's attention was drawn away from the two bodies. Mikki looked up to see what the noise was about. She took in the slim, tall figure of a striking-looking young girl arguing with Ramankaka and a couple of her other uncles in the portico leading into the hall. 'My God! What an attractive female,' thought Mikki before wondering who on earth she was. She continued to stare while the girl raised her voice and insisted on coming in. Mikki was confused for a minute. Why would anybody try and stop a person from attending a funeral? It just wasn't done. On such occasions, everybody who wished to be present was given free access. Why was Ramankaka stopping her? She didn't look like an undesirable character. On the contrary, this one was a stunner. Mikki looked again more closely. Wait a minute. There had to be some mistake. Wasn't she a relative? Where had Mikki seen her? She couldn't take her eyes off the shapely figure framed against the imposing gates. Mikki thought with amusement—'We could be sisters!' There was a resemblance. A pretty strong one. Except for the girl's lovely long hair, and the way she was dressed, there were many similarities; particularly the way the girl held her head at an angle. And the way she tossed back her hair. Mikki was mesmerized by her. But she knew she couldn't just walk over and solve the mystery. That would have to wait till later. She watched the girl turn her back finally and march away with defiant steps. Mikki liked the way her slim hips swung from side to side. The bright sun filtered through the girl's white Lucknowi kurta and Mikki could see her contours clearly.

Ramankaka seemed very agitated and Mikki could see him talking urgently to the others. At one point she thought she saw them all looking at her pointedly. Oh well! There were other things to think about right now.

*

Ramanbhai was waiting for Mikki in the library. 'Beti, there are many things we have to discuss. I have a lot to tell you. Now that all the condolence visits and ceremonies are over, we need to talk about your future and the future of your father's industries. I have arranged meetings with the solicitors, chartered accountants and, of course, the various boards of Seth Hiralal's companies. We need to get your appointment finalized at the soonest to avoid complications.' Mikki stared at him blankly. 'It's much too soon...' she started to say. Ramanbhai cut her short, 'No, my dear. We have to act swiftly. Have you seen the business papers? The stocks have dipped. Shareholders are getting nervous. The market is down as it is. We cannot afford to waste time. I can understand what you must be going through. But the world is a cruel place. There are enough vultures waiting to pounce on you, I don't want anybody to take advantage of your present state of mind. And remember, do not sign anything given by anyone without checking with me first.'

Thank God for Ramankaka, thought Mikki. He was one person she could always trust. One person who'd have to stand in for her father now that he was no more. He had enough training in that department anyway. On umpteen occasions it had been Ramanbhai, and not Seth Hiralal, who had escorted her and her mother to various functions. She remembered one particular occasion clearly, when it had broken her heart not to have her father present. It was the day she had led her victorious school team. Mikki headed the march-past at the Inter School Athletics Meet. She was Games Captain that year and more than anything else, she'd wanted both her parents, not just her mother, to witness her hour of glory. Mikki's eyes had scanned the stadium stands anxiously, searching for them. Instead, she'd caught Ramankaka's friendly face and her heart had broken. He'd tried hard to make up for her obvious disappointment by taking her mother and her for a grand treat at the Taj Mahal Hotel later that evening. But he had also sensed that the young girl's spirits were not in the celebration. He had patted her head affectionately and whispered, 'Next year, I promise, I'll get him here. I'll make him cancel all his meetings.' Mikki had stared at him, her eyes swimming with tears and sobbed, 'Next year won't matter. Someone else will be Games Captain, not me.' Embarrassed, Ramankaka had looked away, but not before Mikki had seen the tears in his eyes.

Mikki placed her hand on Ramanbhai's arm and stopped him. 'Before we talk about anything else,' she said, her voice suddenly adult and firm, 'I want to ask you something. And I expect an honest answer.'

Ramanbhai looked at her questioningly with a new expression in his eyes. Mikki continued, 'Tell me...I noticed a girl at the funeral the other day. My age. In fact she even looked a little like me. You prevented her from coming in. Why? She seemed like a decent person. Thousands of strangers attended the ceremony. So why was she not allowed in?'

Ramanbhai evaded Mikki's searching gaze. 'We'll discuss this matter some other time,' he answered abruptly, and got up to leave.

Mikki's voice was sharp and loud as she commanded, 'No! Now! I want to know. I have every right to know. And I'd like an answer right away.'

Ramanbhai shifted uncomfortably on his feet before answering slowly, 'All right. Since that is your stand I'll tell you. The girl you saw is your father's daughter from another woman, a long-time mistress. The girl's name is Alisha. She was born four months after you. She lives with her mother in Vile Parle. What else do you want to know?' Mikki did not answer him immediately. Then, softly she said, 'A sister? A half-sister? My sister? Alisha. What a nice name. Why wasn't I told about her? Why did Mummy never tell me—or Gangu? Or Dhondu? Or you, Ramankaka, for that matter?'

Ramanbhai paused for a long time before telling Mikki, 'Your father didn't want me to. He saw no reason for you to know about his other life.'

Mikki's eyes were beginning to flood. She'd never felt this betrayed before. Her father, always distant, now seemed a total stranger. A stranger who'd led a sneaky double life.

'And Mummy? What about her? Did she know?' Ramanbhai nodded his head, 'Yes, Maltiben knew.' 'Why couldn't she have told me?' Mikki choked while asking. Ramanbhai drew her to him. 'You were far too young at that time. You wouldn't have understood. Besides, what was the point in upsetting you?' Mikki's sobs started to emerge in great shudders, 'I hate all of you for this. It's not fair at all. And now Papa and Mummy are gone. I'll never know the truth about what really happened.'

Ramanbhai allowed her to cry, stroking her hair gently and patting her slim shoulders. 'Baby, all that is in the past. The chapter is closed. Your father is dead, and with it, his other life and other attachments. You have to think ahead, plan ahead. We have to talk seriously now about business matters. I'll expect you in Papa's office tomorrow morning, to meet the others. Don't be nervous. And don't commit yourself to anything. If there's something you don't understand, just look at me and delay your answer by saying,

"I'll have to think that over." After the meeting, you and I will go over the whole thing and make the right decisions, OK?'

Mikki nodded absently. As Ramankaka left the room she thought desperately, Oh, if only I had somebody I could really talk to. Anyone. Sean was too far away. In any case, he wouldn't really be able to connect with what was going on at that distance in a country that was so alien to him. Mikki had heard someone use the word 'orphan', Gangu perhaps, during the funeral. What an awful ring it had to it! It was hard to think of herself as that—a rich, little, orphan. Mikki looked up and Alisha's image flashed before her eyes. Suddenly it occurred to Mikki that she was not alone. She had a sister. A younger sister. And she wasn't going to let her go. Mikki rushed back into her room. She was going to find out everything she could about Alisha. She was going to phone her as soon as she could get hold of her number. And she was going to invite her to come home. Mikki was determined to claim the only blood relative she had left.

TWO

'Hello...I'd like to speak to Alisha Mehta, please,' said a female voice when Leelaben groped for the phone, and held it to her ear. It was close to ten o'clock, and Leelaben's head was still woozy. She hated waking up these days. She answered the caller in Gujarati, using her rustic accent. It was far too early in the day for her to remember to switch to the other, more cultivated one. In any case, these calls were such a nuisance. Alisha's friends didn't have the decency to wait till noon before picking up the phone and dialling their number. 'What's your name?' Leelaben asked rudely. There was a slight pause before the person replied, also in Gujarati but the refined, *shudh* variety favoured by snobbish upper-crust Ahmedabadi families. 'My name is Mallika Hiralal. Am I speaking to Leela Mehta?' Leelaben nearly jumped out of bed. She was suddenly wide awake, but her speech was still slow thanks to the pills she'd popped the previous night. She began stammering, not quite sure how to handle the call. 'Yes, yes, yes—that is, I am Leelaben. But, but, I mean, Alisha is sleeping... I mean she has gone to college...let me see if she is at home...maybe she is in her own room… I picked up the extension in my room…hold on, hold on, one minute….'

Mikki waited. She was pretty nervous herself, only she knew how to disguise it, at least so far as her voice was concerned. Her hand, holding the phone receiver, was gripping the instrument so tight that her knuckles were white with the strain. The woman's voice intrigued her. It was crude and slurred, like a *banjaran's*. Just the sound of it made Mikki uneasy. Her father had been such a fastidious man. So finicky about such things. She remembered how he'd inspect her mother thoroughly before stepping out for a party, often asking her to change her sari, or replace an old handbag with a new one. She also had distinct memories of him subjecting her to a similar scrutiny, often reprimanding her for dirty fingernails or for wearing ill-matched socks with her English shoes. Table manners, too, had been a fetish with him. Mikki would suppress the urge to giggle whenever they had relatives to lunch or dinner—particularly Anjanaben who couldn't resist a resounding belch or two after a meal. Mikki's father was an aesthete who responded to beauty—music, painting, flowers and sunsets. This woman didn't sound like his type. Mikki couldn't wait to see her…and her daughter, of course.

She held on to the reciever, overhearing a commotion over the crackling of the bad phone connection. There was a great deal of door-pounding and shouting, before she picked up the sound of stiletto heels click-clacking their way over bare floors to the telephone. 'Hello?' The voice was sexy, slightly hoarse, and low in the throat. 'This is Mikki—Mallika Hiralal—you don't know me, but I've just found out that we are, you know, related…sort of….through Papa, I mean, my father…and yours. I'd like to meet you whenever you are free. Is that possible?' Silence. Mikki tried to picture the girl at the other end. She was obviously thinking. Mikki waited. After a few seconds, Alisha said, 'What for?' Mikki detected the hostility and defiance in her voice. 'Well…' she continued, more sure of herself now that she sensed the other girl's vulnerability, 'I think it's important for both of us to get to know one another. Don't you?' Alisha snorted, 'Really? After all these years? I knew all about you, my dear, even though you may not have known about me. I see no reason why I should go out of my way to meet you when I've survived for so long on my own. In any case, I did see you at the funeral when your people did not have the decency to allow me to pay my last respects to my father.'

Alisha's voice cracked and Mikki hastened to apologize: 'Please believe me when I say I didn't even know of your existence at that point. I saw you, I noticed you, but I didn't know what the problem was or why they'd stopped you from coming in. It was so awkward for me...I couldn't intervene—it was the wrong time. I can only say how sorry I am that such an awful thing took place. Please accept what I'm saying... and let's meet. I'm all alone. We could be friends. That's all I ask....' Alisha hesitated before saying, 'No, I'm sorry too. But I don't trust you. Maybe you are lying to me. Someone must've told you to buy me and my mother off in case we create trouble for you. Don't worry about that. We may not be rich like you, but we have our self-respect. We value our independence. Papa—yes, I called him that too—looked after us for so many years. I'm sure he must have left at least a little for me and my mother. He'd promised to send me to America next year. To study there—like you. Maybe I wouldn't have got admission into Wharton or any other fancy university, but I would have managed to get in somewhere. Now, I suppose, I'll have to forget all those dreams and plans. But I don't give up so easily. I will find a way. I'll apply for scholarships and I'll go on my own. So, Miss Hiralal, I don't need to meet you ever. And please...do me a favour...don't phone again.'

Mikki was taken aback by Alisha's rush of bitter words. As she listened to her she told herself to stay calm and not react. Before Alisha slammed down the phone, Mikki managed to say, 'I'd like to help you. Please...' Before she could finish her sentence, Alisha all but screamed, 'I don't need your fucking charity. Get it?' and hung up.

Mikki continued to hold the receiver for a long while, going over her conversation with Alisha, her half-sister. Almost grudgingly, Mikki had to admit that she liked what she'd heard. She'd already approved of what she had seen. Alisha sounded like quite a woman. And now, more than ever, Mikki was determined to meet her and win her over. She'd find a way. And soon.

*

Seth Hiralal's offices were located at Nariman Point. He owned Hiralal Towers. It was a property he had been particularly proud of. He'd acquired it twelve years earlier as part of a major take-over deal. Before that, his companies' offices had been scattered through the Fort area, with Seth Hiralal sitting in an old-fashioned setting, surrounding by *dhoti*-clad accountants and clerks. With the acquisition of a sick tyre company, Hiralal had swung the deal of the decade—prime real estate in Bombay's most expensive and prestigious business area. He had promptly renamed the high-rise after himself and hired a high-profile architect to re-do and refashion the premises to house all his companies, retaining an entire floor for his own office and the offices of the top executives of his holding company.

When Mikki walked into her father's office for the board meeting she was struck by its opulence. Hiralal's 'suite' stretched over five thousand square feet of highly polished granite. His table, a massive slab of Italian marble, was as big as a room itself, and devoid of papers. Discreetly placed below eye level were a set of buttons that electronically controlled everything, including various doors leading in and out of the vast office. Hiralal had been very proud of all the latest gizmos installed by his interior designer, a high-society lady who mesmerized her clients with an impressive show of cleavage, as much as by the pricey *objets d'art* she talked them into buying. Mikki stared at the silver-framed photographs of herself and her perfectly groomed mother and thought how ironic it was that her father should've spent a major portion of his day with both of them observing him, while his loyalties remained elsewhere—with two other women whose existence she had just discovered. She noticed Ramanbhai looking at her. Almost as if he was reading her mind he said: 'Your father loved you very much. He also loved your mother.' Mikki smiled up at him, 'Yes, Ramankaka, I know. But right now I'm more interested in those areas of his life I didn't know about.' Ramanbhai stood near Seth Hiralal's table and held out his hand, indicating the leather wing chair, 'Please... do sit down. This is where you belong now.' Mikki hesitated before sliding in behind the table and occupying the place her father had so suddenly vacated. 'The others will be joining us soon. But before they arrive, I want to brief you on a few things.' Mikki looked at him questioningly. 'His will...well, I think there are some complications there that need to be sorted out. Your mother's will is fortunately very clear and you inherit everything. All her jewellery, assets, properties. But I'm still in the process of sorting out your father's legal papers. That will take time.'

Mikki was sure Ramanbhai was keeping something from her. 'You aren't telling me everything. All I need to know is, what state has he left his companies in—healthy or not. And if not—what can be salvaged and what dumped.'

Ramanbhai smiled indulgently, 'How simple you make business sound! If only things were so uncomplicated.'

'Aren't they?' Mikki asked, just as she heard the secretary buzz the intercom to announce the arrival of the other board members. Mikki straightened her shoulders. She'd chosen to wear a silk business suit with softly contoured lines. Sexy without being blatant, yet severe enough to be taken seriously. Her cream-coloured silk shirt felt sensuous next to her skin. She was wearing her mother's pearls. She twisted her father's signet ring which she had taken to wearing, to give her confidence. 'For good luck,' she'd told herself while dressing that morning, little realizing just how badly she was going to need it.

Amazingly, the board meeting went off smoothly. Mikki had expected hostility, resistance, even scorn. But as she faced the ten men across the Italian marble table of her father's impressive board room, she sensed sympathy, yes, but also a grudging sense of respect as she addressed them. Her voice had sounded ridiculously small and kiddish to her own ears, especially during the first two minutes. And then, she'd found some hitherto unknown strength as she held forth confidently and firmly, outlining her resolve to head her father's empire and steer his companies towards the path of even greater success. Frequently murmured 'hear hears' reassured Mikki that she was saying all the right things—and more importantly, that she was being taken seriously. Or, if all ten of them were pretending, they were doing a bloody good job of it!

She made eye contact by turn. With each sentence she spoke, she knew she was saying goodbye to all her previous dreams. There was no going back any more. She had committed herself to Hiralal Industries for life. That was going to be her future, her destiny. While she continued with her speech, the images from her immediate past flashed by: goodbye Sean, she thought. And goodbye Wharton. No more campus life. No more chasing an MBA, no more being a student on one of the best campuses in the United States. Mallika Hiralal was all set to make her way in the corporate world as the undisputed queen of a cluster of companies her father had built from scratch. Mikki squared her shoulders and raised her chin as she made her concluding remarks. She thought she saw approval in Ramanbhai's eyes as he watched her.

She was glad she'd woken up earlier than usual that morning to prepare herself. At first the stack of company reports and balance sheets had confused her completely. But she had told herself they had to be scanned. Her father would have done it that way—and she'd plunged in bravely. Half an hour into the sheafs and the figures began speaking to her. With increasing excitement she discovered a clear picture was beginning to form in her mind about companies whose names she'd barely heard. She'd decided to concentrate on the holding company—named after her—and base her talk on that. She'd also familiarized herself with the backgrounds of the board members making sure to memorize their names.

Now, as she stood around with the men over cups of coffee brought in by her father's old secretary, Mrs D'Souza, she felt a peculiar thrill coursing through her veins as Mr Shah, Mr Alimchandani, Mr Jeejibhoy and Mr Chopra, spoke to her without a trace of condescension. She was glad for Ramanbhai's unobtrusive but constant presence by her side. It was almost as if he was standing in for Papa.

After the others had left she turned to him and asked, 'So, Ramankaka, how did I do?' He put his arm around her and said, 'I'm very proud of you. So would your father have been. You deserve a special lunch. Shall we go to the club? I need to talk to you at length. There are certain aspects that have to be discussed in privacy. I didn't want to raise these issues in front of the others.' Mikki looked at him quizzically, searching for clues. But his expression was impassive. He placed a kindly arm around her shoulders and led the way out of the office. Mikki thought she saw Mrs D'Souza pull a face.

The lunch quickly dampened Mikki's high spirits. Ramanbhai revealed figures that were startlingly at variance with those printed in the balance sheets. She tried to probe and question Ramanbhai but he deflected all her inquiries with a polite but firm, 'Not now. I'll let you know the correct picture later, after I've had meetings with the solicitors and accountants.' Ramanbhai again avoided giving her a direct reply when they discussed her father's will. Finally, in frustration, she put down her fork and said, 'I expect forthright answers from you. Do not fob me off with vague figures.

Facts. I'm looking for facts, Ramankaka. I should've known my handling of the board meeting this morning wouldn't have convinced you of my capability. I'm in charge now. And I'm capable of dealing with whatever it is you have to tell me.' Mikki didn't realize she'd raised her voice sufficiently for other members to stare at their table. She stopped herself, flushed, and apologized. The bearer was bending low to remove their plates. Mikki could smell the coconut oil in his hair. She looked around her and noticed the others in the dining hall. A few members smiled and waved. She didn't recognize anybody. In any case, she was the only woman there. Giving herself time to think she ordered a black coffee and sat back wondering whether or not to light a cigarette.

Mikki didn't really enjoy smoking. In fact, she didn't even inhale. Yet it was a pose she rather fancied and it gave her something to do with her hands when she was nervous. Like right now, facing Ramanbhai and waiting for the next bomb she was certain he was going to drop. He waited till the bearer had served the coffee before saying, 'Your father had formed a trust ten years ago.' Mikki took a sip, grimaced and said, 'So?'

'Well…the thing is the trust is not in your name, or your mother's name,' Ramanbhai added looking uncomfortable. Mikki looked out at the emerald green golf course and then back at him. 'In that case, it must be in Alisha's name, right?' Ramanbhai nodded. 'Well…I don't grudge her that. She was his daughter, after all. Poor girl, she could never get that recognition, let her at least have some money. There's a lot of it to go around surely… ' Mikki started to say, then stopped when she saw Ramanbhai shaking his head and fidgeting with his napkin, 'That is the problem, my dear. That is what I have avoided telling you.'

Mikki stared hard at him, 'What do you mean? What are you trying to tell me?' Ramanbhai answered slowly, deliberately, 'The simple truth is this—Alisha has all the money. You don't.' Mikki clutched the sides of her chair. The signet ring began cutting into her fingers. 'But that's impossible. How can she have all the money when it's mine?'

Ramanbhai signalled to her to keep her voice down. 'It's complicated. The trust was set up ten years ago. A great deal of money had been transferred into it. That was reinvested many times over. The clauses of the trust were such that the money couldn't be touched. Alisha was to inherit it all when she turned twenty.

Nobody had access to that money, not even Alisha's mother. It was a fund set up by your father to see her through college, take care of her marriage and, perhaps, provide her the capital if she wished to go into business. This was done in a way that protected your interests in his companies. Alisha has nothing to do with those and Seth Hiralal had made sure she wouldn't be in a position to make any claims at a later date. But things have changed. We've had a very bad year. Our profits have plummeted this quarter. Last year was also bad. Two consecutive bad years can play havoc with a company's finances. Your father had borrowed heavily from financial institutions in an effort to pull out of the rut. We have huge debts on our hands. He lost heavily on the Malaysian joint venture. He also burnt his fingers in the Singapore deal. Our American collaborators pulled out at the last minute from that huge plant we were setting up in Orissa. All in all, it was bad luck for your father. His *jyotish* had told him his stars were bad, very bad. He was at the tail end of his *sadesati* period—you know that seven-year cycle when Saturn rules your life? He'd been advised not to travel, not to go into any new business and not to take any risks. But your father was a headstrong man. I tried to warn him. He was off to Baroda to sign a new deal. A deal he had been advised against by all of us. Anyway, he is no more. And there is no point in looking back. We have to face the truth—and the truth is this—Hiralal Industries is in trouble. There are huge loans to be paid off. The interest is mounting every day. There is virtually no capital. Your father had diverted funds into several high-risk projects in the hope of raising money to pay off creditors. His public issue was a flop even though we managed to cover up, using our pull in the press. Soon, very soon, news would have been out in the market that the companies were on the brink of financial collapse. Just last month the share market was buzzing with all sorts of rumours about a possible take-over or a merger. We can keep this quiet for just a little while longer. But not much more than a week or a fortnight. As it is, the newspapers have been phoning and carrying small reports about the uncertainty in the wake of your father's death. We have to plan a future strategy immediately. I'm afraid the news is bad, Mallika, and we might have to consider liquidating a few assets to raise the money required.'

Mikki's hands were ice-cold. She snapped open her tan-coloured handbag and pulled out a cigarette from a silver case. One flick of the Cartier lighter and it was lit. She watched the smoke curl into a snake above her head and get sucked in by the air conditioner. Finally, she said tonelessly, 'I'm broke. Flat broke. That's what you're telling me. Right?' After a pause she heard Ramanbhai's voice. 'Right.' It was time to tip the bearer discreetly and leave the club. As the two of them waited in the foyer for her father's Mercedes to drive up, Mikki started to laugh. Ramanbhai looked at her in alarm. 'Are you all right? What are you laughing at?' Mikki pressed her fingers into his arm and said, 'Life.'

*

Mikki's chance to meet Alisha came soon enough. She had finally accepted her old friend, Navin's, invitation to spend an evening at The 1900's—the chic nightclub favoured by the richie-rich kids of city industrialists, starlets on the make, social prowlers and other nightbirds who danced the nights away to the insistent throb of international chart-busters played by a chatty deejay. It wasn't Mikki's kind of place at all. After her five years in the US, she preferred her outings elegant and quiet. A gourmet meal in a romantic setting, or a light supper at an efficient brasserie. Sean had initiated her into enjoying forbidden pleasures such as non-vegetarian delicacies her mother would've disowned her for tasting, and champagne with peach brandy, which had become her favourite cocktail ever since she'd sipped it at a trendy off-campus bar six months after arriving in the United States.

But Navin's persistence had made her relent. In any case, Mikki thought she'd earned a night in town, after her high pressure existence of the preceding days. For the evening she opted for a black taffeta outfit. A daring little dress with a beaded bodice, which was cut slyly to push her breasts up and pinch her waist in. She liked what she saw in the mirror as she dressed, lingering over her accessories—black silk stockings, black patent leather heels and a Chanel bag to match. Her hair looked all wrong with such a sophisticated ensemble. On an impulse, she squeezed some gel on to her palms and sleeked it over her head. Hair taken entirely off her face. The new look went perfectly with the dress and high-lighted her delicate bone structure to advantage. She snapped on her mother's ancient Van Cleef and Arpel's diamond earrings (bequeathed by Mikki's grandmother) and smiled at her image in the mirror. She looked smashing and she knew it.

Navin was speechless as he watched Mikki climbing down the curved marble stairway as he stood in the portico waiting for her. 'You look great,' he exclaimed. 'So do you,' she said with a laugh. 'Terrific! Now that we have our mutual admiration society going, let's go kick up a riot…' Navin said, helping her into the front seat of his BMW. He swung in easily beside her and switched on the ignition. 'Here's to a ride I hope you won't forget,' he said before leaning forward to kiss the nape of her neck. Mikki stiffened, aware that the night-watchman was staring at the two of them and would pass on what he'd just seen to all the other security-men, drivers and domestics. She gently pushed Navin away saying, 'Let's hit the road first, O.K.?' He grinned back at her and shifted the powerful car into gear.

When they reached the hotel the *Sardar durwan* took the car keys and Navin smoothly slipped him a tenner greeting him with a cheerful, *Sat Sri Akal*. Mikki slid out gracefully making sure to keep her knees together. Some of the low-slung cars these days required great expertise to get in and out of without flashing your panties, she thought, as she tugged at her hemline. Navin self-consciously adjusted his cropped-off evening jacket and flicked back a strand of moussed hair. They walked up the marble steps of the Taj Mahal Hotel and into the crowded lobby. Mikki could feel the eyes on her as they walked across the long stretch of marble before getting to the poolside and into the dimly lit discotheque, where they were greeted by half a dozen voices.

'Mikki,' said a cat-like creature in a sequined sweater, 'we didn't expect to see you so soon after…I mean, I'm sorry, *yaar*, but I thought you *gujjus* have a long-long mourning period or something.' Mikki ignored the outstretched hand and moved towards one of the more secluded alcoves. She didn't need this. Not now. She was aware she had broken the rules by stepping out in public so soon after her parents' deaths. But she'd decided she wasn't going to be a hypocrite and sit around at home pretending to be in mourning like the others from her community, who used this period more as an extended gossip-session than anything else. She didn't want to get involved with aunts and uncles and cousins whom she wasn't at all close to. Anjanaben had tried to move in and take over the kitchen telling Mikki she was too inexperienced to handle such things, particularly in her state. But Mikki had firmly rejected her offer and just as well. Anjanaben's slimy son was coming back to town and Mikki guessed he was dying to worm his way into her favour.

She ordered a fresh orange juice for herself while Navin opted for a whisky ('Single Malt, please'). Mikki began wondering what she was doing in this place. Two years ago, she would've given anything to be there. And now, as she surveyed the dancers gyrating on the small floor and glanced at the people in adjoining alcoves, she wanted to get up and leave. With a start Mikki realized how much she'd changed in the five years she'd been away. This used to be 'her scene'. This was 'her crowd'. She should have been entirely at home in this place. And yet, she felt alienated and alone. Mikki shuddered involuntarily as she thought of the person she'd been. How shallow she must've appeared to casual observers. And how spoilt. She remembered her mother's disapproval each time she breezed into her bed-room to sing out, 'Bye.... I'm off...see you later, Mummy,' dressed in outfits her mother considered outrageous. God! She must've looked pretty awful—like all those creatures boogeying on the dance floor, she thought, her critical eye sweeping the floor. And yet she'd revelled in that life. Looked forward to flirting lightly, discarding boyfriends and designer outfits with equal nonchalance. She suppressed a smile at the memories...at the hearts she'd broken and the money she'd blown up. Just then, she spotted Alisha. She was with an escort—a good-look-ing one. Mikki noted her clothes—sexy but in a trampy way—and disapproved of what she'd done to her long hair. How much better she'd looked on the day of the funeral, she mused. Spon-taneously she got up and started walking towards her table. Navin called after her, 'Hey...where do you think you're going, babe? Don't tell me you want to groove all by yourself.' Mikki paid no attention to him.

Alisha could barely concentrate on what the handsome young man was saying to her above the din of the music. She had watched her half-sister walk in and then resolutely turned her face away. The dance floor was crowded as it generally was on Wednesday nights. It was the one night of the week when the entrance fee to the disco was halved to attract the crowd that stayed away on weekends, intimidated by the 250 rupees per head charge. Alisha was wearing a hot pink mini dress in clinging jersey. The sort of outfit her papa would've disapproved of. 'So what...he's dead now,' she'd said to herself as she'd dressed. Her mother had looked up from her glass of rum and Thums Up ('I need something to help me through the next few hours') to ask, 'So...where are you going...and dressed like that?' Alisha had replied shortly, 'I'm going out. And there's nothing wrong with my dress. Everybody wears clothes like these. Even the precious Mallika.'

'Don't talk about her. She is nothing to us. I don't know why you keep bringing her into our life. From the time you were a child, you used to compare yourself to her. How many times had Papa told you, "Mikki is Mikki and you are you?" But no! Always jealous. Always angry. And going to the funeral when I'd forbidden you. Disobedient, that's what you are and always have been. Did you enjoy being insulted by that *haraami*, Ramanbhai? Who is he? Papa's servant, an employee. And he dared to shout at you in the presence of all those people. I'm so ashamed....' With that she'd trailed off, her mind wandering on to some unrelated topic.

Alisha knew she'd lost her to another world, a world made hazy by booze and pills. Her contempt for her mother was growing with every passing day and it was hard for her to disguise it. All that show of sorrow! Huh! It wasn't as if she'd been true and faithful to Papa. How many scenes, how many tantrums this very room had seen! Alisha recalled some of her mother's lovers, including a family chauffeur. She remembered her father storming into their apartment and confronting her. And her mother's drunken giggle before Papa's hand came smashing into her face. Alisha shuddered at the memory of the countless times her mother would sneak into her room followed by some awful looking man she'd probably picked up at a party. And Alisha would like awake in her bed listening to their tinny laughter followed later by grunts and moans. The chink of glasses with the clink of ice and the smoke of cheap cigarettes curling out from under the door. Alisha had accepted the fact a long time ago—her mother was a slut.

Alisha switched back to the present and her companion. 'Guess who's walking our way? That Mikki something whose fat cat father just died. Hey, do you know you resemble the rich bitch?'

Alisha glared at him, 'Don't ever say that to me again. Get it? I am me. Alisha Mehta. I have nothing to do with that other female.' The young man held up his hands, 'Cool it! I just thought you looked alike. That's it. You could pass off as sisters.'

'Fuck you, wise guy,' Alisha snarled, turning her back on her escort—and found herself staring straight at Mikki's slim midriff.

'Hi!' Mikki said, her voice friendly. 'I'm Mallika—Mikki. We spoke to each other over the phone, remember? What a surprise!' Alisha jerked her head up and looked into Mikki's eyes. 'Bitch!' she hissed. Her companion put his hand on her arm. By then Navin had sauntered over, muttering, 'What's going on? What's the scene, man?'

Alisha got up. Mikki thought she was going to hit her. Instead, she stubbed out her cigarette and headed for the door. Mikki waited before following her, guessing she was on her way to the loo. She found her there, freshening her lipstick.

'What do you want?' Alisha demanded. 'Why don't you just leave me alone?'

Mikki looked at her quietly before saying, 'I want us to be friends, Alisha. Just that. Nothing else. I'm reaching out to you as someone who is a part of my life, whether you like it or not. You can't just walk away. Not after you know and I know the truth. Why are you so angry with me? What have I ever done to you? We are sisters—nothing can change that, don't you see?' There were tears in Mikki's eyes and her voice was breaking.

Alisha began brushing her hair vigorously, staring back coldly at her image in the mirror. 'Yes,' she said 'I do see we are sisters. You have all the money, all the status, our father's name, his home, everything. And I have nothing. That is the difference.'

Mikki tried to put her arm around her. 'That's what I want to change—if you give me the chance. Please. Let us not fight. We need each other….'

Alisha arched an eyebrow, and said, 'Do we? I don't need you, baby. If you need me, it will be on my terms. And when I decide I need you. Got that?' Alisha checked her lipstick, adjusted her dress and left without sparing her another glance.

*

'We will have to do something quickly,' Anjanaben spoke urgently to her myopic husband leaning over his crossword puzzle. 'Are you paying attention?' she asked impatiently. He looked up vaguely. 'Do what?' he asked squinting up at his wife, whose eyes were darting around their cramped flat. 'Call Shanay back immediately. This is our chance. Why waste time in Antwerp hanging around like a servant in some diamond merchant's office when he can come home and get into Hiralal Industries?' Her husband filled in the word that had been eluding him. Anjanaben roughly pulled the newspaper out of his hands. 'When are you going to learn to look after your family? We've had such a useless life. One servant, two bedrooms, no car, nothing. What is the point of living like this? Don't you want your son to succeed? Or do you think he should also be like you...a failure? Mallika is alone. She is young. She needs people. She needs a husband. Shanay will be right for her. They've known each other since they were children. We shouldn't waste any time. Before some other man grabs her, we should send a proposal. Or no. She might not like that. But we should get Shanay to live here with us and then approach her. If it works out properly, he will take over Hiralal Industries. Can't you understand such a simple thing? The girl is like a small mouse with vultures all around just waiting to pounce on her. I'm going there today to see her, offer my help. Poor thing. How will she cope with all those many servants, drivers, ayahs, *bais*? Her mother was good at all that. But then Maltiben was a *rajkumari*, she'd been taught how to manage a large house by her mother. *Maharani sahiba* was a wise woman. Got Maltiben married quickly before anybody discovered her secret. Anyway, not that having a weak heart is something so bad. Now she's dead in a plane crash. Otherwise also, she would've died young. Her maids from the palace had told me the truth at the wedding itself. Nobody listened to me. I don't know about her daughter. She looks quite strong. Anyway, let us get Shanay back first and then we shall see.'

Himanshubhai, Anjanaben's husband, looked at her ample figure as she went into the bedroom to change into a better sari. He hadn't heard most of what she'd said. He'd been far too busy searching for a seven-letter word that meant seclusion.

THREE

'Baby…it's me. Remember? Shanay? Long time no see, hunh? You know how *Ba* is—she said, "Phone, phone." So I said, "O.K., *chalo*, no problem. I'll give her a buzz. Why not?" As soon as she phoned me, gave me the bad news about Uncle and Aunty, I returned. Really bad, isn't it? You must be so lonely? Should I come over? Or maybe you can come to a hotel? We'll have a cup a coffee or something? What say?'

Mikki heard him out. She was barely awake. She had a tough day at the office ahead of her, and here was this pest. But she didn't want to be rude. 'Why don't you meet me at the office first and then we'll talk about our coffee date,' Mikki said sleepily. The eagerness in his voice was unmistakable—same old Shanay, she thought. Always eager, like an over-enthusiastic puppy. She climbed out of bed and started on her morning routine. There was just so much to do, it sometimes depressed her thinking about it. A few weeks ago she'd been a carefree student romping around an enormous campus with Sean. And now, each morning, she awoke with a huge weight on her shoulders. She would have a rushed morning as usual. She figured she'd just have to fit in Shanay somewhere.

As she dressed quickly, in yet another sober pin-striped business suit, she marvelled at her local *darzi* who'd copied a Lauren design to perfection. She preferred to dress in these suits rather than saris, but it seemed to bother her father's employees. It had been brought to her attention by Mrs D'Souza who had hesitantly put it to her that perhaps she'd fit in better and quicker if she switched to Indian clothes. Mikki had immediately rejected her suggestion, but now, as she slipped into her hip-length, double-breasted jacket, she began to wonder whether it wasn't worth considering an ethnic make-over—perhaps one of those super-exclusive *salwar-kameezes* with padded shoulders that made a woman look like a cross between a *Dallas* bitch and a local cabaret star.

Mikki got to the office around ten o'clock—which was early by her father's standards. He arrived close to noon, which used to puzzle her. He did leave their home at nine-fifteen sharp! But now she'd got it figured out—obviously he'd used the time to visit Alisha and her mother! No wonder her own mother had hated to receive calls asking, 'Is the Seth still at home? We are waiting for him…meeting with marketing people at ten-thirty.' It was hard for Mikki to visualize her father in bed with Leelaben…or rather, any woman. Most nights her mother slept in another wing of the house with her personal maid in attendance. Mikki rarely saw her father in the evenings, though he made it a point to be home for an early dinner—eight p.m. sharp—and always the same menu—vegetable soup, two dry *chappatis*, salad, roasted *pappads, moong dal*, a spoonful of rice and lightly sweetened dahi after his thali was cleared. Her mother's rich and elaborate meals were served simultaneously and hardly eaten, since Mikki herself preferred lighter food, without red chilli powder. The cook prepared three separate menus, occasionally four, if there was a visitor. But the pattern never altered. Conversation at the table was kept to the barest minimum as uniformed but barefoot bearers padded around, bringing and removing dishes, whisking away unwanted delicacies and rushing to sweep the smallest crumbs that dared to fall on the Italian marble floor.

*

Mikki met Ramanbhai for their daily morning conference. His expression was grim. Mikki was beginning to tire of his pessimism.

She also felt he was keeping things from her. She'd decided she was going to fix a one-on-one meeting with the solicitors and chartered accountants to find out a little more about the precise state of affairs at Hiralal Industries. Someone had obviously informed Ramanbhai about her plans. He didn't seem too pleased about them. 'Why do you want to bother with all this, Mikki? Leave it to me. I can handle these people. Your father also didn't get involved in day to day matters. He concentrated on policy-decisions.'

Mikki looked at him barely concealing her impatience. 'Before I get to the policy-making level, don't you think I should first familiarize myself with the basics of the business, starting with things as elementary as what it is that we actually manufacture?' Ramanbhai shot her a sharp look but immediately altered it to suit his words, 'Beti,' he said deliberately, 'I appreciate your method of trying to start at the bottom and I agree it is the best way to understand any business. But your case is different. You have been thrown into an unusual situation on the death of your great father. This changes the picture. You don't have time on your hands for apprenticeship. Had you been a son, your father might have taken you into his confidence from a young age and guided you properly from the beginning. But as a daughter, all he wanted for you was a good husband—that is all. Your training, if there was one, was to become an obedient daughter-in-law in some prominent business family.... Beti, the problem is nobody takes you seriously...why waste time with solicitors and accountants? What will they tell you? Nothing. They will give you a cup of tea, compliment you on your nice dress and send you home. My advice is—leave these serious matters to me. I am there to handle them. Trust me. I will guard your interests like a father. But you will make things difficult for yourself if you do things without consulting me.' Ramanbhai tried to put a paternal arm around Mikki's shoulders but she shrugged him off before saying, 'Thank you for your advice, Ramankaka. I appreciate and value your words. But I'd like you to hear a few of mine now. I can't change my sex, unfortunately. That is the one thing all of you will have to accept. But I can change just about everything else...and I intend to. Fate has left me in my father's shoes. Had I been the son he never had but constantly longed for, perhaps I might have had more success with the likes of you. I don't expect you or the others to give up your prejudices— but I want you to know that I will not let that stand in my way. This is going to be my show and I intend running it on my terms. If these old solicitors aren't prepared to talk turkey with me, I'll sack them. That goes for the accountants and anybody else who wishes to treat me like a simple-minded, spoilt little girl out to play at being a businesswoman. My genes are the same as my father's even if my gender isn't. I'm determined not to let the companies go by default. I will learn whatever I have to and I will hire whoever I think fit. But before I set about doing that, I need facts and figures. And I'm depending on you to give them to me.'

Ramanbhai smiled softly, 'Mikki...sorry, Madam...you are your father's daughter. I have worked in this company for thirty long years. I'm willing to extend the same sort of cooperation to you as I did to your father.'

Disarmed by the sudden switch in Ramanbhai's temper Mikki held his hands gratefully, 'The corporate world is full of sharks, Ramankaka. I'm so glad that I have you on my side.'

*

Shanay was certain Mikki wasn't going to be happy when she saw him. He had tried to talk his mother out of her absurd plan. But Anjanaben's steely determination was one thing Shanay had long given up on. When his mother made up her mind, nobody could influence it—least of all Shanay. But this time it was not his mother he was worried about—it was his cousin, Mallika. She'd always been such a difficult girl. He had tried so hard to make friends with her, particularly after they were grown up. But each time he went over to her bungalow, she'd send the servants to tell him she was out, or in the middle of her tuitions, or taking a nap. Shanay knew she was avoiding him and he used to wonder why. He didn't want to annoy her, but he did enjoy her company. Besides, she was the prettiest girl he'd ever seen. 'Pretty and spoilt,' his mother would snort. 'So what?' Shanay reasoned, 'which girl in her position wouldn't behave that way?' But he also knew she could be loving and kind. She had demonstrated this aspect of hers one Diwali when she was ten or twelve, and he, a little older. The family had been seated at the unending table right after the *'Chopda pujan'* in the main hall. This was a real treat for Shanay and other poorer relatives who only got to meet and eat with Seth Hiralal on this special occasion. Shanay had been seated across from Mikki who was looking exceptionally pretty in a bright pink *chaniya-choli*. Cold coffee in silver glasses was served for the first time that year. Shanay had taken one sip from the glass and exclaimed, 'Ugh! What is this bitter thing? Has the milk gone sour?' His other cousins had laughed mercilessly while Seth Hiralal had glowered at him. It had been Mikki who had piped up in his defence. Spiritedly, she'd put down her own glass and announced, 'Shanaybhai is right. This stuff is awful. I think I'm going to throw up. Come on, Shanay....let's go to the kitchen and drink some water.' Shanay had pushed back his chair gratefully and run behind her. Near the refrigerator, he had squeezed her hand and tried to say something but Mikki had brushed him off playfully with a, 'Stupid! Always saying silly things in front of everybody. Haven't you tasted cold coffee before? I love it…especially with vanilla ice cream in it. See… try…it's great when you get used to it.' Hesitantly, Shanay had taken a sip from an extra glass in the fridge and pulled a face. 'No, Mikki, I still don't like it.' Ever since that incident, whenever Shanay was offered cold coffee anywhere in the world he'd think of Mikki and that Diwali. It always brought a wry smile to his face.

Anjanaben was aware of Shanay's soft spot for his cousin. That was one of the reasons she was so certain he'd jump at the chance to come back and help her. When he didn't, it was her turn to be surprised. 'Are you mad?' she'd screamed at him long-distance, 'Think of the future. This is just the opportunity you need. You can easily rise in the company. Mikki is just a foolish young girl. She has no idea of business.' Shanay had been adamant about staying out of Hiralal Industries initially. Then Anjanaben put his father on the line. Still screeching shrilly in the background, prompting her husband each time he was at a loss for words, 'Tell that son of yours not to be a fool like you. One in the family is enough.' Finally, Shanay had given in on the condition that he'd take the first plane back if it didn't work out his way. Anjanaben had backed off smugly. Once her boy was here and installed in Hiralal Industries, everything else would follow. Shanay may be a little crude, she told herself, but he was shrewd. Yes, he had been careless, unable to clinch the odd deal during his early days but everybody learns through mistakes. He wouldn't err again. Not when the stakes were this high. Anjanaben's eyes shone at the thought of the future and the untold promises it held for all of them. Mikki wasn't exactly her idea of the ideal daughter-in-law…on the other hand, if the girl was willing to listen and learn, why not? It could work. Anjanaben would make sure it did.

*

When her secretary announced Shanay a frown of mild irritation creased Mikki's brow. Reluctantly, she pushed some files away and told her secretary to send him in. The sight of his 'leisure suit' (as shopping malls in New Jersey described those hideous outfits) put her off instantly. There he was, grinning from ear to ear and saying, 'Howyoudoin'?' in an accent that was a cross between Jamnagari Gujarati and a Texan drawl. 'You are looking swell,' he added still slobbering like an ecstatic pooch. 'Thanks,' Mikki said briefly before buzzing for some coffee. Shanay, she noted, had gained weight. Not too much, just enough to fill out his rangy frame. He didn't look all that bad, Mikki mused, taking in his thick hair, angular jaw and eyes with the longest lashes she'd ever seen. Maybe if he hadn't been wearing that ghastly suit he might have looked passable, she figured. He had certainly been quite nice-looking when they were young. The cutest looking male cousin in the clan. And he had always been so touchingly devoted to her, even when she had acted mean with him. So many incidents, so many slights in the past, and yet here he was, cheerfully telling her about his experiences in New York and how easy it was to find homemade *dhoklas* and spicy *chivda* in Queens these days. But his accent grated and she couldn't help thinking he was coming on a bit too strong. It was only when he stopped mid-sentence to say, 'You are making me nervous. Why are you staring at me?' that Mikki snapped out of her reverie and tried to pay attention to what he was saying.

Her room was filled with some overpowering fragrance. Abruptly, she asked him, 'Is that your after-shave that's smelling so much?' Glowing with pride, Shanay confessed, 'It's the latest in men's perfumes. Everyone in the States is using it. It's awesome, no?' Mikki sniffed the air and screwed up her face, 'It is horrible,' she said and immediately regretted her words—Shanay was crest-fallen. 'Next time I'll use something else,' he said slowly. Mikki leaned across the table and softly apologized, 'I have no right to talk to you like this. I'm sorry.' Shanay recovered quickly, 'No. No. No. You have every right. Say it. Say anything. I don't mind.' Good old Shanay, Mikki smiled. Still the same worn doormat lying at her feet with a large 'Use me' written over him.

'So,' he said to her, 'tell me everything. Are you liking it here?' Mikki hesitated before replying. She suddenly thought of Sean and their times together. She pushed the thought away. Sean had been sympathetic enough over the phone the few times they'd spoken. But both of them knew there was no going back.

Shanay was staring at her, barely able to conceal his admiration. 'Mikki, I have to say you look great!' he finally blurted. Mikki smiled and spontaneously reached across to place her hand over his, 'You look good yourself, Shanaybhai,' she said.

Mikki asked him what brought him back. He looked at her in surprise, 'You're kidding? I don't believe you, *yaar*. I came for you.'

*

'You know, Mikki darling…if you want to be taken seriously in business circles, you'd better start attending all these corporate parties…you know…the p.r. things organized by bankers. What about The Chambers and The Belvedere? I hope they've invited you to become a member?'

Mikki listened attentively while the sophisticated lady in a crisp *chanderi* sari spoke to her. Mrs Kumar had been a close friend of her mother's. Mikki liked her, despite the auburn rinse to the hair and the excessive amount of jewellery she always wore. Mrs Amrita ('Amy') Kumar was a gracious, well-connected woman…another princess who'd married a commoner…in her case, an armyman who'd gone on to become an ambassador. Mikki enjoyed their regular lunch meetings these days. In the beginning Amy had tried to treat Mikki like a close friend's young daughter…with just that hint of a patronizing air that had put off Mikki sufficiently to tell her politely that they needed to rework their personal equation. Amy had laughed with relief, 'Oh, darling…thanks a lot. I was beginning to get worried…I mean, I do absolutely adore you, of course. But imagine having to play mommy forever!'

Mikki had reached across the round table they had been occupying, and kissed her on the cheek. 'I'd rather we were friends…and if you don't mind, I'll drop that irritating "aunty" after your name. I'm much too old to call the friends of my parents "uncle" and "aunty".' 'Call me Amy, darling,' Mrs Kumar had promptly suggested, 'that way I feel young too. I detest all this aunty-uncle business myself.'

It had been terrific after that. Amy didn't have any children of her own. She had all the time in the world for her friends...and she had dozens of them stretched all over the world. She led a leisurely existence in an enormous apartment which she referred to as 'my Bombay base'. It was anything but a transit flat, yet given her background, she couldn't ever get herself to call it 'home'. For her, that was a red stone palace cresting a hill set amidst acres of lush agricultural land in the Punjab. It was considered an architectural jewel internationally and often featured in plush publications devoted to grand living.

Amy was proud of her ancestry, yet very discreet.

Her Bombay apartment reflected all this. Old silver frames from her own state with sepia-tinted photographs of her legendary father, Prince Paramjit; her beautiful mother, Princess Urmilla, and her brother who died before the age of ten of some undetected viral infection. There were priceless antiques which had come from her parents as a part of her dowry, including miniatures, salvers, chandeliers, Persian rugs, gold goblets, silver services emblazoned with the family crest, carved furniture and an exquisite collection of old firearms.

Mikki saw flashes of her mother in Amy, and yet the two couldn't have been more different. Mikki didn't really understand what it was that made her recoil whenever she thought of the lonely woman who had given birth to her. Even as a child Mikki had shrunk away on the rare occasions her mother had tried to caress her, hold her, kiss her. Perhaps because she had sensed what a strain it really was for the older woman to make that effort. Touching, physical contact, put her off. She avoided even formal handshakes, preferring a *namaste* at all times. Mikki remembered her father's irritation in the presence of foreign collaborators who'd stick out their hands only to be greeted by her mother's primly folded ones. 'It is not our custom to shake hands with strange men,' her mother would say later, to which the Seth would reply witheringly, 'Why strange men alone? Obviously it is not your custom to touch even the man you took as your husband.' And it would be Mikki's turn to blush and look away.

Amy was right, of course. Mikki needed to move around much

more in business circles. She'd tried attending a couple of Rotary Club meetings and had been talked into signing up with the ladies' wing of the Indian Merchants' Chamber. At the former, she had yawned through boring speeches and endless golf-related conversations. And at the latter she'd shrunk away from over-dressed women with phoney ideas. So these were the chaps she'd watched teeing off over the club green for so many years. And now she was sitting with them trying hard to feign interest in their shop talk. The ladies' wing experience had been even more tedious. Earnest, conceited, self-conscious women playing at business and spending time impressing one another with their latest acquisitions. She'd felt out of place and impatient listening to the snide remarks and the sly bitching. The women had made sure to isolate her, maintaining a polite distance while they discussed the wholesale price of out-of-season *mosambis* and always-in-season diamonds.

At the office, uncertainty still hung over the future of the companies. Ever since her talk with Ramanbhai, he had stopped shutting her out and going into huddles with 'his men' for long closed-door meetings that yielded nothing as far as Mikki could see. She had also sensed that he was intensely unhappy over her induction of Shanay, even though he never said much. Without saying anything definite Ramanbhai had made it obvious however, that he did not approve. There had been pointed references to his 'immaturity' or his 'lack of experience in such matters'. Mikki had chosen to ignore the barbs. She'd reasoned it was inevitable. Ramankaka, despite his avuncular ways, was extremely possessive about Hiralal Industries. And why not? thought Mikki. He was responsible for their success and he was totally committed to seeing that Hiralal Industries' reputation was maintained even after Seth Hiralal's death. She only wished he'd stop being so considerate towards her: in his extra-protective attitude, and his zeal to to shelter her from the seamier aspects of business, she couldn't help feeling that Ramanbhai was holding some things back from her. And the lawyers and accountants were either too spineless or a bit too beholden to Ramanbhai to to tell her the entire truth.

The more she thought about it, the more inviting it became to ask Amy on the board. She needed an ally. Someone she sort of trusted. At least someone who spoke her language. But before that she had to be convinced of the health of the empire she had inherited. And the only way to find out the truth was to go into the market-place and ask, since nobody within Hiralal Industries was willing to tell her.

*

'Tell me the truth, Mummy,' Alisha demanded, 'Exactly how much money do we have? What has Papa left for us… *if* he has left anything. Or has that bitch got everything?' Her mother stared at her, unable to grasp the question. Alisha looked at Leelaben in disgust, 'What is this? Do you know the time? Nearly lunchtime. And just see yourself…like a bloody ayah. No…even they'd feel ashamed to slop around like this.'

Leelaben clutched her housecoat to herself and began to cry. Alisha was tempted to strike her. 'Stop it, Mummy. Stop it! I can't bear your stupid attitude, what's the point in crying? Will it get us out of this lousy place? No. Why waste your tears like this? I'm sick of you. Sick of our life. You sit there boozing, feeling sorry for yourself. But what about me? You may feel your life is over…but mine is just beginning. I'm not going to waste it sitting in this dump with you. The minute I know we have enough to buy me a ticket out of this garbage heap, I'm going. And listen to me carefully—I'm not coming back. You hear? I'm not going to let my life rot along with yours. I'll be gone, gone, gone. Go on…tell me. Where is the money?'

Her mother waved her arm limply in the direction of the cupboard in her room.

'Forget it. A few thousand rupees. That won't get me a ticket to Kathmandu. I mean the *real* money. Or have you drunk it away? No…knowing what a fool you are, you've probably given it to some bloody boyfriend. Which one? Last week's lover? The week before's? Or is it the man I found in your bed last night—eating rice like a starving dog, spilling food all over the place and over your half-naked body? Did he take it all? Tell me!'

Her mother shook her head vigorously, looking scared, 'No, no…please don't shout at me…please. I don't know what money you keep talking about. Your father never used to tell me anything. He used to say I didn't have the brains to understand all this…but, but, but…one man from his office had phoned last week. One man…' and she trailed off. Alisha caught the edges of her frayed housecoat. 'Which man? What man? Who had phoned? And for what? Pay attention to me…listen…think…concentrate…who was it?' Her mother looked blankly at her. 'I have seen him before…twice, thrice…with your father. He was there when we bought this flat…and when you were born…yes…I remember him…his name also…I will tell you…please…don't shout…I'll tell you…he phoned.'

Alisha began pacing up and down the small room. Her mother was getting on her nerves these days. Not that they'd ever got along. But now she could barely stand the sight of her. 'Ramanbhai,' she heard her shouting triumphantly, 'Yes…baby…did you hear that? Ramanbhai…he had phoned. That was him. He gave his name…I recognized his voice…he asked about you also. He said there was something important he had to tell us…very important. Baby…why don't you phone him? His card is somewhere. His number also…Papa always spoke to him from here. Always. Four times, five times in one hour.' Alisha was barely listening as her mother rambled on. She'd got the name she wanted. That man who had thrown her out from the funeral—funny that he should have called. Something must have come up. Something must have changed. Alisha's mind was racing. She wouldn't wait for him to phone again. She would reach him before that.

She walked towards the phone purposefully. Her mother was whimpering away in a corner of her bed. She still hadn't stirred or made any attempts to change out of her night-clothes or make her rumpled bed. Alisha averted her eyes. She couldn't bear the sight. She dialled the number she found in the well-thumbed phone book with pages falling out and her mother's childish scrawls all over it. She heard the nasal accent of the receptionist who answered.

'May I speak to Ramanbhai?' Alisha asked, her voice sounding uncertain to her own ears. The receptionist spoke in Gujarati, 'Who wants to speak to him?' Alisha replied, 'Please tell him it's Alisha— he'll know who it is.' The receptionist hesitated before checking with Ramanbhai. Within seconds, he was on the line. Alisha didn't know what exactly she'd phoned for. For a moment her mind went blank as his face and expression on that fateful morning flashed before her eyes. Then she took a hold on herself and her voice took on a confidence she wasn't feeling as she said, 'I understand you had phoned my mother last week. Unfortunately, she isn't well enough to speak to you and has asked me to do so on her behalf.

You mentioned you had some important information to convey to us. I've called to set up a meeting.'

Ramanbhai's voice was guarded but pleasant, 'Allow me to apologize to you my dear girl...for that rather unfortunate incident at our Seth's—your father's—funeral.' Alisha let that pass without responding to it. She waited for Ramanbhai to continue. 'Well...' he said, his tone more business-like, 'Yes...there are a few matters I'd like to discuss with your mother and you. They are related to the business affairs of your father, as you must have guessed. Please suggest a time and place, I shall be there. The sooner the better.' Alisha hesitated: was this the same man who had been so rude to her? Something must've happened between that time and now. His tone was different. She could sense the change in his attitude. She replied coolly, 'I shall consult my mother about a convenient time and get back to you. The venue will naturally be our home, which I presume you know the address of. Do we need to request our lawyers to be present at the meeting?'

Ramanbhai paused before saying, 'That won't be necessary...for the moment.'

Alisha replaced the receiver and reached for a hair-brush. She began brushing her tresses vigorously. It helped her to think. An old habit that used to amuse her father. Everytime he saw her with the brush in her hand, he'd tease, 'So...what's cooking in your mind now?' Oh God! sighed Alisha. Why did he have to go and die?

FOUR

'How is it going, *dikra*?' Anjanaben asked Shanay. 'What?' he countered knowing all along just what his mother was getting at. 'You know…you and Mikki and all that,' she said, looking slyly at her son. 'Why don't you concentrate on your *theplas*,' Shanay said as he looped a polka-dotted tie around his neck. 'Take that stupid tie off,' Anjanaben instructed. 'Wear one of Papa's old ties—silk, English. Very good quality.' Shanay snorted, 'What do you know about ties? Or do you think you know everything?'

Anjanaben went to the small wash-basin in the corner of the living-cum-dining-room and washed her hands. She didn't say anything. These days her son was behaving peculiarly, being short and rude with her. That's what happened when parents sent their boys abroad. Too much independence too soon. In six months they forgot their manners and came back showing no respect to their elders. Shanay used to be so good, so obedient. Everybody used to tell her, 'Your son is made of 24-carat gold. Such a good boy.' Anjanaben would glow with pride. True, he had gone to a vernacular Gujarati school unlike his rich cousins who'd gone to convent schools in South Bombay. But Shanay was better than all of them. She could see the envy in the eyes of other women when they met on Diwali or at family weddings. Their sons smoked, drank liquor, drove fast cars, wasted money, went to the races, gambled, had girlfriends and, worst of all, didn't listen to their parents. Anjanaben used to say to these women, 'Look *baba*, my son is not a *badey baap ka beta*. He knows his place in life. He will marry the girl I find for him and live with us in our humble flat. She will take over the kitchen and both my husband and I will retire, attend *kirtans* and look after our grandchildren. What more can we ask of God? What more can he give us? We are blessed, I tell you. We may not have wealth—but we have health and a son who will take care of us in our old age.' But now this seemed a long time ago.

'What time will you come back from office?' she asked Shanay, her tone slightly sharper now. 'Can't say,' Shanay replied sullenly, still fussing with his tie. 'Means what?' she demanded. 'Means…I have a lot of work pending in the office. Mikki needs me. I cannot leave before she leaves. Sometimes she is there till eight, nine o'clock. I have to stay with her.'

Anjanaben was secretly pleased to hear that. Good, good. They must be getting closer. She decided to be blunt, 'Achcha, so tell me… you have impressed Mikki, no? So don't you think we can start making some plans now…? Your father and I are waiting for the good news. If you say it's O.K. I will go and approach her directly.'

Shanay swung around, 'Are you mad, Mummy? What are you saying? Please do not spoil everything. I'm enjoying my work. For the first time in my life I feel as if I'm not wasting my time. Mikki trusts me. I respect her. Forget it! I will not forgive you if you spoil everything by interfering in my life.'

Anjanaben sat down heavily on the scruffy sofa, 'Wah! Wah! Now I'm getting a lecture from my own son! That is the trouble with you modern people! A little freedom and *bas*, you forget your parents, your duties. Don't ever think you can talk to me in this fashion again. All my hopes are pinned on you—on your future. This is your chance. Mikki has everything. Today she trusts you, depends on you. Tomorrow she may find someone else. Then? Then you'll be left staring! Another man will walk away with her—some loafer like that Navin. And you—like a stupid pumpkin—will come crying to me. Don't be a fool. This is your opportunity to better your own life, and ours. If you marry Mikki, just

think of where you will reach! Your cousins will die of jealousy—
yes, yes, all those spoilt boys who have done nothing but fritter
away generations of wealth. They will envy you. You shall have
power. You will become somebody. I will be proud of you.'

Anjanaben's eyes were shining as Shanay slipped on a blazer
and picked up his briefcase. 'Stop dreaming, Mummy,' he said. 'In
any case your dream could turn into a nightmare if I really married
Mikki. Do you know what they are saying in the office? That
Bachchoobhai's "accident" was not an accident at all. He was
killed. Do you hear—killed. It was a case of murder.'

Shanay looked at his mother and thought she would collapse.
She looked so foolish at that moment, with her mouth wide open
and her eyes shut. Irritated, he left the room. As he ran down the
stairs he could hear her screeching, 'Wait—baba, wait. Why would
someone murder him?' He didn't bother to answer her. It was a
question that didn't have any answers. At least not just yet. But
Shanay intended to find out—not just for Mikki's sake, but his own.
With a start, he realized he was back in love with Mikki.

Shanay knew his love for his beautiful cousin was doomed. That
he was dreaming a hopeless dream. And yet he'd never really got
her out of his system. Not since that first time he had clumsily
caught hold of her while playing 'chor-police' in a darkened room
of her rambling bungalow, and she'd struggled out of his grip
saying angrily, 'Shanaybhai...what are you doing? I'll tell
Mummy.... I'll tell everyone. And then they'll all beat you.' Guiltily, Shanay had released her. But the memory of that touch continued to linger over the years. They'd been children then. But even
at the age of eight, Mikki had exuded an irresistible appeal that had
had him under her spell ever since.

Shanay had tried to get over her. He'd thought it would be easy
with his Belgian girl. But it was Mikki who kept him awake at night.
And it was Mikki he longed for. Sometimes, he wondered whether
she was aware of just how strongly he felt about her. At such times
he told himself to stop hoping... stop dreaming... stop caring—
Mikki would never be his.

Shanay got into the white Maruti Mikki had given him and put
the key into the ignition. Just being in the car—her car—made him
feel close to her. He could smell her perfume, see the sexy mole on
the nape of her long neck, watch her move lithely across the room
to check on something, hear her laugh.... His spirits soared as they

did each morning, at the thought of getting into the office, and being near Mikki.

When Shanay arrived he noticed that Mikki seemed very tense. 'Have you heard anything?' she asked Shanay as soon as he all but ran into her office suite after she buzzed him on the intercom. 'A few rumours,' he answered guardedly. 'Like what?' she demanded impatiently tugging at the white pin-striped jacket that ended just above her knee. 'Like…well, I don't know if I should say this… but everybody at the office now knows about your sister, I mean Alisha…I'm sorry, Mikki…but how could I not tell you?' Mikki twisted a lock of her hair impatiently as she sipped her morning coffee. Now that she and Shanay spoke to each other in Gujarati, it was easier to talk to him. Besides, it helped when the conversation was informal. She was glad Shanay had dropped English. Poor chap used to be in a mess trying to impress her and getting it all wrong. She needed practice with her Gujarati too, so the switch had worked out fine for both of them. Mikki looked directly at Shanay with a defiant tilt to her chin, 'What is there to know about Alisha?' Shanay seemed uncomfortable, 'Well…the thing is…someone in office has been in touch with her. The telephone operator told me yesterday she heard some of the conversation but was unable to trace the call.'

This was news, but Mikki didn't want to show her interest. She pretended to be absorbed with some files on the desk. Without looking up she said in a bored-sounding voice, 'What else?' Shanay answered, 'Also…there are rumours that Bachchookaka's plane crash was not an accident. It was a case of sabotage.' Hearing that Mikki looked up sharply. 'What do you mean? What are you saying, Shanay?' He continued, 'Maybe you should just ignore it. You know how people love to gossip…but this is what I heard in the executive lunch room. I should not be saying this, but I think Ramankaka has started all these stories.' Mikki came up to Shanay and spoke in an urgent, low voice, 'Listen, Shanay. I want you to report everything you hear to me, no matter how trivial it seems to you. Every rumour, every bit of gossip, every little story. Find out where it starts, follow it up. If necessary, let's hire professionals. I want to get to the bottom of this. Why would anybody have wished to kill my father?'

'I think Bachchookaka had a lot of business rivals. There are stories about loans and bad debts. I don't know how much of all this is true. But people are saying that the company stock had crashed and that he borrowed heavily....' Mikki looked thoughtful, 'I have to investigate the details, but yes, some of what you're saying is certainly true. He had made a few bad business decisions just before he died. But that does not mean someone would kill him for them. What would his enemies get by doing that? Not their money....' Shanay was quiet for a bit, then he added slowly, 'Mikki...did you know he was trying hard for that 1500 crore project in Andhra Pradesh? The one Amrishbhai was also interested in?' Mikki nodded her head. 'Did you know that Amrishbhai had almost succeeded in getting his licence whereas Bachchookaka's efforts had been stalled for two years and his files had disappeared in Delhi?' Mikki nodded again. 'I didn't have the details...but I knew about the project. I'd heard him discussing it with Ramankaka often enough. He was obsessed with it.' Shanay said, 'Perhaps there is a clue there somewhere. We'll have to find out a little more.' Mikki shook her head in disbelief, 'This is insane! Murder? Sabotage? Over a business deal?' Shanay said, 'It isn't the first time, you know. It happens all over the world. We may be completely off-track, but we should find out more about the crash. Do you have all the reports? Post-mortem? Civil aviation?' Mikki said, 'I'll have to reactivate everything all over again. I was too shocked by the tragedy to even think of such things. I wasn't interested in the damned reports. Besides, Ramankaka was handling everything. He'd told me not to worry about it. You remember how horribly the press was behaving? Ramankaka took care of all that, including the reports. The papers will be with him. The inquiry into the crash is likely to take a while, you know how slowly things happen here. But we can certainly find out more...I'm sure Ramankaka will cooperate.' Shanay looked steadily at Mikki. 'That is my biggest fear. Will he?'

*

Things at Hiralal Industries were soon moving fast. Mikki's new team of executives comprised bright and sharp young men and women, most with MBA's from good management schools. She looked forward to her daily interactions with them and to their weekly brainstorming sessions. She'd appointed a three member core group and given them control of the operation to bail out

Hiralal Industries. It was code-named Operation Salvage and the project was cloaked in secrecy. Shanay was meant to oversee the strategies and monitor the progress. Mikki was pleased to note that nobody in her set-up questioned her authority. When she addressed meetings, the rest listened to her attentively and, she imagined, with growing respect.

But Shanay was still caught up with his murder theory. Mikki was getting impatient with his obsession and told him so late one evening when they found themselves alone in her office, after the 'hot shots' (as she mentally referred to the MBA's) had gone. 'Listen…let's be realistic,' Mikki began. 'Maybe you've got something there, but we aren't making any headway. Let's concentrate our energies on saving Hiralal Industries before some shark swallows us up. Have you heard anything—what does the business grapevine have to say about the state of our affairs?' Shanay shifted from one foot to the next uncomfortably. Mikki urged him on, 'Come on, Shanay. Don't play games with me. Give it to me straight. I'll take it on the chin. We're up shit creek—I know that. How much worse can it get?' Shanay cleared his throat, 'There's that chap in Dubai with business connections in Singapore and America…and God knows where else. You know the man I mean? Punjabi. Rather, half-Punjabi. His mother's a Sindhi from Lahore. Anyway, I've done a check on him. I suspect he's fronting for them…the same people who killed Bachchookaka.' Mikki groaned, 'Shanay, stop it! You are getting paranoid about this. Stop speculating. Just give me the facts. Who is he? Where does he operate from? What is the source of his income? Who are his business associates? What is his standing in the community? That sort of stuff. Just dump this murder business. We don't have the time to play Sherlock Holmes—you know that.'

Shanay was hurt by Mikki's brusque put-down. He shrugged and continued, 'You don't seem to realize, Mikki, that the whole thing is a part of the same puzzle. "Chibs" Chotlani is a smooth operator with no known assets. He doesn't have a stake in anything, and yet he is considered a big fish. His friendship with the Khinlanis is well-known. He has fronted for them before. He was the man involved in their failed bid to take over the doddering food company along with the sick rayon mill. You remember that? It was a major scandal.'

Mikki looked vaguely at Shanay before saying sweetly, 'Sometimes, just sometimes, you tend to forget my age. I was sixteen at that time and the last thing on my mind then was to keep track of hustlers and wheeler-dealers.' Shanay smiled, his eyes glowing with love for Mikki. She looked so vulnerable, so beautiful when she allowed herself to relax. Timidly, he asked her, 'So…any plans for dinner?' Mikki glanced at the Piaget on her slim wrist and said, 'Navin was to meet me at home for a quiet evening and then we'd planned to drive down to RG's for a drink.' Seeing Shanay's crestfallen expression, she quickly added, 'But I can get out of it. Shall I?'

Shanay nearly jumped with joy as he reached for his jacket, held out his arm and jauntily escorted her out of the office and into the waiting car.

*

Alisha was suspicious the moment she saw the flowers in Ramanbhai's hands. 'For you,' he said smoothly. 'Please accept them. It is a small way to say sorry.' Ramanbhai looked rather impressive in his *bandh-gala*. There was a slight nip in the air those days. The weather bureau described it as a 'cold wave'. Alisha's mother refused to open even a single window and lay around in bed all day, shivering and cursing. She looked such a sight. Alisha was disgusted seeing her slop around—making tea in the kitchen or listlessly watching T.V. She'd requested her to get dressed for Ramanbhai's visit, but Leelaben had laughed, 'Get dressed for him? That man? Forget it! He was like a servant to me. That's how I treated him. I never liked that fellow. I would tell Bachchoo, "Be careful. He is a dangerous person." But your father…do you think he listened to me? Never! He'd shut me up saying, "Woman, watch your words. Don't interfere in these matters. They do not concern you." I'd say "O.K. but mark my words. This man will betray you one day."'

Alisha had given her mother a gentle shove, 'I don't care what you thought of him or how you behaved in the past. I have a feeling he is going to be of use to us now. And I will get what I can out of him. Why would he come otherwise? That too after what happened at the funeral? Get up, get dressed. I don't want him to think we live like beggars.' Her mother had laughed again, '*Arrey baba*, that man knows everything. If I ask him my bank balance just now, he

will give it to me right down to the last *naya paisa*. He handled all
the money affairs in your father's companies. Even our expenses
went through him. If I bought a new diamond set the money was
sanctioned by him. If Bachchoo ordered saris from Kala Niketan
the bills went to him. You can't fool Ramanbhai.'

Alisha squared her shoulders and told her mother quietly, 'I
don't wish to fool him. I just don't want him to fool me, that's all.'

And then he was there, in their stuffy little flat, standing very
still, staring at Leelaben. He held out his hand with an envelope in
it. 'Please… I have brought this for you. It's nothing…but I know
how difficult it has been since Seth's death.' Leelaben stared at the
packet. She knew what it contained. Hesitantly, she reached out
her hand to take it but before she could touch the envelope, she felt
a sharp slap on her wrist. 'Don't,' Alisha said curtly, and then
turning to Ramanbhai she spoke rapidly, 'Whatever it is that
you've come here for, get on with it fast. We don't need your
charity. We aren't beggars. However, my father owed us some
responsibility and I hope you have come here to discharge it on his
behalf.'

Ramanbhai liked the young girl's spirit. 'I have come to you with
good news. And for that I have brought some *pedas*. Before I tell
you what it is, let's share some sweets together. Surely, you will
not refuse?'

Alisha looked at the small box in his other hand and reluctantly
went towards the kitchen to fetch a plate.

'May I also bother you for a glass of water?' Ramanbhai asked.
Leelaben smiled vacantly at him. He patted her on the shoulder
and without a warning she burst into loud sobs. Startled by the
sound, Alisha whirled around to find her mother in Ramanbhai's
arms. She rushed towards the two of them, 'What the hell is going
on, Mummy?' she hissed, her eyes ablaze. 'Get a hold of yourself.'
Ramanbhai continued to comfort Leelaben, as she rested her head
against his chest, her body heaving. 'It's all right, Alisha. Your
mother is very upset…as we all are. Such a tragedy. Such a great
man. Gone…leaving so many orphans behind.' He started stroking
Leelaben's untidy hair and making soft, clucking noises. As her
sobs subsided gradually, Leelaben pleaded with Alisha, 'Please,
baby. I'm so cold, and so upset. I need a drink. *Bas*, just one drink.
Anything. Get me a brandy.' Alisha stared at her mother and then
her eyes met Ramanbhai's. She wondered how many similar

scenes he had witnessed in the past. How many times had her mother made a fool of herself? How many times had he held her while she wept? This man, whom her mother had just a short while ago dismissed as a servant. Seeing their intimacy, she also wondered how many times they'd slept together. The idea revolted her. And she wanted to throw Ramanbhai out of their home that very minute. But she stopped herself. She needed him. And he obviously needed her or he wouldn't have bothered to come there at all.

Alisha waited for her mother to stop crying, and then, assuming her most businéss-like manner, she turned to Ramanbhai, 'Let's get on with it. So, what did you have in mind?'

He looked at the young girl in front of him admiringly, recalling the day Bachchoobhai had phoned him at 3 a.m. to ask him to rush to an exclusive maternity home in the suburbs. *'Bhai*...please rush immediately. Leelaben is in labour. I will see her in the morning. Do whatever is necessary. Take ten thousand rupees with you. Tell the doctors not to spare on expenses. She must receive the best treatment. And...Ramanbhai...I don't need to tell you...this news is strictly between us.'

It was Ramanbhai who had first cradled the infant girl in his arms while Leelaben lay back in her bed, exhausted after a long and tiring labour. Ramanbhai, who was childless, was enchanted by the little girl as she squirmed and squealed in his arms. She had been beautiful then...and as he stared at her now, he realized that she'd grown into a beautiful woman. So much like Mikki—and yet, so different. Harder, sharper, with the instincts of an alley cat. 'Right,' he said, reaching for his battered briefcase, 'your mother is, of course, aware of the trust fund your father set up for you. When you turn twenty, you will have full access to the money—which, by the way, has grown to a substantial figure thanks to some wise investments. I have your portfolio right here. We can examine it later. What you may not be aware of—and this is the purpose of my meeting—is that Hiralal Industries is in a bad shape. Your father made some hasty decisions during the last two years and borrowed heavily. He also got involved in ventures floated by entrepreneurs of dubious character. He lost a great deal of money on his Malaysian adventure. In other words, H.I. can be described as close to bankruptcy. Your half-sister, Mallika, at this point has virtually nothing to her name other than her mother's jewellery and certain other fixed assets such as properties, which are likely to be attacked shortly. What you need to know is this—your stock right now is much higher than hers. You have the resources, the liquidity, the means to acquire a hefty share. I have a proposal for you. With the help of other interested investors, you can gain effective control over the companies. Till such time as you are not ready, I will run the business side on your behalf. We already have backers standing by for the take-over.'

Alisha was far too stunned with what Ramanbhai had revealed, to react immediately. She looked at her mother, who seemed in a daze herself. Finally, Alisha snapped out of her reverie and said evenly, 'It's too much to absorb in such a short time, I need to think about what you have just told us. I shall speak to my mother and then consult a lawyer before getting back to you.' Ramanbhai chuckled mentally at the young girl's stand. He liked her for it. Any other person would've jumped for joy or at least betrayed some emotion. But here was Alisha, her head thrown back proudly, giving nothing away, saying very little. Smart girl, he concluded.

It was only when Alisha heard the door shut behind Ramanbhai that she threw up her hands, let out a lusty yell and danced around her mother singing, 'We are rich. We are rich. We are rich, rich, rich!'

*

Mikki was in a gloomy mood sitting at The Brasserie with Navin and another couple. These sort of evenings were beginning to bore her. The same old crowd saying the same old things. But this was still preferable to staying home. God! That house seemed so desolate these days. Just the sound of her CD's as she knocked around the place waiting for Navin to turn up. She hated to be home. And she hated going out. Mikki told herself to snap out of this ridiculous state. She reminded herself that she was young, known and desirable. She should've been making the most of her evenings in town—evenings like this one. But she'd have given anything to escape. She stopped herself from drumming her fingers on the table and reached for a cigarette instead.

She surveyed the other diners, mostly foreign residents of the Oberoi Towers, tucking into bloody steaks and stuffed chicken breasts. As her eyes swept the crowd, they suddenly stopped at a small table in the far corner. It was occupied by a man in his late forties—attractive in an unkempt sort of way. His hair looked blow-dried at a fussy salon, but fortunately it wasn't dyed. He was expensively but conservatively dressed. Mikki liked the little she could see of his silk tie. He was smoking a cigar and nursing a Bloody Mary. Catching Mikki staring at him, he raised his glass. Mikki blushed and looked away. Five minutes later a steward appeared carrying a wine-chiller with a bottle of Moet et Chandon in it. Navin interrupted his conversation with the other two at the table to look up impatiently and say, 'I'm sorry...there must be some mistake. I didn't order champagne. But while you are here, get us another round of the same....' The steward smiled and handed Mikki an embossed card with a message on it: 'To the most beautiful lady in India. I wish I could write a poem or sing a *ghazal*. Champagne is a poor substitute, but it's the best I can do for now.'

Navin raised his eyebrows questioningly. Mikki silently handed the card to him. He read it and looked around to spot the man who had sent it to their table. His eyes met the stranger's. Navin relaxed...he wasn't some young stud making a play for Mikki. This man was ancient! He turned to the steward and signalled to him to open the bottle. When their champagne flutes were filled, he raised them saying, 'To us...and to loaded admirers.' Mikki, embarrassed by all the attention, looked away while her companions clinked glasses.

Later in the evening, Mikki excused herself and walked carefully out of the restaurant, heading for the ladies' room. On her tall heels and wearing a risqué mini that hugged her thighs, she was afraid she'd slip on the polished granite. Once inside the spacious bathroom, she fixed her hair, applied fresh lipstick and stared at herself in the full-length mirror. The thought of spending the rest of the evening with Navin and the other couple bored her to tears. She contemplated inventing a headache and going home. That was it...she'd tell them she'd developed a migraine...something to do with champagne and her system. That decided, she walked out purposefully and ran straight into the stranger from the corner table who was emerging from the men's room next door.

He stepped back, but held out his arm to steady her, smiling amusedly at the obvious awkwardness of their unexpected encounter. 'What a way to meet.... outside a toilet! Hardly a romantic setting for such a momentous occasion,' he laughed. Mikki liked his voice: low, cultivated, brimming with humour. She liked the way his light eyes crinkled as he spoke to her. She steadied herself, but couldn't find any words to deal with the situation. He continued to hold her arm, steering her gently away from the two entrances and towards the bookshop. 'Don't tell me three sips of champagne do this to you...I counted, you know—three sips. That's all you had. By the way, in case you didn't read my card, the name is Binny Malhotra...and don't bother to introduce yourself...I know who you are...as I'm sure everybody else here does.'

Still flustered, Mikki tried to pull her arm away. 'Don't run. I won't bite. Promise. But if I may be permitted to say so, you looked terribly bored with that bunch of juveniles. Why don't you dump them and allow me to make the evening more interesting for you?' His eyes were travelling brazenly over her face and her body. Mikki found her voice finally, 'I'm sorry...Mr...Mr...Malhotra...I was thinking of going home. And I do not accept invitations from total strangers who accost me outside rest rooms.' He laughed and said, 'Atta girl! I can see your father raised you well. I like that! I confess I would've been disappointed if you'd accepted my brash suggestion. But I must warn you that I do not give up easily. I mean to pursue you, woo you, win you...remember, you have been warned. And by the way, in case you didn't know it, you have a run in your stocking.' With that, he strode off briskly, leaving Mikki standing outside the bookshop, astonished by his approach.

*

Two nights after that strange encounter Mikki received a call at eight in the evening, just as she was about to leave for a splashy party arranged by one of Navin's movie-star friends. Mikki was excited at the prospect of meeting some people from the younger set—they looked rather interesting in the pictures she'd gazed at in fan magazines while getting her hair done. She had taken up Navin's suggestion that she wear something glamorous and glittering. Amy had accompanied her on a shopping trip which hadn't yielded much. Finally, Mikki had settled for a fuschia, off-the-shoulder evening dress (one of her New York buys) and combined it with contrasting emeralds from her mother's jewellery box. Her hair was pulled back into a sleek chignon, which made her look older and more sophisticated. The phone rang while she was

dabbing on her mother's favourite perfume, Shalimar, and surveying her image in a full-length mirror. She recognized the voice and
immediately got flustered.

Binny sounded amused as he said, 'Did I take you by surprise?'
Mikki, thrown by the unexpectedness of the call, forgot to feign
annoyance at his taking it for granted that she knew who he was
despite his not bothering to identify himself. She swiftly collected
her wits about her and said, 'I'm sorry, you've caught me at the
wrong time, Mr Malhotra. I was just about to leave and I am
running behind schedule…so, if you'll excuse me….' He laughed
and she was tempted to put down the phone. But she didn't. She
waited for him to say something, intrigued that he'd taken the
initiative so soon after their first encounter. Binny said, 'I'll keep
this short. Yes—I know you're going to the Puri party tonight and
I'm sure you'll steal the show from the tarty actresses there—but
the reason I'm calling is because I'd like to see you. Soon. Immediately. Perhaps tonight itself. After that young man—Navin?—is
through with showing you off and impressing his friends. And,
before you snap "how dare you" and hang up on me… it's business. Strictly business. I think you need me. You are in a tight spot,
young lady, and I'm your man on a white charger. You'll just have
to take my word for it. I am not a rapist so you can leave your
bodyguard at home.'

Mikki was left standing foolishly with a dead receiver in her
hand. She didn't know what to make of the call. But she knew she
wanted to see Binny again. Already the party had slipped into
insignificance, and she couldn't wait to see the mysterious stranger
who had made her so acutely aware of being a woman.

Navin whistled when he caught sight of Mikki. They'd decided
to use her car for the night since Navin hated the bother of finding
parking space, and there were going to be hundreds of invitees
flocking to the Puri party that evening.

The venue was the main attraction. Deepak Puri, the hot hero of
the day and his wife, Munni, who resembled a child-bride, had
hired an abandoned Studio for the event. The theme was nostal-
gia—and an expensive art director had gone to town recreating the
ambience of a bygone era of movie-making. Enormous black-and-
white or sepia posters from silent films covered the Studio walls,
while the sound system played recordings of popular film songs
from the Forties and the Fifties. Most of the guests had adhered to

the dress code and worn elaborate costumes, especially created for the occasion. Mikki was the one woman who stood out in her contemporary outfit, but somehow she didn't feel self-conscious at all, even when photographers clicked away as she emerged from the Mercedes on Navin's arm. She would've felt far more aware of her appearance had she come dressed as Anarkali or Chandramukhi or Noorjehan. Navin, too, had not bothered with a costume and was looking rather dashing in a black *sherwani* with a blood-red silk kerchief sticking out rakishly from his breast pocket. He beamed at the cameras, his arm possessively around Mikki's waist. It was obvious he revelled in the attention the two of them received whenever they went out.

Mikki could barely concentrate on all the 'happenings' being staged at different levels within the cavernous Studio. Her eyes swept disinterestedly over the crowd, spotting a retired heroine, the latest stud, the newest starlet, the overnight sensation, the darling of teenagers, the singing star. Her focus was on the person she was scheduled to meet later. She hadn't broken the news of her early departure to Navin yet. But when he saw her glancing at her Rolex for the fiftieth time in the first half-hour, he finally asked her what she was tense about. Mikki told him she had to leave in another hour. Navin stared at her uncomprehendingly. 'Leave? For where? What for?' Mikki smiled mysteriously and said, 'I'm sorry Navin...but something came up urgently. It's business, of course.' He looked at her and said, 'Bullshit! I don't believe you. It's some other man, isn't it?' Mikki was about to deny it hotly, when she stopped herself and said more sharply than she'd intended, 'What if it is? Do I owe you an explanation?'

Navin looked pained as he turned away. His arm, which had been on hers, fell to his side. He said slowly, 'No, I suppose you don't. But I thought we had something going. Something special. As a matter of fact, I was going to speak to you about it tonight. I wanted to make it official. I love you, Mikki, and I was going to ask you to marry me...after the party, when we were alone.' He looked like a little boy who'd lost his favourite kite, and Mikki found herself feeling sorry for him. She reached out and touched his cheek. 'I'm sorry, Navin. This is so unexpected. I don't know what to say. Or how to react. I'm really not ready for marriage. I like you. And at this point, I'd rather be with you than anybody else. But marriage? It's too soon after...you know...after the tragedy. I need time....'

Navin smiled wanly. 'So long as it isn't a straight refusal! And Mikki—it isn't too soon. You need someone. You need me. You are so alone right now.' Mikki smiled secretly. Two men in one night had told her that. Which one of them would she finally choose?

Binny's driver recognized her as soon as she walked out of the Studio. She left her own car for Navin and followed the chauffeur, who was wearing the insignia of Binny's flagship company embroidered on his uniform's epaulettes. He opened the door of a frosted silver Rolls-Royce. As Mikki climbed into the car, she was overwhelmed by the smell of roses. The entire back seat was full of them—long-stemmed yellow ones tied with a white satin bow. A small card said, 'Welcome to my world, Mikki.'

Mikki sat back, her heart thumping expectantly. She didn't know where this man lived or why she'd agreed to see him. The car pulled out of the parking lot smoothly and silently, as Mikki stared ahead of her, excitement mounting with each passing kilometre. They were headed south, which was just as well. She felt safer being that much closer to her own home. She'd been half-afraid that Binny was going to whisk her off to some distant destination miles out of Bombay.

In twenty minutes, the car was pulling into a long driveway just off Peddar Road. It was an unfamiliar stretch and Mikki wasn't sure she'd ever been on it, even though it was a magnificent old house, probably an old Parsi residence originally, with lights ablaze. As the chauffeur held the door open for her, she was greeted by a black Great Dane. She noticed two Dobermans, their eyes glowing like coals in the dark. But they were chained and had armed keepers next to them.

'Princess, how beautiful you look tonight.' Mikki whirled around at the sound of Binny's voice. She'd expected him to receive her at the door Instead, he'd surprised her by emerging out of the dark shadows of the garden, from behind the car. He walked over briskly and held both her hands in his, his lips lingering on her cheek as he bent to kiss her. Mikki was acutely aware of his staff watching this little tableau. Holding her by the elbow, he steered her firmly into his home saying, 'I'm honoured to welcome you to my humble abode.' Mikki suppressed a small smile at the facetiousness of his tone.

As she walked into the mansion her eyes quickly took in the priceless *pichwaiis* on either side of the huge door, the etched glass windows, the Persian carpet that covered almost the entire floor of his spacious living-room, the old French chandeliers and the coloured Italian marble. He seemed to favour Greek statues and somehow they didn't look too out of place in this setting. She noticed other *objets d'art*—English carriage clocks, porcelain, silver. Obviously, her host was a man of taste. He saw her taking in everything and said, 'Please, do not embarrass me. Compared to your late father's renowned collection this is nothing.' Mikki said simply, 'Not at all. It is wonderful to be surrounded by so much beauty. You have a discerning eye, Mr Malhotra.' He bowed, 'Thank you, Mademoiselle, I thought I'd established that the first time we met.'

Binny led Mikki into a study adjoining the living-room. They settled comfortably into two well-worn leather armchairs. Binny reached for a decanter and poured himself some port. He looked at her questioningly, before saying, 'I'm sorry—I'm as ill-mannered as I'm old-fashioned. I just assumed that a well brought up girl like you stays miles away from evil indulgences like these.' Mikki didn't respond, but she was beginning to feel a little uncomfortable. She knew nothing about this man and she had accepted his invitation on a crazy impulse. Was he married? There was no wife around and no evidence of one either—not a single photograph or even a feminine touch in sight. No tell-tale signs of children either: no bicycles in the driveway, no forgotten doll in some corner, no torn comics on a table, or sneakers in the hall—nothing.

'You look incredibly desirable tonight,' Binny said, raising his glass. Mikki shifted in her chair, aware of his eyes as they travelled hungrily over her bare shoulders and down her legs. She heard a discreet knock and heard Binny say, 'Enter'. A security-man in a grey safari suit walked in dragging a cowering boy with him. Momentarily Binny looked startled, but recovered quickly to wave them away saying, 'Later, later.' 'What was that?' Mikki asked curiously. 'Nothing, princess,' Binny answered dismissively, 'let's concentrate on you…and us,' he said, reaching once again for his port. 'Don't you offer even a cup of coffee to well brought up young ladies?' she finally asked and Binny jumped up immediately to ring a bell. The bearer who walked in was holding a silver salver with a remote control phone receiver on it. 'Sir… ' he said softly. Once again Binny got rid of him after ordering coffee for Mikki.

From nowhere as it were, soft strains of music wafted in. Mikki was still on her guard, unsure as to what the evening was about.

'My dearest girl,' Binny said again, right after she'd been served coffee from an exquisite Limoges set, 'you are in trouble. Big trouble. I suppose you are aware of it. But I doubt that you know just how big.' Mikki sipped her coffee wordlessly. Binny continued, 'I have made it my business to mind other people's—not just anybody's, mind you, but people I like. People I fancy. As it happens I both like and fancy you. And my executives tell me your father's industries are likely to collapse soon, unless someone comes along to rescue them from sure disaster. And that someone, in case you haven't guessed yet, princess, is me.' Mikki refused to react. Binny studied her calmly saying, 'It's amazing how cool you are, under the circumstances. You must be aware of the implications. To put it plainly, if you don't watch out and take remedial steps you will be tossed out of your position and house, on that pretty little butt of yours. Out on the cold streets, with not even those green rocks you wear around your neck to keep you warm. It will all be gone before you can blink. Think about it—an orphaned young girl—beautiful but broke, with nowhere to go, nothing to do and nobody to help her. Sounds like the script of one of the Hindi films produced by the crowd you just left, doesn't it?' Mikki set down her delicate cup on the table and asked him bluntly, 'What's your deal?'

Binny laughed, 'I like that, princess. You are a woman after my own heart. No wasting time. No wasting words. To the point. All right…since we are treating the whole thing in such a business-like fashion I'll give it to you straight…I'm prepared to take on Hiralal Industries with all its current liabilities on two conditions. The first—that you marry me. The second—that you relinquish complete rights in all your father's affairs to me—and that includes properties and any other assets my lawyers will come up with.'

Mikki rose to her feet and held out her hand with a smile, 'I like your style, Mr Malhotra,' she said, 'but not nearly enough to want to become Mrs Malhotra. Thank you for the interest shown—but no, Hiralal Industries is not on the market and neither am I, even if the bidder is quoting the highest price. And now, if you don't mind, I'd like to get home. I believe you have a car waiting for me. Good night and thank you for the coffee.'

Binny tried to put his hand on her shoulder to stop her from leaving, but Mikki shrugged it off and continued walking towards the door. She still found him maddeningly attractive, despite his offensive approach and insolent suggestions. But she was determined not to be swayed. Everything about the man told her he was a shark, ready to snap up the first fish in the ocean.

*

Amy was her usual clear-headed self when they met a week after the Binny encounter. Both of them were seated on the mezzanine level of a fancy new Chinese restaurant that had opened recently. 'Listen, darling...I don't know the man, but I know his type. Binny Malhotra sounds like the new breed of Indian businessmen. In our time we used to call them hustlers. He has obviously done his homework, and let's make no mistake—he probably *does* fancy you—indeed, which sane man wouldn't? You are a stunner and a winner, darling. Just look at you—even dressed in a simple *salwar*-kurta, without any make-up, you look absolutely gorgeous. And take your background, your family's reputation, your wealth and the aura surrounding you—I'm surprised you don't have a stampede outside your door. Let's not make any bones about this, Mikki, you are the most desirable woman in the country right now. Certainly one of the richest and, without a doubt, the smashingest, to coin a word. You don't have to look so worried or bewildered. I know just the man who can tell us more about the Mysterious Malhotra. Let me call Pesi Dinshaw when I get back. He is two thousand years old and knows just about every ant that crawls into the business world. He is really quite incredible—you must meet him some time. Old money—tons of it—no known business, but enormous clout. President of this and chairman of that. On the board of countless blue chip companies. Yes—good old Pesi would know. Till then, relax and enjoy your King Crab—it's the best in town.'

Mikki heard Amy out, and toyed with her noodles. Her mind just wasn't on food, not even on the excellent slow-fried tiger prawns with a black bean sauce that Amy was devouring with such relish. Mikki wasn't answering Navin's calls. Nor had she bothered to brainstorm with her whiz kids at the office. She was feeling inexplicably morose and distracted about the mess around her. Hiralal Industries, despite her best efforts, was facing collapse.

Amy polished off her bowl of steamed rice with baby corn and broccoli before turning to Mikki again, 'Darling, listen to an older woman. You need a man in your life. A steadying influence who can take care of you and give you all the things you've missed in your young life—attention, affection and interest in you as a person. Let's find out more about Malhotra. For all you know, he just might be the man. I admit his approach was wrong. Maybe he lacks finesse, sophistication, refinement. But I've known real bastards who've had all that and who've remained bastards nevertheless. Sometimes the Malhotra type of men are better—aggressive, take-charge fellows, blunt and crude, men you can't walk all over. Perhaps you need someone like him. An older man, an experienced one. And together you'd make quite a team.' Mikki was secretly thrilled to hear Amy's words. She hadn't been able to get Binny out of her mind. And she'd been furious for he hadn't bothered to call or send her flowers and an apology, after that one date together.

And then there was the Navin issue to deal with. Mikki knew she was merely postponing it and that she would have to face his sulks sooner or later. But right now her mind and heart were filled with thoughts of Binny. Binny the Bastard, as she had dubbed him when she had walked out on him that night—a night she so desperately wanted to forget. But couldn't.

*

It was Navin who struck first. The formal proposal came from Navin's mother and it was Anjanaben who received it. First, a phone call and then the visit itself. The intermediary had said rather apologetically, 'I know you also have a son who would be suitable, but you see, I have been asked to approach you by Sudhaben herself and how could I refuse? You are now Mallika's closest female relative, so we would like to make this a formal visit. Please do not misunderstood…see… I'm only doing my job…you know that I've been in the marriage brokering business for so many years now. It's a nasty business *ben*, but what to do? I'm in it, so I have to deal with difficult situations like this one.'

Anjanaben bit back her tears. She was furious. How dare she! How dare Sudhaben come to her with the proposal knowing it would clash with Shanay's interests? But the rules of the community were such, she couldn't snub the lady. Tradition demanded that she see her and convey the proposal to Mikki. But before doing that Anjanaben wanted to tear her son to pieces. What a fool! There he was in Mikki's office, practically on a night and day basis. What an opportunity! And he'd thrown it away. Just thrown it! He could have approached Mikki directly months ago. She had told him to repeatedly. But that ass had refused, saying he couldn't do it. And now Mikki was likely to slip out of their hands and life. She knew Navin was seeing the girl. She was also shrewd enough to see why Shanay had lost out in the race. The boy was a wimp! No go in him. Just like his father. Both farts. But Anjanaben wasn't the kind to give up so easily. She would convey the proposal all right, but she had her ways too. Mikki would hear the sort of stories about Navin's family that would shock her. She would tell Mikki all about Navin's mother and her affair with a boy as young as her son. And she'd tell Mikki about Navin's father—a no good specu-lator who had flung away his money on horses and whores. Yes, the family had had money once upon a time. Money and prestige. But that was two generations earlier. Today, they were known for nothing but their decadent lifestyle. Drinking from daybreak, liv-ing off the grandfather's investments. Soon those would be gone too. And then what? Navin was not like his parents. He'd been brought up by his grandmother. Poor Mangalaben—a saintly lady. But what could she do? The boy was lonely, neglected and sad even though he tried to hide it. His father encouraged him to follow in his footsteps. Fast cars, fast women, and all the money he could spare for the boy's 'hobbies'. No time for his only son but plenty of loose cash to pamper him with!

Anjanaben shook her head. No morals. No values. Serves Mikki right! If she was foolish enough to accept, she'd become like one of them. Anjanaben bustled off to phone the bungalow. It was a daily ritual. She'd call after she was sure Mikki had left for the office. And then she'd question her mole. Who came to the house? What was cooked? What was bought? Any phone calls? She liked to know. After all, her son's future was at stake.

Anjanaben dialled impatiently, her fat fingers getting stuck as Mikki's number yielded a busy tone. Damn. She dialled again. This time, she got her man. And she also got some important information. Sakharam told Anjanaben about a man called Malhotra. Binny Malhotra, whose driver had arrived in a big car that morning carrying an enormous bouquet of yellow roses and what looked like a jewellery box. Anjanaben chortled with glee. Good, good, good. Mikki obviously had another suitor in the picture. *Theek hai.* She'd still go ahead and convey the proposal. But as and when the chance came, she'd tell Navin's mother about this Malhotra fellow. An outsider. A Punjabi. Anjanaben shook her head. The family was jinxed. Poor Mikki. And then, with a start, she remembered, it was the same girl she wanted her son to marry. She shook her head again. Poor Shanay.

*

Mikki was more amused than anything else when Anjanaben told her about the proposal. 'Why couldn't Navin have asked me himself?' she wondered aloud. 'It's not as if he's an old-fashioned guy. We've been going out for some time. I didn't know people still went about it like this.'

Anjanaben's face was impassive as she said, 'Look, Mikki, I didn't want to get involved in this *chakkar* at all. But since I was approached by the boy's side...I am here as a messenger, nothing else. After all, now with your dear mother gone, who else can people turn to? At least you have me...our family...all of us...Shanay...' and she trailed off. A bearer came in with a tray. Anjanaben surveyed it and said, 'Oh, you've stopped making *farsan*...your dear mother always had four, five different snacks for visitors...some savoury, some sweet...but of course, you are a working woman. I don't suppose you have the time to look after the house. These days it is the same story everywhere. Girls are busy outside, everything gets neglected inside.'

Mikki let that pass. It was no use making the effort to defend herself in any case. She changed the subject, 'Shanay is doing very well at the office. Aren't you glad he is now living in India with you?'

Anjanaben looked at her through narrowed eyes, 'Yes...but you know, I had to force him to come back. He was happy, very happy abroad. He had learnt to cook, wash his clothes, everything. But I was the one who phoned him and said, "Come back, come back," when your parents passed away. I did it for you, Mikki, I hope you know that. I thought you needed us...someone.... Shanay is an obedient son. He came back as soon as I said he should. Anyway...now I can only look forward to his marriage. What more does a mother want besides a good *bahu* in the house? Someone who will make her son happy. If you know of any young girl…just like yourself…you let me know.' Anjanaben sighed deeply, looked around the bungalow, and ran a finger over the sideboard. 'Dust,' she commented, leaving a trail on the wood. Mikki looked guilty. 'Oh God! I must get Dhondu to organize the polishing and cleaning of the furniture.' Anjanaben nodded, 'Yes, especially before Navratri.'

It was true. She had been neglecting the house. She'd left it all to Dhondu and Gangu to supervise. She didn't even know the names of all her servants. She'd seen a couple of new faces but she hadn't bothered to find out who had hired them and for what purpose. It used to be her mother's department. And now Mikki just presumed it was handled by Dhondu and his wife. She'd have to take more interest in the house and look into the daily running of the place. She'd been signing vouchers and bills blindly. The amounts were staggering. Where was all that food going?

Anjanaben walked with her, lifting cushions, surveying the corridors, checking behind heavy doors for cobwebs. While pacing restlessly, Mikki asked her, 'So…what should we say to Navin's parents?'

Anjanaben looked at her, slightly startled by the question and said, 'Well, that depends on you, doesn't it? What do you want to do? Are you interested in the boy? Shall I go ahead with it?'

Mikki paused and said a little absently, 'I don't know. I do need someone around this place to organize things. I'm bad at it. I suppose I could hire another property manager or something.'

Anjanaben snorted, 'Mikki, please be serious. We are discussing a husband for you, not a manager. You know this boy. His family is good, quite good. Not as good as yours, but they have money. The boy, I'm told, is a little wayward, but that is to be expected in rich families. Take my Shanay—steady as a rock. We may not have money, but we have values, culture, traditions. These things are important.'

Mikki stopped in front of her aunt and asked bluntly, 'Why don't you just say it? You want me to marry Shanay not Navin. Why are you being so evasive? The reason you asked Shanay to return was because you were hoping he would hook me. Come on, be honest about it. Look…I like Shanay very much, but I don't love him. He is a good man and I can trust him. But he would fail as a husband, or maybe I'm afraid I would fail him as a wife.'

Later that evening, Mikki met Amy for a quick consultation. 'What do you think?' she asked. 'Do you love Navin?' Amy demanded. 'Love? Why should I love him? I'm looking for a husband, marriage...not an affair.' Amy's eyes twinkled, 'You are right. You don't have to love the person you marry. The important thing is—do you feel this will be the right decision? No point in getting hitched in a hurry. It's Navin today. Tomorrow can bring a Hiten, Jatin or a Jai.'

'Yes, I know,' Mikki replied, 'but Navin is well off. He may help me with Hiralal Industries.' Amy said seriously, 'That's not reason enough. Let's face it, right now your market value is very high. You are the most eligible girl in the community. You can afford to wait. Don't rush into anything stupid.' Mikki looked thoughtful as she said, 'What real difference is it going to make? If it's not Navin it will be some other rich man's son. And they are all the same anyway. Like my father.'

Amy looked at Mikki searchingly, 'I thought you'd flipped for the other one...what did you say his name was? Binny something. What about him? He's rich too!'

Mikki blushed, 'Oh, don't be silly. I can't marry someone like him. He's a rogue. Much older. Not my type at all. You know what happened that evening...how can you ask after that...?'

Amy teased her, 'You can't fool me. I can tell from your face, your eyes. Look, it's very simple—if you think Navin is the man for you even if you aren't in love with him—then go ahead. Get engaged, at least.'

Mikki got up, 'As soon as I get home, I'll call Anjanaben and tell her to say "yes". I'm surprised at Navin. The silly fool could've called or something. Here we are dating, dancing night after night and he sends his mother to propose to me—and that too through an aunt I can't stand. How unromantic....'

Amy interrupted her, 'Not unromantic—correct. That's the way it's done if you believe in an old-fashioned, conventional arrangement. And I think all that is very important to Navin's family. Now you can expect his mother to organize a huge engagement party where they'll show you off—the catch of the season. Make sure you get a fabulous ring out of them at least.' Mikki laughed, kissed Amy and went home.

*

When Mikki's car swung into the driveway she was slightly surprised to find Navin's car in the compound. She asked the gurkha, 'Navinbhai *kab aayey*?' He told her he'd been waiting for an hour. Mikki walked in to the living-room but he was nowhere to be seen. She rang the bell and Dhondu appeared. He informed her that Navin was in her bedroom. She walked up to her room and opened the door slowly. Navin was sprawled out on her silk coverlet, his arms behind his head, his shoes resting on the bed. Mikki's first reaction was to say sharply, 'Hey—take your feet off my bed.' Navin laughed, 'Baby—don't start bossing me around so soon. There's enough time to make me a hen-pecked husband.' She stared at him coldly, 'Whatever gave you the idea I've accepted?…besides, I'm disappointed that a modern man like you should need an intermediary to fix your deals.'

'Deals?' Navin smiled, walking over to her, 'What are you talking about, sweetheart? I love you.'

Mikki was too taken aback by his declaration to say anything. She allowed him to hold her in his arms and kiss her. He took his time over it, his hands moving across her back and down to her hips. He clutched her bottom and pulled her towards him as his mouth came down on hers, again and again, more roughly each time. She tried to push him away, especially when she felt him growing urgently against her. 'Stop it,' Mikki managed to splutter. 'What's the matter with you?' Navin swept her into his arms and carried her to the bed. Mikki was kicking furiously and pounding his back. He placed her down and stood over her grinning broadly. 'Don't worry…I'm not going to rape you. I'll wait. This was just a test. I'd heard you were quite a fast babe. I'm happy to see you like this. That's what I'd expected from my future wife. I don't like *chaalu* women. So, Mikki, you've passed with flying colours. Now, I can go home and tell my mother to announce our engagement.' Before Mikki could respond to the absurdity of the remarks, Navin had walked out with a swagger.

Two days later, their enagement was formalized with a simple ceremony, attended only by Navin's large family and a few relatives of Mikki's. While Mikki stared down at the six carat diamond on her ring finger, she heard Amy whisper, 'Mikki, please, try and look cheerful. You are supposed to be happy on this day.' Mikki straightened up and adjusted her exquisite Paithani sari. Navin was about to pop a *peda* into her mouth. The video cameraman lost the moment just as she opened her lips to bite into it. 'Please...repeat...don't mind...repeat...repeat...' he said. So they did.

Later at home, after the engagement ceremony, Mikki felt she needed to get away from it all. The enormity of the step she had just taken hit her with full force. She needed to clear her mind. Stepping out into the cool night air, she opened the door of her old Jaguar and slid in, rolling down the windows and stepping on the accelerator. She wanted to break all speed limits and tear down the road watching the lights of the Queens Necklace twinkling dangerously past her.

It was near the overhead Chowpatty bridge that she sensed she was being followed. There were two men in the car, both young. As the white Contessa drew up, headlights blinking, she tried to accelerate. The car refused to pick up speed. Hell! She remembered the driver mentioning he wanted to send it to the garage for extensive servicing. One of the men gestured to her to pull over. The street was empty of cars apart from the stray taxis cruising along. Surreptitiously, Mikki reached for the can of mace she always carried in her handbag—a practice drilled into her by Sean. She was being forced to the kerb and it wasn't going to be much use trying to escape or resist.

With her heart thudding, and one hand gripping the can, she pulled over and waited. The two men rushed up to her door and signalled for her to lower her window further. Before she could aim the can in their faces, one of them caught her hand, while the other spoke to her in a low, urgent voice:

'We don't want to harm you. Don't create a scene or raise an alarm. This is strictly business. And the deal involves your cousin, Shanay. Refer to these files...' the man continued, pushing some papers at her. 'You'll find all the details there. That bastard is avoiding our calls. The money involved may not be big for Hiralal Industries, but for small traders like us, six lakhs is a lot. Pay it or else we'll be forced to do something you won't like.'

Mikki stared at them coldly, 'This is not the way we conduct business in our organization,' she said. 'If you need something phone one of my financial managers during work hours and fix an appointment.'

The other man pushed his face up close to hers. She could smell the whisky on his breath. 'Forget all that, madam. We're tried everything. This deal is between you and us now. You have seven days to pay up. Six lakhs—or you're dead.' With that they were gone, swallowed up by the night as mysteriously as they'd appeared before her.

Mikki found herself shaking all over as she restarted her car. She'd have to check this out with Ramanbhai first thing in the morning. Or better still, as soon as she got home. She looked at her watch. It was past 2 a.m. No—she'd let him sleep peacefully tonight.

*

The next morning Mikki was at her desk bright and early. She'd asked Mrs D'Souza to dig up the relevant files. After half an hour, Mrs D'Souza came in to say she couldn't locate them. 'No correspondence—telexes, letters, nothing? We must have something on record,' Mikki said exasperatedly.

'Nothing at all,' Mrs D'Souza repeated.

'Send a peon to see whether Ramanbhai is free,' Mikki said and sat back at her desk, her mind whirring. How could Shanay have hoped to set away with a fiddle like this? And what had he expected—that Mikki wouldn't find out? What a fool!

A small knock and Ramanbhai was in front of her. It was so reassuring to see him. Mikki greeted him warmly, 'I'm so glad to see you. I need to talk to you urgently, I phoned in the morning but you were out. I don't know where to begin, but I had a rather unpleasant experience last night.' And she recounted the entire drama for Ramanbhai without skipping a single detail. Ramanbhai's face remained calm and expressionless through out.

At the end of her story, Mikki exclaimed, 'Well, what do you think?' Ramanbhai took his time to answer. 'Shanay is young, ambitious, perhaps immature. We'll have to tackle this nasty business in the right way—maybe involve the police or a private security agency. It's a simple matter, you leave it to me. What should we do with Shanay?' Without pausing Mikki said, 'Fire him. There's no alternative. He got his chance and he ruined it. Shanay has to go.'

Ramanbhai looked down thoughtfully at his shoes before saying, 'Is that the only option? That would make it too easy for him.

You'll allow him to get away so lightly? No. We mustn't take hasty decisions. Sooner or later, he will get into a deeper mess from which nobody will be able to save him.'

Mikki said, 'You are right. One can't be so emotional. I am prepared to give him the benefit of the doubt. Another chance, even. Let's first hear his version. I'll sleep over it….' Ramanbhai bowed slightly, 'As you wish,' he said and went out briskly.

*

Mikki thought Shanay looked particularly sheepish as he stood awkwardly at her table, shuffling his feet nervously. 'Well?' Mikki demanded, 'do you want to tell me what this mess is all about?' Looking over his shoulder to make sure nobody had walked into the room, Shanay said hoarsely, 'Look… let me explain….' Mikki looked at him stonily, 'That's what you are here for. I can tell you I don't enjoy being followed and threatened by goons in the middle of the night. I'm so mad I could fire you. But I decided to wait till I talked to you first. So…what's the story?'

Shanay sat down heavily and muttered, 'It's all a terrible mis-understanding. Actually, it doesn't involve you at all. It's between me and them. Some old diamond debt. I was stuck with a dud consignment. But I had to pay up. That's how it works in that business. I couldn't come up with the money on such short no-tice…and I thought…' he trailed off limply. Mikki waited before saying, 'And you thought you could fiddle my accounts and "borrow" the money. Is that it?' Shanay shook his head miserably, 'Fire me,' he whispered. But something about his crumpled up stance touched Mikki. She softened suddenly before saying in a voice that was harsher then she intended, 'Look…the next time you are up shit creek, don't mess with me. Tell me about it. You could have asked for a loan. I'd have arranged it for you. With interest, of course. But this was a low-down thing to do.' Shanay looked at her gratefully, 'Mikki…I don't know what to say or how to thank you.' 'Don't,' she said brusquely. Shanay got up to leave. 'Does…does Ramanbhai know all this?' he asked. 'Ramanbhai knows everything that goes on in this office.'

Shanay nodded, 'I figured that out. I wish you hadn't told him, that's all.'

After Shanay left, Mikki ordered a cup of coffee and thought about her decision. She'd been far too soft on him, she'd never make a good businesswoman if she carried on like this. But something about him had made her rethink her position. And it wasn't just the desperation in his eyes. She told herself she'd give him time. Another crack at it. They'd grown up together, and she'd always been fond of him. She'd recently begun to trust him. After getting him to give up his business and join her, Mikki's conscience did not permit her to terminate his services over this incident. But she knew what she had to do. She would get Ramanbhai to monitor Shanay's schedules and projects more closely. And she'd take away some of the key areas of responsibility from him. These, she'd handle herself. Clipping his wings, in the long run, would prove more beneficial than sacking him. Satisfied with her calculations, Mikki buzzed for Mrs D'Souza. A terse inter-office memo would do the trick, she figured, as she began dictating it.

FIVE

Binny read about Mikki's engagement in the announcements column of the *Times of India*. He'd already seen photographs in the two evening papers. One had misspelt Navin's name and the other had got Mikki's age wrong. He re-read the brief paragraph. So, she'd gone ahead and done it. Binny summoned one of his men, 'Find out more about this man,' he instructed, pointing to the circled-off item. He turned to make a couple of quick calls—first to Dubai, then Hong Kong. Binny had been depressed for the past week or so. Those bastards were at it again, stalling his plans. Bureaucracy, huh! It was so frustrating to do business in India. Nobody allowed an entrepreneur like him to function freely. He called up his consultant and barked, 'How did it go at the bank meeting, Wagle?' The man answered, 'Not as well as we'd have liked it to, sir,' 'Why?' Binny demanded, impatiently running a hand through his thick hair. 'Well, sir, there seems to be a slight credibility problem... you know with that last take-over mess.' Binny snapped, 'I don't need to hear excuses. I want results. Get it?'

Wagle hesitated before venturing to say, 'But, sir...I have some good news. Ramanbhai from Hiralal Industries approached me through a common source.' Binny sat up immediately, 'Yes?' his voice was expectant. 'What did he propose? I have a fat file on them. You've seen the papers also.' Wagle, encouraged by the words, carried on, 'We have studied the working of two of their companies closely, sir. And I can tell you, their affairs are in a complete mess. Their finance man, Amrish Dalal, and I were together in college. We apprenticed in the same firm. He was telling me the time to move is now. But what Ramanbhai came up with was different. He didn't give too many details. Should I follow it up, sir?' Binny was standing up now and nearly shouting into the receiver, 'Listen, Wagle, you just move as fast as you have to. Set up a meeting with this man right away. Don't bring me into the picture at this point. Perhaps, after the third meeting. Find out everything from him, particularly how the companies are structured. I want to know more about the holding company.' Wagle kept saying 'Yes, sir' to everything Binny said. He could sense the urgency in his voice. When he put the receiver down, Binny permitted himself a small smile. Things might improve after all.

Binny had been getting a bad business press lately. The two leading economic papers had run uncomplimentary profiles on him. Binny had been enraged by the implications. They'd called him a shady character, a wheeler-dealer and more, suggesting that he had been set up as a front man by Indian industrialists engaged in fraudulent foreign exchange transactions. They'd dug into his antecedents and come up with a rags to riches angle that people seemed to lap up. Binny frowned, recalling some of the slights. There was nothing wrong in making it from scratch, he'd reasoned. So what if he'd started at the bottom of the heap? Did these people bother to learn more about his past or about how his father had to flee Lahore during the Partition, taking nothing but his family with him? Binny's father had died when he was at school in Delhi. He'd been raised by a friendly 'uncle' next door. An uncle who finally married his widowed mother. Not a bad fellow, but somehow Binny had felt betrayed, and left home soon to start life on his own, working in the overcrowded Karol Bagh area with a paper merchant. He'd done everything from trading in second-hand car parts to starting a small business fixing electronic equipment. And now, twenty years later, he was a tycoon. He had made it. He had money, power and access to anybody he wanted to meet in the government. The only thing he didn't have was acceptability in society. It was the one thing Binny craved for more than anything else. And no one was going to deny him the status of being Mallika Hiralal's husband—and the owner of Hiralal Industries.

*

For Mikki, being engaged to Navin involved an endless round of parties, particularly those hosted by his countless relatives. Mikki found Navin's people crude and upstartish, starting with his mother who had taken to calling up every morning, or worse, visiting the bungalow without warning. Mikki mentioned her irritation to Navin who made a joke of it saying, 'Mother-in-law problems already? Don't be silly, baby. She wants to take care of you. That's all. She still treats me like a kid.' Mikki smiled, and her voice dripped sarcasm as she said, 'Don't I know it!' Navin was a bit of a brat and very juvenile in his tastes. He laughed too much and too easily and his attention span didn't stretch beyond two minutes. This evening they were on their way to an all-night *dandiya-raas* party in the suburbs.

'Navin, be careful,' Mikki urged him as they drove at a reckless speed. 'What for?' he said. 'Other chicks find it sexy. They get all horny in the next seat and practically tear my pants off.' Mikki let the remark pass and concentrated on the narrow road. She hated it when the car stopped at traffic lights and people gaped at the two of them. They were an attractive couple. She glanced at Navin, rigged out in fashionably ethnic gear for the evening. He caught her looking at him and patted her thigh, 'Not bad, huh? This dhoti idea is *maha* convenient. No zips to bother about. Lift it up and in you go... ha! ha! Feel, feel...that's what a joy-stick is for.' Mikki turned away, mildly disgusted. Navin didn't wait for the lights to change and shot past the other cars. This time he just about avoided a child crossing the street. Mikki was thrown forward roughly and her nose hit the dash-board. 'Shit!' Navin exclaimed. 'You're bleeding, man... shit!' Navin pulled over and offered her his silk kerchief. 'No, I couldn't mess up your Dior hanky,' Mikki said, and reached for some tissues in the glove compartment; instead, she came up with a carton of imported condoms. Navin grinned sheepishly, 'Just in case...you know...rainbow colours. One for every day of the week. Fun, no?' She pushed away the box of condoms and found the tissues. Once again she asked herself what she was doing with this man. Some of the blood had dripped over her clothes and they were too far from her home for her to change. Navin surveyed her under the street light and said lightly 'Chalega,chalega. In any case, you are so pretty nobody will notice your clothes. And even if they do, I'll say we decided to stop in a dark corner for a quickie and discovered you were a virgin! Ha! Ha!' Mikki was tempted to punch him.

Mikki and Navin's marriage had been fixed for December—two months from now. The thought of spending the rest of her life listening to similar cracks was making Mikki seriously dread her decision. She'd confessed as much to Amy. Amy had been slightly evasive, but she hadn't discouraged Mikki either, 'Darling, the boy is still young. We women mature faster. It's up to you to mould him, groom him, teach him how to behave in company and that sort of thing. It's much better that way. You'll be able to control him in the long run. You aren't the type to take orders from anyone. Navin seems—what's the word—malleable.' And Mikki thought of plasticine figures in kindergarten schools. The image depressed her. But she told herself Amy was right. She was better off with a slightly dumb husband than somebody like…like…and immediately Binny's face floated up in her mind.

*

Alisha's mother couldn't wait to lay her hands on the money Alisha had come into. The day Ramanbhai had produced the legal papers, Leelaben had swung into action ordering him to hand over the money immediately. Ramanbhai tried explaining to her that it wasn't such a simple matter. Buying out an established company took time, manoeuvring skills, manipulation, persuasion…so many things, so many factors. As he put it to her: 'Leelaben, you must understand…Hiralal Industries is not some corner *paan-bidi* shop that you can go and offer a good price before someone else does. There are shareholders, banks and financial institutions involved. I will move as fast as I think is necessary to corner shares. But even that takes time. We will have to persuade other shareholders to back us. We will have to prove that we have the confidence of the financial institutions and minority shareholders. These are complicated business decisions that will require years for you to understand. What I'd like is for Alisha to sign a piece of paper—a simple document granting me the power of attorney to manage her affairs. Once I get that, I will be able to control her interests. I can get to see Mikki privately, I will convince her that this is the only way to keep Hiralal Industries in the family. She's a sensible girl. I'm not so sure about her fiancé. But I have a feeling I can win him over…there are ways. And nobody in this world is beyond temptation.'

Leelaben nodded vacantly. All this was too much for her to absorb. But she knew Ramanbhai was a canny, ruthless businessman. After all, he'd been the one to dissuade Seth Hiralal from divorcing his wife and marrying her when their affair had been at its peak. She'd cursed him then and had gone to the extent of falling at his feet, begging him to change his stand. To this day she couldn't forget the disgust in Ramanbhai's eyes as he'd roughly pushed her away, hissing, 'Get away from me, you whore! You've trapped him…but your charm won't work with me. I am his friend, his adviser. It is my duty to tell him what I think is in his interest. As for you—women like you change with the seasons. Seth has everything and he can get any woman—even the Queen of England. You are nothing more than a passing fancy. Don't fool yourself. Divorce? Hunh! Who would leave a *rajkumari* for a *rundi*?' And with that he'd turned around and walked off.

Seth Hiralal had never raised the subject of marriage after that. And true to Ramanbhai's prediction, he had moved on to his next woman—a young Anglo-Indian hairdresser from Calcutta…and the next…and the next. Oh yes, he'd come back to Leelaben's bed from time to time. And he'd made sure the baby was cared for. But that was about all.

When Ramanbhai left, Leelaben poured herself a drink and attempted to organize her thoughts. She refused to believe that Ramanbhai would do anything that might benefit either her or Alisha. Leelaben made a mental note to warn Alisha. Even though she knew that if anybody could deal with Ramanbhai it was her daughter.

*

Amy had advised Mikki to return the jewellery Binny had gifted her: 'Darling, you don't need trinkets. Even expensive ones. I mean, it's just not classy to accept baubles from men you aren't going to bed with and have no intentions to marry...unless I've got the whole thing wrong, silly me.' Mikki looked at her with amusement. They were drinking tea at Chambers, whose membership Mikki had been invited to join after Amy had dropped a subtle hint to one of the directors. 'I haven't closed my options yet,' she teased while Amy pretended to look scandalized. The place was deserted at that hour. A lone shipping tycoon was busy shuffling papers at one of the tables. The waiters, trained to leave members alone, hovered discreetly in the distance, alert and ready to jump, in case service was required. Mikki liked the place even though she was one of the youngest (and certainly the prettiest) persons around. Amy narrowed her eyes and said, 'Naughty, naughty! What would your poor mother have said? Anyway, darling, there's absolutely nothing wrong in playing the field. But it does seem rather crass to me that this gentleman—and I'm assuming he is one—should ply you with something as grand after one horrendous meeting. By the way, are you sure those are diamonds and not zircons? These days it is so hard to tell, even for someone like me. I could practically smell out a fake. Instincts, I suppose. Well...to come back to you, darling, are you certain about the young man who is about to become your husband? I've heard he's something of a Mamma's boy. I must say, darling, he seems perfectly sweet, but I'm not at all sure about his parents. I mean, his mother haggles over tips with the hairdressers! Would you agree there is a slight problem about class? Never mind. It's so rude of me to be even discussing this with you. You must involve me in your trousseau shopping, darling. With your mother gone, who else can help you—and don't you dare mention that aunt of yours—what's her name—Anjanaben? Forget her, darling. Let's do it all by ourselves. Really, really splurge and feel wicked. Wouldn't you just love that? I know you don't need any more jewellery. But let's be reckless with your wardrobe. The wedding sari—have you ordered it yet or not? You know how long weavers take these days. Those Festivals of India have really spoilt them.'

Mikki took a sip of her tea and said, 'Actually, I don't want to go into a super-production. I'd prefer a quiet wedding, possibly at the bungalow itself, with a lunch to follow. The reception can be slightly larger, but definitely low-key. Navin's mother doesn't agree. She wants to hire the Turf Club and all that.'

Amy screwed up her nose, 'Well...she is rather vulgar. I'm sorry to be such a beast, darling. But low-key is not her style at all. If she could, she'd take over a floodlit football stadium.'

Mikki laughed out aloud, 'How did you guess? Do you know, that was just what she'd suggested initially! Fortunately, Navin shot it down.'

Amy asked quietly, 'And what does the young man plan to do with the rest of his life once the wedding is over? I assume he'll be working for you? Sorry, again. How gauche of me. I mean to say, helping you with the business like any husband would?'

Mikki loved Amy for this. She said seriously, 'Well, we'll just have to get him something worthwhile to do with his time. I'm sure once he finds the right slot, he'll settle down. I thought I'd let him sort of float around and then find his own level, if you know what I mean.'

'Perfect,' Amy pronounced, 'but while he's "floating", as you so charmingly put it, I'd make sure to monitor his time. And, darling—don't get me wrong—but sign all the cheques yourself, you know, until Navin gets his teeth into the business. Oh, help…there I go again…that sounded awful.'

Mikki patted her jewelled hand and said, 'Stop it, Amy. You don't have to keep apologizing to me. You are a friend. I trust you. You mean well. You are on my side—and God knows I can do with as many allies as possible. Just be your self…really. I appreciate your being candid. Very few people tell you what you need to know honestly.'

Amy smiled, 'You are a clever girl, Mikki. I must admit I hadn't thought that earlier. I'd expected you to grow into a spoilt foolish woman filling your head with frivolous fashion, parties and inappropriate boyfriends.'

Mikki laughed, 'I have had my share of all that, and I confess, I enjoyed it. But circumstances have changed. And whether I like it or not, I'm hoping Navin will help…but even if he chooses to do his own thing, that's fine. It's not as if he needs my money….' her voice trailed off.

'No?' Amy asked, her eyebrows arching.

'No,' Mikki answered firmly. 'He has plenty of his own. Come on, Amy, your bridge club must have told you that.'

'Yes and no, darling,' Amy said. 'His father has made a pile. Nobody knows exactly how. Not that it matters all that much these days. I'm not a snob about new money, so don't look at me like that. What I'm saying is Navin and his family tend to throw money around a bit too splashily. In my experience the only people who do that are those who've made it in a hurry and are afraid to lose it in a hurry. If I were you, I'd be careful. Cautious is the word actually.'

'Thank you, Amy, for warning me. But funnily enough, it isn't Navin who is worrying me, but Alisha. She has been on my mind constantly. I don't know what she's up to. Or even where she is. Ramanbhai seems a bit pre-occupied lately and I can hardly ask Shanay to keep tabs on Alisha. Would your bridge girls know anything about her, do you think?'

Amy said, 'I'll definitely ask around. Very quietly, of course. I hope that girl hasn't been bothering you. Or that poor wretched mother of hers. Alisha means trouble. You'd better watch out for her.'

'Why do you say that?' Mikki asked.

'Well, my dear, let's just say we women of the world have our instincts.'

The bill had arrived, and after signing it, they left the club. When the lift finally arrived the first person out of the door was Binny Malhotra. The lady receptionist sprang up from behind her desk to greet him, 'Good to see you, sir. You haven't been here for a while.' Binny ignored her completely, and walking up to Mikki held her by her shoulders, as Amy watched interestedly—'I still mean what I said. Marry me.' Just as abruptly he dropped his hands and strode off leaving Mikki transfixed. Amy waved her hand in front of Mikki's face and chuckled, 'Snap out of it, kiddo. It was just a line.'

Mikki straightened her *dupatta*, blushed and said softly, almost to herself. 'Was it? I'm not so sure.'

*

Shanay buzzed her on the intercom: 'Busy?' Mikki answered quickly, 'Yes. What's it?' 'Something I think you should know...I need ten minutes.' 'O.K. but keep it brief,' said Mikki and closed the files in front of her. She'd spent the last week going through what seemed like hundreds of files, a lot of which seemed to be in a highly disorganized state. Taking Mrs D'Souza's help, she'd managed to get through nearly half the files of the previous year.

Noticing that a few were missing, she'd asked Mrs D'Souza to locate them and update the whole cabinet. Now, with the newly installed computer systems, Mikki planned to revamp her office and cut down on inefficient, time-consuming methods. But for that she required all the information she could get. And the missing files were vital. Mrs D'Souza spent more than a week looking for them before reporting uncomfortably that they seemed to have disappeared. Nobody could provide any clues, neither the clerks nor the peons. Finally Mrs D'Souza said rather hesitantly, 'Madam, if you don't mind…I think the files were probably taken by Shanay with the help of the old Mehtaji who used to look after our Seth's private matters. Mehtaji had the keys to your father's office and access to all his personal files, drawers, everything. Your father trusted him completely. He told me he was working on a project with Shanay.'

Mikki had figured out as much on her own. But she'd needed independent confirmation of what she suspected. She nodded, dismayed by the news, but impatient to get on with the rest of the mess. God! She hadn't realized how distracted her father must've been over the last year. And how seriously disturbed. Some of his letters made no sense, and Mrs D'Souza had told her reluctantly that there were days he used to ramble on and dictate incoherent letters that she'd quietly destroy later. His appointment book was equally puzzling—with names and time schedules that made no sense to her. She'd found regular appointments with a Dr Snehlata Sheth and made a note to call her up when she herself was slightly more free. The telex files also had papers missing. But even the ones still there indicated a grim picture with urgently worded messages reminding her father of overdue payments, overdrawn accounts and serious shortfalls. Mikki tried to piece some sort of a picture of her father from all his papers, including a few letters written, she imagined, by Alisha's mother. They were in Gujarati and unsigned. Minutes of meetings, lawyer's notices, supplier's ultimatums…it was a wonder her father hadn't cracked up. Or had he?

*

Shanay walked in carrying an armful of files. Mikki noted he had altered his attitude towards her since the incident on Marine Drive. He was more formal and deferential, treating her like a boss rather than a friend. Mikki preferred it this way. It made their interactions that much simpler. But today Shanay looked almost grim, his face set and his forehead creased. 'Some problem?' Mikki enquired. 'Yes,' Shanay answered curtly. Mikki was slightly taken aback by his tone. He continued, 'I have found major irregularities in several departments that you need to take note of on a priority basis. I think Hiralal Industries is heading towards catastrophe unless we do something right away to stall the process.' Mikki got to the point immediately, 'Ramanbhai, you are going to say it's him. Isn't it? And it was always him? I don't know why you feel so hostile towards the old man. Without him, our companies would've gone down the drain. Forget it. I trust him completely. Tell me something new.'

'Well,' Shanay continued, 'if you'd rather not face the truth, that's fine by me. But look…I have all the evidence you need right here.' And he tapped the files.

Mikki refused to glance at them, 'I don't know what it is about the two of you. But I'm getting pretty tired sorting out your hassles.'

Mikki was finding it very hard to conceal her irritation with the two of them these days. Ramanbhai was not as obvious but he made his dislike for the younger man quite clear. It was hard for Mikki to figure out who was being threatened by whom. Or was it just the generation gap? Shanay, with his new-fangled American-style approach to business succeeded in rubbing the more conservative old man the wrong way. But Mikki knew that it went beyond that. There was deep distrust and mutual hostility that was beginning to make her most uncomfortable. She'd tried to talk about this prickly issue to Ramanbhai but he'd been dismissive. Shanay was only to eager to rubbish his senior. But it was a trait Mikki didn't care to encourage.

Shanay pleaded with her, 'Mikki, just hear me out, that's all. Let me show you that I'm not just talking through my hat. That old man is cheating you.'

'Rubbish! I bet your mother has been filling your head with all these nasty stories. But since you are here…let me see what you've come up with.'

Shanay grabbed the first of his files, 'Here…take a look. He has managed to milk two of our subsidiary companies dry—the oil unit at Bhavnagar and the biscuit factory at Baroda. They were shut down last year showing major losses which were absorbed elsewhere. But it seems that the entire thing was manipulated to run the companies aground. Look at these invoices, for example,' and he shoved the other file under her nose.

She took one quick look and said, 'Go on.'

Shanay said, 'There have been fiddles almost everywhere. He has converted the losses cleverly to his own advantage and indulged in God knows how many *benaami* transactions. The money has been grabbed by him, and I'm sure he managed to take it out of the country in various *havala* deals. There are also two big FERA violations and I have found the CBI correspondence on them. Ramanbhai had a powerful contact man in Delhi who is identified only by his initials. But I think I know who he is. We have to get to the bottom of this and fast. Personally, I think there's no point in resorting to conventional methods, you know, filing charges, law suits, police cases and that sort of thing. It will take too long. Besides, we don't have any evidence. He has destroyed all the papers. The day after your father died, Ramanbhai came to the office late in the night to shred a lot of stuff. The night-watchman told me so himself. We'll have to get him on something else and through someone he is scared of. We need a quick breakthrough.'

Mikki listened to Shanay attentively. She realized she couldn't really afford to lightly dismiss what he had just told her. Yet, she wasn't entirely convinced. Ramankaka must be getting old and goofing up, she told herself. But even so, these 'mistakes' couldn't be ignored. Assuming half of what Shanay had come up with was true, Hiralal Industries was in trouble. Big trouble. The weight of his words descended on her and strangely enough, she wasn't nervous. Thinking aloud, she said, 'What we require immediately is funds. We need to be bailed out fast. I know the banks won't look at us. And we cannot afford to borrow from the market—the interest rates will kill us. Maybe I could tap Navin. After all, he has a direct stake in ensuring Hiralal Industries doesn't sink. Let me talk to him...' and Mikki reached for the phone.

Shanay stopped her by putting his hand over hers. Startled by his action, Mikki looked at him questioningly. He said slowly, 'Don't get me wrong. But I don't think that's a good idea. I mean...he is your fiance...but I have a feeling he may not want to get involved in our affairs.' Mikki snapped, 'What do you mean by "our affairs". They are also his affairs—or, will be soon. It's in his and my interest to salvage what we can. Besides, he won't be donating the amount. I'll work out a loan arrangement that won't kill us.'

Shanay continued to look sceptical. Finally, he shrugged and left the room. Alone at her table, Mikki went over his words. What if he was right and Navin refused? Mikki hadn't even considered the possibility. She knew that had the situation been reversed, she would have willingly extended whatever help she could to Navin. Isn't that what marriage was supposed to be all about? Her mother had seen her father through a bad patch and sold a part of her jewellery, plus mortgaged her shares and other assets. She distinctly remembered snatches of their conversation during that period. Mikki had assumed it was taken for granted between partners to stand by each other when the going got rough. She was counting on Navin and his family to pitch in. She decided to call him, anyway. Navin's secretary informed Mikki that he was in a meeting but she'd interrupt him to put Mikki through. Navin sounded cheerful as he jauntily greeted her. Mikki didn't want to discuss such a delicate matter over the phone and asked whether she could come by his office later in the day to talk about some important developments. Navin laughed, 'Don't tell me you are chickening out?'

Mikki quickly clarified, 'Navin, be serious for once. This is business.'

Navin sobered up sufficiently to say, 'Well…in that case, I'd better get my mother to sit in with us.'

Mikki was dismayed to hear this and couldn't keep her annoyance to herself. 'Why do we need her around, Navin? Surely the two of us can sort it out on our own? We *are* adults, remember?'

Navin hesitated before replying, 'Look, baby, when it's business, she calls the shots. That's how it works in this set-up. I'll need to have her and the finance manager. You can bring your guys along if you wish. Any or all of them—except that creepy cousin of yours—what's his name—Shanay. I can't stand the bugger. And I don't want him drooling over my carpet, it's new.'

Mikki considered what Navin had said and rang off with a resigned, 'I'll see you at five.'

Mikki didn't see the point in involving her 'hot-shots', at this point. She decided to tackle it on her own. Shanay asked her whether she'd like him to accompany her. 'No,' Mikki said,'I know it isn't going to be easy now that Navin's mother is in the picture.

But I'll give it my best shot. Wish me luck.' Shanay raised his thumb and added, 'Sure, Mikki. But I'm also working on an alternate plan of action. A back-up strategy in case we need one.' 'You are a sweet guy,' Mikki smiled, 'did you know that?' Shanay looked away and swiftly left her room.

*

When Mikki walked into Navin's plush office suite in Cuffe Parade, she wasn't prepared to face the nearly ten people arranged around an elliptical conference table. It wasn't the first time she was there and yet she felt like a stranger. The room was cleverly designed to intimidate and overpower visitors. Navin's mother had hired the best people in the business to re-do the floor she occupied along with her top executives. The place stank of money, with highly polished granite everywhere and expensive art on the walls. The lobby looked more like the reception area of a five-star hotel than a place where businessmen waited briefly before being summoned into spacious cabins. The main area was divided up in the modern work-station manner, with open cubicles, modular furniture and plenty of green everywhere. Definitely an office designed to impress.

Mikki turned her attention to the gathering. Navin's mother came rushing up and gushed over Mikki's artfully simple trouser suit. She asked where she'd got it from and Mikki, embarrassed by the attention, lied that it was locally tailored. In any case, Anne Klein wouldn't have made an impact on the lady in front of her, whose eyes were racing over her body, taking a rapid inventory and pricing everything right down to the gold Rolex she was wearing that evening.

Navin smiled goofily at her and waved his hand by way of a friendly greeting. She could sense he was desperately trying to convey that he was on her side. Mikki found that rather sweet, but not of much help. The atmosphere was tense with only Sudhaben, cackling and giggling, underplaying her hard-nosed business woman instincts and resorting to a flighty, flirtatious manner that was as fake as the zircons on her earlobes. Mikki sat on the chair one of Navin's men held out for her and pulled out her papers. Navin had started smoking nervously. The room was silent while Mikki re-arranged her files and began her presentation, a slight tremor in her voice. Sudhaben was watching her closely, listening keenly to every word. Mikki stated her case with increasing confidence, reading out statistics and pointing to neat charts her men had hastily prepared. Navin had begun fidgeting with the ash tray and tapping his lacquered Mont Blanc against the silver pen-stand. Mikki stared pointedly at him, and his mother glared. Navin guiltily put the pen down and feigned interest in the proceedings. But it became obvious to Mikki that Navin's presence was merely decorative and that eventually any decision that had to be taken would be taken by his mother and her henchmen, who, in any case, weren't giving anything away by their bland expressions. At the end of her twenty-minute monologue, nobody spoke. Finally, Sudhaben came and placed a motherly arm around Mikki and said to the others, '*Bachchi hai*. She is young and new to all this. We must encourage her, now that she has joined the business community.' Mikki felt the colour rushing to her cheeks. The bloody bitch! It was a crushing put-down she wasn't prepared to counter. What could Mikki have said to redeem herself anyway? She sat back, shuffling her papers self-consciously, furious that Navin had not intervened on her behalf or said a single word by way of a token contribution to the proceedings. The other men were smirking and looking towards Sudhaben for cues. She carried on in a honey-sweet manner, with condescension underlining every sentence she uttered. After five minutes of this, Mikki decided there was no point in subjecting herself to further humiliation. They were getting nowhere. It was obvious Mikki had failed miserably in her mission. She got up and thanked all of them for their time and attention. Navin resolutely refused to meet her eyes. Neither did he offer to walk her to the car. And Mikki was relieved she didn't have to pat his hand or comfort him for the ordeal she had been through.

*

Shanay was waiting for her at the office. He strode up to her as she walked through the dimly-lit, deserted corridor towards her room. Both of them were silent as she shrugged off her jacket and fell heavily into the huge chair her father used to fill so easily. 'No go,' she said briefly. Shanay nodded. She was glad he was there. If he hadn't betrayed her that once, she thought, there would be so much she would like to confide in him, but….

Mikki wasn't as disappointed in Navin, as she was in herself. How could she have misjudged the situation so completely? How could she have overestimated her own position in Navin's life? She hadn't felt this small or this let-down ever before. 'Let's go get ourselves a drink,' she said, smiling wanly at Shanay.

They headed for The Library Bar at the President Hotel. Mikki liked the place. It was informal, friendly, quiet and comforting. They settled into her favourite corner table and ordered. Mikki never had to make a choice in this place. The barman knew her tastes. Within seconds a refreshing daiquiri was in front of her. Shanay settled for an orange juice. Mikki took three large sips and felt better. She leaned towards Shanay and said, 'Cheer up. It isn't the end of the world, you know. We'll find someone else to help us out. But before that, I have a little business to complete.' She waved her hand and a smart young waiter appeared immediately. 'A letter pad, please,' she said. Minutes later she was busy scribbling a short note.

It was to Navin. The engagement was off, she stated simply, without going into elaborate explanations. She added she'd be returning the ring and all the other presents the next morning. She couldn't resist a line advising Navin to hitch up with someone more credit-worthy the next time round. Surprisingly, Mikki didn't feel bitter at all. On the contrary, she was ready for another daiquiri...and another. Something, somewhere told her she'd had a narrow escape, and never mind the cost. She raised her glass and clinked it with Shanay's. 'To life,' she said. Shanay's heart broke to see her perfect teeth as she threw back her head and laughed.

*

The news of the broken engagement travelled fast. And along with it, the news of the precarious financial position of Hiralal Industries. Mikki was amused to note that the latter had created more ripples within the Gujarati community than the former. She also knew that her name had probably been struck off most society lists, to say nothing of the marriage bazaar where she'd been rendered instant poison. Amy, who had invited her over for a drink the same evening she had heard the news, was sympathetic but worried, 'Darling, having a sense of humour is fine. But you have to push on as we all do. What now?'

Mikki smoothed the creases from her crêpe-de-Chine sari—one of the few 'office saris' she'd acquired on Amy's advice. 'Any ideas?' she asked lightly.

Amy was looking thoughtfully at her. 'You know...that Malhotra man... after we ran into him at Chambers, I asked around. I rely absolutely on the bridge club grapevine as you know. He doesn't sound too bad...you can't hold his background against him. He is a buccaneer, but what can be worse than a fortune-hunter, which is what Navin turned out to be? Perhaps you should phone this man one of these days. Do be sensible, darling. Women like us can't possibly be expected to slum around after being used to certain, very basic, comforts. We both like our travels abroad, our personalized bedsheets, trinkets, servants, cars. It's absurd to give all that up. Right now, your stock is low. The quickest way to shoot to the top is to tie up with Malhotra. And I'm being very practical when I tell you this—what's the worst thing that could happen in that alliance? A disastrous marriage can always be put behind you, darling. These days divorce isn't what it used to be. You are young and attractive. There will be dozens of Malhotras later. You need a knight, even one in tarnished armour, right now. So, be a good girl, get home, have a long hot bath, wear your sexiest negligée and call the man.'

Mikki didn't have to. He called her. It was so uncanny, she nearly jumped out of her skin when the extension near her bath tinkled. 'What are you doing?' he asked her conversationally. 'Soaking,' she answered and then nearly choked on the words. She hadn't meant to be provocative. 'Wonderful,' Binny replied, 'I intend seeing you tonight. My car will be there within an hour. And before you ask too many questions, dry yourself and wear something pretty, I'm taking you to a very special place. I hope you aren't scared of water....'

A mystified Mikki replaced the receiver and got out of the tub. Water? What did Binny have in mind? She went to her wardrobe and surveyed it. Just the sound of his voice had acted as an instant pick-me-up.

Feeling strangely elated she picked a black Spanish style tore-ador jacket with a black slit skirt. She wore it with a soft, pearl-grey silk shirt and raided her mother's jewellery drawer for the ropes of pearls which would set off the simplicity of her outfit perfectly. She took her time to dress and debated over the perfume. Finally she picked Estee Lauder's White Linen. It was feminine without being overpowering, yet very sexy. Mikki admired herself in the mirror and then called for Gangubai. When the old servant appeared she asked for some orange juice. When she reappeared a short while later with a glass of freshly squeezed orange juice Gangubai said in a voice Mikki could barely hear, 'Dhondu and I are thinking of retiring in December.' Mikki stopped sipping and nearly screamed, 'What? Retiring? But you can't! Don't I look after you? How can you leave me?'

Gangu's eyes were full of tears as she spoke, 'The bungalow isn't the same without Seth and Sethani. We feel alone... you will get married and leave for your husband's house. What will become of us then? It's better that we go right now while you are still the *malkin*. Otherwise our fate will get us nowhere. We are too old to look for other jobs. Our lives have been spent here. Once you aren't there, we will be at the mercy of that man.'

Mikki caught her by her frail shoulders and shook her, 'Which man? What are you talking about? You and Dhondu do not have to report to anybody but me. Who has been bothering you. Tell me.' Gangubai looked beseechingly at her, 'Please, baby, don't do anything or say anything. Or that man will kill us. As it is, he has been threatening Dhondu. Baby, you don't know what is happening in this place. There are such stories we can tell you. But we have kept quiet...for your sake and ours.'

Mikki rang the call bell and summoned Dhondu. When he arrived, he was looking decidedly nervous. He stood before her, hands folded, and said, 'Please...make some arrangements for us to go back to our village. We cannot stand the tension any longer.'

'What tension?' Mikki said impatiently.

Dhondu lowered his voice and said, 'Strange things are happening in the bungalow these days. All sorts of people come here when you aren't at home.'

Mikki was startled to hear that. She demanded urgently, 'Which people? And who lets them in? You are in charge here, Dhondu. Plus, we have security staff, the *gurkhas*...Sakharam.' At the mention of his name, the old couple exchanged furtive looks and glanced over their shoulders. 'It is him. Him and two new watchmen he hired. You were too busy to notice, but so many changes have taken place in the last few months. We even have a new *maharaj* in the kitchen.' Mikki took in her breath. Had she been so preoccupied with her affairs that she hadn't noticed what was going on right under her own roof? She felt ashamed of her own negligence. Just then, someone knocked on the door and the three of them jumped. It was Sakharam, announcing the arrival of Binny's car. Mikki waited for him to leave before turning to Dhondu and his wife. She told them, 'Look, you are all I have left in this world. You are like my father and mother. There is nobody else I can trust. You cannot leave me alone and go. Please...don't talk of retirement. As soon as I get back, I'll look into what you've told me. Don't worry, I won't mention your name. But the first thing in the morning, I'll get rid of Sakharam. I never did like him. Once he goes, the people he has hired will also be sacked. I'll reorganize everything and spend more time looking into the affairs of the house. Have faith in me. It will be like the old days again...I promise you.' She gave Gangubai a quick hug and left the room.

*

Twenty minutes later, Mikki was in a speedboat, skimming the waves at forty knots. Binny studied her face in the moonlight, then looked at the dappled water around them and announced with a shrug, 'Don't look like that. I'd said it was going to be a surprise, right?'

Some surprise, Mikki thought, as she hung on to the narrow seat, and surveyed the rapidly receding lights of the Bombay skyline shrinking into tiny dots as she and Binny sped over the sea towards Mandwa. The jagged line of the crazily angled jetty appeared before them within fifteen minutes. The cool breeze had blown her hair all over her face. Binny looked very dashing in a blazer worn over crotch-tight jeans as he manoeuvred his tiny boat deftly into the bay which had several sailing boats anchored in it. Mikki was amused by the name he had given his high-powered speedboat. It was called '*Sexy Lady 1*'. He told her he had another bigger model which was called '*Sexy Lady 2*'. So far, Binny hadn't said a thing about where they were headed for, or why. As he dropped anchor a rubber dinghy with a small outboard motor was brought along-side '*Sexy Lady 1*'. Two men in smart uniforms helped Mikki into the dinghy. The water looked so dark and ominous, she nearly didn't climb in. But Binny's hand was at her elbow, steadying her. 'We are nearly home,' he said, pointing to the lights along the shingled shore. 'Home?' Mikki asked puzzled. 'Let's put it this way, princess, this is my principal home. The one you've been to in Bombay is just a town house. Oh yes…don't wear heels next time, princess. They look very glamorous but you can't walk over rocks in them,' Binny said, as the dinghy bumped into a boulder and Mikki clambered off, stumbling as she came ashore. Binny leaned over and picked her up with one easy movement. Mikki thought of protesting but gave up the idea. Binny was right. She would never have made it to the sprawling house by the sea on her own without breaking either the heels of her shoes or her ankles, or both.

Mikki heard dogs barking excitedly at the sound of their voices. The two men were following them at a respectable distance and behaving as if they were used to seeing Binny carrying attractive young women across the narrow strip of rocky beach to his shack by the sea. Perhaps they were, and she wasn't the first, but as they approached the low walls of the property, she struggled out of his arms saying, 'I can manage.' He mocked her, 'Can you, really? I'm not so sure.'

Mikki surveyed his spectacular set-up and whistled apprecia- tively. Binny laughed, 'I like that, princess. So…even you can and do get impressed.'

Mikki shrugged and started walking around the paved garden, lit up with hand-crafted lights that threw a soft glow on the erotic stone sculptures placed between bonsais. A uniformed bearer appeared out of nowhere, carrying a silver tray with two cham- pagne flutes on it. 'This is your night, princess,' Binny said, toasting her. Mikki raised her glass and clinked it softly against his, 'Make that "our" night,' she said. And at that moment, Binny knew he'd won her. He stared sardonically into her eyes. 'Trust me?' he asked. 'Not a bit,' she replied, reaching for his lapels and pulling him towards herself.

After a lavish lobster dinner, he led her to his split-level bed- room wordlessly. Mikki was beginning to feel woozy after five glasses of Brut. He proudly pointed out the finer details of the master bedroom—the textured walls with exposed boulders, the rugged roof with enormous beams, the shaggy throw rugs over the russet coloured flooring and the gigantic, canopied bed which looked out on to the sea that lay a few metres away. Mikki could hear the wind through the casuarinas and the waves lapping against the compound wall. The moon was low in the sky and had a rainbow halo around it. Binny gestured towards it, 'A good omen. An auspicious one,' he said, as he took Mikki into his arms and kissed her gently at first, and then with increasing passion. She felt her heart thudding against his chest. Slowly, he unbuttoned her shirt and cupped her breasts. Mikki caught her breath as Binny hauled her on to the bed and nearly tore off her clothes. He kept repeating, 'Beautiful, beautiful, beautiful,' while she lay back and closed her eyes. At that moment the only thing that mattered was the feel of him over her slim body, the touch of his fingers inside her, and the slow, deliberate movement of his tongue as it explored her mouth and kept up a steady rhythm, while his legs parted hers and he began his final assault on the woman he had already claimed as his own.

*

'So, how was it, darling?' Amy asked the next afternoon on the phone.

Mikki blushed before replying, 'Like in the movies.'

'That good?' Amy said. 'We must meet and you have to tell me all about it. My place later tonight.'

Mikki hesitated. She wasn't really free to speak, surrounded as she was by her crack team. 'Let me call you back,' she said and rang off. The young executives, who'd been pretending to be totally absorbed in their files while Mikki conversed, snapped back to attention as she said, 'So…where were we?' One of them grinned cheekily, 'Well, to put it very bluntly, in the dumps. The business papers have been going for us all of last week. This morning again there's a piece which looks planted, predicting an imminent take-over. The interesting aspect of this report is that for the first time Ramanbhai's name has been mentioned in print.'

Ramanbhai, who had been standing quietly through all this, acknowledged this bit of news with a smile. 'So far he was always identified as a "shadowy figure" working in the wings,' the young man carried on. 'There is also a mention about a mysterious person who is legally entitled to a large chunk of Hiralal Industries.' Mikki narrowed her eyes on hearing that. She didn't have to think too much to know who that was. So…Alisha was at it again.

Ramanbhai was not unduly distressed by the news. He said

softly: 'We at Hiralal Industries shouldn't pay attention to cheap bazaar gossip. Our loyalty is to Madam. We should strive hard to get over the present troubles. Our mission should be to defeat these betrayers at their own dirty game.'

Mikki studied Ramanbhai's face as he spoke, but his expression was inscrutable. Shanay's suspicions may be false. But there was no way to ignore the number of weekly resignations at all levels. Labour trouble was brewing in the factories and all the union leaders were spoiling for a showdown. This year, like the previous one, Hiralal Industries had skipped paying dividends. The bonus issue, too, was unresolved. Her finance manager had hinted at a severe cash flow crisis within a fortnight. Mikki knew she had to move and very quickly at that. She faced her young team and on an impulse made an unexpected announcement, 'I have something important to share with all of you,' she began. 'Within the week, you'll be hearing of my marriage to...' and she paused, suddenly conscious of what she was about to say, '...to Mr Binny Malhotra.'

There was a stunned silence in the room. Her eyes sought Shanay's. His jaw had dropped. A small voice piped up after what seemed like forever, 'Congratulations, Madam.' Mikki smiled at the young executive gratefully, and carried on, 'There will be an immediate transfer of funds to ride over the present emergency, and thereafter, we shall be looking at a future take-over. I'll be convening a board meeting tomorrow, followed by a general meeting soon after the motion is passed. Mr Malhotra will be in full control...and I cannot think of placing the companies built up by my dear father in better hands.' The unenthusiastic applause was slow in coming. When it had died down, Mikki dismissed the others and requested Shanay to stay behind.

Shanay looked devastated. As soon as they were alone, he said to her, his voice breaking, tears in his eyes, 'Oh Mikki! why did you have to make such a big sacrifice?' Mikki burst out, 'Sacrifice! How can you use such a word, Shanay. I'll be proud to marry Binny and become Mrs Malhotra. Please do not think I'm doing this only to save the companies.' Shanay shook his head disbelievingly, 'Whatever you might say...I still think it's a mistake. Your life is more important than the fate of Hiralal Industries.' Mikki smiled gently at him, 'Dear, dear, Shanay. You really are so sweet and true. But I know what I'm going in for and what's good for me.' Shanay's face was devoid of all colour, 'I hope you understand, I cannot work here any longer. When Mr Malhotra occupies the chair you are in, I shall submit my resignation. I will not be able to work for him…or anybody else. My old bosses in the diamond business will be happy to have me back.' Mikki understood and didn't say anything. She knew she'd be wasting her time trying to persuade Shanay to stay on.

Ramanbhai was waiting outside the door. 'This is preposterous,' he spluttered, rushing in as soon as Shanay left. How could you do such a thing? This will be the end of Hiralal Industries. Your marriage is your own affair… but here we are discussing…'

Mikki interrupted him, 'We are discussing my father's companies and their future. As it turns out my marriage is linked to both. I'm sorry you feel this way, Ramankaka, but the decision is mine and I strongly believe it's in everybody's interests.'

Mikki could see a mixture of a rage and disbelief in Ramanbhai's eyes as he struggled to control himself. Unable to hold back his words, he let them pour out, for once dropping his cold, detached manner and snarling in a voice that was full of anger, 'This is the reward I get for all the years I've spent working for your family. This is what happens in the end to loyal employees. I didn't think that one day I would be ordered around by an immature chit of a girl like you. A girl I've seen in her cradle. If only your father had given birth to a son—a responsible son instead of you, I wouldn't have had to stand by helplessly and see my life's work being thrown away so casually. You are making a big, big mistake, my dear. And you shall pay for it.'

Mikki regarded him coolly, 'Thank you for your concern and all you've done for my family, Ramankaka. I want you to know that I value you and your advice at all time. And now if you'll excuse me.…' She walked off leaving him to stare after her retreating back.

*

Mikki seemed to be facing problems on all fronts. Two nights after Binny had whisked her off to Mandwa, Dhondu had been threatened and beaten up by the new night-watchmen when she'd gone out to a party at Amy's house. She'd come home to a hysterical Gangubai, who'd bundled together a few clothes and was waiting for Mikki to tell her that Dhondu and she would be leaving for their village near Mahad at dawn. Mikki had tried hard to make her change her mind but it had been impossible to speak to her rationally. Seeing their state, Mikki had gone to a cupboard, removed five thousand rupees, and thrust it into Gangubai's hands, telling her driver to drop the two of them to the ST bus-stand. Then she'd gone to their living quarters to comfort Dhondu and check whether he required the services of their family doctor. Dhondu was more in shock than anything else, though he was badly bruised. He refused to say anything…. She could see how damaged his dignity was. Mikki told him she would send for them as soon as the troubles were sorted out. Both Gangu and Dhondu touched her feet before she could stop them. Her last memory of them was that of Gangubai wiping a framed picture of her parents with her sari *pallu* and placing it reverently into a tiny aluminium trunk, alongside framed pictures of her favourite gods and goddesses, as Dhondu looked on.

The first thing Mikki did the next morning was to summon Sakharam and sack him. She'd worked out his severance pay and other dues. He was probably expecting the action and his face was impassive as he took the envelope from her hand and walked out. She also sacked the new security guards—the ones who had assaulted Dhondu. They tried telling her they had only been following Sakharam's instructions but Mikki was in no mood to listen to explanations. She called a hurried meeting of the rest of the staff and told them she would not tolerate any indiscipline or acts of insubordination. One of the senior bearers was instructed to track down the old *maharaj* and reemploy him on better terms. Henceforth all servants were to report directly to her each morning and receive orders for the day. She was to be informed in case of any change in schedules or duties. They looked a dispirited and sullen lot, and Mikki realized just how much she'd taken them for granted. She resolved to involve herself more in the day-to-day running of the house and starting going back to her room. Just as she dismissed her staff she saw a strange sight…there, driving into her imposing compound was a beautiful car—a Mercedes 500. It had an enormous satin bow tied around it. And the compact coupé was filled with yellow roses, leaving just enough space for the driver to see the road ahead of him.

Mikki's eyes shone as she rushed to read the tiny card that had come with the car. It said, 'To my bride-to-be. A wedding present. In memory of that night and all the nights to come.' Binny! She had

had little time to even think of their unbridled ardour that magical evening, but the gift brought back memories of those moments when the waves crashing outside hadn't been able to compete with their passion, as they'd devoured each other's bodies uninhibitedly, oblivious to everything as they'd savoured each other's smells, textures, tastes, and had surrendered themselves simultaneously and totally.

SIX

All of Bombay was abuzz with the news of Mikki's forthcoming wedding. Anjanaben rushed over as soon as she heard (Shanay hadn't divulged anything to his mother). She could barely keep her disapproval from showing. 'What would your parents have said!' she started off, 'first of all, this man is not even from our community…and then…and then…the age difference. I've asked everybody….His reputation is also not good.' Mikki smiled sweetly at her aunt and said, 'Oh, I know you mean well. Who else do I have left? I need your support… your help. You must give me that. And I'll personally request Himanshubhai to perform my *kanyadaan*. I know what I'm doing. Besides, where was my community when the Navin fiasco took place? Nobody bothered to call me or meet me after the engagement broke off. And you know how badly that family behaved? Anjanaben…please do not oppose this.' The older woman was left without any words, her rage swallowed along with the *paan masala* in her mouth. 'Very well,' she said grandly, 'since you have decided to go ahead with this. But let me tell you, I'm not doing this for you but for your dead parents.'

'Of course,' Mikki answered, 'do it for them…and you'll get their blessings from wherever they are.'

Anjanaben summoned the *bai* who had replaced Gangu and one of the senior *hamaals* she was familiar with. She asked for a pad and pencil and started listing what had to be done on a priority basis. 'You will be married according to our Gujarati traditions by our priests. None of this Punjabi nonsense. It is always the prerogative of the bride's family to decide such things. Your mother would have liked to perform all the rituals—the *mehendi* ceremony, *garba, grihashanti*—everything. I'll arrange all that, of course. Don't worry, Mehtaji will maintain a correct *hisaab* of all expenses. We will sit together with the other relatives and decide on whom to invite and whom to leave out. The presents will also be worked out according to who gave what on previous occasions. Leave that to me.'

Mikki suppressed a laugh. Maybe she'd been wrong about her aunt. Maybe she wasn't all that much of a schemer. She was happy to see her so involved. For the truth was Mikki was so busy working out the details of the imminent take-over of Hiralal Industries by Binny that she hadn't had the time to bother about her own wedding.

*

Binny, the ardent lover and enthusiastic suitor, left Mikki exhausted. There wasn't an hour when something or the other didn't arrive at her office. He had instructed his jeweller to design one-of-a-kind modern pieces for his bride, besides acquiring collector's items from down and out Maharajahs and Ranas looking for discreet deals. Weavers and sari merchants came bearing exquisite silks and brocades which they left for her approval.

Binny teased her, 'I bet you thought I was another one of those Punj-pappey types who'd bombard you with Karol Bagh silks and Chandni Chowk trinkets. Darling princess, you deserve the best and you are going to get it. I realize how alone you must be feeling right now without a mother or a sister to help you with the shopping. But just because we don't have anybody does not mean that my princess will get short-changed. My philosophy is simple—if you don't have them, hire them. For a price, you can get even relatives!'

*

Late one afternoon, just as Mikki was about to plunge into some lengthy correspondence, an embossed letter-head was hand-delivered, bearing two words: I'm waiting. Puzzled, she looked up at the bearer. It was Binny's chauffeur. '*Saab* is in the car downstairs,' he announced. Mikki picked up her bag and rushed. Binny greeted her with a broad grin. 'Where to?' Mikki asked slipping in beside him. 'Office,' he replied with a wicked gleam in his eyes. Ten minutes later they found themselves in the elevator taking them up to Binny's floor. Once inside his room, he shut the door with a soft click. 'Take off your clothes, princess,' he commanded as he efficiently stepped out of his own. 'What?' Mikki wasn't sure she'd heard right. 'Off, off, off,' he gestured impatiently.

Mikki could hear busy office sounds coming through the door. Seeing her hesitation, Binny walked over and undid her buttons swiftly. Mikki tried to stop him but his urgency was obvious. And by this time she knew that Binny Malhotra generally got what he wanted. She abandoned the fight and helped him with the skirt zipper. 'This has been my fantasy from the day I saw you,' Binny said with a satisfied laugh. 'I wanted to take you right here, on my table...not on a holiday...and not after office hours....but bang in the middle of a hectic work day, with my secretary buzzing the intercom and people waiting to see me.'

Mikki smiled indulgently. The man she was going to marry was clearly crazy, but it was precisely this sort of madness that turned her on. Binny picked her up and placed her on the enormous table with great delicacy. She felt like piece of rare porcelain as his fingers stroked her body. The phone rang—Binny's direct line. He ignored it. It rang again. And again. With each ring his ardour grew. An impatient sweep of his arm flung various papers and files to the floor. He pushed up her knees and pulled her to the edge of the table. 'Perfect!' he commented as he entered her smoothly while standing squarely on the plush carpet, his body close to her prone form. Mikki looked up at the ceiling briefly and saw the two of them reflected in the glass covering the overhead lights. Binny's head was thrown back while his body arched gracefully at the point where it joined hers. 'This is like a dream come true,' he repeated thrusting into her vigorously. 'Don't come, princess...or come again and again,' he panted, his hands over her breasts, his eyes tightly shut.

Mikki was ready to lose herself in the act of love when he abruptly withdrew and jerked her up into a sitting position. 'Like that?' he asked, still out of breath. 'Why did you stop?' she complained, drawing him into her again—being rougher than she intended. Her nails dug into his back as he carried her to an upholstered couch on the other side of the large room. 'This is the ultimate joy-ride,' Mikki crooned, feeling him inside her as he walked. He put her down without getting out of her. 'Straddle me, princess,' he said, as they sat across each other, legs and arms entwined. 'Pretend I'm your rocking horse,' he prompted as Mikki moved her bottom back and forth till she couldn't contain her desire any longer. Grabbing the back of his hair, she allowed the moans to escape, uncaring that the sounds would carry outside. 'Yes, princess, yes...do it,' Binny encouraged, as Mikki moved energetically, her body glistening with sweat in his air-conditioned room. She felt Binny's index finger entering her from the back at the exact moment when she was at the pinnacle of passion. She cried out at the exquisite pain of the sensation as the two of them climaxed together—noisily, wetly, exhaustedly—in perfect tune with each other's rhythms and needs.

Their nights were equally hectic: with Binny, the inexhaustible lover taking her forcefully again and again, often changing locations and laughing at her reactions. She enjoyed his experienced approach and found herself discovering aspects of her own sexuality she hadn't guessed existed. Binny also relished talking sexily to her over the phone and driving her into a semi-frenzy with the explicitness of his words and the limitlessness of his imagination. Mikki found herself getting jealous of his expertise and questioning him about previous lovers. Binny stopped her by covering her mouth roughly with his own before pushing her head further down his body, till she had him between her lips while her tongue flicked over him and her teeth nibbled hungrily along his length. 'Don't let's go into flashbacks, princess. They aren't relevant. There's no room for them in our life. My world begins and ends with your body now. Who I had or how many is not worth discussing. Enjoy the moment. Enjoy us.' And Mikki smiled, nuzzling his chest and kissing the crook of his arm where her head was resting. It was true. He hadn't asked her about any of her previous boyfriends. He hadn't even mentioned Navin.

Mikki squeezed his hand affectionately. They were spending a quiet evening together at his town house. She was overwhelmed by the attention Binny paid her. There was no time to step back and review her decision. There was no time for anything. The evenings went by in a blur of endless cocktail parties for the two of them. The crowd was far older than the one she was accustomed to, and she found their business gossip boring. The women were syrupy and uninteresting, ceaselessly discussing their latest acquisitions. But as long as Binny was there, close to her, exchanging a conspiratorial wink, leaning over to kiss her lightly or just looking at her over the heads of overdressed strangers, Mikki felt good. In love.

Mikki felt guilty about her earlier reservations. She had misjudged him. Beyond the rough exterior and gruff manner, Mikki had found an attentive, loving man who didn't spare any expenses to please her. It made her feel so much better about her marriage and herself. She wasn't selling out. She was buying in. It was a thought that comforted Mikki as she treated herself to a long bath before getting into an elaborate embroidered *lehenga* that had been specially flown in from Delhi for that night. The night Mikki was to meet Binny's family.

*

It was less of an ordeal than Mikki had imagined. Binny had converted his home into a *mela* for the occasion, abandoning the European ambience, camouflaging the marble bird-baths and statues by draping *phulkari* covers over them. Under an enormous, Delhi-style, brightly coloured *shamiana*, over a thousand guests had been assembled. Mikki had a small group of relatives with her. On Amy's advice, she'd kept out most of the distant aunts, uncles and cousins preferring to restrict it to just Anjanaben, Shanay, his father and two other uncles she was fond of. Amy was on hand to steer her nimbly though the crowds while providing an entertaining commentary throughout. Mikki whispered more than once, 'But who are all these people...they're so different from us.' 'Of course they are, darling,' Amy giggled, 'they are Punjabis.'

Mikki's eyes searched for, and finally found, Binny. She'd barely seen him that night. She caressed his body with one, long, sweeping look that took in the well-tailored *sherwani* that glittered with uncut-diamond buttons. He looked like a swarthy warrior. Mikki knew that he was the most impressive man in the gathering. She felt her face burn as she clutched Amy's arm, whispering, 'Isn't he gorgeous! 'Amy exclaimed, 'Yes…I suppose he is. But just look at who he's with, if it isn't that bitch—Urmi.'

Mikki hadn't even noticed Binny's companion, who he was so absorbed in conversation with. But now she looked and her eyes settled on a hard-faced woman in her mid-thirties.

'Who is she?' Mikki asked curiously,

'Very attractive…don't you think?' Amy said by way of reply, 'and equally lethal. I thought she was living in London these days. I heard she'd hitched up with some Sheikh.'

Mikki found herself staring. The woman was quite stunning: dressed in an aquamarine chiffon that displayed her curves to advantage.

'What a figure!' Mikki said, and added, 'I'm jealous.'

'Don't be,' Amy said, 'you've got him—not her.'

Mikki laughed, 'I suppose that's the right way to look at it. Let's move along. Maybe I'll find someone to make eyes at too. Perhaps Binny will notice me then.'

Amy steered her though a dense group of over-dressed women attacking their *gulab-jamuns* ferociously. 'Darling, you have to keep reminding yourself that you'll be marrying a man of the world, not some inexperienced youth. He must have his own life. And in time, you will have yours. That is the civilized way to handle marriage. Binny is not a love-struck teenager. He is a shrewd businessman, and I'm sorry to say this, since it is a harsh judgement, but he is something of an *arriviste* and therefore a social climber. Nothing wrong with that. But you should realize your own worth in his life also. Don't undersell yourself, ever. And that's Aunty Amy's advice to you.'

Mikki gave Amy a big hug and they went across the lawns to watch a group of men dancing the *bhangra* with great gusto.

The last of the guests left at dawn after an enormous Punjabi breakfast of *aloo parathas* washed down with tall silver tumblers of *jeera* flavoured *lassi*. There was fresh *gajjar-ka-halwa*, *jalebis* and thick cream to go with all that. Mikki felt sick just watching the people eat, while Binny played the perfect host—attentive, charming, warm. He was also pretty drunk. But Mikki found herself making excuses: 'If not now, then when?' she said to Amy who left soon after pleading a migraine. It was obvious to Mikki that

Binny's crowd hadn't exactly impressed her older friend.

And now, Mikki herself was beginning to flake off, but Binny was in no mood to call it a night, even at 7 a.m. He'd gathered four or five of his cronies around him and was busy ordering Bloody Marys when Mikki gestured that she wanted to leave and catch up on some sleep. Binny roared, 'Sleep? Nobody sleeps till I say so.' Mikki thought he was play-acting. She smiled and started to collect her handbag. A sudden crash behind her head startled her and she jumped instinctively to one side just as a few shards of glass flew past her face. Alarmed, she stared at Binny who was laughing uproariously while his hangers-on watched the scene, uncertain of the response expected from them. '*Saali* Urmi *kidhar gayee? Bulao usko*...' Binny slurred. There was an embarrassed pause as the flunkeys shuffled around looking uncomfortable. 'Urmi!' Binny shouted and lunged towards the door unsteadily, 'Urmi....Urmi....Urmi....' Mikki watched in horror as Binny staggered out into the compound and waved for his chauffeur. In a minute, his car glided up. Binny fell into the back seat and was gone.

*

'Darling, all brides get cold feet,' Amy soothed her, 'and don't let these men fool you...they get them too. Binny must've been nervous. And a little high... that's all. Forget it.'

Mikki wasn't exactly convinced by her explanation. She'd seriously considered calling the wedding off. Binny had been appropriately contrite and nearly drowned her in yellow roses, which had been accompanied by an exquisite Patek Phillipe jewelled watch. The small note had said simply, 'Forgive me. I love you.'

Amy had also harped on the business complications now that Mikki had impulsively signed over practically the dress off her back to Binny. 'Either way you are screwed, darling,' she'd said gently. 'So you may as well go through with it.' Mikki knew that what Amy was saying made sense. She had placed herself in a situation in which she was at Binny's mercy, stripped clean of all her assets, her businesses, her properties—just about every conceivable possession. She'd traded in all that for love. Everlasting love. And now it seemed to her that she'd been short-changed. Cheated. A sense of panic convulsed her. It was too late...too late... too late. The new watch on her slim wrist was ticking away softly…while the countdown to the marriage *mahurat* had already begun. Trapped, scared and terribly alone, Mikki reached for the phone. There was just one person she felt she could turn to. Just one person whom she hoped against hope would understand her. Alisha. Her sister Alisha. She prayed fervently while the phone rang. 'Please don't turn me away…please don't let me down. You are the closest person left for me in the world. We share the same blood. We had the same father. I need you…help me, help me.'

*

Alisha's voice on the phone sneered, 'So…you beat me to it once again. Bitch! And now you're the one crying on the phone. *Wah!*' Mikki didn't know what she was talking about, 'Beat you to *what*, Alisha?' she asked, her voice breaking. 'Don't pretend,' Alisha countered, 'You knew very well that I was on the verge of taking over Papa's companies from you.'

Mikki caught her breath, 'What are you saying?'

'Go on, pretend some more. You should've been an actress. You can still become one, after that bastard throws you out….As if you weren't aware of the situation. I had the money to buy you out. Papa had left it to me. It's me he loved. I was the one who inherited a trust. You inherited debts. That's all. My money was safe. Papa saw to it. That's the way he'd planned it. All my life I had to do without all the things you took so much for granted. And just as I was about to get everything, you sold it off to a stranger, an outsider, a vulture who will devour you and spit out the bones. Serves you right. Go ahead and marry him, or don't. But leave me alone.' With that Alisha banged down the phone and turned triumphantly to her mother. 'Showed her nicely, didn't I? God knows what she was really after…crying and all that on the phone. All *nakhra*, all *natak*. She really thought she could fool me and that I would melt. I'm sick of her. Everywhere I go I hear nothing else. Mikki this, Mikki that. "Has anybody told you you look like Mallika Hiralal?" Shit! I wish she'd die.'

Alisha left her mother's room and went into her own. Now that the grand take-over plan had fallen through she'd have to think of other things. But first, she would use some of her money to move out of this dump, and into a decent building. Alisha pulled out a brochure left by a prominent builder. 'Luxury penthouse in

Versova.' Too far. 'Four bedroom duplex in Worli.' She circled that. 'Three bedroom flat with sea-view. Cuffe Parade.' Too small. 'Terrace flat with garden. Malabar Hill.' Worth considering.

It was in the course of her own house-hunting spree that Alisha discovered she had a nose for real estate. She could literally smell out good properties. It was a line that fascinated her. And the money was big when you knew how to roll it. Over a couple of weeks she managed to establish a quick rapport with a developer—a young man called Altaf, who had just started out in the business himself. Intrigued by the quick returns this business allowed, she'd partnered with him on two small deals and made enough to want to back his next project—a shopping complex in Nalasopara. Within a month Alisha found herself on the threshold of an exciting and challenging career. She enjoyed site inspections and was learning rapidly about building material and where to get it at the best prices. Now, with two or three projects off the ground, clients were beginning to approach her directly. All that was required was a telephone and some desk space. Altaf managed to acquire both. They split the costs of running their 'office'. Alisha was keen on getting into big time quickly while Altaf was more cautious. They had two building co-operatives to finalize, plus a modest resort at Khandala. Once that went through, they would consider other jobs, maybe even a luxury hotel in Goa, which had asked for bids in the open market.

Ramanbhai was aware of her involvement in this business and had warned her against it. 'This is not for us. It is not for respectable people. The building trade is controlled by thugs, smugglers, gangsters—all sorts of anti-social people with jail records. It is dangerous. Builders use *goondas* to evict people from sites. Enmities are settled through violence. Why do you want to dirty your hands?' But Alisha had been far too elated to listen.

Yet, absorbed as Alisha was in her own activities, there seemed to be no getting away from Mikki's shadow. Everywhere she went she faced the inevitable questions and the inescapable comparisons.

With each encounter, Alisha's rage against the injustice of her situation only grew. She promised herself that one day the balance would alter in her favour. One day, people would feel sorry for Mikki. One day, she, Alisha, would be on top of the situation, looking down on all those people who didn't give her the time of day. They would, she swore, oh yes, they would. They owed her that much. But first, she'd finish Mikki.

*

Alisha's business was expanding at unimaginable speed. At the rate she was growing, it didn't do to operate out of a hole in the Lakda Bazaar. She'd been offered a *gala* at Nariman Point in a building right next door to Hiralal Towers. The estate agent was asking for an absurd amount, most of it in an unaccounted for cash transaction. That wasn't the tough part for her, because in her rapidly expanding business, most of the deals were sealed with fat wads of notes that weren't reflected in the books. But a *gala* wasn't Alisha's idea of a swanky office. She wanted the entire floor. Perhaps a dual deal with her dream apartment tied into it would solve the problem. She walked into Altaf's cubicle and asked him to sniff around for a bargain. A distress sale, perhaps. With her luck and instincts, she'd know immediately when she found both. Her office would be bigger and better than the suite Mikki functioned out of. And soon…she'd throw her out of that as well. Mikki along with that suitor of hers. Alisha frowned, thinking of her mother's harsh words that morning. The invitation to attend all the ceremonies had arrived, hand-delivered by Mikki's chauffeur, along with an ornate golden box containing a kilo of *kesar barfi*. As soon as the chauffeur left, Leelaben had flung aside both and commented bitterly, 'See…she has beaten you again. Mikki is getting married. The man must be a millionaire. Look at this card. They must've spent no less than five hundred rupees on each piece. And God knows how many lakhs or maybe even crores will get spent on her wedding. Will I live to see the day when you have *mehendi* on your hands? Without a father, without even his proper name, who will marry my girl? Nobody in the community….'

Alisha had fumed, 'Do stop your meaningless *bak-bak*. I don't want to get married. You hear? But if I choose to, I'll be able to get whosoever I want, even Prince Charles. Yes, yes, don't make a face. Money can buy the best husband in the world. And today I have it. I have more of it than that girl. Besides, who has she ended up with? Some unknown character. Maybe even a smuggler. These days it's hard to tell. As for your great community, you can keep it. I wouldn't want to marry some *gujjubhai* in any case. I'd rather die a spinster.'

Her mother sniffed, 'With your reputation you probably will. I've given you a good education, good clothes, good food, everything. Why? Because I didn't want you to suffer the same fate I have suffered. I wanted you to enjoy a respectable life. Get married into a decent family. Be a gentleman's wife. Go to good clubs in good clothes. Have nice children. What else can a mother want for her daughter, tell me?'

Alisha turned away abruptly and picked up the phone. But her mother wasn't through with her. 'Go on...talk to the *mussalman*. Marry him too. Complete the disgrace. Out of all the Gujaratis in this business, you could only find some Muslim fellow. People are talking. Just yesterday I got a call from Pratimaben. She asked if it was true. That is how a girl's name gets spoilt. Don't blame me later when nobody is ready to even look at you.'

SEVEN

O n the day Mikki was to be married, the headline in the morning's paper shocked the city. 'Was Seth Hiralal murdered?' asked the tabloid and went on to quote 'a source close to the family', who had divulged the rumour that was doing the rounds in business circles. Rivalry with an unnamed group was given as the reason for the 'heinous crime' with a request to the investigating agencies to re-open the case which had been closed as a straightforward one of an accident. The dead pilot's wife had been interviewed and she expressed her doubts over the accident theory. 'My husband was a cautious, experienced pilot with an excellent service record. Unless somebody had tampered with the engines, it is impossible for his plane to have crashed. He never neglected to complete all pre-flight checks. Besides, he had flown successfully under far worse weather conditions and over difficult terrain when we were posted in Assam. He used to pilot the chairmen of tea companies. They entrusted their lives to him. I believe this was not a simple accident. I think it was a plot to kill Seth Hiralal. My husband has been wrongly blamed. He was a good pilot with a clean record. And I would also request the authorities to reopen the case and clear my husband's name.'

The lady added that she had received neither insurance nor compensation after her husband's death.

It was obvious who was going to get hurt the most by this—Mikki. Amy phoned her as soon as she read the report to say she must ignore it. Mikki was too shell-shocked to reply.

'Darling, we are brought up to deal with muck-raking with dignity. Don't let such evil gossip ruin your big day. Keep your head high. Look beautiful. Show the world the stuff you are made of. If nosy, insensitive, boorish people ask you, treat them with the contempt they deserve. I'll be over as soon as I can get my face on.'

Mikki read and reread the piece dozens of times. She couldn't make any sense of it. The motive she could understand: to get her upset enough to call off the wedding. But why would anyone want to stop her from becoming Mrs Binny Malhotra?

*

Binny called sounding concerned and solicitous, 'Princess, we'll fix whoever has done this to you later. But today is our day and nothing and no one can ruin it for us. Look your best. That will be the perfect revenge. Don't answer any questions. And don't accept any calls from press-*wallahs*. I can't wait to see your naked body. I'll be stripping you with my eyes throughout.'

Mikki wondered whether she should speak to anyone else but decided she could do without insincere sympathy. Strangely enough the one person she really felt like talking to was Shanay. But he had distanced himself totally from her. She hadn't seen him in days. How she missed his quiet presence and unflinching devotion. She wondered how Alisha was taking the awful news. After all, he was her father too. Unless, of course, whoever it was had made her a party to the newspaper plant and she was a part of the conspiracy to embarrass Mikki on her wedding day. Mikki dismissed the thought as being far too uncharitable. Finally, she made a determined effort to get the whole business out of her mind. She knew Amy and Binny were right. She would have to square her shoulders and face the world looking more dazzling than she ever had before.

As Mikki treated herself to a long soak in a bathtub filled with fragrant oils, fragments of the article returned to haunt her. The report had talked about her father being involved in a multi-crore scandal. It mentioned a deal that had soured and money that he was unable to pay back. Loans to the tune of eighty crores. Licences that had been acquired under suspicious circumstances. A rival whose project had been stalled using pressure tactics in Delhi. Was her father such a manipulator? Or had he become a victim of his own ambitions in the end? Was his death orchestrated by rivals? Or an insider? Who had miscalculated? And by how much? Mikki wished she had at least some of the answers. In another few minutes from now, her bedroom would be taken over by stylists, hairdressers, beauticians. And from that point on, she wouldn't be alone for even a moment. Mikki felt she had to do something, enlist some help to get to the bottom of the story, starting with tracing the source. Who had given it to the tabloid? And how much money had changed hands in return for the favour? Once again, Mikki found herself thinking of Shanay. She told herself not to let pride get in the way...and dialled his number. She got Anjanaben on the line, who informed her that Shanay had left town the previous night.

*

Binny had insisted Mikki dress like a traditional Punjabi bride. She hadn't really minded. Red and gold were her colours and she vastly preferred them to the white and red she'd have had to wear had she opted to go *Gujju* for the ceremony. Mikki missed her mother desperately even though they'd never really been particularly close. She missed Dhondu and Gangubai, who seemed happy enough in retirement. The house loomed over the tiny bride, and Mikki began to feel depressed at the thought of leaving it permanently. Her bed, her room, her cupboards, her bathroom, her place at the dining-table, her swing in the garden, her old clothes, her servants, her drivers, her area...her sense of self, as it were. She began weeping uncontrollably as Amy ran to fetch a box of tissues, saying, 'Your make-up. The mascara! Oh God! Why didn't the woman use water-proof stuff!' Mikki muttered, 'Fuck the mascara. Fuck everything. I don't want to go through with this. I want my room, my home. I don't want to marry Binny. Amy...do something. Ring him up...call it off. I don't care how it'll look.'

Amy ignored her completely and went about organizing her jewellery, getting dozens of red bangles, arranging the two main sets Mikki would be wearing and packing an overnight case with a new negligée, toilet case, and a fresh change for the next day. Mikki couldn't understand her indifference and finally screamed, 'Listen to me! Look at me!' Hearing her scream, Anjanaben rushed in from outside where she'd been busy with the few guests and relatives from Mikki's side who'd assembled there to accompany the bride to the *mandap*. Amy tactfully hustled her out of the room and came back to Mikki. She shook her hard and then forced her to sit down on the bed. 'You are behaving like a spoilt brat, darling. Get hold of yourself. You aren't some twelve-year-old marrying a man against your will. You have chosen Binny. This is your decision. Every bride feels nervous and unhappy to leave one part of her life behind, but this is ridiculous. Now, go blow your nose. It's almost time to leave. We will miss the *mahurat* otherwise....'

Mikki's sobs subsided. She looked at her face in the mirror. God! the make-up woman's hour-long efforts had been completely washed off. In any case, she'd made Mikki look like a vamp from the Hindi screen. Mikki went into the bathroom to scrub her face clean and start again, from scratch.

*

The wedding was a spectacular affair, a super-production done with amazing taste. Binny had arranged for a European lady of great refinement to organize everything, down to the choice of music. Mrs Maria Lal was an Austrian who'd come to India ten years earlier. She was married to a corporate bigwig and moved in the best of social circles. Somewhere down the line, she'd become involved with Indian handicrafts. She'd owned a string of successful boutiques that specialized in one-of-a-kind *objets d'art*. She also ran a roaring export business dealing in fakes—fake antiques, fake jewellery, fake furniture. But above all, she was the 'Ambience Empress'. She orchestrated grand happenings—auctions, parties, charity balls and occasionally, weddings. Binny had courted her ardently through mutual friends. Maria had succumbed eventually...for a whopping fee. The setting was dignified and understated, with plenty of natural coloured *khadi* silk and fresh jasmine blossoms everywhere. Binny himself, looking stately, was cold sober. Mikki exchanged glances, remembering to keep her head, weighed down with the *ghungat*, appropriately lowered. Fortunately, Binny had dispensed with the standard trappings of a typical Punjabi wedding and so this bridegroom did not arrive astride a decorated mare, accompanied by a noisy *naan khatai* band blaring the latest disco hit. He had also hand-picked the invitees, leaving out the rowdier elements from his crowd. The assembled guests represented a good mix of business and the arts. Mikki had left almost everything to him, thankful when he'd told her, 'Princess, your job is to look beautiful. Taking care of all the arrangements is mine.'

Anjanaben had got her way on a few things though. The priest was Gujarati and the rituals were being performed according to the traditional rites of Mikki's community. Binny looked very bored through the múmbo-jumbo of chants that nobody really understood. As the priest got the holy fire going, Mikki felt her eyes smart. She looked up and saw Binny with tears streaming down his face. The priest ladled some more ghee into the crackling flames. Mikki resisted the impulse to giggle and paid attention to his instructions. At one point he placed a *supari* on Binny's palm and got Mikki to put hers over it. A silk scarf bound their hands together as some more *mantras* were chanted. Binny's finger scratched Mikki's palm as he whispered to her, 'You know what that sign means, don't you?' Mikki smiled, 'Don't tell me, let me guess. You're horny, right?' The priest looked at the two of them sternly as he walked around wrapping them in a sacred thread that had the bride and bridegroom tightly bound in its fragile web. 'He isn't taking any chances, is he?' Binny said under his breath as the bare-torsoed *pujari* took one end of Mikki's sari *pallav* and tied it into a firm knot with Binny's *angavastram*. Mikki teased in a low voice, 'Try running away from me now, Binny Malhotra.' Surreptitiously her husband of a few minutes reached over and pinched her bottom. The *saat pheras* around the fire were finally over. 'This is where you belong from now on, princess,' Binny said solemnly. Mikki did not look up to see whether or not he was joking.

As they exchanged garlands Mikki could hear a distinct sob followed by a long wail coming from amongst the guests observing the ceremony. From the corner of her eyes, she saw Urmi being escorted out of the *mandap* with a young girl by her side. What on earth was she doing here, Mikki thought, with irritation; Binny's face hadn't twitched a muscle throughout the little scene. Mikki decided to ignore it and concentrate on the ceremony.

Three hours later, it was all over. The *baraat* had been modified and shortened to exclude those endless songs of lament, cheating elderly relatives of the sadistic pleasure of making the bride cry her eyes out whether she felt like it or not. Binny had instructed the priest to stick to the basics and get on with the formal part of the long drawn out ceremony as briskly and briefly as possible. Even so, given the lavish dinner that followed and the *ghazals* sung by Begum Zenia (imported from Pakistan for the night), it was well past the witching hour by the time Binny nudged his lovely bride and asked mischievously, 'Shall we run away?' They slipped away quietly leaving their guests to enjoy what was left of the party. Binny ignored the flower bedecked wedding car and slid in behind the wheel of his Peugeot. 'Princess; this is our night,' he said, kissing Mikki passionately. 'Let's make the most of it.' Successfully evading the crowd of drivers, he pulled out of the parking lot and headed straight for the Gateway of India, where '*Sexy Lady* I' was waiting for them.

'But, darling...what about my things, my clothes, my tooth-brush?' Mikki asked.

'You aren't going to need any of that....' Binny replied.

It was a night Mikki would remember forever. There was a slightly mad edge to everything Binny did, from the time they left the shores of Bombay, till they awoke, close to noon, the next day. She couldn't quite put her finger on it, but Binny seemed differ-ent...all charged up and excitable. His laughter was exaggerated as was his love-making. He took her again and again, making her ache with pleasure as well as physical fatigue, as his seemingly inexhaustible desire kept driving him to make love minutes after they'd both collapsed drowsily in each other's arm. He bathed her in a bottle of champagne, he massaged her with bath oils, he poured a flacon of Joy on her limbs and crushed rose petals between her breasts. He licked honey out of her and passed straw-berries, half-eaten, from his mouth to hers.... His expertise and imagination were boundless as he excited her in a hundred differ-ent ways, touching, licking, nibbling, sucking...he turned her over, he stood her up, he had her on all fours, and he even had her upside down with blood rushing in a gush into her head. It was unreal, pleasurable, but also a little frightening. Mikki didn't have time to do anything but savour the myriad physical sensations sweeping over her pliant body as she surrendered to this man who was now her husband. There was no resistance left. And she was happy. They had broken all the rules and every taboo she had ever known.

She felt liberated, uninhibited and aroused to the point of primitive abandon. If this was what her man wanted, if this was what made him happy, she would give it to him. She would give him every bit of herself, her body, her mind, her soul. She was in love with him. And he was finally hers.

The honeymoon in Bali was short—just four days—but Binny promised her a longer one as soon as their business affairs were sorted out. 'Besides, princess, I want our life to be an unending honeymoon,' he teased as they lay contentedly on the beach, sipping tall drinks with hibiscus flowers floating in them. Mikki was in no mood to complain, though she had been hoping they'd get to be together exclusively for at least ten days before rushing back to the frenetic life they'd left behind in Bombay. 'What am I going to do when we return?' she asked Binny, pouring a fistful of sand over his belly.

'Be my slave, of course,' Binny answered.

'Full time?' she pouted.

'Full time,' he confirmed.

Mikki said, 'Darling…be serious. I am used to a busy schedule, a business to run…I can't just sit around doing nothing.'

Binny answered casually, 'You won't be doing nothing. Looking beautiful is serious business. Women work hard at it. And full time.'

Mikki pushed herself up on her elbows and looked at him. 'You're teasing, aren't you?' she asked seriously.

'No,' Binny replied shortly. 'I haven't married a business tycoon. One in the family is enough. I want a wife who stays home and looks after me. That's it.'

Mikki traced her fingernail down the length of his arm and persisted, 'I can look after you and look after at least a part of the business. We could work together, jointly. That way we won't be separated. I won't have to wait hours to see you.'

Binny pulled his eyeshades over his eyes and said tersely, 'No. That's not how it works in my family. Our women stay at home and make sure the place is perfectly run. They fulfil their husband's every need and look good when their men get home in the evening. No office-going. No business meetings. And you'd better get used to it.'

Mikki realized she'd be wasting her time pursuing the topic at that moment. She told herself she'd bring it up again once they'd settled down to their new life at home. Binny's home. And now hers too.

*

Alisha finally found the home of her dreams. And it happened to be right across the road from Mikki and Binny's Bombay bunga- low. Perhaps that was one of the reasons she grabbed it even though an astronomical price was being asked. Her mother pro- tested, whining, 'Baby, why do we need a palace? Let's not spend so much.' But Alisha knew she just had to have it and didn't waste any time clinching the deal. She didn't want to wait around while the place got fixed up either. She gave orders to her contractor to go ahead and ready one section of the house for her to move into with her mother, while the electricians, plumbers and carpenters hammered away at the rest. She got a marble plaque done for the outside which said 'Alisha's Hideaway' in gold letters. Landscape designers went to work on the grounds while Alisha strode around impatiently, clad in skin tight jeans, tossing her long, silky hair and screaming orders at workmen to finish, finish, finish. 'What's the hurry, *baba?*' her mother kept asking as she watched her daughter behaving like a woman possessed. 'I want it now. And want the best, 'Alisha crowed, supervising masons as they fitted granite slabs into the main lobby and started on the parquet flooring for the living-room.

Alisha dreamed about inviting Mikki over one day to see all the grandeur for herself. Grandeur that owed everything to the gener- osity of her father…and Mikki's. She imagined the interiors of the bungalow across the street and visualized Mikki moving around languidly inside, and swore to herself that 'Alisha's Hideaway' would put Binny's residence in the shade.

Meanwhile, most of her other projects were taking shape on schedule and Alisha was enjoying her work. She'd hired an attrac- tive young woman called Sapna to oversee details and go on sites for inspection. They'd struck up an odd sort of friendship. While Sapna was careful enough to maintain her distance and act defer- ential in the presence of outsiders, she had taken to offering Alisha gentle advice on her own home as well as on the more sophisticated aspects of living—such as reorganizing her trampy wardrobe or throwing out some of the junky 'antiques' she'd been conned into

buying by unscrupulous dealers. Alisha quite enjoyed these informal meetings and the two of them fell into a pattern where they
started going off for an occasional drink after work.

Sapna was close to thirty and a divorcee. She'd married a
computer engineer in Chicago and had returned once the split had
become inevitable. Her ex-husband had opted to stay on and work
for a small software company. Alisha grudgingly admired the
manner in which Sapna had managed to put her life together after
a particularly nasty divorce. She'd handled the proceedings with
dignity and humour, while wasting no time in reacquainting herself with the professional discipline she had abandoned to follow
her husband to America. She'd started off with a five-star hotel as
a p.r. woman, moved on to special projects, developed a couple of
winning concepts while there and had then began working for a
high-profile gay architect, with clients all over India. It was fatigue
that drove her to quit her job and team up with Alisha. Her old boss
had driven her to exhaustion and while Sapna had valued the
experience and exposure, she found she hadn't had a moment to
catch up with the other areas of her life. She hadn't even found the
time to enjoy her success. When she spotted Alisha's ad in the
appointments' page of the *Times of India* she applied on an impulse,
and to her surprise, bagged the job after a gruelling session with
Alisha, who, far from offending Sapna, had actually amused her.

Alisha appreciated Sapna's calm and steadying presence
around the place. Given her years of working for an American firm
as a glorified office girl, Sapna's strong point was her organiza-
tional ability. She introduced methods and systems into Alisha's
set-up that altered the entire functioning of the company and gave
it the professionalism it had previously lacked. Plus, Sapna was
great at client presentations. It was her personality combined with
the smooth patter and all the charts she'd get done that impressed
people not accustomed to this sort of an approach.

It took a while for Alisha to lower her reserves and Sapna
shrewdly didn't push her. Working late, poring over blueprints
and models, fixing coffee or just taking a break before getting back
to their desks, they gradually developed a rapport that went beyond a working relationship. Sapna introduced Alisha to the rich-
ness of Indian textiles, the limitlessness of their design, the
refinement of local craftsmanship and the sheer skill of artisans
with centuries of tradition behind them.

Initially, the subtle change in Alisha's attire was barely discernible to those who didn't know her. But Sapna recognized the signs and smiled to herself. She was, after all, over ten years her senior. And she had seen life in the raw. She sensed Alisha's insecurity and made allowances for her sudden flashes of temper or the impetuousness of some of her business decisions. But Sapna also recognized that behind the bluster, Alisha's native instincts were shrewd and well-honed. It was only a matter of application and experience. Sapna was happy to provide both.

'Alisha's Hideaway' threw open its doors with a lavish housewarming party that was largely orchestrated by Sapna who had supervised everything from the elegant invitation cards to the menu, which featured an array of sea-food along with unusual salads. She'd also gone along to pick the right outfit for Alisha's big night and the two of them had eventually settled for a marvellously simple, yet very effective, *angarkha* in natural tussore silk.

'Don't let's go for clutter and heavy embroidery,' Sapna had suggested as they inspected one exquisite creation after another at Ensemble, the priciest boutique in India. Against Sapna's advice, Alisha had flown in the hottest rock group from Goa, featuring Franz, who had hit the top of the Indian pops with his single, 'Goa for the Gods of Love'. Sapna herself was demurely dressed in white but looked 'bewitching' as someone put it. 'The only thing missing is a full moon, *yaar*,' someone else commented as the party swung on outdoors, lit by thousands of tiny lights in the trees. Alisha laughed, 'Sapna...why didn't you fix it...or did I forget to order the moon?' Sapna waved her hand from where she stood, chatting quietly with a grey haired ad tycoon. The guest list had been drawn up by her too and it was an interesting bunch of people, some of whom Alisha had only read about in the glossies. Complete strangers walked up to pay the hostess extravagant compliments. The comments ranged from, 'You have quite a set-up,' to 'If your firm can come up with an identical property, I'm buying.' It was clear to both Sapna and Alisha that the party was a triumph both in social and business terms.

After the crowd had melted away, leaving just a handful of colleagues and Sapna's grey haired friend, a post-mortem was conducted over glasses of champagne. Sapna asked Alisha quietly, 'I noticed you dancing with Navin. Like him?'

Alisha looked at her blankly, 'Navin? Which one was he? I've danced with so many cute guys tonight, I've lost track.'

Sapna laughed, 'He was cuter than most. In fact, I'd say he was the cutest…the one with the gelled hair and bedroom eyes. In black. His fiancee was in red…also cute. But he ignored her right through the evening.'

Alisha was suddenly all there. She perked up and asked interestedly, 'Oh, that guy! Yes, he was kind of cute. But I thought he was coming on a bit too strong. I like the caveman approach. But he carried on in a slightly *filmi* way. I thought he was a movie-star in the making. Sexy chap.'

Sapna smiled mysteriously, 'Yes…rather. I would've thought so ten years ago. Now, of course, he seems like a *bachcha*. Wonder why his earlier engagement broke off.'

Alisha took a swig and asked casually, 'Who was he engaged to?'

Sapna paused before saying slowly, 'Oh… I believe her name is Mallika Hiralal.'

Alisha nearly dropped her glass. 'Him! So, he was *that* Navin! How dumb of me! I should've known right away.'

Sapna continued to stare amusedly, 'You've heard of him, then?'

Alisha grabbed her arm and whispered, 'Heard of him? Of course I've heard of him. Don't you know who Mikki…I mean Mallika…is?'

Sapna shook her head. Alisha bit her lip and sat back in her chair, 'Doesn't matter…it's not important. She's…she's…someone I know vaguely. Anyway…she isn't a Hiralal any more. She got married to some Malhotra fellow. In fact…they live right there,' Alisha finished, gesturing towards the bungalow across the road.

'Really?' Sapna said, 'what a coincidence!'

Alisha was silent for a while, 'How did Navin get here anyway?'

Sapna replied, 'Like the others…he was invited. A friend of a friend of a friend. You know how these things work.'

Alisha nodded, 'Interesting. Very interesting.'

Sapna asked lightly, 'Did he…you know…suggest a meeting or anything?'

'Yes,' Alisha replied, 'as a matter or fact, he did. But I didn't know he was engaged. I mean to this new girl, whoever she is…. I didn't know he was the same Navin to begin with.'

Sapna said, 'So…you accepted?'

'Sort of,' Alisha smiled.

'And now?' Sapna continued.

'And now nothing. Let him call...I'll see what I feel like doing at that point.' She clicked her fingers and a waiter walked up quickly, 'Some more champagne for everybody,' she said gaily, 'Let's all have fun....'

Alisha got up and floated towards the dance floor. 'Music...music,' she waved her arms, as the exhausted band picked up their half-packed instruments. 'Let's dance...' she said to a startled Franz while the band broke into a jazzed up version of 'I Could Have Danced All Night'.

Sapna sipped her champagne and looked up at the stars. She spotted Venus. The Goddess of Love had been playing games again that night. She turned to her companion and held out her hand, 'Shall we...' 'Why not?' he said suavely as he got up and escorted her to the floor. Alisha winked as Sapna swung past her. The music had changed. The bands' back-up singer had started to croon an old favourite, 'Black Magic Woman'.

Alisha turned around to look for Sapna. For a flash she thought her white sari had turned black. She blinked. Franz was staring at her. Alisha laughed, 'It must be the song...it's playing tricks on me,' she said as she led him off the floor and into the house. The music continued to float up to them as Alisha lay in her brand new bedroom, on her brand new bed, with a brand new man beside her.

EIGHT

In her new status as Binny's wife Mikki hardly got an hour or two of his time. When he wasn't travelling, he was working long hours at the office, often over the weekends as well. 'This is crazy,' she said to him one morning at the breakfast table.

'What is crazy, princess?' he asked absently as he read the financial papers.

'I hardly see you,' Mikki cried. 'We've been married over six months now and I probably saw more of you during our absurdly short honeymoon.'

Binny didn't bother to look up. 'That's marriage,' he replied shortly.

'No, it isn't,' Mikki said, her voice rising, 'at least it isn't the sort of marriage I'm looking for. I thought we'd be doing things together. Enjoying life. Nowadays I get to see you only at parties. Isn't that funny?'

Binny put his paper down slowly. He looked at Mikki sitting across him and asked, 'What did you just say?' Mikki stared into his eyes. They were ablaze. His voice was low and cold. She felt herself shiver involuntarily.

'Nothing,' she answered and reached for the butter knife. Fixing his single slice of toast was something of a daily ritual. Suddenly Binny grabbed Mikki's arm and slapped her wrist sharply. The small knife fell out of her fingers and landed noisily on the floor. Holding her slim wrist with one hand he pushed her chin up with the other, 'Listen very carefully, princess. This is no longer your father's home and you are no longer the pampered child. You are Binny Malhotra's wife. And you'd better start behaving like her. In our family women are trained to obey their husbands. Thank your stars you don't have a mother-in-law to please. You will never, I repeat, never, question me…or complain. You have nothing to complain about—got that? Your life is perfect. You have every-thing…everything. Where I go, what I do, when and with whom, is my business. I will spend as much time with you as I choose to. There are social duties and obligations which you will fulfil. If I feel it's necessary for you to travel with me for some purpose, it shall happen that way. If I have to attend parties on my own, it shall happen that way. Your job is to look beautiful. I told you that when I married you. Buy clothes. Buy jewellery. Go to the beauty parlour. Play bridge. Learn golf. Attend cooking classes. That's all. But, no questions—you don't have the right. And none of this cheeky business. I will not tolerate it. You have spoilt my morning. My day will go badly now. I have tensions at work. I don't need tensions at home. Understand? When I say, "Butter my toast", you butter it. That's all.'

Binny released his grip on her wrist and turned away leaving his slice of toast untouched. Mikki looked down at the white marks left by his fingers on her arm. She was shaking with fright as she rang the bell for the bearer to clear the breakfast table. As Mikki stared stonily at the elaborate flower arrangement on the dining-table, she thought of her mother and her father and the countless breakfasts they'd shared like characters in a silent film, with just a puzzled child as their audience.

Amy was curiously unsympathetic when they met later in the day and Mikki was disheartened by her reaction. 'Don't you un-derstand how awful this makes me feel?' she asked plaintively.

Amy played with her many rings and bracelets before saying, 'Darling…I really don't know what to say. I mean, what did you expect? Romance? Don't be naive. All marriages turn like this. Perhaps not quite so quickly. But certainly after a year or so. Besides, the man is really busy. I don't know what women like us are looking for. Why don't you listen to Binny and get involved with charity work and things? Get out of that home of yours. You sit there day in and day out like a moping canary in a gilded cage. What's the point? You've married a man of the world...not a poet. Be realistic. Don't expect him to mollycoddle you—he has better things to do.'

Mikki stared at Amy, just about managing to keep herself from crying. 'This isn't what I wanted,' she said sadly. 'What was it you were looking for?' Amy asked, gentle again. Mikki searched for the right words, 'I don't know, Amy, I wanted someone with whom I could share my life. Is that such an impossible expectation?'

Amy snorted, 'Not for us women, darling. But men are different. They are in search of something else. Sex, for instance. I don't mean to be overly personal, darling... but are you sure...you know what I'm getting at?'

Mikki was quiet for a while. Then she spoke hesitantly, 'It was O.K., I mean, it was great in the beginning. We were averaging five times a week. Often more. And then...I don't know what happened. Binny seemed to lose interest. We'd start off well and suddenly he'd turn away—go to the bathroom. Switch on music. Start reading. Or even leave the house in the middle of the night and drive off somewhere.' Mikki caught her breath, 'I thought we'd make love every night...and that he'd want me to get pregnant.'

Amy asked tenderly, 'And he doesn't?'

Mikki shook her head, too overcome to reply. 'Maybe he isn't ready for fatherhood just yet,' Amy said, patting her hand, 'give him time. Be patient. You have youth on your side—enjoy it. Let him enjoy you. Why do you want to saddle yourself with the responsibility of a child just yet? Wait. Let the marriage settle down first. Be free to travel...there's enough time for you to tie yourself down with babies later.'

Mikki couldn't control herself any longer and burst out, 'It's not that simple, Amy. I think he doesn't ever want me to have children. He told me so himself.'

Stunned by what she'd heard, Amy kept quiet and gave Mikki time to compose herself. Slowly Mikki began to pour out the whole story of that nightmarish evening two months ago—an evening she'd never forget. She'd missed her period that month and decided to see her mother's kindly old gynae—the same one who'd performed a hysterectomy on her mother three years earlier. 'Congratulations,' the old man had beamed after examining her. Mikki had blushed, barely able to conceal her excitement—she'd rushed to the florist and ordered up the shop. She'd gone to the gourmet cheese and salad store at Kemp's corner and picked up her favourite nibbles. The next stop had been her reliable booze man from whom she'd bought a case of hers and Binny's familiar Bordeaux then a good crunchy fresh French loaf from the patisserie at the Taj. She'd breezed through the best stocked store in town, Rustom's, and bought fresh mushrooms, a great paté and baby corn. She couldn't wait to get home and cook them a special meal and her kind of food. She knew the candles were at home in the top drawer of the teak sideboard. What else did she need? Sexy lingerie. She had that too—the virgin one from 'Victoria's Secret'. Binny had given it to her before the wedding and she'd been saving it up for just such an occasion.

Mikki was flushed and glowing with joy as she whipped up one dish after another in a kitchen she wasn't familiar with. The cooks watched with indulgence and amusement as memsaab pottered around asking for wine vinegar one moment and tarragon mustard the next. By seven she was through. She'd rushed upstairs for a long shower using her favourite Guerlain bath gel. And then she'd changed into her sexy, plum coloured *peignoir* and waited for her husband—the father of her unborn child.

Binny had got home late as usual, and seemed tired and irritable. She'd waited to tell him till after dinner, which he'd just picked at. When she finally did…he exploded. She'd thought he was going to hit her. He'd been violently upset and started cursing Mikki crudely in Punjabi. Mikki relived the horror again as she said to Amy: 'I was so stunned…I started crying and hitting out at him. He caught my hands and flung me across the room. I kept pleading with him and asking why he was so upset. Didn't he want our child? And he bellowed, "No! No! No!" I caught his feet and begged, "What about me? I want to become a mother. I want someone to call my own." Binny looked at me with so much hate in his eyes I thought he'd kill me, and said, "Then you should have married that pansy who ditched you…but I doubt that he would have filled your belly." I kept crying. And as usual, Binny walked out of the house and disappeared. I waited up for him. He had had a lot to drink when he got back at around four o'clock. It was no use trying to talk to him then. So I pretended I was asleep. Next morning, he told me to arrange for an abortion. When I refused, he said it was that or a divorce. I was too frightened when I heard that horrible word! Where would I go? I have nothing left to my name. I asked him to give me a reason why he wanted me to get rid of his baby. And that's when he told me,' Mikki broke down and collapsed into Amy's arms.

The older women soothed her by stroking her hair which had grown now and fell around her shoulders. 'We'll find a way out of this, darling. It can't be that bad.'

Mikki wailed, 'Amy, you don't know the whole story…it doesn't end here. It's much worse. Binny already has a family…he is the father of two children—a boy and a girl.'

Amy raised her eyebrows and asked, 'Oh? and a wife too?'

'A mistress. He never married her…she wasn't classy enough for him.'

'And do you know who this woman is?' Amy asked.

'Of course I do. I mean…I found out. And that night Binny himself told me all about her. It's Urmi. You saw her at our wedding. You even recognized her. But you didn't tell me a thing. I knew it had to be her. And their children, Urvashi and Nitya. That's the reason he doesn't want me to have my own. And, like he put it crudely, he wants me to remain firm and tight for his pleasure.'

Amy hugged her and said, 'My poor child. What a mess you've got yourself into. But don't despair…this man sounds like a low down bastard. But there are ways to fix people like that.'

Mikki whimpered, 'Amy…you aren't going to believe this…but I don't want to fix him. Trouble is, I love the man. Call me a doormat, a slave, a victim, anything. But, I feel hopeless and helpless. It is as if I've forgotten what pride is…or ever was. He can, and does, trample all over me.'

Amy threw up her hands and looked heavenwards. Finally she said gently, 'In that case, darling, make the best of it. But if I were you I'd still hire a good lawyer…just in case…you know.'

Mikki smiled, 'Yes, Amy, I know. But I have nothing left to lose. Binny has control over everything. All my assets were signed over. That was part of the deal.'

Amy smiled wryly, 'I'm glad your mother isn't alive, darling. This is no position for a girl like you to find herself in. No money, no husband, no baby. But it's your life, and I wish you well. I'm there whenever you need me.'

Mikki kissed her warmly and said, 'Thank you, Amy. It means a lot to me.'

The two women stood quietly, waiting for their respective cars to come. The club was nearly deserted. Even the diehards at the bar had gone home. It was still too early for the card players. They watched as a bunch of teenagers drove in for a game of squash. The sound of laughter from kids splashing around in the swimming pool came floating up to them. Amy tapped Mikki lightly on her shoulder saying, 'That's where you should be—in an azure pool with people your own age. Not crying on an old woman's shoulder.' And she was gone, leaving Mikki groping for sunglasses in her smart new Chanel bag.

'Looking for something?' she heard a familiar voice ask. Mikki looked up to see Navin standing in front of her, twirling his car keys. She didn't know how to react, so she said, 'Hi!' instinctively. Navin leaned over and kissed her cheek. Mikki pulled back hastily. Navin laughed and said, 'Oh...by the way, congratulations. I know I'm six months late...but then you didn't invite me to the big event.' Mikki stared coldly at him. Her car had rolled up by then. 'It wasn't a zoo party...animals weren't on our guest list, I'm afraid,' she snapped and got into the waiting car. Navin was still standing there, twirling his car keys, as she told the driver to take her home.

*

Alisha had seen Navin twice since the night of her party. He'd told her he was footloose and fancy-free despite the well-publicized engagement to the Arora girl. 'Oh...that's a formality,' he told Alisha as they dined at the Zodiac Grill. Alisha smiled to herself at the obvious lie. She hadn't made up her mind about Navin. He was fun in his own way. But her attraction was on a different level altogether. She wanted him only because Mikki had had him. Perhaps he sensed it, but Navin was smart enough to make his moves without revealing too much about himself. He hadn't brought up Mikki's name even once during their dates. And Alisha was waiting for the right moment to raise the subject. Meanwhile Sapna was encouraging her to see more of Navin. And Alisha was beginning to wonder why. One of these days, she'd ask her directly.

The first time Navin and Alisha made love it was a disaster. Both of them had had far too much to drink, and what started off as passionate groping in the car with Alisha tearing at Navin's fly as they sped down a deserted Marine Drive after dancing tirelessly at RG's , ended up with both of them snoring noisily in Alisha's bed at dawn. When they woke up around eleven, they regarded each other with surprise. 'What happened?' Alisha asked groggily. 'Search me,' Navin replied, his eyes barely open. 'Did we…?'Alisha left the question half-phrased. Navin reached for her under the sheets and said, 'No, we didn't…but let's not waste time.' He rolled over her and pushed his knee between her thighs roughly. Alisha struggled out from under him. 'Hey! Cool it, lover boy…I've got to pee and brush my teeth first. I'm a hygiene-conscious girl.' Navin smiled lazily, 'Well…while you're at it, you can order some tea for me. I prefer to do it when I'm more awake.' Alisha pulled a face and walked languidly into her gleaming bathroom which resembled a movie set with dozens of lights focused on the wall-to-wall mirror, a jacuzzi which was almost obligatory, a bidet and shower room, all done up in lavender colours. She'd also put in a rockery and a miniature Japanese garden just outside the large picture window. An oval-shaped skylight cast a diffused glow over the area when the lights were not on. This morning, sunlight filtered in gently. From the window she could clearly see the top of Mikki's bungalow and a portion of her terrace garden. It used to amuse her that she could keep an eye on Mikki while seated on the potty—'Spying as I shit,' as she put it to herself.

Alisha stretched and surveyed her body critically. Now that she had all the privacy she needed, she preferred to sleep nude. The image reflected in the mirror was an attractive one. Alisha pinched her tummy to check whether she'd put on weight. She had been over-indulging herself recently. She stepped on the scales…they were steady at 52 kilos. She began brushing her teeth systematically with Neem toothpaste. Her father had started her off on it and she just hadn't wanted to switch. She liked the slightly acrid taste it left in her mouth…it went well with the hot tea she gulped down right after. Her eyes looked puffy. Damn! she thought. I must go easy on the whisky sours. After brushing her hair carefully, she strolled out to find Navin jogging on the spot. 'Don't tire yourself out too much,' she said and sat on a cane chair watching him. She took in his flat stomach and broad chest approvingly. She liked his boxer shorts. They were cute, with little sailboats on them. She spoke to the kitchen on the intercom and asked the bearer to bring up breakfast for two. Navin finished off with a brisk toe-touching routine and stood up to observe her. 'You have well-trained servants,' he commented, 'they seem used to this breakfast-for-two business.' Alisha didn't respond to that. She knew she was looking ravishing in her soft white dressing gown and she was in no mood to break the spell. 'Shower?' she suggested, walking to the wardrobe and handing Navin a smart terryrobe. He raised his eyebrows. 'Do you have them to suit all tastes?' he asked. Once again Alisha kept quiet and busied herself with fluffing up the pillows.

Last night was a total haze. She couldn't recall a single detail...when they got in, what they did or even if they undressed, though that was obvious in the morning seeing that their clothes were strewn carelessly all over the carpet. She picked up Navin's Versace jacket and folded it over the chair. She put her own outfit away. Strange, she thought, as she hung up her dress, she was dressing more and more like Mikki these days. Often, people would stop her in a restaurant or at the theatre mistaking her for her half-sister. Half-sister! Alisha thought mockingly. And here was that half-sister's ex-lover bathing in her bathroom and lustily singing a Hindi film song.

A knock on the door announced the arrival of breakfast. Alisha let the man in and dismissed him saying, 'No phone calls till I tell you. Take instructions from *bhabi* as usual about what's to be cooked, marketing and all that.' The man melted away just as Navin emerged from the bathroom, fresh and fragrant. 'I like your taste in men's toiletries...Hermes, Gucci, Klien. Very nice,' he said as he rubbed his thick hair with a fluffy towel. Alisha indicated the tea service and asked, 'Sugar?' 'Of course—three,' Navin said as he came up to kiss the top of her head. He looked at the tray and laughed, 'Hey...behind all that big act you are a real *Gujju*, aren't you. What is this? *Khakras* for breakfast? I'd half-expected griddle cakes or croissants.' 'Too fattening,' Alisha said and started nibbling on a crisp *khakra* which she had lightly buttered. 'Shall I make one for you?' she asked Navin. 'I'd rather pass. I'll have some toast instead,' he said.

Alisha scanned the headlines of the newspapers in the tray and immediately found what she was looking for. 'Hiralal Industries, now rechristened Malhotra Enterprises, has shown a slight improvement this quarter. Shares are being quoted at 135 rupees against 52 same time last year. At a press conference, the new Chairman and M.D., Rakesh ('Binny') Malhotra announced a series of expansion plans, plus a new project approved by the government of Karnataka. He also added that the Malaysian collaboration was finally showing healthy profits.'

Navin was getting restless. 'Hey, how about mixing business with pleasure?' Alisha put down the papers, turned around and pulled open Navin's bathrobe. She stared pointedly and said, 'What pleasure?' 'Let me show you,' Navin growled and pulled her to him. They fell down on the plush carpet as Navin tugged her hair roughly and jerked her neck back. He stuck his forefinger into her mouth and forced it open. 'Suck me off,' he commanded as Alisha stared at him open-eyed. 'You first,' she said. 'No. Together then,' he added as he turned around over her body and forced her thighs apart. Alisha felt aroused enough to grab him and let her mouth work, but her mind was on something else. She was visualizing Mikki doing the same thing to Navin. Her tongue moved sensuously over him and she nibbled gently. As she moved rhythmically she kept thinking, 'Did Mikki? Did Mikki? Did Mikki?' She wanted to obliterate any memory Navin might have retained of his love-making with the woman she hated. The woman who consumed her. Navin was clumsy at what he was doing. Alisha winced as his teeth hurt her. But she moved under him, writhing and simulating a pleasure she did not feel in any way. 'Come, come, come,' she mentally urged him as her mouth pulled urgently on him. She was willing to do something she had never done before: she was ready to swallow his ejaculation. She felt sick when the slightly brackish, viscous fluid filled her mouth. But she took him in, as he lifted up his head from between her legs and rested it on her flat stomach. 'Wow! Baby!' Navin said gratefully, 'You really blew my mind.'

Alisha smiled. 'No, sweetheart, I really blew you,' she said and went off to gargle the remnants of his passion down the oyster shaped basin.

*

Binny had made it clear to Mikki that she'd have to accept Urmi in their life. Now that she was no longer a secret, Binny often phoned her or received calls while Mikki was present in the room. There were some social occasions that Binny felt required Mikki's presence and he'd instruct her accordingly or get his secretary to do it.

And on some informal evenings he'd get Urmi to accompany him. Mikki was astonished at her own meek acceptance of this arrangement. Amy questioned her one day over lunch at her house and couldn't believe what Mikki was telling her in a voice filled with submission and pain. 'Where is the question of pride when you love someone? I cannot explain it rationally…but I feel content just to share the same roof. It makes me happy that he is there in my life. That he is my man…at least in the eyes of the world.' Amy shook her head disbelievingly. 'This is not the woman I know. Have you been hypnotized? Does he drug you? Are you sure you aren't on tranquillizers? Where is your self-respect?'

Mikki smiled a sad smile, 'Some women are made for this. All my life I wanted to admire someone. I wanted to admire my father and never could. Now I've found the person. Don't ask me to explain. He is like a God to me. I don't care who he sleeps with. All I care is that I am his wife and that he comes home to me.'

Amy was silent for a while. 'He has a free body for his use in his bedroom whenever he wants one. No wonder he isn't complaining. You are nothing more than a legitimate prostitute, don't you realize that?'

Mikki looked at her thoughtfully, 'Amy, let's discuss something else. I don't expect you to understand. Sometimes these things are too complicated for an outsider. All I know is, I satisfy him; he satisfies me. I don't care how that makes me look. Besides, all wives are prostitutes to some extent. Weren't you? Didn't you use your body to reward or punish? What's the big difference?'

*

Leelaben, far from enjoying her daughter's new found riches, found herself completely alone and sinking into a depression. In their cramped suburban flat Alisha and she had had no choice but to run into one another constantly. Now, the situation had changed. Alisha hardly saw her mother. She had engaged a full-time housekeeper to look after the efficient running of her impressive new mansion. Besides that lady—a homeless, educated widow from Cochin called Mrs Panniker—Leelaben also had the services of a maid who was instructed to stay with her round the clock. Alisha found herself getting increasingly snappy and short on the few occasions her mother and she met. Still, the signs hadn't escaped her. Leelaben had resumed her heavy drinking despite the blanket ban and was popping pills constantly, often bribing drivers and bearers to get her both, the booze and the tranquillizers. Alisha had already dealt with five employees for falling for the bait—fat tips stolen from Alisha's own handbag. She tried to persuade her mother to go out, contact some of her old acquaintances, but Leelaben couldn't get herself to dress up for anything any more. She slopped around the house in a nightie most of the day and passed out by nightfall. She ate sporadically, often skipping meals for days together, and then suddenly screamed for some particular delicacy out of the blue. Three cooks had quit in a huff, unable to keep up with her demands. Even so, thanks to the calm, reassuring presence of Mrs Panniker, who smoothed things over, Alisha's little palace ran like a well-oiled machine.

The crisis, when it came, occurred one night when Alisha was out with Navin. They were seeing each other regularly now, even though Alisha confessed to Sapna that the sex 'could be better'. Navin was working on it. Meanwhile, they made as attractive a couple as Mikki and he once had. They were seen together everywhere, often in colour co-ordinated clothes.

By the time Mrs Panniker managed to reach Alisha at the new night club in the suburbs which was celebrating its opening with a splashy party for potential members it was 2 a.m. Alisha and Navin were dancing to Madonna's 'Vogue', when a smartly-dressed steward tapped her lightly on her bare shoulder and whispered, 'It's an emergency.' She could barely hear him above the cacophony of the state-of-the-art sound systems, but she instinctively knew something had happened to her mother. The colour drained from her face as Navin stared at her with a 'What's wrong?' expression. 'My mother,' Alisha answered shortly, 'let's go.' Both of them rushed out of Zebra's and into Navin's latest acquisition…a fiery red Amtrax.

As they sped down the Western Express highway, Alisha surprised herself by beginning to pray. And then she realized she wasn't praying for her mother. She was praying for herself. As Navin raced past Breach Candy hospital where she knew she'd have to bring her mother, she thought of what would happen if Leelaben were to die. She'd already guessed that it must have been a lethal combination of whisky—or even country liquor—with Calmpose that had done it. She was hoping it wouldn't be too late before they arrived. At the back of Alisha's mind was one thought—if she lost her mother, she and Mikki would be on par—parentless. No, she didn't want that to happen. Mikki had nobody to call her own. She did. She wanted it to stay that way. She wanted to be one up on Mikki on that score at least.

When Navin's car screeched to a stop at the gates, Alisha took one look at Mrs Panniker's composed demeanour and knew her mother wasn't dead. She rushed up to her and asked, 'Is she all right?' knowing the answer. Mrs Panniker replied evenly, 'Yes, madam. If you don't mind, I contacted a doctor I know. He is from my village but he practises in Bombay. He came immediately and took *bhabi* to a nursing home close by. We couldn't wait for you to arrive and I didn't have much money with me. *Bhabi* was in no condition to give us any. But please don't worry. She is all right— perfectly all right. Dr Kurien is with her and I was waiting here to escort you.' Alisha looked at her gratefully and said a soft 'thank you'. She made a mental note to give her a hefty increment the following month. She looked at Navin who was whistling tune-lessly and staring at the sky. 'I'll be down in a minute,' she said and ran into the house to change out of her strapless velvet dress into a demure *salwar kameez*. Stepping out of her clothes she noticed the tinsel in her hair. Damn. Those chaps at Zebra's had got carried away and sprinkled the stuff on all the dancers at midnight. She brushed out as much of it as she could and ran back to join Navin and Mrs Panniker.

Navin dropped the two women off at a neat, small polyclinic down the road and asked indifferently, 'Do you want me to wait, I've got a pretty heavy day tomorrow.' Alisha whirled around coldly and said, 'Get lost, pal,' and took Mrs Panniker's arm as they went into the building and straight up to the ICU. They were met at the door by Dr Kurien and Alisha took an immediate liking to him. He couldn't have been more than thirty-five, but he seemed older, with a sprinkling of grey in his thick hair. Alisha appreciated his quiet manner and the way he took charge of the situation, explaining gravely to her that her mother could have died had it not been for Mrs Panniker who went into her bedroom to check on her and found her lying unconscious on the bed. Alisha couldn't help noticing the lilting cadences in his heavily accented speech. She tried to concentrate on what he was saying but kept getting distracted by his swarthy good looks, dark eyes and the graceful hands with tapering fingers, which he used so expressively. She continued to stare up at him since he was so much taller than any man she'd known. She realized she hadn't heard a word of what he'd said when Mrs Panniker nudged her gently and said, 'Madam, the doctor needs some details to fill in *bhabi*'s medical history.'

Alisha snapped out of her reverie, telling herself it was all the white wine she'd drunk and the sharp night air that was making her head swim. Carefully she provided details about her mother's age and other facts. Dr Kurien informed her that he had engaged a day and night nurse to stay with Leelaben on Mrs Panniker's instructions, and that there was really nothing for Alisha to do but go home and get some rest herself. Mrs Panniker was insistent about staying at the nursing home, 'Just in case *bhabi* gets up.'

Alisha reasoned with herself that there wasn't much she'd be able to do by hanging around and in any case her mother was sound asleep and heavily sedated. 'Her pulse is a little slow,' Dr Kurien explained as he walked Alisha to the door. She turned around, hand extended, to thank him for all his help and started to reach for her handbag to pay him what she owed. Dr Kurien stopped her, saying firmly, 'It can wait. I'll be seeing her through till she is well enough to go home. Please, let's not discuss fees right now.' Alisha shrugged and turned around saying, 'See you in the morning, doctor,' when she remembered she had got rid of Navin. Dr Kurien asked, 'Do you have a car to take you home?' Flustered, Alisha said, 'Well… I did. But now I don't!' He straightened up, saying firmly, 'Give me a minute. I'll get my car keys,' and strode off down the narrow, dimly-lit corridor. As Alisha watched his long legs carrying him to the office room at the end of the passage she shivered involuntarily. It was still dark and the strong smell of antiseptic mingling with the scent of *raat ki raani* sent a frisson of excitement up her spine.

*

Leelaben took her time to bounce back. She was far more frail than Alisha had realized. Her weight was down to the lowest it had ever been and she looked ancient lying back on clean white sheets, her eyes staring vacantly at the ceiling. Alisha spent as much time with her as she could snatch from the office. She'd more or less given up her nightly outings, preferring to rush to the nursing home after work. It was the exhilaration of going there that made her ask herself why she felt the way she did when she got dressed every morning with such care, making sure to avoid her more outrageous outfits in favour of conservative *salwar kameezes*, even saris. It was Sapna who drew her attention to it when she commented, 'I must say you are glowing these days. Can't be just the nip in the air. And it can't be your mother, though I'm sure you are happy she's pulled through. So…what is it? Or should I ask, "Who is it?"' Alisha blushed as she dismissed Sapna quickly saying, 'Don't be ridiculous. You know my life is reduced to playing nursemaid to my mother. I don't see anybody and I don't go anywhere. Check with Navin, if you don't believe me.' Sapna chuckled, 'I did. He is wondering too.'

Alisha grabbed her bag and sailed out saying, 'Profits. Concentrate on profits. And projects. And leave my glow alone.'

She was feeling so much better these days. Fitter, too, now that she'd cut out all the late nights and the cocktails and cigarettes that went with them. She was looking good, as everyone remarked, and functioning well at the office given that she went there with a clear head these days, after eight hours of sleep in place of three. But Alisha was honest enough not to fool herself. She knew her state of well being had everything to do with Dr Kurien. She looked forward to seeing him, talking to him, and had been very embarrassed with herself to discover she'd taken to showing off like a school-girl, bragging about her achievements or pointing out some magazine write-up, about her, in a childish attempt to impress him. It was foolish and she knew it. They belonged to entirely different worlds. He was polite but distantly so. Alisha looked for little signs of interest but none were forthcoming. Now that her mother was on the mend, there was really nothing much he could do other than visit her twice a day and monitor her recovery. Yet, Alisha would wait for the moment, her eyes shining in anticipation. She'd try and draw his attention to her mother's condition, hoping to engage him in a longer conversation. It was stupid and futile but she couldn't stop herself from fantasizing. There was little she knew about him or his background and she certainly hadn't reached the level of cross-examining Mrs Panniker. She wondered where he went after he'd done his rounds. She was curious about his life. She didn't even know whether or not he was married, though in all probability he was….She devised little tricks to get some information out of him. 'Where can I reach you in an emergency, doctor? I mean...once my mother gets home. Who knows, she may repeat this little stunt...and you've taken such good care of her. She wouldn't want to go to anybody else. She feels so confident with you,' she'd asked once, as innocently as she could. Dr Kurien laughed self-consciously and handed her his card. Alisha stared at it looking for clues. There were none. 'But...it doesn't say anything,' she said, and he asked, 'What doesn't it say? My telephone numbers and qualifications are on it. That's all a doctor needs to state.' She felt intensely silly as she stammered, 'Of course. But you know how telephones in Bombay are. What if I can't get you quickly and have to send my driver?' He reached for his wallet and pulled out another card, 'This is my personal one,' he smiled. Alisha took it eagerly, her mind racing to think up new topics with which to engage him in further conversation. 'Doctor...I'm worried about my mother. How can I make her permanently well...you know?' He looked at her steadily and took his time before saying, 'I hope you don't mind my saying this, but what she needs is your time...and even more importantly, your love. There is nothing wrong with her physically. Yes, she is a little weak at present. But it's not a serious condition. She requires reassurance and understanding. She is a lonely lady. And an insecure one. She has been feeling extremely rejected and unloved.' Alisha looked at the doctor sheepishly and asked, 'Did she tell you that?' 'She didn't have to...though she did mention loneliness. Especially after your father's sudden death...it was a great blow to her,' he told her. Alisha was thoughtful for a while. More than anything else, she wanted the doctor to hold her in his arms and rock her gently. She longed for his touch and was prepared to settle for anything—even a warm handshake. She jerked herself out of the reverie and said, 'Thank you for telling me this. I've been so wrapped up in my own life, I just haven't paid enough attention to her, poor thing. But now I will,' she hesitated and then asked him, holding her breath as he replied, 'Doctor...you must have a family...I mean...' 'Yes,' he answered gently, 'I do have a family—they live with me. My parents....' Alisha kept looking at him, her eyes full of questions unanswered. He hesitated before adding, '...and my wife...and children...two of them.'

Alisha thought she was going to burst into tears. Not wanting him to see her intense disappointment, she turned away and started to leave hurriedly. She nearly stumbled on the stairs and would have fallen down, but his arm caught her in time. He pulled her up and she glared at him, angry tears swimming in her eyes. She tried to jerk his hand away, but he held on, steadying her, his eyes pleading with hers. She burst out, 'Why didn't you tell me from the start? I hate you.' He kept holding her, looking into her eyes as she fought to free herself. 'Let me go,' she all but screamed. And abruptly he did. 'Listen to me,' he started to say. But Alisha put her hands over her ears and ran into her car. 'Navin *saab ke ghar*,' she instructed the driver and rolled up the tinted glass windows to shut out the world...to shut out Dr Kurien.

NINE

A little over a year into their marriage, Binny announced he was going away on a business trip to London. Mikki asked timorously, 'Alone?' He looked at her impatiently and snapped, 'I never travel alone.' She bit her lip and persisted, 'Take me with you.' Binny was busy fixing his Hermes tie. He tugged at it savagely and threw it on the bed. 'You've done it again. Spoilt my mood first thing in the morning. Didn't your parents teach you anything? Never ask a man stupid questions when he's going to work. It brings bad luck and God knows I don't need any more of that.' Mikki whimpered, 'I'm sorry...really sorry, darling. Let me make it up to you.' She came up to him and knelt on the carpet. They were in front of his wall-to-wall mirrored wardrobe. He did not look at her while Mikki reached for his fly. Roughly, he pulled her kimono off her shoulders and closed his eyes briefly as she took him into her mouth. He gave in to the sensation for a minute, but then suddenly caught her hair and pushed her away. Surprised, Mikki asked him, 'Don't you like what I'm doing?' Binny answered gruffly, 'I do. I want you to look at yourself at the same time. Look....' And he jerked her head towards the mirror. 'Go on...' he said. Mikki slipped out of her kimono, knowing the sight of her naked body would stimulate him further. She forced him to lie down on the carpet as she continued to kiss him...but without urgency. Once he was on the floor she climbed on him, sat astride his thighs and took him into her. He had his neck to the side, watching her as she started to move lithely, throwing her head back so that her breasts stood out, 'Beautiful...beautiful....' Binny muttered, getting a little out of breath, 'You are a little whore...you know that?'

Mikki moaned and quickened her pace. She could sense his excitement mounting as she increased her speed rhythmically. She took his hands and placed them over her breasts. He held her taut nipples between his thumb and forefinger and squeezed till they hurt. She leaned over him till his mouth was close enough to hers. 'Kiss me, Binny,' she said, panting lightly. But he turned his face away. 'Kiss me, Kiss me...' she kept pleading, while he squeezed his eyes shut and concentrated on the paroxysms of passion that were wracking his body as Mikki moved expertly over him, her thighs gripping his waist, her hands in his hair, spurring Binny on to gush into her as her own body shuddered with the intensity of their love-making, while her heart thumped wildly for the man whose mind was already somewhere else...on someone else.

*

When Binny left without bothering to tell Mikki about his plans, she decided to move back into her home till his return. Binny's servants seemed increasingly sinister to her and even though they did not openly challenge her authority, it was understood that they took their orders from Binny whom they referred to simply as 'the boss'. There wasn't a single friendly face around. And not a single female servant. The men, dressed in dark safari suits, strode around the premises checking things as if on a military exercise. Mikki could never figure out why a private residence required staff to carry walkie-talkies or even why all the rooms were fitted with sophisticated electronic devices monitored from a control room to which she didn't have access. When she'd asked Binny about all this, he had told her to mind her own business, adding, 'Wives should not concern themselves with matters of this sort. It seems you learnt nothing in your parents' home. Not even cooking.' Mikki tried to protest saying, 'I've done a lot of cooking in the

States. Of course I can cook,' but Binny scoffed her, crushing her with his remark, 'I don't call that cooking. We Punjabis don't eat that shit. We like real food. Tell me—can you make *dahi-wadas, aloo parathas, mughlai mutton*? That is called good eating, not a few raw vegetables and some silly sauce with two prawns floating in it.'

Mikki took advantage of Binny's absence by enrolling in a six-week crash course in gourmet cooking being conducted by a visiting French chef in a suburban five-star hotel. She'd always enjoyed cooking but in her mother's fastidious kitchen there was just no room for teenage girls to potter around and experiment. The *maharajs* would have fits and her ayahs would go hysterical, thinking if there was any accident, they would be held responsible. It was thanks to Sean and her stay in America that Mikki had been able to indulge her culinary interests. Sean had a long shelf filled with cook books and the two of them had spent several happy hours in their compact kitchen trying out exotic, international recipes, often with great success. They'd acquired quite a reputation on campus and were often invited to cater for informal parties. Initially, Mikki found herself feeling horribly embarrassed at the thought of accepting money for their efforts. It was Sean who convinced her that it was a good way for both of them to earn pin money and indulge their passion at someone else's expense. It had reached a stage where they had bookings right through the term on practically every weekend. It was a lot of work but Mikki had revelled in it. Sean and she had become status symbols of sorts as they cooked and served elegant meals around the place, very stylishly taking care of table arrangements, flowers, settings, everything. Sean would joke that if they flunked out they could always get someone to set them up as restaurateurs. Mikki harboured no such dreams. She knew her parents would've been horrified if they'd discovered her off-campus hobby. It was a secret she hadn't divulged to any one back home.

And now she found herself enjoying every two-hour session as she brushed up on her basics and then went on to learn more sophisticated dishes. Monsieur Laurent shrewdly guessed that his other Indian pupils, no matter how eager, were basically there to kill time and impress friends. Most of his students were well-heeled socialites who didn't know elementary beef cuts. As a matter of fact, most of them had never come anywhere near beef. He adapted his course swiftly and began teaching them what was

derisively referred to as pseudo-continental cuisine. It meant com-
promising with his art, but M. Laurent was no great chef and he
knew it. Back home in Lyons, he worked for an American couple
who ran an American restaurant for American tourists. He knew
the meaning of the word 'adapt'. So, he improvised his repertoire
and concentrated on popular dishes such as *coq-au-vin* and threw
in favourites like cous-cous which wasn't even French. But in
Mikki he found someone with refined tastes and a definite talent
which went beyond mere aptitude. Mikki was quick, eager and
efficient. She picked up skills the others struggled with for days
and still couldn't master. She added her own little touches which
lifted the dish from the ordinary to the special. M. Laurent began
taking interest in her progress and passing on tips he didn't bother
to give the other students. Mikki looked forward to her classes.
She'd made one or two friends and found herself drawn in particular to a shy, young Goan boy called Lucio, who was hoping to open
his own restaurant in Goa someday.

It took a while for Lucio to open up to Mikki but a ruined pastry
was what brought them together. At first they despaired over the
mess, and then they laughed. M.Laurent was not amused as he
admonished them, cursing in French and carrying on like it was a
major catastrophe. Lucio and she exchanged guilty glances as they
started over. He admired her rings and she admired his shirt.
Somewhere along the way they found out they shared a passion
for Heavy Metal music and Lucio invited her out. Mikki accepted
promptly. It was ages since she'd been anywhere with anyone her
age. More so, with someone she felt comfortable around. Or could
crack silly jokes with.

'Where shall we go?' she asked when they strolled out of the
class. Lucio suggested a newly-opened jazz cafe, adding, 'The
owner's son was in class with me. We'll get a discount.' It was only
when her car drew up that Lucio whistled and then said solemnly,
'Holy shit! You some kind of a rich bitch?' Mikki smiled and caught
hold of his arm. 'Come on…don't ask too many questions.' Lucio
got into the car reluctantly, sliding stiffly into the back seat. Mikki
told the chauffeur to play her favourite cassette of the moment and
sank into the plush seat with her head thrown back. 'Relax,' she
whispered to Lucio, who was busy staring at the road ahead of him.
'You never told me,' he said accusingly. 'Told you what ?' Mikki
asked. 'That you were loaded,' he answered. 'I thought you knew,'

she said, adding, 'everybody does.' Lucio looked at her curiously, 'Are you famous or something?' Mikki replied, 'In a way, yes. I suppose I am.' Lucio took in his breath and said, 'S-H-I-T', through clenched teeth. 'Is that a problem?' Mikki asked. Lucio replied, 'I'm not sure. I mean, I haven't ever known anyone rich. Or famous. Except that folk singer—you know who I mean. And that's because he is from the same village in Goa.' Mikki tried to change the subject but she could see Lucio was too awed by her riches to snap out of it. 'It's O.K. I don't bite or anything. And if it makes you feel better, next time we can walk or take a cab,' she joked, but she noticed Lucio didn't laugh back. He was sitting with his arms pinned to his side, staring fixedly at the road ahead of him.

When they reached Café Trinca's, he shrank out of the car furtively, as if he didn't want anyone to see him. They went inside and found a table quickly, but Lucio continued to look hunted. Abruptly he said, 'Look, I don't know how to behave with society types. I thought you were one of us. Now all these guys will make fun of me.' Mikki couldn't understand his anxiety and tried to probe. But Lucio lapsed into a sullen silence and looked like he was being punished. After half an hour, Mikki asked for the check. They'd had two cups of coffee. Lucio sprang up and reached for his hip pocket. 'Look, lady, you may have all the loot. But I don't let chicks pay for me. Get it? I have the bread.' Mikki was getting a bit fed up. She rose to her feet and said, 'Thank you, Lucio. A pity you ruined what could have been a great evening with your silly hang-ups,' and walked out.

Next day at class, Lucio averted his eyes when she walked in. Later, between sauces, he came up to her and held out his hand which had some egg yolk stuck on it. 'Like…I'm sorry, O.K.? Really sorry.' Mikki smiled and held out hers, which was full of stiff egg white. 'I'm sorry too.' Their hands made a soft, squishy sound as they came together. Monsieur Laurent looked over his bifocals sternly and said, '*Merde*! Now we have an omelette nobody wants.'

*

Late one afternoon, while Mikki was in the midst of a much needed siesta, Ramanbhai called. The servants refused to disturb her. Mikki was enjoying being home again. Dhondu and Gangu had returned when she sent for them, and pampered her. The old *maharaj* had resurfaced and insisted on feeding her round the clock. Some of the bearers and drivers who had been asked to retire by Binny's accountant after the take-over, came regularly to meet her. Some of them had landed jobs, while the others were scrounging around for any work they could get. Mikki felt a sense of shame for letting down her parents' old and faithful staff and subjecting them to the shabby treatment Binny had insisted on. But she also realized that she couldn't have kept them on her own, and that it didn't make sense to run a house that nobody lived in.

Binny had spoken to her about cut-backs, hinting that eventually he'd have to sell all her properties. At that point she hadn't paid much attention to his words, but now, as she luxuriated in her own environment, she couldn't bear the thought that one day her bungalow would belong to someone else...would be occupied by strangers. At Hiralal Industries, too, Binny had got rid of most of her father's executives, her own M.B.A. group and Mrs D'Souza. Ramanbhai had been stripped of most his powers, while Shanay had left. He'd ripped the office apart and replaced the old fittings with new fixtures, false ceilings, Rexine sofas and artificial waterfalls gurgling over fibre glass rocks and plastic ferns. Mikki had been there just once or twice and had rushed out, sickened by the tasteless changes. She couldn't recognize anything or anyone. The old board room was redone beyond recognition. Her office suite now resembled a cheap hotel lobby. Mrs D'Souza's cabin had tinted glass and leatherite walls. Yet Binny's home was a far cry from such atrocious taste. She couldn't reconcile the two images. Finally, she decided that Binny must have spoilt the office just to spite her. Later she was told that Urmi had given the redecorating assignment to a friend she had wanted to oblige. And Binny hadn't stopped her.

The servants told Mikki about Ramanbhai's call while she was having her evening cup of tea. She wondered why he was calling her after so many months. He called again just as she was getting dressed to go to her cooking class. 'It is urgent,' he said shortly, 'and important. Mikki, I know you have heard stories that I have been trying to get Alisha to buy out Hiralal Industries, and I don't deny the charges, but my intentions were good. I know you love Alisha, and that she was the one person you could sell to, and still keep the company in the family. Mikki, to me Hiralal Industries has always been more important than anything else. And now I know how Binny has been treating you, and I fear that some of your most trusted personnel are in his pay. Mikki, your life is in danger. I need to see you for fifteen minutes. No more. Not at your house. Not at your husband's house. Not even in mine. We are all being watched and followed. Our phones are being tapped. Even this conversation may in all possibility be overheard. You will receive a message from me about when and where. It has to be before Mr Malhotra's return. Remember my words…. Your life is in danger.' There was a short click and Ramanbhai disconnected. Mikki stared at the receiver puzzled by what she'd heard—danger? Of what kind? And from whom?

Preoccupied and worried, Mikki was five minutes late for her class. Monsieur Laurent admonished her lightly and Lucio winked. Mikki scarcely noticed them—her mind was entirely on Ramanbhai. He had sounded sinister and desperate. Was he threatening her? She remembered past conversations and meetings. She decided to seek Shanay's help. She knew he was back in town. He had successfully re-entered his old diamond trade and now had a firm of his own, a small one, but doing a fair amount of business.

Mikki found it difficult to concentrate on the simple *pot-au-feu* that was being demonstrated. She kept fumbling with the meat cleaver and went overboard with the pepper mill. 'What's wrong, love? No call from hubby?' Lucio asked in a whisper. Mikki was too distracted to indulge in their usual banter. She just smiled vacantly and carried on with the beans and carrots at hand.

Lucio had decided he was very bored with the proceedings. Half the fun of attending classes was to be with Mikki and then to go off to some small eatery later. They discussed food and fashion mainly, but sometimes Lucio spoke about his life in Goa and his dream of opening his own place on a small strip of beach favoured by Europeans. Mikki had sensed early that he wasn't interested in her as a woman even though he took the trouble to undertake a detailed critique on her appearance each time they met, correcting her make-up, advising her on colours, giving her unusual tips on beauty care and generally indicating that he was involved with her as a person. She had asked him about it one night after two glasses of Matheus, drunk at one of her favourite five-star bars. Mikki, in a kittenish, coquettish mood, had scratched her long fingernail against the grain of his stubble and purred, 'Tell me something truthfully, Lucio…don't you find me desirable…sexy…attractive...irresistible...most men do, you know.' Lucio leapt like he'd been stung by a wasp, 'Darling, don't be perfectly absurd. I thought you knew!' Mikki, her head swimming slightly, leaned forward and grabbed the front of his shirt, 'Knew what, baby? What is it that I should have known?' Lucio seemed stuck for words. Finally, he caught her hand and hissed, 'Oh, for heaven's sake, sweetheart, I'm gay. I thought everybody in class realized that.' Mikki recoiled at his words. 'Gay? Don't be ridiculous,' she said before she could stop herself. Hastily, she added, 'I'm so sorry. I shouldn't have said that. What I meant was, you are such an attractive man. I find you great to be with as a date. I couldn't have dreamt...anyway. Now that I know, I won't fantasize or grab.' They sipped their drinks thoughtfully and Lucio told her about his lover who had died a miserable death in Goa the previous year. 'After that, darling, I've been on a downer. Only my cooking saved me. That's why it is so important, you understand?' Mikki nodded. She felt a surge of affection for the slim, handsome man sitting across her. She leaned over and kissed his cheek. She saw a few heads turn to watch the two of them. She recognized Anil Jethani—Binny's business associate. He was staring at her in a peculiar way. Mikki was beyond caring. She waved jauntily and blew him a kiss. Lucio turned to see who it was and gulped. 'Jeez! It's him!' he said, his expression changing. 'You know the guy?' Mikki asked. 'Of course I do. Every gay in this city does. He is the Queen of Queens. He cruises the beaches and bars, picking up whoever's interested.' Mikki stared at the man and then at Lucio. 'Have you...?' she asked. 'Yes...' Lucio replied. 'He was vicious. I swore to myself...never again.' Mikki turned away and asked for the check.

*

'He is planning to kill you,' Ramanbhai's words rang in her ears. They were sitting on a parapet on Worli Sea Face, their cars parked close by. 'Why should Binny want to kill me?' she asked him. She'd been completely unprepared for what Ramanbhai had told her. It had taken him twenty minutes to unravel a complicated plot which began with her parents' mysterious plane crash and ended with this—the latest revelation involving her. 'I don't believe you...' she said slowly. Ramanbhai pressed his fingers to his forehead desperately trying to make her believe him. 'You must believe me, Mikki.

I have no reason to lie. I will gain nothing. And I want nothing. Material things do not matter to me. I lost my only son years ago in a car accident near Bangalore. He was all I had. He was the one thing that mattered in my life. After his death I dedicated my life to Hiralal Industries, and to you. Remember that school function I attended, Mikki? That time when your father couldn't find the time to come? I saw the hurt in your eyes and I thought you needed a parent as much as I needed a child. I can't bear to see you in danger.' Ramanbhai had closed his eyes. He seemed to be lost in thought. The sea breeze was getting stronger as monsoon clouds began rolling in towards them. Mikki felt the first few fat drops of rain on her face. She turned to Ramanbhai and caught his arm, 'Let's get out of here. I think there's a storm coming,' she said and the two of them ran to take cover in their waiting cars. The thunder rumbled and a violent sea churned up against the spot they'd been occupying moments earlier. An enormous wave swept over the parapet and crashed against the sides of the cars but by then Mikki and Ramanbhai were safe inside.

*

Binny returned in a foul mood. At the airport, where she'd gone to meet his plane, he'd nodded to her, handed over his briefcase and overcoat to one of his minions and wordlessly got into the waiting Mercedes. Mikki, who had spent the previous three days attempting to get Binny's sullen servants to prepare the house for his return, felt humiliated and crushed; perhaps, she thought, he's only suffering from jet leg. Binny had asked the driver to switch on a tape of Mehdi Hassan's soulful *ghazals*, put his head back against the head-rest and shut his eyes. Mikki had reached across to link her fingers through his but Binny had brushed her away with a sharp, 'Leave me alone.' In any case, intimacy was out with the driver in the front seat frequently turning around to check on Binny.

Back in the house, Binny had gone straight to his study, poured himself a large drink and had started going through his papers. The 'ping' of the fax machine was the only sound to disturb the silence of the night. Mikki had asked whether he wanted coffee, before going to her own bedroom. Binny had instructed her one day to shift into the adjoining wing, saying shortly that he wasn't used to sharing his room with anybody and that her presence in it distracted him. That had bothered her for a long time even though she'd grown up seeing her parents occupying separate rooms. In any case, he was rarely home and if he did choose to spend the night there it was well past 2 a.m. by the time he retired. But the day he got back from his long trip Mikki was hungering for him. She wanted to seduce him, devour him. She'd missed him physically and had planned a night of sensuous love-making. Binny's rejection hurt her terribly but Mikki was getting used to being hurt by him.

As she lay on her own bed, Mikki wondered whether or not to tell him about her strange encounter with Ramanbhai. She still wasn't sure whether to dismiss what he'd told her as the rantings of a deranged man or to take serious note of his warnings. But at that point she was so desperate to grab Binny's attention, she was willing to compromise her own life if it meant he'd notice her, listen to her, acknowledge her existence. She decided to tell him the following week…on his birthday.

*

Two days after his return from abroad, Binny came home unannounced in the afternoon. He found Mikki and Lucio happily experimenting in the kitchen. A scared looking bearer walked into the pantry and whispered, 'Memsaab…the boss is looking for you.' Mikki's hands were full of flour, while Lucio was whisking egg whites. Mikki was surprised to learn her husband was home at that hour and even more surprised that he had asked to see her. She raised her eyebrows across the table at Lucio, who smiled back encouragingly and gave her a thumbs up signal saying 'Ummmmmm—sexy things ahead for you baby…you deserve them.' Mikki blushed and turned to go towards the sink to wash her hands. That was when she saw Binny framed against the swing door that led into his enormous, hotel-style kitchen from the adjoining pantry. 'Who's that man?' he said striding into the room in a menacing manner. Mikki forgot all about the flour on her hands and rushed towards Binny to stop him. Lucio stood frozen, the egg whisk in his hand hanging in mid-air. Two kitchen assistants fled through the back door leading to the servants' quarters. Binny pushed Mikki aside roughly and went up to Lucio, whom he lifted up effortlessly by his shirt front and practically threw across the room. 'Get out of my house before I break every bone in your body, you bloody homo,' he snarled as Mikki tried to intervene. One swing from Binny's arm and she fell to the floor taking heavy copper-bottomed pots and pans with her. A pastry cutter landed on her arm and cut it as a tall stool overturned hitting her on the head and temporarily dazing her. 'Binny please...' Mikki cried out. 'Stop it. Lucio is a friend of mine. We were baking something special for you...for your birthday.' Binny whirled around, 'Fuck my birthday, bitch. And fuck you. If he is such a *yaar* of yours, you can leave with him. Defending another man in my home, you have guts. Don't tell me who he is, I know all about your so-called cooking classes with some French fellow. God knows what else he taught you both there. Don't deny anything. I've got proof. Photographs. Bills. That's what you were up to while I was away. I knew I couldn't trust you, whore.' Binny went back to Lucio who was cowering behind the oven. He grabbed him by the hair and turned him around to face the oven which was hot. With one arm against the back of his neck, he reached out and grabbed a rolling pin. He held that to Lucio's face and taunted, 'This is what you'd like shoved up your bum, wouldn't you? Let's try it for size.' Lucio began crying while Mikki crawled to where Binny was and held on to his legs. 'Please, darling. Don't do anything to him. Punish me. But not him. It's not his fault. Please Binny, please, darling.' Abruptly, Binny released Lucio and disengaged his leg from Mikki's grasp. Quietly, he surveyed the two of them and commanded, 'Get out of my house this minute. Both of you.' Then turning to Mikki he said, 'It's over. You can send someone for your filthy things—I don't want them to pollute my house. Out! And take that pansy boyfriend of yours with you.' Mikki raised herself up from the floor and pleaded with him, her eyes full of tears, 'Binny, why? Why are you doing this? What have I done? I love you. Only you. I'm innocent. Please Binny...I can't live without you.' He sneered as he swung out of the door, 'Women like you don't die so easily. Now get out.' And he was gone.

Lucio picked up Mikki tenderly and said, 'You need some ice for that love...it's beginning to puff.' He traced his artistic fingers lightly over her bruised forehead and looked around for a kitchen towel to mop up the blood flowing from her arm. Then he suggested firmly, 'You need a lawyer straightaway. I mean right this minute. Someone who can see the state you are in. You need to have yourself photographed with all those nasty cuts and bruises. We'll fix the animal, don't worry. I've seen bigger and worse bullies. I've been abused and beaten by gorillas next to whom your husband looks like a pet monkey. I know how to handle this. Leave it to me....'

The full moon shone down on them as they hailed a passing cab and headed for Lucio's home. Out of Binny's house, and his life.

*

'Sit down first, have a cup of tea...and then we'll do some serious talking,' Lucio instructed the still shaken Mikki. 'Anybody you'd like me to call?' he asked solicitously. 'Yes,' Mikki nodded, 'please call my cousin Shanay...no one else...but he hasn't been returning my calls...I don't know whether he'll come. I know he is in town though...his mother told me....' Lucio took the number and dialled and when Shanay answered, quickly briefed him before handing the phone to Mikki. She was comforted to hear the concern in his voice. Mikki filled Shanay in on everything that had happened and asked Shanay whether he knew of a good lawyer. Shanay asked for Lucio's address and said he would be there immediately. Repeatedly he inquired, 'Tell me...are you all right? Are you badly hurt? Shall I get a doctor along?' Mikki assured him that the injuries were superficial and Lucio's mother, a trained nurse, would look after her, but her voice sounded small and broken even to her own ears.

Fifteen minutes later, Shanay was at Lucio's. He hugged Mikki and it occurred to her that it was the first time they'd shared any sort of physical intimacy. Then he got down to business. 'I have heard of a Centre which deals with such cases specifically. It's a...it's a...I don't know what the home is...but before I left India I'd read about it in a newspaper...we should phone them.' Mikki perked up, 'Yes...it's a voluntary organization. Amy has a lawyer friend who works there. Phone her and get the number.' Amy was stunned when she heard what had happened and insisted on coming to Lucio's.

Half an hour later, there was a full-fledged conference on with Bhawna, the activist-lawyer friend of Amy's in total charge. 'Wife abuse,' she informed the group, 'is a criminal offence. We can file a complaint straightaway—if that's what you want—but I must tell you that it will attract a great deal of publicity, given the social status of the two people involved. Does Ms Hiralal want that?' Mikki shook her head vigorously while Lucio kept repeating, 'Give it to that bastard. Fix him.'

Mikki spoke privately to Shanay, who agreed with her that a scandal was something she didn't need. 'Can't I just document for the moment what he did to me and then produce the evidence in court during the divorce proceedings?' she asked Bhawna. 'That decision is up to you. But we can create quite a stink right now if you want to. I have a lot of friends—activists—working in various newspapers. They'll be more than willing to take this up for you in print. We could file charges tomorrow itself, as soon as the courts open.' Something in Mikki resisted—which Amy summed up in one word —class. 'Mikki is far too private a person to air her grievances in public,' she explained to Bhawna. 'She only wants to protect herself in case he decides to get nasty in court which she is sure he will.' Bhawna nodded and asked briskly, 'Do you want to claim alimony, maintenance and all that? In which case, we could take him to the cleaners.' Again, Mikki shook her head. She explained how she'd signed over everything to him. Bhawna shook her head unbelievingly, 'You must be crazy. Didn't anybody advise you against it?' Mikki smiled a tired smile and said softly, 'A lot of people did...but the problem was I loved the man...and I still do.' Amy nearly exploded, 'Stop that, Mikki! Don't you have any pride left? Look at you—black and blue from his blows, and still pining for him! I don't understand this. Can someone please explain?' Bhawna took her aside for a private conference. When the two of them returned, Bhawna said, 'For the moment let's just record the event as it happened. Lucio was a witness to the whole incident and we've all seen the injuries. Let Mikki sleep over it and we'll talk tomorrow.' Amy looked at her young friend questioningly and asked, 'Do you want to spend the night with me? Lucio quickly interjected and said, 'No, Mikki, stay here with us. Mother will take care of you...and we have a spare bed. It's not a palace, but our home is clean and comfortable.' Mikki nodded weakly, 'Yes...I'd prefer to remain here.' Then she turned to Shanay and pleaded, 'Stay with me for some time. There so much I have to talk to you about.' He gripped her hand and nodded. The two women went away promising to phone first thing in the morning.

Lucio left Shanay and Mikki alone after fixing himself a stiff shot of rum. They sat down on a diwan and Mikki burst into tears. Shanay held her till her outburst was over. Practical as always, he reached for a pad and pencil and asked her to list what she could of her known assets—mother's jewellery, property, shares, anything else she could think of. There wasn't very much she could come up with. Shanay shook his head in wonder after Mikki had run out of possessions she could rightfully claim as her own. 'Silly girl! Throwing your life away on a no good fellow—a criminal.' Mikki hushed him mid-sentence by putting her fingers over his mouth. 'I know everybody thinks I'm crazy...but, Shanay...you don't say harsh things to me, please. Not now. I can't take it. I need you to be on my side, to lend me your support. I'll have to begin everything all over again. And I want you to help me. Just promise me that much.'Shanay nodded and pressed her hand, 'Tomorrow, we'll look at all aspects—legal,financial, everything. Don't worry. I'll be by your side always.' Mikki's eyes were moist as she held her cousin's hand tightly and said, 'Thank you.'

*

Binny's lawyers moved before Mikki's could. By eleven o'clock the following day she was served a notice. The divorce petition put forward seventeen charges including adultery. But what got her was the one that said her marriage to Binny remained unconsummated and therefore the marriage stood annulled. She gasped in disbelief as images of their passionate love-making at Mandwa, the beach in Bali and at home, kept flashing through her mind. How could Binny have sunk so low? That, more than anything else he accused her of, hurt the most. She called Bhawna promptly and asked her what to do next. Bhawna wasn't at all surprised or thrown by Binny's papers, 'These men do it all the time when they want a quick and inexpensive way out of a marriage. Don't worry, we won't let him get away with this. Send the papers to me or better still, bring them with you. Take down my office address.'

Mikki arrived at Bhawna's poky little apology of an office in record time. She could barely wedge a foot in for the place was crowded with petitioners, most of them labour class women, sitting on every available stool and chair. Bhawna, assisted by a group of young, earnest lawyers, was attending to clients while handling two telephones that didn't seem to stop ringing. The place was crammed with law books and files. And in the midst of this chaos, there was Bhawna calmly juggling people and calls, looking fresh and cool in a simple black and white sari, her arms full of old silver bangles, and her hair kept in place with a couple of pencils to hold up the carelessly knotted bun. She gestured to Mikki to sit down where she could and wait. Someone thrust a chipped mug full of tea into her hands. 'Taarini!' exclaimed Mikki recognizing her old school friend. They embraced awkwardly and stood staring at each other.

Taarini was fidgeting with her sari *pallav*. Mikki noticed perspiration stains under her arm. Also, that her eyebrows looked as if they hadn't been strung for days and the polish on her toe-nails was chipped beyond redemption. Still, the sight of an old dear friend comforted her, and before she knew it she'd blurted out the whole sordid story to her former room-mate. Afterwards she blew her nose and said, 'I'm sorry I burdened you with my problems. I won't do it again. I should have realized you have problems of your own.'

Taarini smiled wanly, 'That's what I'm here for. Yes, I do. I do have problems. Do you want to hear them? Then listen...do you know I'm having an affair and it's driving me crazy? Don't look at me like that. Does it shock you so much? Why? Because you can't imagine a middle class working mother betraying her husband and children? You think only rich socialites are entitled to other relationships? Well, let me tell you that the man I'm involved with is not rich or powerful like your husband or like any of the other men you know. He is a humble trade unionist. He works in my office and I admire his guts. Of course, he is married. But so what? He is honest, principled, committed to his cause. And I love him so much, I could die for him. Surprised? Shocked? Don't be...I'm also a woman like you.'

Mikki kept staring at Taarini. She tried visualizing her frumpy friend in bed with a lover. It was impossible. Mikki blinked and looked at her again. How would she be without her clothes? Which man would get turned on by her? Mikki observed her friend's blue-veined breasts which sagged tiredly in an ill-fitting bra And now this woman was telling her that she was involved in a passionate relationship with some fiery trade unionist! It seemed unbelievable.

Taarini was smiling as if to herself. A secret smile. Like she had read Mikki's thoughts. Finally, she spoke, her voice filled with amusement, 'So…suddenly you think you don't know me, right? You are saying to yourself, "It's not possible. How can this funny-looking woman have a lover? What does he see in her?" Don't feel embarrassed. I would've said the same thing in your place. But you see, Mikki, it isn't only glamorous, beautiful women who have affairs. Even an ordinary woman like me sometimes finds someone who loves her, cares for her, wants to spend his life with her. I just thank God for Shashi. For allowing me to experience what love is. What sex is…with the right person. Now my husband is saying that I am a woman of loose, unstable character. That I can't even visit my children on weekends. I'm here trying to get custody of the little one at least…he's so small.'

*

Bhawna was brisk and to the point as she went over Binny's papers and told Mikki that he had obviously pre-planned the entire operation. 'What I can do is organize a *morcha* designed to embarrass him. That's easily done. But it won't get you anything in real terms. What you've told me indicates that your position is very weak. You obviously don't want to continue with the marriage. What you need is a fair settlement. Frankly, I don't think you'll get one, unless you are prepared for a long-drawn-out battle—say, extending over the next ten years or so. I wouldn't advise it. Your next best option would be to wait for his next move. Meanwhile, move back into your own house—do not give up your claim to that. I know he owns it. Chances are he'll lock you out. If you can reclaim it before that, it will be difficult for him to dislodge you—we'll file an injunction to prevent that from happening. He could resort to muscle power, even send *goondas* to frighten you. Are you prepared for that?' Mikki nodded her head. 'Let me send my court clerk, Vinayak, with you. Go home to your father's place. If you wish we could ask for police protection saying you fear you'll be assaulted, O.K.?' Bhawna said. Mikki stared at her blankly. She felt exhausted. The thought of her own bed and the possibility that she could collapse into it, cheered her up a little. She picked up her handbag and said gratefully, 'I appreciate what you are doing for me.' But Bhawna's attention was already elsewhere. A slum-dweller was showing her a deep gash on her forehead, inflicted by a drunken husband the night before. An infant was wailing on the woman's hip and another young child was pulling at her nine yard sari. Mikki turned away. Was there such a difference between her and the weeping woman? The sun was shining brightly through the window. She shaded her eyes against the glare and walked out into the busy street. Her life could have been a lot worse, she thought, as she climbed into a waiting cab and headed for home.

TEN

After learning that Dr Kurien was a devoted family man, a disappointed Alisha had taken up with Navin again. She hadn't got Dr Kurien out of her mind though, and often thought of calling him on some pretext of the other. Leelaben was still frail and in low spirits. Alisha had made sure to lock up all the booze in the house. The pills had been thrown away too. Leelaben was watched round-the-clock by hired nurses who sat around, watching video and eating all day. Alisha tried to spend as much time as she could with her mother, but it was a terrible strain. Leelaben was depressed and withdrawn most of the time. She'd taken to talking to herself and laughing out loud for no apparent reason. Alisha organized little drives and other outings for her but her mother seemed disinterested and apathetic as she stared vacantly out of the car window, muttering sadly to herself.

Sapna was managing things at the office and Alisha appreciated her supportive attitude. Sapna had taken over most of the executive functions and often presided over client meetings when Alisha couldn't make it. She travelled to Goa frequently, trying to clinch a project larger than anything their firm had handled before. Alisha was enthusiastic, but reluctant to accompany her, fearing her mother would attempt something drastic in her absence. Navin made for relaxing company in the evenings, often escorting both Sapna and her to concerts or any of the other cultural events Alisha was being initiated into.

Sometimes, Alisha wondered why Sapna seemed to be pushing Navin on her, subtle though her methods were. But Alisha dismissed her own suspicions as neurotic, and forced them out of her mind. She knew, of course, that Mikki's marriage was over. She'd heard the gossip at the hairdressers and relished listening to all the gory details. Without commenting on it, she'd found herself thinking, 'Serves the bitch right. Miss High and Mighty deserved to be pulled down. Now let's see what she does and where she goes.' On another level, Mikki's leaving Binny's palatial home created a strange vacuum in Alisha's life. It deprived her of the thrill of knowing her half-sister was a stone's throw away—these days when Alisha used her bathroom, she couldn't gaze out of the large window and imagine Mikki in her home. Alisha felt cheated, as if the entire exercise of getting this place had become futile without Mikki to torment her. Bitterly, she thought, 'Once again I've been defeated by her.'

*

One morning, Alisha noticed Leelaben sitting very still, her gaze fixed on nothing in particular. She went and tapped her but got no response. Alisha thought it was gloom, nothing more. She had become increasingly uncommunicative these days. And then, suddenly, the comb Leelaben had been holding in her right hand fell to the floor, and she slumped over in her chair. Alisha screamed for the nurse on duty while she frantically slapped her mother's face saying repeatedly, 'Mummy! Speak to me…say something…for God's sake, open your eyes…look at me.' Leelaben just lay on the ground. 'Oh God! I hope she isn't dead,' Alisha said to the nurse and then realized it was a stupid remark since they could both see Leelaben breathing regularly. The nurse took her pulse and said quietly, 'Call the doctor. I think your mother has suffered a stroke.' Alisha had never forgotten Dr Kurien's number and dialled quickly. The moment she heard his voice, her mother's condition receded into the distance as she hung on to his every word, barely understanding his instructions as she shut her eyes and imagined his quiet presence beside her. Finally she heard him ask, 'Hello, are you there, Miss Mehta?' She hastily covered up by saying, 'I'm sorry, doctor, I was a little distracted…Mummy just wet herself,' which wasn't a lie for in reality Leelaben had done just that. Dr Kurien rang off after telling her to stay by Leelaben's side till he got there.

Alisha waltzed off to her room to change into something attractive. She knew she was being absurd and unbelievably selfish, but her entire focus was on the man who was going to walk in through the door within the next fifteen minutes and turn her life upside down.

Leelaben was moved back to the nursing home. Nothing could have suited Alisha more. Overnight she became a dutiful daughter, barely stirring from the mother's bedside. Everybody commented on the change in her. She'd begun to dress and act differently as well. Gone were the provocative little outfits she used to favour, replaced by sedate saris or chaste *salwar kameezes*. She'd also developed a sudden interest in Kerala. She asked Sapna for books, any books, that would give her a glimpse into Dr Kurien's background. One of Sapna's friends had just returned after a trip to Cochin. Alisha badgered the man for details, asking him to describe in precise terms exactly what he'd seen and experienced. 'Are the women beautiful?' she asked anxiously, picturing the doctor's wife. 'Not particularly,' the man answered and she breathed a sigh of relief. 'Good boobs, though—huge,' he added as an afterthought and off she went imagining Dr Kurien making passionate love to a woman with enormous breasts. She went to the extent of asking her video-library man for art films from Kerala, with or without sub-titles. She was stunned by their content and especially by the explicit sex scenes which she was told had been inserted later by unscrupulous film-makers. She started reading the poems of Kamala Das and made a mental note to attend the famous snake boat race during Onam. Every day, Alisha picked up something new about Kerala and every day she tossed it casually at the doctor. The more Alisha tried to initiate a dialogue, the more he withdrew. She thought she saw a tortured look in the doctor's eyes when they met and fervently believed he was stopping himself from getting involved with her since he was a 'good' man. But the fact still remained that he gave her no encouragement at all.

One evening, he didn't show up at the nursing home. Alisha

panicked. It had to be something serious that had prevented him from coming, or else he would've informed the staff as he normally did, when he went out of town. She sat by the phone imagining all sorts of awful things—accident, heart attack, car crash. She thought of him lying stretched out on the road, with her image on his mind and her name on his lips. At last. At last, she would know that he had loved her all along just as she had loved him. The world would know the truth about them. Maybe, if she rushed to meet him, he would finally confess to her that yes, he too couldn't live without her.

The phone rang and she nearly jumped out of her skin. She grabbed it before the receptionist could. 'Yes?' she said eagerly. It was him. He sounded remarkably relaxed and happy. 'I'm sorry I couldn't come on my rounds this evening,' he said. Alisha wailed, 'I've been waiting for you. What happened? Is anything wrong?' He laughed, 'No. No. Nothing at all. It's just that I had another patient, if I can call her that. At home.' Alisha held her breath. He continued, 'My wife.' She was tempted to ask, 'Is she dead?' Maybe he sounded so relieved because the one impediment that stood in the way of their happiness was finally removed. Her heart soared. He sounded slightly bashful as he confessed, 'She's just had a baby—a baby boy. Our third child and first son.' Alisha bit back her tears. No. This wasn't possible. It wasn't true. He was fibbing. It was someone else impersonating Dr Kurien. This man was lying. He wanted to hurt her. It just wasn't possible. Stupidly, she heard herself ask, 'Are you sure?' 'About what? The baby?' he laughed. She recovered swiftly and said, 'No, I mean—are you sure you won't be coming by to see Mummy?' Dr Kurien said, 'You'll have to excuse me tonight. She's fine, isn't she? Nothing out of the ordinary I hope? She's had a comfortable day, I know that much, I'd checked with the nurse. Don't worry about her, she'll be fine. Just fine.' Alisha wanted to scream, 'Yes, she will. But what about me? Will I also be fine, just fine?' Without another word, she put down the phone and rushed out of the nursing home not bothering to say good bye to her mother. Leelaben died the same night of a massive cerebral haemorrhage. Alisha didn't blame herself. She blamed the doctor.

*

Leelaben's obituary notice in the *Times of India* was almost over-looked by Mikki. It was Amy who called her and brought it to her notice. 'I'd like to offer Alisha my condolences, but I don't know how she'd react. What do you think?' Mikki asked anxiously. Amy pondered over this and said, 'Decency demands that you make the gesture. It's up to her how she reacts. Go there. I believe the *uthamana* is tomorrow.' Mikki thought about another funeral, not so long ago and what a fiasco that had been. She was reluctant to go. For one, it would mean going across the street from Binny's home—that was going to be painful enough—for another, she'd have to risk being snubbed publicly by Alisha. Even so, Mikki reasoned, she'd brave it and put in an appearance. Like her, Alisha too was orphaned now. They just had each other. She debated whether or not to get Shanay to accompany her and then decided against it. She'd face this alone and risk Alisha's wrath.

Mikki dressed with care, making sure not to overdo or under-play anything. She wore one of her mother's 'safe' saris. Fortu-nately, with Bhawna's help she'd managed to obtain a stay order, stalling Binny's plans to throw her out of her father's home, which he now owned. 'Play for time,' Bhawna had advised and that's precisely what she was doing. There had been several attempts to use strong-arm tactics against her—threatening phone calls and menacing visits from the very men who surrounded Binny, and who not so long ago, addressed her as 'Madam'. But Mikki had re-hired her sacked security staff who'd agreed to work for her on reduced salaries. Dhondu and Gangu had also come back. For the moment, her life seemed reasonably safe.

Mikki looked at herself in the long Victorian standing mirror. Her hair had grown out and fell flatteringly over her shoulders. The blond streaks had disappeared. She'd gained a little weight, but it suited her. The figure was more full, more womanly. 'Less like a mannequin and more like a wife,' she thought wryly, patting the extra inch around her slim waist. She'd discarded most of her old business suits as well. The ones she'd had a local *darzi* pains-takingly copy from *Cosmo and Vanity Fair*. In any case they were sadly out of style now. Her wardrobe continued to be handpicked, but it reflected a more subtle taste. She'd taken to wearing *bindis* and bangles. Long earrings, too. But for this occasion she'd opted for her mother's dependable pearls and solitaires. She didn't want to overwhelm or offend Alisha—by her appearance at any rate.

Mikki gave Lucio a quick call before leaving. The two of them had decided to set up a classy home-catering business, making full use of her enormous kitchen and vast social contacts. 'The Gourmet Experience' had just about got off the ground, with attractive mailers sent to the 'right' people. They'd done their first few society parties and rejoiced over the oohs and aahs that had greeted their well-put-together menus. Mikki realized, of course, that half the thrill of having them cater was to see Mikki slaving away in swanky kitchens located in the homes of people she'd not even condescended to visit before getting into this business. But it didn't matter. She knew Lucio and she were good at what they were doing. Besides, she needed the money and so did he.

Lucio reassured her, 'Don't worry, baby. I'll hold the fort. Nothing major lined up for tonight. A small cocktail at the Swamy's—simple *hors d'oeuvres* and cold cuts. I can handle it. Mummy will help. You just go ahead and do what you have to.' Mikki thanked him, adding, 'I love you, Lucio.' 'I love you too, darling. Now run along like a good girl.'

Mikki's heart was sinking as her car negotiated the steep turn leading to Alisha's house. There were more than twenty cars in the driveway already. She glanced up the road at Binny's mansion. She caught her breath at the memory of her time there. She hadn't mustered up the courage till then to even drive past the road, and had taken elaborate detours to bypass her former residence. Slowly she adjusted the pleats of her sari and started climbing up the stairs which led to the enormous sitting-room. She could feel the eyes on her. She hadn't spotted Alisha so far. Hastily, she removed her Armani sunglasses and looked around for a place to sit in the ladies' section. An attractive, dusky woman came up to her and said softly, 'You must be Mallika. I don't know whether it's a good idea for you to be here. You know how Alisha feels about you.' Mikki nodded, 'Yes, I do know. But I felt it was important for me to come here today and express my condolences. We...we only have each other now.'

The woman nodded and indicated a place for Mikki to sit. 'I'll go and tell Alisha,' she said and disappeared upstairs.

Sapna knocked on Alisha's bedroom door with urgency. 'Who the hell is it?' Alisha asked impatiently. 'It's me,' Sapna said, adding quickly, 'She's here. Like you thought she would be. What do you want me to do and say?'

Alisha smiled. She was in bed with Navin. Slowly she wound her arms around his neck and kissed him lazily, 'Say nothing,' she purred, 'I'll deal with the bitch my way.' Navin pushed her away and said, 'Don't tell me you're planning to create a scene...come on...not at your mother's *uthamana*. Grow up, baby.' Instead, Alisha grabbed Navin by the waist and pushed her crotch against his, 'How much should I grow? This much?' And she started to rub herself against him, making sure Navin got aroused. 'Stop it. Stop it. People are waiting for you downstairs.' 'They can wait,' Alisha said as she began tearing his pyjamas off hungrily. '*Uthamanas* turn me on,' she continued as she pushed him down on the carpet, and sat astride him, her negligée pulled up to her waist, her panties around her ankles. 'Do it. You want to...go on! Do it,' she commanded as she expertly slid him into her. Navin had shut his eyes and was moaning as much with rage as pleasure. 'Bitch!' he muttered, as Alisha quickened her pace. 'Strike me. Hit me,' she instructed, as Navin clutched her bottom savagely and finally struck her. Alisha squealed and dug her nails into his shoulders. 'I like it,' she repeated, 'Do it, do it, do it.'

Outside, the Bengali lady who'd been hired to sing soulful Rabindra Sangeet, began her monotonous lament describing the dark passage of monsoon clouds across the parched countryside. Navin was grunting noisily as Alisha rode him faster and faster. Downstairs, Mikki was transported by the singer's voice to another land and she found herself shedding tears for a woman she hadn't known but whom her father had once loved.

Alisha spotted Mikki before she saw her. She grabbed hold of Navin's hand in hers and sauntered up to where she was sitting. Snapping her fingers, Alisha said, 'Up! Get up! You are not welcome in my house.' Mikki looked up, startled out of the reverie she'd slipped into. She noticed Navin beside her tormentor. Alisha was waiting. 'You heard me, Miss Hiralal. Or do you still call yourself Mrs Malhotra?' Mikki rose to her feet and tried to reach out for Alisha, who stepped back making Mikki stumble clumsily over the mattress she'd been sitting on. Navin leaned forward and caught Mikki's arm. Alisha immediately slapped his wrist and said, 'Hands off. I know your hands are well travelled over her body. But not now! And not on my turf!' Mikki picked up her bag and started for the door. She heard Navin's voice calling out, 'Mikki...wait. Please, I'll come with you.' 'Oh no, you won't mister,' Alisha screeched, holding him back. He shoved her away roughly and ran behind Mikki. 'I'm sorry for what happened,' he said, 'I'm through with that piece of shit.' 'Don't talk about my sister like that,' snapped Mikki as they ducked into the car and drove off. 'Some sister,' snorted Navin, reaching for a cigarette. 'Some friend,' Mikki said, rolling down her window to let the smoke escape.

*

Even though Mikki hated herself for it, she fell right back into her old relationship with Navin. As she told Amy, 'I know it's terrible of me. But I need a man around. I don't mean sexually. I feel lonely and distracted. Of course Lucio is a sweetie, but he is more like a girlfriend. Besides, both of us are cooking nearly everyday now, and are booked through the entire festive season. I need to unwind, relax. With Navin, I'm with a known devil, I can handle that.' Amy was sympathetic, 'You must be a brave woman to live alone in your huge house with that monster after your blood.' Mikki smiled, 'That's another reason why I feel slightly reassured with Navin around the place. Not that he has moved in or anything...but he's there, and Binny knows it. I don't care if he uses that in the divorce petition as well. He has already accused me of the foulest deeds— so what's another lover?' Amy shook her head, 'Darling, I think you are being far too passive. You should've hit back. Look at him—it's all your money, your father's companies and he's lording it over you. I hope you are protecting your interests. Do you have anything on him yet? Bhawna said she'd advised you to hire one of those shady fellows—what are they called—business spies or something. Have you done that?' Mikki said, 'No, Amy, I just can't get myself to sink to such levels. I was married to the man—I can't play dirty with him.' Amy let out her breath, 'But he can with you! It doesn't make sense, Mikki. And don't tell me you still love him and all that.'

'O.K. I won't tell you then,' Mikki laughed, 'but the fact remains that I do.' 'And Navin?' Amy quizzed. 'He's an escort and an occasional companion—a bed mate twice or thrice a week. Nothing more.' 'What if he re-proposes?' Amy asked. Mikki answered confidently, 'Oh no, he won't. He isn't such a fool. He'll end up marrying a prosperous *Gujju* girl from an established family—like the girl I once was. He knows I'm broke now.' Amy searched her friend's face. She was amazed to note how calm Mikki looked. Mikki smiled,'There are days I feel like giving it all up and walking off into the Himalayas. But, dammit, my life has barely begun— why should I give up on it so quickly?' Amy hugged her, 'You are pretty tough, aren't you?'

As the two women were chatting the phone rang harshly, cutting into their memories. It was a stranger's voice Mikki heard on the line. He sounded frantic, 'It's about your sister, Alisha.'

Mikki clutched her throat and moaned, 'No. Don't tell me…is she…is she….' The voice added more briskly, 'She is alive. Just about. But we need you here urgently. My name is Dr Kurien. I used to treat Alisha's mother. Your sister tried to kill herself. She slashed her wrists in the bathroom earlier today. She's at my nursing home, in the ICU. She'll pull through…here's the address. Please rush….' Mikki was half way out of her house before the doctor had finished his last sentence. She was praying for her sister's life and, in a way, her own.

ELEVEN

'W here's she? Where's my sister?' Mikki said as she burst into the hospital and siezed Dr Kurien by the lapels. The doctor explained to her calmly that for the moment her condition was reasonably stable. Mikki stammered, 'But what happened? How was she hurt?' As she asked all her questions in a rush, she noticed the same dusky beauty she'd been met by at Leelaben's *uthamana*. She was sitting quietly outside the ICU, watching Mikki and the doctor. Suddenly, a red light began blinking and a nurse ran out summoning the doctor urgently. 'Oh God! Oh no!' Mikki cried and clung to Amy. Sapna came over to where they were and put her arms around Mikki. 'It was horrible, horrible. But I'm sure she's going to pull through this. Relax.' Mikki all but screamed at her, 'What do you mean, "relax"? How can I relax? That's my sister out there. And she may be dying, and I don't know how or why.' Sapna looked at her steadily and said in a quiet, authoritative way, 'No she won't. She isn't a quitter. This would never have happened if it hadn't been for Navin. Son of a bitch.' Mikki froze. 'Navin? What does he have to do with it?' Sapna was reluctant to speak, 'I'm not sure you are ready to hear all this just now. It can wait.' Dr Kurien emerged from the ICU looking grim. He called Mikki aside, 'Miss Hiralal, I'm afraid there has been a slight set-back. Your sister's pulse is rather low. She's lost a great deal of blood. We are going to require transfusions. You might be aware that she has a relatively rare blood group—A Negative.' Mikki broke in to say breathlessly, 'Doctor, that's my blood group too. Here…I have my donor card in my bag somewhere. You can check it. I can give her as much blood as is required.' Dr Kurien scrutinized the card and instructed the nurse, 'Sister Annie, that solves our problem. Please prepare Miss Hiralal. We'll need two bottles to begin with. I'll phone the blood bank to check if they have any reserve. If not, we might have to flash an appeal on television and radio.' The nurse rushed off to get the bed ready. Dr Kurien looked at Mikki, 'Your sister is not just another patient to me. She is very special. Very special,' he said, awkwardly. Mikki looked into his eyes and could see the depth of his feelings for Alisha. She was glad he was there right now. 'Can't I see her?' she pleaded with him. 'Just for a second—no more. I promise I won't touch or talk to her.' Dr Kurien relented seeing Mikki's anxiety. He put a finger on his lips and cautioned, 'Very quietly please.'

Mikki was shocked to see Alisha lying helplessly on a hospital bed with tubes running in and out of her body. Her face was ashen as she lay limply, her beautiful, sparkling eyes shut and her face and hands slightly blue. Mikki took in the bandaged wrists and her heart broke. Poor, lonely, lovely Alisha. Mikki bent over her and touched her fingers. How delicate they were, with perfect ovals for nails. She pushed back a strand of hair that had strayed across Alisha's pale forehead. She thought she saw Alisha's eyes flicker. The nurse came in and asked Mikki to follow her, leaving Dr Kurien to monitor Alisha's pulse and keep his eyes glued to the green graph that kept moving irregularly. Mikki left the room after briefly praying by her sister's side. She blew Alisha a kiss from the door before it swung shut behind her.

For two days and nights, Mikki didn't leave the nursing home as Alisha hovered precariously between life and death. And as her sister battled to live, Mikki prayed for her recovery. From nowhere grew a certainty that this was one battle she would win.

On the second afternoon, just before Alisha regained consciousness, Sapna told her what had happened that awful morning when Alisha locked herself into her fancy bathroom and used Navin's razor to slash her wrists. 'He had spent the night with her. It was the first time after their showdown at her mother's *uthamana*. Alisha had been pining for him. I could see how miserable she was. She couldn't concentrate on anything in office. Which was O.K., I handled everything, as I have been doing for some time now. Alisha had been visiting the office erratically or not at all. She hasn't been herself. I thought it was because of her mother—or Dr Kurien. Or Navin. Or even you. But it was something else. I still don't know what was eating at her. She'd shed a lot of weight and seemed very depressed and distracted. She was desperately lonely too, in that huge bungalow. So…it was my mistake…I phoned Navin and asked him to contact Alisha. Initially he was reluctant. And then he agreed. She called him over and I suppose they had their usual fight. Over you. Alisha knew he'd started seeing you again and, that was destroying her too. I think he taunted her about—I don't know how to say this—about you being sexier in bed. That did it. Alisha flew into a rage and started breaking things. Navin wouldn't stop. He kept on and on, describing your body in intimate detail. And what you two did when you were together. It was too much for her. She rushed into the bathroom and locked herself in. Navin helped himself to another drink and bolted after banging on the door a few times. The servants didn't dare go into her room. It was only in the morning when she didn't ask for her usual *chai* that they went up and found her bedroom door open, as Navin had left it. They knocked on the bathroom. When she didn't respond, they phoned Dr Kurien and me. Both of us rushed there. And you know the rest….'

Mikki sighed, 'How do you know all this?' she asked. 'Navin,' Sapna said. 'It's all my fault,' Mikki said finally, 'I should never have allowed Navin back into my life. He caught me at the wrong time. When I was feeling weak, low and defenceless. Damn!'

Sapna caught her hand and said, 'Please…don't blame yourself. This would've happened sooner or later. Alisha is such a fragile person, she's constantly on edge. Poor girl.'

Mikki nodded, 'I have to make sure it never happens again. Ever. I'm going to look after her from now on. Let her protest and fight. I won't listen to her. She needs me. And I need her too.'

*

It was obvious to everybody that Dr Kurien was doing much more than just a doctor's duty. He was by Alisha's side throughout her ordeal. It made Mikki wonder whether Alisha was his sole patient. But she was grateful for his presence and told him so. He hesitated before speaking. But once he started, the words came out in an unstoppable torrent. 'I love Alisha. I love your sister,' he told Mikki, who nodded and said, 'I know you do.' Dr Kurien wrung his hands and carried on, 'I'm a middle-class man with a family. I don't know anything about you rich people. I've been brought up differently. I have three children, a wife, old parents. I'm helpless. I cannot do anything at this stage to change my life. I cannot hurt my family. And I cannot hurt Alisha. We have not spoken about this subject so far. I would have tried to forget her…tried to get her out of my life, but then this happened…now I feel it's too late. Destiny has played its part…I will not let her go. I will tell her how I feel. Seeing her near death made me realize my love. But I'm afraid—for her and for myself. I do not know what to do. I only know I love her. That's all.'

Mikki heard Dr Kurien out without interrupting him even once. She knew this relationship had no future. But she didn't want to tell that to the anguished man who had saved her sister's life. She decided she'd be more candid when Alisha was better and she'd had a chance to talk to her about the doctor. At that point Mikki had no inkling about Alisha's feelings towards him. It was possible he'd imagined it all. Alisha was easy to fall in love with, after all.

On the fourth day, Alisha opened her eyes just as the sun was setting. The first person she saw was Mikki. A slight frown creased her forehead. She tried to speak but the words wouldn't come. Mikki bent over her eagerly and held her face, 'Alisha. It's me—your sister,' she said. Alisha turned her face away and scowled. 'Please, Alisha—look at me,' Mikki pleaded, 'I'm here to look after you. You are fine. We are going to live together from now on.' The nurse came in and beamed. When she saw that Alisha had regained consciousness fully, she rushed off to call Dr Kurien.

Alisha looked at Mikki blearily and asked, her voice just a whisper, 'What happened? What am I doing here? Was there an accident? Navin? Sapna? How did you get here?' Mikki shushed her and said, 'Let Dr Kurien tell you. He'll be here in a minute.' He walked in just then, his eyes shining with happiness. Without warning, he bent over Alisha and kissed her all over her face, like an over friendly puppy. The nurse blushed and looked away. Mikki decided to leave them alone and left the room.

Twenty minutes later Dr Kurien emerged from Alisha's room with an overjoyed expression on his face: 'She's happy. I have told her everything. She wants to see you.' Mikki's heart did a somersault as she asked him, 'Did she really say that—that she wants to see me? Are you sure?' Dr Kurien took Mikki's arm firmly and escorted her into the room saying, 'Here's your sister.' Mikki, her eyes bright with tears, stroked Alisha's wan face gently and hugged her. After a minute, she felt Alisha's arms creeping hesitantly around her shoulders. The two sisters held each other close and cried the lost years away.

*

Once home, Mikki took charge of Alisha's life. It hadn't been all that easy. Alisha had resisted her for the first couple of days till physical exhaustion had forced her to abandon the fight. Mikki had sat herself down on her bed that first morning home and said gently, 'Look, Alisha...let's learn to trust each other. You need me now...just as I need you.' Alisha had turned her face away and scowled, 'Big bloody deal. So I made a hash of things. So what? I still hate you.' Mikki had been silent for a bit before saying, 'I can understand your anger. But let it be in the past where it belongs, you and I are innocents in this complicated mess we are in. And the man responsible for it—my father and yours, is dead. Forget what happened, I'm prepared to blank out everything and start everything from scratch.' Unexpectedly, Alisha had burst into tears. Loud, angry sobs wracked her body as she lashed out at Mikki blindly. The words were harsh and crude. But they were so uncalculated, it was easy for Mikki to forgive her. She'd sat quietly waiting for the tantrum to end. Fifteen minutes later, Alisha was blowing her nose in Mikki's hanky. She was still holding back. Still stiff with all the old feelings she couldn't shake off. Mikki waited a while and then explained, as one would to a spoilt child, that in her present fragile state, Dr Kurien had advised Mikki to look after her sister. At the mention of his name, Alisha had softened sufficiently to agree to staying on, adding, 'But only till I'm well enough to go back to my own home.' Mikki had nodded eagerly and said, 'Of course, let's leave it to the doctor to say when.'

'Now...how about working out a schedule to get you back to full health,' Mikki said to Alisha one evening, as they sat eating breakfast a week later. Alisha was still wan and weak. Dr Kurien had said it was going to take her at least a month to regain her weight and, more importantly, her confidence. Mikki had smiled and said, 'No problem, doc. We have all the time in the world now.' He came by twice a day often staying for over an hour. Mikki would leave the two of them alone and go and try out new recipes.

Lucio's enthusiasm combined with the long hours he put in had reaped rewards that both he and Mikki were enjoying. They were still an item on the party circuit and Mikki sportingly went along with the 'exploitation' of her image. 'Come on,' she joked, 'if it gives these fat cats a thrill to be served their canapés by Mallika Hiralal, that's fine by me—provided they pay for their thrills.' And pay they did. Lucio and Mikki ran the priciest show in town even without the frills. But they also delivered the choicest dishes made with the finest ingredients.

Each day Mikki would leave Alisha reluctantly and go off to supervise orders before rushing back home and straight to wherever Alisha was. Often she'd find Sapna there, blueprints spread out on the marble top table in Alisha's room. Mikki would watch admiringly, silently, as the two women pored over their projects, completely absorbed in the work on hand. Apart from these work commitments all others stood cancelled. Alisha's animosity almost completely gone as a result of Mikki's determined effort to break it down, the sisters now spent their time catching up with each other's lives. Alisha's curiosity was insatiable as they went through trunks of old albums, gazing at photographs of their father, giggling at some of the poses struck by him and his friends and generally trying to reconstruct those areas of his life they knew so little about. 'I still can't get over it,' Mikki exclaimed once when Alisha squealed at the sight of a woman peeping out of a corner of a party picture. 'Hey! Look! Here's Mummy.' Mikki grabbed the album from her excitedly, saying, 'Show me! Show me!' Both of them stared hard at Leelaben who looked like a frightened deer caught off-guard. 'Amazing,' Mikki said, 'how Papa managed to keep it a secret from me all these years!' Alisha nodded her head and teased, 'But I knew all about you!' Mikki gave her a friendly shove and they turned more pages, brought up more memories, rediscovering their past, rediscovering themselves....Alisha gazed at Mikki's childhood pictures for a long time before saying pensively, 'I'd be lying if I didn't tell you how jealous I feel, even now, as I see you in these photographs looking so happy. You had so much more of him.' Mikki looked at her and said, 'Are you kidding? I have a feeling he spent more time with you and your mother than he ever did with me and mine. We hardly got to see him—especially during the past five years. He was gone before I woke up and by the time he checked in for dinner, I was asleep. Later, I had my own plans. Besides I was at a boarding—and so were you. Yes, I remember a few summer holidays well—in Europe, Japan, America and that African safari with his business partners from Nairobi, which was such fun. Other than that...' and she trailed off. Alisha recounted her happy days with the man who led such a duplicitous existence. Strangely, both women bore him no grudge. 'He was what he was,' Mikki concluded philosophically and Alisha agreed.

*

It was time for Dr Kurien's visit and Alisha was tense. 'Don't be depressed,' Mikki had said to her before leaving for a large theme party at Mrs Lalwani's new beach house. 'He's a nice fellow, but I don't think he can leave his family, so, Alisha, don't pin your hopes on him, there are other men....'

Mikki stopped when she saw the look of distress on Alisha's face and left quietly. After she'd gone Alisha brooded about Dr Kurien. She knew, deep down inside, that he could never be hers, but that didn't stop her from loving him desperately. He'd taken her off all drugs and recommended a holiday. 'A change of environment is essential,' he'd said. But Alisha didn't have the energy to go anywhere. First her father, then her mother, and it could've been her next. If it hadn't been for Dr Kurien. And Mikki.

Alisha watched Dr Kurien's Maruti drive up and observed him as he emerged from it. His step was light as he ran up the stairs. She knew the sight ought to have excited her but there was a peculiar sinking feeling in her stomach...a sense of foreboding. He came up to her enthusiastically and held her close. Alisha felt her eyes welling up with tears. No, she told herself, no she mustn't. 'What's wrong?' he asked softly, 'Oh—nothing...everything....' She broke down suddenly. He continued to hold her as she wept. He knew what was troubling her. But he also knew this was one area where he couldn't help her. Not without destroying his own life, the life of his small, happy, unsuspecting family. 'There is really no future for us, is there?' Alisha cried.

'Calm down, darling, calm down,' he crooned. But Alisha fought him off. 'You should have let me die. At least I wouldn't have had to suffer this.' He propped up her feet and asked, 'Shall I get you some warm milk?' 'Fuck your milk,' Alisha lashed out. 'And fuck you, too.' He held her hand between warm palms and said, 'Look at me, Alisha, look into my eyes. What do you see? I love you. Darling, I love you. You must believe me. You must.' Alisha's face was wet with tears. 'I do believe you. I desperately want to. But I'm a selfish woman. I can't share you with your wife and family. I don't want to fall into the same trap as my foolish mother and end up like her. She wasted her youth on a man who said exactly what you just said to me. And she also believed him. If you want to continue the relationship—get a divorce and marry me.'

The doctor was thoughtful for a while. Abruptly, he got up and went towards the door. Alisha cried out, 'Wait! Don't leave me.' He turned around and said, 'You are making this impossible for both of us. I am a Catholic. There is no divorce for me. I'm also a believer. It would break my father's heart. For women like you— men are playthings. Today you want to break up my marriage. Tomorrow you'll get bored and move on to some other man. Where will that leave me?'

Alisha was absolutely distraught. She phoned Mikki, who, wondering what the problem was, came home immediately. When she got back, she was relieved to find Alisha was all right; then she noticed Dr Kurien, and the tension in the room. 'Lover's quarrel?' she asked casually. Alisha sobbed into the pillow she was clutching while Dr Kurien stood around sheepishly. Then, without saying goodbye to either of them, he walked out, slamming the door behind him. 'What am I to do?' Alisha cried as Mikki comforted her. 'Get well,' Mikki commanded. 'That's top priority right now...everything else, especially the doctor, can wait.' Alisha's tears wouldn't stop. 'Give me something to calm my nerves,' she pleaded. Mikki dismissed her pleas with a harsh, 'Rubbish! Behave yourself. I'm in charge around here. Take a nap and if you're a good girl, I'll get you a fun movie to watch later.' 'Big deal,' Alisha said, pulling a face. But she knew she didn't really have a choice.

*

Two weeks after Alisha had regained consciousness, Mikki called up and told Navin, 'I never want you to call or try and see either of us again. Do you understand? You're nothing but a low down S.O.B. Stay out of our lives permanently. You could have killed my sister!'

Navin laughed a mocking laugh. 'Ha! Ha! Killed that little bitch? She deserves to die. If you don't watch it, she'll kill you.' Mikki hung up on him. When she turned around she found Sapna watching her closely. Before she realized what she was saying, Mikki snapped at her, 'What the hell do you think you're doing here?' Sapna apologized calmly, adding, 'I thought I owed you that. You see, if it hadn't been for me, Alisha would never have met Navin. I introduced the two of them at her housewarming party.' Mikki looked at her absently, her mind elsewhere. 'So? It can happen.' Sapna paused, 'It wasn't just a coincidence. In a way, I'd planned it all…to get even with you.' 'Even with me?' Mikki asked, puzzled.

Sapna smiled, 'You may not know me…But I've known you, or rather known about you, for years. Through your father. He and I were…you know…you understand. I was very young when I met him. Barely out of college. I'd gone to his office for a job. He spotted me in the lobby as he walked into his own office and sent for me. After talking for a while, he said, 'I'm very impressed by you. When can you join? I need a personal assistant.' I told him I hadn't come there looking for a clerical or secretarial job. I gave him my quali-fications. He looked even more impressed as he scanned my re-sumé. He made me another offer in one of his divisions. I jumped at it. I needed the job badly. We fell into a relationship soon after. This was while he was still seeing Alisha's mother, but had lost interest in her. After a few months, I got knocked up by him and was terrified. He suggested an abortion. I refused. He sacked me on the spot. Just like that. I was on the streets. That's when I met my husband and got married immediately. Yes, I had the abortion without anybody's knowledge, neither your father nor my hus-band knew about it. I went to some awful quack in a filthy clinic and he butchered me good and proper. Ruined my insides. I can never forget the nightmare of those days as I lay bleeding all by myself in the Working Women's Hostel, where I used to stay. Your father didn't even bother to find out what happened to me. If I hadn't met my husband, I might've tried to take my life, just as Alisha has now done. I hated your father with such intensity, it used to hurt physically. I'd have nightmares about him. It was that bad.

'After my divorce, I came back to India and joined Alisha. At first I didn't make the connection. But when I found out whose daughter she really was, I began plotting my revenge. Then something else happened. I started to like her. She is very likeable in her own crazy way, you know. But by then it was already too late. Navin and she were too involved. At one point I thought of confessing to Alisha. But then I had to think of my own career. I hadn't found an alternative job then. I have one now. I came by to submit my resignation. And to say goodbye.'

Mikki was far too taken aback by what she'd heard, to react immediately. She kept fiddling with a corner of her *dupatta*. Sapna filled in the interval by adding, 'One more thing. Ramanbhai knew about me and your father. Ramanbhai knew everything. I suspect he was blackmailing Seth Hiralal. He'd even come to see me quite recently—after I started working for Alisha. He told me he was very sorry about what had happened. He wanted to know if the child was alive, if someone else could stake their claims to the Hiralal legacy. He was very disappointed when I told him about the abortion. He said, "You know, you could have used the child to get you something out of Hiralal."'

Mikki held up her hand to silence Sapna and said, 'Look, at this moment I don't need any of this. I have to first make sure that my sister gets back on her feet. I'll deal with what you've told me later.' Sapna said, 'As you wish,' but did not leave. Mikki added, 'I don't wish to upset Alisha by revealing all this to her. Once she is strong enough to get back to work, she'll decide what to do with your resignation. Meanwhile, I expect you to do whatever you have to at the office. You are paid for it, after all.' With that Mikki dismissed the older woman and went back into her bedroom to brood over what she'd heard. She knew her father had been a real bastard. But it was only now that she was discovering newer and blacker aspects of his personality. Poor Mummy, she thought, for the first time in her life. And poor us, she concluded, thinking of Alisha and herself.

*

Alisha sold her property for a huge profit, which she promptly reinvested in a hundred acres close to Pune. She also bought a small flat near Mikki's home but Mikki wouldn't hear of her moving into it. 'Are you crazy? What for? Where's the hurry, anyway?'

'Darling, much as I love you, we can't go on behaving like Siamese twins for the rest of our lives. Eventually, you're going to remarry. And I hope not to remain a spinster forever. I'd like kids, lots of them,' Alisha said, and Mikki laughed, pleased to see her revived spirits. But she was still afraid to leave her alone. Alisha's moods swung dangerously from high euphoria to deep depression. Mikki feared that, left to herself, she'd resume her old wild ways. Alisha reassured her saying, 'Look, big sister, you can't mother me like this—you have your life and I have mine. Let's split while we still like each other. Who knows...too much togetherness might create problems. What if I start getting on your nerves?'

Mikki looked at her lovingly and said, 'Don't be crazy. I've waited for so long for this to happen. And now you want to throw it all away. Why? We need each other. Or at least, I need you.'

Alisha tossed her long hair and teased, 'Yes, yes. But what about my sex life? And yours? At this rate we'll die old maids—dried up bags.' Mikki interjected, 'I don't interfere with your love life, do I? I'm not cramping your style. As for me, I'm too busy cooking to have time for love-making.' But listening to Alisha chattering on animatedly, made Mikki feel glad. It was an indication that she was getting back to her old self. She encouraged her to say naughty things and laugh. Mikki knew that behind the facade, Alisha's heart was aching for Dr Kurien. He had not called since that dramatic day when he'd staged a walk-out. Mikki felt somewhat relieved. She hoped that Alisha would finally be able to get Dr Kurien out of her system. She wasn't sure why, but she didn't really trust the guy. Anyway, business was booming and her catering outfit—now expanded to over twenty-five full-time employees including two junior chefs from a catering college who did marvellous things with pasta—kept Mikki busy enough to not worry unduly about Alisha. Mikki no longer attended all the events personally. Neither did Lucio. But the two of them oversaw everything down to the smallest details. Mikki was busy all right. But also desperately lonely. Miserably, she realized she missed Binny despite everything that had happened. She was surprised at his silence. Apart from a few notices from his solicitors which she promptly passed on to her own, he seemed to have disappeared. She knew he was travelling a lot and flying in and out of Bombay. She also knew he'd installed his woman and the two children in a farm house outside Bangalore, but other than business snippets that appeared here and there, she had no real information. She waited, knowing that, sooner or later, he'd make his move, since it was he who was keen on a divorce and not her. Till then, her instincts told her to sit tight.

Mikki's suspense ended abruptly one afternoon when she found two of Binny's senior executives on her doorstep. She went to receive them, her hands full of the dough she was kneading for exotic *vol-au-vents* required later in the evening. 'Something wrong?' she asked, searching their grim faces. One of them nodded and stepped up to her. 'Mrs Malhotra, we are very sorry to inform you that…that…Mr Malhotra is dead.'

'What?' Mikki said, leaning back to support herself against the door. The men moved forward, and guiding her gently by the arm, put her down on a roomy Chesterfield. 'Water !Get some water,' they shouted to one of the bearers. Alisha heard the commotion from her room upstairs and rushed to the head of the stairs. 'What's up?' she demanded. 'What's happened to Mikki?' As she came rushing down, she tripped over her gown and fell headlong, landing with a heavy thud at the bottom of the staircase. One of the men rushed to help her up, but her eyes were shut and she appeared to be lifeless. The other man asked the servants agitatedly, 'Doctor? Do you have the number? We need a doctor.' The bearers scampered off and came back with Mikki's thick leatherbound telephone book. They scanned the pages frantically and found Dr Kurien's number which had been highlighted with a fluorescent felt-tipped pen. They got him on the first ring and briefly told him what had happened. 'I'll pick up an ambulance and be there as fast as I can,' he said and rang off.

*

Mikki was wide awake and alert as the doctor ran in with his team. But Alisha was still unconscious. His eyes took in Mikki as he rushed past to examine Alisha. 'Her pulse is weak,' he growled to the nurse. 'Check her B.P. We'll have to move her quickly...but very gently. It could be a head injury. We'll need to do a CAT scan at once.' Two attendants with an emergency stretcher walked in and began lifting Alisha gingerly. Mikki's voice rose weakly above the commotion as Dr Kurien was busy phoning the nursing home, 'Doctor, please...doctor...where are you taking my sister? Is she all right?' He nodded absently in Mikki's direction and mumbled, 'God willing, she'll be fine. I need someone here to attend to you. I am so very sorry to hear the terrible news....'. Mikki nodded her head and reached for the phone. The first number she thought of was Shanay's. 'I'll be there,' he said tersely when he heard the news.

The two men from Binny's office were waiting silently for her to compose herself. 'What happened?' she asked at last. 'Car accident,' one man explained. 'While driving from Bangalore to Ooty, Mr Malhotra, Miss Urmilla and...and...the children...they were all killed. Head-on collision with a truck. Instantaneous. Driver also dead. Very bad. Very bad.'

Mikki still couldn't believe what she was hearing. 'Early morning. They were going to the races. Mr Malhotra's filly, Sugar Plum Fairy, was running. Odds on favourite.'

Mikki nodded mechanically and stared at the men not knowing what to say. She felt hollow and numb. The tears just weren't there. They stood around awkwardly. Finally one of them began shuffling towards the door, saying, 'Is there anything else we can do...Mrs Malhotra? The funeral is in Bangalore tomorrow morning. Your ticket has been booked on the last flight tonight—in case you want to be present. Mr Malhotra's close associates thought you may want to absent yourself.'

Mikki looked up sharply and said, her voice rising without warning, 'Absent myself? What nonsense! He was my husband. As his widow I would like to oversee all arrangements for the funeral. Please make sure you ask your people in Bangalore to speak to me right away and I'll instruct them. Oh yes—we will provide the same facilities to the lady and the children who also died with my husband. And his driver, of course. I want the best of everything for Binny. He lived well and loved life. I would like his funeral to be remembered by all those who attend it. It will be grand, dignified and beautiful. I'll see to it. And...I need to meet our solicitors to sort out new developments. Get Ramanbhai on the line for me someone. Let's not waste a single moment more.'

Ramanbhai's voice over the phone was solicitous but distant. He sounded distracted and aloof, as if his mind was on something else. Mikki jolted him into paying attention by shouting, 'Ramankaka are you listening to me? Please concentrate on my words. This is a very significant development for us. I need to meet our lawyers on my return. In the meantime, I want you to keep an eye on things in my absence.' Ramanbhai spoke up, 'Yes, I'm willing to intervene and do whatever is necessary...but you are surrounded by people who manipulate you, use you, are not loyal to you. Under the circumstances, it's difficult for me to be effective.' Mikki was in far too much of a hurry to listen to him grumbling. She cut him short saying, 'Oh Ramankaka, this is hardly the time to discuss office politics.' He butted in swiftly, 'I'm not wasting your time on cheap gossip. I have specific information on Shanay. If you wish I can give it all to you on the way to the airport.' Hurriedly, Mikki rang off after agreeing to pick up Ramanbhai en route.

'That boy is no good,' Ramanbhai began as soon as he got into the car. Mikki looked at him exasperatedly, 'Is that all?' He assumed an injured air, 'I have been warning you about him all along. From the first day that he walked into the office. He's strange...nobody trusts him in the organization and nobody likes him. They put up with him because of you. But it has come to my notice that he will stop at nothing to get you. And your money. It is an old, old plot hatched by that scheming mother of his.'

Mikki waved off his remarks and said irritatedly, 'Let's talk about something else.' But Ramanbhai was determined to go on, 'Do you know...people are suspecting he is involved in the accident? Mr Malhotra's death.' Mikki snorted, 'That's ridiculous and you know it. Why would he want to commit such a crime?' Ramanbhai said softly and deliberately, 'So that he can finally have you.' Mikki sighed, 'If that were so, he would have tried hard after my divorce. I was free and available, remember?' Ramanbhai laughed dryly, 'You are so young and so gullible, my dear. Do you think we all couldn't see how impossible that was for any man? You were still in love with that husband of yours. You may have been divorced, but your heart was not free. And it would never have been free so long as Mr Malhotra was alive. That's why Shanay had to kill him.'

Mikki's head was reeling, 'Are you saying Shanay murdered

Binny, Ramankaka?' she asked, emphasizing each word. 'Precisely,' he said, rubbing his hands, 'these things are easy to arrange...for a price. Drivers can be hired for the job...any number.'

Mikki looked at him thoughtfully, 'How come you know so much about such things?'

Ramanbhai stared out of the window, 'When a person has been in business as long as I have, he gets to know everything—that is his job, and now please drop me off at the nearest taxi stand. You can choose to ignore what I've just told you...but at your own risk.' Mikki instructed the driver to pull over. Ramanbhai hopped out nimbly and waved to her 'Don't worry about anything in Bombay. I'll take care of it,' he said, leaning against the window. She smiled at him gratefully. The airport lights were shining in the distance as she drove off. Shanay? A murderer? Mikki mused. Impossible! Maybe she had a lot more living to do before she could believe such a charge, she concluded, as the car drove in to the terminal.

TWELVE

Mikki arrived in Bangalore late at night and wasn't surprised to find nobody had been sent to meet her at the airport. Her travel agent in Bombay had made all the arrangements so she found her hired car waiting for her right outside the arrival lounge. 'Windsor Manor,' she instructed the driver and collapsed into the back seat. She hadn't had the chance to catch her breath or even think clearly. On Amy's advice, she'd worn an ivory coloured silk sari rather than a stark white one and her hair was pulled back into a simple pony tail. She'd applied a touch of lip gloss over her dry lips. The tears still weren't there and she was dreading the moment when she'd actually have to confront Binny's body.

Once she reached the hotel, she checked into her suite and got on to the phone. First, a call to Shanay to check on Alisha. 'Thank God!' she exclaimed when he told her that the CAT scan was clear and Dr Kurien was confident there was nothing major to worry about. Besides, Alisha was fully conscious and asking for Mikki frequently. 'Haven't you told her about Binny?' Mikki asked. 'No. The doctor felt it would be too much of a shock at this stage. He advised us against letting her know. We just said you had to leave on an urgent business trip to Bangalore and that Binny had had an accident.' Mikki was silent. She wished desperately that someone could have come with her. She was going to face the ordeal all on her own. Amy had some guests over and Lucio's mother was in hospital with a broken hip. Mikki told Shanay to convey her love to Alisha saying she'd phone back the next morning before leaving for the funeral. 'He's very considerate, for a murderer,' Mikki thought to herself about Shanay, remembering Ramanbhai's grim warning.

Mikki decided to take a long bath before going to bed. She'd asked Room Service to send a large hot chocolate. She needed her sleep and she wasn't going to pop a pill to get it. The phone rang while she was shampooing her hair. She picked up the receiver and heard a familiar voice which she couldn't place immediately. It was a Gujarati-speaking man and he was talking in such low tones it was difficult to catch his words. 'Listen to me carefully,' he said, 'your husband…was murdered. It was not an accident. It was a planned case of hit-and-run. Just believe what I'm saying. The people who killed your father also killed your husband. Your father's accident was also not an accident. And you are next. They are going to kill you too. And that illegitimate sister of yours. Be careful…be very careful…be very careful….' Mikki's hand was frozen on the receiver. 'Who are you?' she started to say, but the caller had already rung off. She tried to place the voice. She'd heard it before several times. She knew the accent, and that unmistakable lisp while pronouncing words with an 's' in them. Who could it be? Shanay? In any case, he was away in Bombay, where she'd left him. But of course, it didn't have to be Shanay. It could've been a hired thug. But if it was Shanay who was killing everybody why would he warn her? And yet, whatever Ramanbhai had told her about Shanay kept echoing in her mind. Shanay—her cousin Shanay. Would he do such a thing to her, even out of love? And did he really imagine she'd marry him after all this? It seemed totally absurd. A bit too far fetched. And yet, who besides Shanay would want to see her widowed?

*

The funeral of her husband was much like that of her parents'— once again Mikki turned away from the sea of white she found herself in. It brought back horrible memories of the other funeral, still so fresh in her mind. She'd dressed deliberately in beige, knowing it would lead to gossip. But Mikki was beyond caring, as she surveyed the four, flower bedecked coffins laid out neatly on the emerald green lawns of Binny's bungalow estate. Fortunately, nobody had rushed at her or tried to create a scene in any way, as she stepped out of the car and walked slowly towards the throng of strangers standing in hushed silence around the bodies. She'd worn enormous wrap-around glasses, thinking how absurd they were even as she put them on. But she needed to shade her eyes from the prying ones of other mourners.

An elderly lady came up to her and held her hand, 'I'm Urmi's mother,' she said haltingly before bursting into tears. Mikki held her frail body as she wailed and began beating her breasts. 'Why has God punished me like this? What have I done to deserve such a fate?' she cried, setting off a chain reaction. Several other women joined the chorus, while Mikki stood there, stiff and self-conscious, not knowing what to do. The men were staring at her from the other side of the lawns. She knew she was expected to break down and perhaps faint as well. But Mikki stood straight and tall as the priests began the ritual chanting.

It took more than an hour for the ceremony to conclude, during which time Mikki got the chance to survey the place and observe the people present. She assumed most of them were staffers. Binny didn't really have too many friends. There was a large contingent from Urmilla's family—weeping noisily and fanning the old lady who was exhausted by her earlier efforts and was now lying on a sofa, moaning softly to herself.

Mikki couldn't wait to get out of that place. She was booked on the evening flight. As she looked at the largest coffin, she imagined Binny lying inside with a sneer on his face, laughing at the grotesquerie of life, laughing at her. She suppressed the desire to join in his laughter. She thought of happier times and her expression automatically softened. Suddenly, it dawned on her that she didn't resent anything about him at all. Not even his brutality towards her. Perhaps that's what they call 'true love', she thought wryly, a soft smile on her face. She looked at the other coffins and found herself feeling strangely happy for Urmi and her children. They were all together at last. Something they couldn't be when they were alive. Mikki shut her eyes and fell into a light reverie induced by the heady smell of spider lilies, roses and incense combined with the insistent beat of tiny cymbals as the priests droned on...Mikki had a beautiful vision of Binny, dressed in his sharpest suit, ascending heavenwards, floating up like he was in a gently rising hot-air balloon. He was acknowledging the crowd gathered for his funeral with a jaunty wave of his hand, his lips twisted...she thought she saw his family—his real family—Urmi and her kids, floating happily around him, also waving and showering flower petals on everybody. Mikki felt a few descend on her shoulder...and then she jerked out of her trance as she realized the coffins were being lifted up and the people had begun throwing rose petals at the departing procession. Mikki watched as the men moved gracefully away, their white kurtas and dhotis standing out starkly against the bright green of the grass. It was just too beautiful. And she was glad for Binny. He would have approved....

Back in her suite, Mikki began packing hastily. It was strange how nobody had bothered to speak to her apart from the one woman who should have shunned her the most—Urmi's mother. Mikki looked around to check whether she'd forgotten anything and suddenly the enormity of Binny's death hit her. On a whim, she called the operator and cancelled her flight to Bombay. And drove up to Mercara instead.

*

Mikki finally came to terms with Binny's death in the solitude of her cool, airy room on a lush coffee plantation. It was a simple object that triggered it off—a perfectly formed acorn that had been left behind by the previous occupant. As she held it tenderly in her palm, Mikki couldn't stop the flood of tears that streamed down her face. She just stood there, clutching the acorn and crying.

She cried till she thought her lungs would burst. And then just as suddenly, her tears stopped. A gentle rain had started to fall outside. Mikki listened as the raindrops created their own music on her roof. It was the most soothing sound she'd ever heard. She stepped out of her room and a tiny frog jumped nimbly out of her way. Mikki stared up at the sky and noticed a luminous rainbow stretched between the trees. It was Binny's smile she saw in the seven colours. Mikki smiled back. The crickets took up their song where they'd left off. Mikki went back into the room, cradling the acorn next to her cheek. She put it into her bag, next to a beige sari that had been Binny's favourite in those early days when he'd string *mogras* in her hair, and kiss the mole on her ankle. Suddenly, Mikki wasn't sad or defeated any more. She packed for the final time and summoned a jeep to drive her down to Coimbatore. 'I'm ready to go home now,' she beamed at the startled old manager as he hastily prepared her bills. She paid up and before climbing into the jeep she sang out to him, 'Oh yes—before I forget—thanks for the acorn. It saved my life.' He watched the tracks in the wet mud made by the jeep tyres and shook his head. Some of the young women who stayed with them these days were quite mad, he told himself, and went back to his register.

*

'You look wonderful,' Alisha said, hugging Mikki as she met her at the arrival lounge of Bombay airport. Mikki noticed Dr Kurien hanging around sheepishly in the background. A slight frown creased her clear forehead as she scrutinized Alisha's face. 'And you? Are you all right? You're looking a little tired yourself.' Alisha squeezed her hand and the two of them started to walk towards the car.

Mikki asked Alisha about the doctor, who'd gone on ahead to summon the driver. 'Alisha…we have to talk about this. What are you going to do with him?' Mikki made her disapproval a bit too obvious. Alisha tried to joke it off saying, 'Oh Mikki, don't ask it in that way—as if he's some little cockroach I'm supposed to squash or something.' Mikki said quickly, 'I'm sorry—I didn't mean it like that. But you know as well as I do there's no future in this. So why waste time?' Alisha burst out laughing, 'Help! You're beginning to sound just like Mummy. Who cares about the future? I don't want to think any more. Nothing is certain. Let me enjoy what I have for now.'

They'd reached the car and Dr Kurien was busy fussing with her bags. Mikki noticed the flowers in the back seat—long stemmed yellow roses—like the ones Binny used to send her. Without a warning her heart lurched and she felt tears stinging her eyes. Alisha gripped her hand and asked, 'Mikki—what's wrong?' Mikki shook her head, 'Nothing…it's nothing…I mean…those flowers…the yellow roses…reminded me of someone…something.' Alisha hit her forehead with the palm of her hand, 'Shit! I knew I shouldn't have! The florist told me you loved yellow roses—so we decided to get you a bunch. Really...I'm so sorry.' Mikki got into the car and placed the flowers carefully in her lap. She told Alisha, 'Forget it. It was so silly of me. I'll have to get used to it, won't I? I might as well start right now.'

*

It was back to solicitors and assorted advisers right away. Mikki felt horribly alone as she walked into the old office the next morning to keep the first of her appointments. It was going to be a crazy day. There was the press to deal with, apart from her own friends and relatives who felt obliged to call and condole.

The first thing she did was to phone Mrs D'Souza and re-hire her. Fortunately the old lady hadn't taken another job and sounded delighted to hear Mikki's voice. 'Can you join straightaway—I mean like, in an hour from now? I need you,' Mikki told her. 'I'll be there,' Mrs D'Souza said simply, and rang off.

Ramankaka was waiting in the adjoining room and came in as soon as Mikki buzzed. 'How are you?' he asked, his voice heavy with love and concern. 'We were all so worried...but now that I've seen you, I can tell you are fine.' Mikki waved her hand to tell him to sit down, while she phoned Amy's trusted solicitor to request an urgent appointment. The call over, she went to the other side of the massive desk and sat on the edge, swinging her legs girlishly. 'Everything is in a huge big mess again, Ramankaka. And I don't have to tell you that I need you. But I feel so guilty about uprooting you like this and disrupting your life. Can you help me again? I can't do this without your help—you know that. We'll have to reorganize on a massive scale. Re-hire all the old people who still want to work for us. Fire the new ones. And one more thing—I want Alisha to be co-chairperson. She has as much right to Papa's legacy as I do. And I want this for her. I haven't told her my plans so far—but I will...this evening. Won't it be wonderful? We'll finally have the chance to work side by side and make something of Papa's empire. I think she'll accept—'

Ramanbhai looked at her fondly before replying, 'Alisha is your family. Your sister. An outsider like me has no right to express an opinion. But since you asked, I feel I should tell you. Alisha is not like you. She is unsteady. Not stable. Yes, I know she is shrewd and hard—perhaps more than you are. I also know she has a head for business, again more than you do. She has already made a success of her own. But you should also think about yourself—your own life. Your own future. You are not her mother. Only an older sister. You cannot look after her forever. Eventually, she'll marry…you'll marry. And then what will happen to the business? She may suddenly walk out leaving you in the lurch. Then what? I'm concerned about you.'

Mikki thought this over, then said, 'I am aware of all that you've just told me. Don't think for a minute that these doubts haven't crossed my mind as well. No…I don't want to play Alisha's mother. What I do want to do is to make her feel loved and wanted. One of the family. I owe her that much. That girl has suffered more than anyone will ever know. I can see the hurt and pain so clearly I want to make up for it. I want to do this for her. What she chooses to do with the opportunity in future, is up to her. You understand? She is my sister. And I love her very much.'

Ramanbhai got up and held out his hand, 'I wish you all the best—you know that. And you can count on me. I'll help you restart the whole organization. But Mikki, I'm not some selfless saint. It is very hard for me to work. Now it's my turn to think about myself selfishly. I have a counter offer. Give me a stake in the business—a share holding we both agree on.' Mikki smiled, 'Ramankaka you know this business inside out—much better than I ever will. Of course you have a free run of everything at Hiralal Industries—now and always….'

'About Shanay…' Ramankaka began, and Mikki cut him off with a wave of her hand. 'Please let's not talk about him. I'm very confused about his motives, and there are things about him, which I can't believe, but which are horrifying me…' Mikki trailed off, unable to finish as the vision of Shanay deliberately plotting her parents' and husband's death, stunned her momentarily.

*

Alisha called the office to chat with Mikki and told her cheerily that she had a dinner date with the doctor. Mikki was glad to find her in such an upbeat mood after all she'd been through in the past month though she despaired of her dalliance with the doctor. Alisha was also back at work in the office, with a bunch of new recruits. Sapna had quit abruptly, leaving Alisha at a time she needed a responsible person to hold the fort and run the show. But her leaving had also revealed a few home truths to Alisha who realized how trustingly she'd handed over the day-to-day running of the business to Sapna. Behind the facade of slick efficiency and hard-nosed decisions, Sapna had been a sloppy and careless administrator. Alisha was aghast to discover dozens of untidy deals which she'd thought were all wrapped up but were in fact left with several loose ends waiting to be tied up. The account books were similarly messed up as were the filing systems. Correspondence alone was going to take an age to sort out. But Alisha was tackling the daunting tasks with ferocious enthusiasm and energy.

Mikki wondered at their similar predicaments. Both of them had been left in the lurch by trusted employees. And both of them needed to start all over again. But while Alisha seemed charged and raring to go, Mikki felt bone-tired, physically and otherwise. She vaguely made a mental note of going for a full medical check up and told herself she'd get Mrs D'Souza to coordinate it with the hospital. But before all that she had a lot of wading through tiresome paper-work to do.

Binny's beneficiaries—his children—were dead. And there was no will. Mikki was told that under the circumstances, and given the peculiar situation of a separation but no divorce, she stood to inherit everything—all of Binny's assets, which included her father's old companies. Just the thought of the new responsibilities was wearing her down. Her short life as a full time wife had spoiled her a little. She realized with a small shock that she'd got out of the work ethic. Catering wasn't really big business—it had been a pleasant distraction and relaxation. In any case, Lucio had been dumped with the orders so many times, he was used to going solo and now had a team of efficient helpers to assist him at large events. Mikki knew she'd have to give up the catering business and she felt regretful. She'd enjoyed the stint while it lasted but now there'd be no time for parties—either catered ones or her own.

THIRTEEN

Mikki's parents' third death anniversary was two months away. Mikki wanted Alisha to participate in organizing an appropriate function to mark the occasion. Perhaps an evening of Rabindra Sangeet like the one she'd organized for her own mother. Mikki hadn't really done anything in memory of her father and mother. This year, she thought the two of them could lay the foundation stone for a hospital—Hiralal Hospital. Eventually, she hoped to build a home for Bombay's street children and aged destitutes. Alisha could be given the responsibility of constructing and looking after the charities.

Mikki had big plans for consolidating what she could. Binny had, in his aggressive fashion, infused enough new capital into the ventures and placed them on the path to rapid recovery. He would've turned them around in another year. The market was buoyant after a five year slump. And investors were showing bullish tendencies. This was the time to come out with a public issue. Mikki had hired an outside agency to help her arrive at a few decisions. Raising money through non-convertible debentures had been one of their recommendations. She was studying that and other proposals. The optimistic business climate was attracting several interested foreign collaborators. A few feelers had reached her from two U.K. head-quartered companies looking for Indian participation in a food processing plant. A lot of work would go into swinging that deal, including several trips to Delhi, but Mikki was keenest on bagging this particular contract. She decided to assign two of her whiz-kids to the job. She needed a comprehensive feasibility report before going ahead with the negotiations. There was work to be done. Plenty of it. Mikki wished she felt stronger. She reached for the call bell to ask for a cup of tea, as she felt herself flaking off.

The shrill ringing of the telephone jerked her out of her lethargy. She was not going to answer it this time. Let it ring, she thought as she leaned back and shut her eyes. After a minute or so, it stopped...only to start again. Damn! Mikki said to herself and picked up the receiver impatiently. 'Yes...who is it?' she demanded. There was no response, just a hollow laugh followed by heavy breathing. But something about that laugh made her stop. She'd heard it before. Mikki waited. The person at the other end wasn't in a hurry. After a pause, she asked again, 'Who's on the line? Speak up or I'll disconnect.' A man's voice sneered, 'Why do you ask questions to which you already know the answers? You are not speaking to a stranger, are you? We know each other, right?' Quietly, Mikki asked, 'What do you want?' The man replied, 'What I want? Nothing. I want to see you dead. That's all.' Mikki tried to figure out the accent. She decided to engage him in conversation, searching for clues all the time. But he was no fool. He cut her short by saying abruptly, 'Enough. I don't have time to waste on meaningless chats. You have inherited all that was yours in the first place. Your husband's death has made you a wealthy woman. People will be after your money. Men in particular. I know who they are. But now isn't the occasion to tell you. One more thing—hire a bodyguard. For yourself and that sister. You'll need one in the coming days.' And he rang off. Mikki contemplated the dead phone in her hands. She wanted to believe it was just another crank caller. But something told her not to ignore the man's words. She rang up an old acquaintance —a police commissioner, a friend of her father's, who now ran an efficient security agency. She asked for an immediate appointment. Mr Gokhale granted it without a single question. Mikki had to get to the bottom of this, and fast.

*

'He sounds like a black-mailer,' Mr Gokhale told her after she'd finished narrating the entire sequence of events. 'So what should I do?' she asked. Mr Gokhale replied, 'We'll open a file for you. Keep us informed about any unusual activity…movements around the house, new servants you hire, suspicious letters…and, of course, the phone calls. Maintain a record. At this stage I wouldn't advice a full time bodyguard. What I'll do is provide two security officers at your office and residence. They will monitor everything and screen unfamiliar visitors. But you will have to be alert yourself and report personally to me in case you notice anything out of the ordinary—anything at all. Even the smallest, most insignificant change. O.K.? Now…chin up. Your father was a brave man. As you know, he had several enemies—powerful ones. But not once did I see him scared.' Mikki decided to ask him the one question that had been troubling her since the accident: 'Did he ever disclose to you that he was being threatened or black-mailed? Was the plane crash really an accident…or was he murdered?' Mr Gokhale was silent as he looked at the earnest face of the beautiful young girl sitting across him. He'd known her since she was a child. And now, he was facing a woman…a very worried woman. Without a word, he moved his chair back and stretched out his arm to pull open a cabinet. 'Look…' he said to Mikki, 'Can you see these files? Over twenty of them. They all concern your father. Over the years, he had had to deal with so many cases and situations. He met me when I was just a sub-inspector at Gamdevi police station. I remember the day he walked in to register a complaint. Somehow, we got along…liked each other…became friends. He wasn't such a big man then. But even when he became one, he didn't forget me. I handled so many of his problems…my men were always at his service. He never forgot me. It is because of him that I'm now running this business. He helped me to get the premises…the business too was his idea. I was going to retire and go to live in Pune. Your father called me and said, "*Arrey bhai*—retire? At your age? Why? Start something. Start your own agency. Become a consultant. I will retain you for our companies." I refused that offer. I didn't want to spoil our friendship. But I liked the idea of starting this agency. So I agreed. His executives prepared all the plans. Your father sent me abroad to acquaint myself with the latest develop-

ments in this field. I received training in Europe. Met my counter-
parts. Learnt so many new things. And now…here I am. Thanks to
him. You see…my problem was…and still is…that I was an honest
police officer. Most people find that difficult to believe. Had I
retired I would have had nothing besides my pension and provi-
dent fund. I didn't want to join some big company as their paid
servant—a glorified gurkha. I didn't want to be at the beck and call
of men who used to see me in my office and called me "sir". Your
father, Mikki, was not a bad man but a misunderstood one. And
now…go home and get some rest. You look tired. Forget the past
and what happened to him. Forget the doubts—murder, suicide,
accident…who knows? Nobody will ever know. There will be
theories and speculation. People will fill your ears with all sorts of
rumours. Ignore them. Rich men have to accept all this as a part of
their lives. Frankly, if you ask me my opinion—I believe it was an
accident. A very unfortunate one. But an accident. It was the timing
that made some people think that your father could've been
bumped off by rivals. But believe me, Mikki, I have gone into the
case thoroughly. See these other files—they are about the crash. I
put my best men on the job. They went over everything—talked to
dozens of people—experts. I have all the reports. My theory is
different. Most people don't know this, but your father used to love
to tinker around in the cockpit. He'd been warned against it several
times. I'd also scolded him once when we were on a trip together.
But he'd laughed—he was like that, childish about some things.
And stubborn. It was all a game to him. He enjoyed danger. He
also enjoyed scaring your poor mother. That day he was advised
not to fly. The weather was bad—visibility low. The pilot himself
was reluctant. Your father personally dragged him from his
house—the pilot's wife confirmed that. It is more than possible that
your father snatched the controls. Perhaps the pilot wanted to
come back to Bombay…the black box does have recordings of
heated arguments seconds before the crash. The voices are garbled.
I'm certain in my mind that your father must've said, "If you can't
fly the bloody thing—let me do it." Once your father took something into his head, there was no way to stop him. That was it. One
fatal mistake and down they went. Also…you must be aware that
your father was suffering from severe depression. He was seeing
a psychiatrist—Dr Sheth. I suspect his mind had become dull with
all the anti-depressants he'd been taking. His speech had started to

slur...even his actions had slowed down. Poor man.'

Mikki had heard what she wanted to. At least one area of her life had been made clear. She trusted Mr Gokhale. He had no reason to lie to her. She thanked him warmly and left, reassured by his words—'Remember, I'm only a phone call away. Day and night service. That's the least I can do for my friend's daughter.'

FOURTEEN

Dr Kurien was late again. Alisha had been waiting in bed for him. Their afternoon trysts had become the high points of her life these days. It was the perfect time for long, uninterrupted love-making with the servants in their quarters taking their afternoon rest, Mikki away at the office, and the head nurse holding the fort in the doctor's clinic. It was the uncertainty of his timings that used to upset Alisha. He'd explain rapidly as he stepped out of his clothes, 'I'm sorry, darling….some stupid patient came in with a head injury. I cou l dn't leave him bleeding on my doorstep.' Alisha would tear off the remainder of his garments and pull him into bed. Sex was always passionate…but rarely fulfilling. And she'd dread the hours that were to follow, when she'd be left to fend for herself and he'd be back in the warm folds of his family.

That afternoon, Alisha was in a black mood. Dr Kurien had already wasted more than forty-five minutes of their precious time together. It was 3.45 now. He should've been there by 3.00—he knew that. And he'd only stay till 5.15—by which time he'd start getting restless and reach for his watch (he always removed his watch before they made love). It was the one moment she detested. The one moment that made her body go tense anticipating the inevitable gesture that signalled his departure. She heard the car. She heard his footsteps. She waited for the peremptory knock on the door before she screamed, 'Get lost, you frigging bastard,' just as Dr Kurien entered, pulling off his tie. 'Don't bother to take off your clothes, you wimp,' Alisha snarled. The sheet had slipped off her naked body. She looked wanton and beautiful in the afternoon light. The doctor ignored her and continued peeling his clothes off. Alisha leapt off the bed and reached him in two strides. She went for him like a wild cat, tearing into his skin with her long nails, spitting and hissing curses while her legs flew at his shins. He caught her wrists and stopped her from scratching his face. She struggled to free herself while continuing to scream obscenities. He pinioned her arms with his hands and pushed her backwards towards the roomy bed. With one leg he tripped her as she approached the edge. Alisha fell back over the heaped up pillows and he fell on top of her. He grabbed her hair and jerked her face back, 'What more do you want from me?' he asked roughly... 'Aren't you getting enough?' His mouth attacked hers and his hands pummelled her body with such force she screamed. 'Go on...yell as much as you want,' he said, biting into her neck savagely. 'There is no one who can hear you.' His thighs pinned down her legs as he entered her in a manner that was so brutal, she felt herself tear. 'Take it, take it, take it,' he grunted, pushing into her. 'All you rich women are the same—you want more all the time. Nothing satisfies you. Here, take it all...it's free.' Alisha was scared by now. She'd never seen him so violent. Almost as soon as he had begun he was coming into her, and she felt violated and abused. There was a dull ache between her legs and she could feel her arms and legs puffing with the pressure he had exerted. 'Why are you doing this to me?' she asked. He didn't answer. Instead, he got up swiftly, climbed back into his clothes and left, leaving her whimpering on the bed.

Alisha didn't blame him. She cursed herself. She'd asked for it. She had no right to speak to him that way. The rules were clear. He was hers for the afternoon. No more. They couldn't go anywhere. They couldn't do anything that other couples took so much for granted. Alisha lay in bed feeling soiled and small. She reached for her tissues to clean herself and recoiled at the sight of so much blood. Bastard! This time he had gone too far, she thought. He had torn her apart—literally.

After the incident Alisha had vowed to stay away from Dr Kurien. But all it required was a phone call to get her anxious and begging once again. 'It's impossible,' she told Mikki finally, 'I can't stop seeing him and I'm not going to try.' Mikki had looked at her sister lovingly and said. 'It's O.K. Let's talk about something else. This is an issue that's going to take time to work out. There is no justification. There is nothing rational about such situations.' Alisha had been grateful but sheepish. Giggling foolishly she'd confessed, 'My God! That man is a brute. He looks like such a lamb. But provoke him and he turns into a tiger.'

Mikki said nothing. She'd noticed the black and blue bruises on Alisha's limbs. Each time she ran in to Dr Kurien, she stiffened at the thought of what he was doing to her sister. The sister she thought was so different from herself. Tougher. Harder. Stronger. But was she really?

*

Alisha and Mikki always breakfasted together and Mikki looked forward to their morning chats—when Alisha entertained her with the previous night's escapades carefully leaving out the intimate details. Mikki suspected she made up half the stories to distract her from asking about the doctor. Even so, her little stories were fun to listen to. The servants doted on their *'chhota memsaab'*, and indulged her every whim. Alisha had struck up a good equation with the crusty Dhondu and bullied him mercilessly. Even Gangubai didn't seem to mind Alisha's quirks and picked up after her uncomplainingly. Sometimes Mikki felt so much older than Alisha, especially when Alisha played childish pranks or laughed uncontrollably over silly jokes. Mikki sensed that behind the couldn't-care-less facade lurked an insecure little girl—a lovable one. The house was filled with her sounds when she was home. The place came alive with her rowdy mannerisms as she bounded around, jesting with bearers, shouting instructions at *bais*, horsing around with whoever was present. In comparison with her sunny, breezy nature, Mikki appeared a prim and proper mistress of the manor, all correct conduct and sober talk. Dr Kurien maintained his distance in Mikki's presence and was almost deferential when addressing her. 'Guilty-conscience,' summed up Mikki. After all, Dr Kurien was no Navin. Scandal was still a dirty word for him. Mikki remembered asking Alisha casually, 'Are you seriously in love or just bored?' Alisha had screwed up her face and changed the subject. He just wasn't Alisha's type, Mikki thought to herself. Unless Alisha had succeeded in coverting him. He'd certainly changed his way of dressing and Mikki knew who was picking up all the bills for his fancy wardrobe. She'd even commented cattily, 'My, my...is the doctor joining the movies?' when he arrived in a snazzy double-breasted jacket one afternoon when she had stayed home.

But despite their obvious need for each other it was plain to see there was something askew in Dr Kurien and Alisha's relationship though Mikki couldn't quite put her finger on it. Amy, with her characteristic perception zeroed in instantly, 'Class, once again darling. Same problem as with Binny. That's what it is. A clash of values. I'm sure he's wonderful...but can you see him pulling on a Davidoffs or sipping Chivas without looking like an impostor? You know what I mean? We girls have grown up with all these frivolous luxuries. We take them for granted. He's learning, and pretty fast by what you tell me. But, darling, his finesse, if he ever acquires it, will always be on the surface—an affectation. He's not really our type at all, is he? Does he even know everything he needs to know about that spirited little sister of yours? He'd be shocked out of his white coat if he found out even half the truth about her old adventures...anyway...I guess she's having a little fun mixing with the masses, so to speak. Let's just regard this affair as a part of her liberal education, shall we?' Mikki had laughed lightly at Amy's barbed observations, acknowledging the accuracy of her assessment. But she continued to feel concerned.

Alisha was not being herself. Mikki had noticed that she'd had a small altar with a crucifix installed in her bedroom. 'What's that?' she'd asked Alisha curiously. 'Oh that...it's well, it's just something.' 'I can see that,' Mikki had said refusing to give up on the topic, 'but what's it doing here?' 'Don't tell me you object, big sister...you with your broad-minded attitudes.' 'I don't object at all,' Mikki answered evenly, 'it's just that I didn't know you had this religious side to you. Have you always been a believer...such a devout one?' 'No...' Alisha replied evasively, 'but that's because I lived in darkness. I needed someone to light up this aspect of myself for me.' 'And I suppose the doctor has been good enough to do this for you...right?' Alisha looked away, tears stinging her eyes. After a brief silence she said, 'I didn't expect you to be this bitchy about my religion. I mean, it's something that's so personal. I don't come and pass comments about your Ganpati collection or the Srinathji you constantly wear around your neck, do I?'

Mikki apologized promptly, 'I didn't mean to hurt you...I never want to do that. But I do feel worried...it seems to me you are so influenced by this man, you are not in possession of your senses. I don't want you to lose your own personality, individuality, values.' Alisha's tone was petulant: 'He hasn't forced this on me. But I know how important his religion is to him...I want to show him that I care enough for his sentiments...I'm...I'm thinking of converting.' Mikki's jaw dropped, 'You can't be serious, darling,' she said in alarm, 'I have nothing against his religion...but you don't know anything about it, you can't treat it as yet another adventure. You can't just convert in order to impress some man.'

Alisha lashed out at her, 'The doctor is not "some man", Mikki—or can't you see that? He is the man I love. I'd give up anything for him—even my life.' Mikki raised her voice a little, 'Don't give me all that bull, Alisha. It's all very well to mouth dialogues straight out of a film. Do you realize the seriousness of what you are plunging into? Tomorrow you want to become a Catholic. Two years from now you'll meet someone else and decide to become a Muslim. Religion is not a tool or a trap to get a man with. Be responsible for once in your life. Break off with this man. There's no future in this for you. He's never going to leave his wife—he's told you that. What will you do then—become a nun?' Alisha began sobbing softly and Mikki felt immediately sorry for what she'd said. Alisha looked so vulnerable and fragile, sitting on her bed, clutching a pillow, with big, hot tears flowing down her cheeks. Mikki hugged her and rocked her to and fro like a child. Gradually, Alisha began to relax. Mikki crooned a song she remembered from childhood and Alisha raised her head, 'Do you know Papa had given me a tape of that...I still have it somewhere. Don't stop...keep singing.' Mikki did, till she felt Alisha's body go limp in her arms and her breathing grow deep and regular.

*

Amy reprimanded her young friend, 'Listen, darling... you've been putting this off for far too long. I can't bear to see you like this.

I don't believe it's just hard work that's making you lose so much weight. Either you make the appointment right now for your check-up...or I'll do it on your behalf.' Mikki smiled at Amy wanly, 'I think it's just...I don't know...maybe I'm...God knows...lonely or something.' Amy smiled, 'Of course you are lonely...but that doesn't affect a person's health so badly. Look at you...have you seen yourself in a mirror recently? You look like a ghost. So pale and sickly. Skin and bones...that's all. I'm sure your clothes don't fit you.' Mikki took a deep breath, 'They don't actually...you're right. I must do something soon. But where's the bloody time for check-ups? You know my schedules...it's work, work, work. So many things to sort out. All those properties to look after. I haven't been back to Mandwa or the old house since Binny's death. I don't know what I'm going to do with them...sell them at some point, I suppose. But honestly speaking, right now, what I need is a break. I don't seem to have the energy to go out once I get home. I just collapse on the bed and pass out. I hardly eat—no time, no appetite, no interest.' Amy stood up and walked towards the telephone resolutely, 'That does it. I don't care what you say—you're going in. Tomorrow. No...don't stop me.'

Mikki hadn't realized just now much weight she'd dropped till she stepped on the scales at the hospital. Even she was shocked. Twelve kilos. She was down by twelve kilos! The nurse was jovial and plump. 'My, my, dearie...aren't you a slip of a thing! I'd love to get rid of all this,' she said clutching a handful of pulpy adipose around her waist. 'But what to do? I like my beer and *sorpotel* too much.' Mikki smiled and went on to the other routine checks—blood pressure, blood sugar, urine, stool and so on. Alisha had sulked briefly when Amy informed her about the decision to move Mikki to Breach Candy Hospital. 'When we have a brilliant doctor in the house with a well equipped clinic close by, where was the need to go somewhere else...or consult someone else?' she asked. Amy explained to her that the decision was Mikki's and that she was likely to require a battery of sophisticated tests that Dr Kurien's clinic was not geared for. Alisha forgot her irritation soon enough and pitched in with all the help needed. Cheerfully, she told Amy, 'Don't worry, I'll hold the fort, handle the servants...and keep an eye on the office.' Amy smiled indulgently, thinking how different the two women were, and yet how alike.

The physician on Mikki's case diagnosed her condition as 'nervous exhaustion'. 'She needs rest—plenty of it. And a lot of relaxation. She should not be bothered by either office or domestic problems. She has been through a very bad year emotionally and her systems have collapsed under the strain. Naturally, we'll be conducting other tests to establish that there is nothing else the matter. She is anaemic, but not alarmingly so. We've already started her off on an iron-rich diet. Don't worry about Ms Hiralal, she's going to be just fine. What she really needs is a change of atmosphere and climate. The pollution in Bombay has been getting a lot of people down recently.'

Mikki had started coughing during the past month and the doctor seemed to have ignored that totally, dismissing it off as a reaction to the dust in the environment. 'It's an allergic cough— dry,' he said reassuringly, while the three exchanged glances. Alisha mentioned it to Dr Kurien who was also not convinced by the other doctor's diagnosis but didn't want to interfere.

Mikki was wasting away. Her eyes were two hollows, her cheeks stretched over her facial bones so tautly that blue veins showed through under the surface. Lying on the hospital bed, she looked frighteningly frail and slight. Alisha had given her a rosary and instructed her to place it under her pillow, adding, 'Do it for my sake, even if you don't believe in it.' She'd also told her that she'd started going to Church to offer special Novenas and light the required number of candles. Dr Kurien didn't accompany Alisha on her daily visits, in deference to Mikki's wishes. He knew how strongly she disapproved of his relationship with her sister. But he made his concern known through Alisha who unfailingly conveyed his messages to Mikki, ignoring her frown of annoyance.

*

'It isn't the "Big C" is it?' Mikki asked Amy anxiously one day. Amy held her tightly and replied, 'Darling, I want to be honest with you…the thing is at this point the doctors aren't saying. They want to run a few more checks before they come up with a pukka diagnosis.' 'Oh no!' Mikki sighed and fell back on the cushions. She opened her eyes tiredly and whispered, almost to herself, 'That's all I need,' before adding, 'who'll take care of Alisha if anything happens to me? She needs me…she only has me.' Amy hushed her gently and sat by her side, holding her hand. 'Darling, think of yourself now. Fight. Fight with all you've got. That's the only way to lick whatever it is that's getting you down. Don't even say the dreaded word. It isn't cancer—I know in my heart that it isn't. Besides…and I know you'll get irked by this…but even Dr Kurien is sure these doctors are way off the mark. He is very keen to examine you himself…but he doesn't want to offend you.' Mikki's eyes were shut. 'I have no fight left in me, Amy,' she said, her voice barely above a whisper. 'It's all up to you and the others. I'm willing to go along with whatever your committee decides…if it's going to be Kurien who's in charge, so be it. I'm in your hands. I trust you.' And Mikki drifted off into an uneasy sleep. Amy stayed with her till the nurse, Sister Dolores, came and escorted her out saying, 'Such a fine young woman…Our Lord plays funny games sometimes. She is kind and gentle. But who knows what's in the Saviour's mind?' And she crossed herself instinctively. Amy squeezed her hand and left to report Mikki's condition to Alisha and the others. One of them always made sure to be around during visiting hours and they stayed in touch constantly through the day, monitoring Mikki's health on a rotation basis, checking back and forth, looking for the smallest signs of progress and recovery.

A few days of rest and relaxation worked wonders on Mikki. Three weeks later, she sat up in bed. 'Let's celebrate,' suggested Amy naughtily, pulling out a bottle of champagne from under her sari *pallav*. From her bag, she produced six champagne glasses and handed the first to Mikki. Alisha hugged Mikki and mussed her hair, 'That was a close call, sister, we couldn't have forgiven you if you'd gone and got yourself seriously sick.' Amy expertly popped the cork, adding, 'Mikki must have got some master strategy up her sleeve…like at the office. They never know what she is going to come up with next.' Everybody laughed and raised their glasses…till Mikki herself said, taking a tiny sip of the well chilled Tattinger, 'Well…if it isn't the "Big C" what the fuck is it? It's good to know I'm not dying of cancer. But something is killing me…and I'd like to know what. Does anybody here have the answer?'

The fizz went out of the sparkling drink, as Mikki's loved ones stared wordlessly at her and then at each other. Alisha broke the awkward silence by saying in a voice full of fervour, 'Only the Lord has the answer. And he shall give it when the time comes.' Mikki softly said, 'Amen', as the others looked away.

*

Mikki had been home for nearly a month, but hadn't recovered fully. She was gaunt and hollow-eyed enough to alarm visitors. 'Darling, you are still wasting away,' Amy said to her anxiously, 'Why don't you consider a longish trip. I have these marvellous Swiss friends—an oldish couple, but great fun. Lovely little chalet on top of a hill—very secluded. Tiny village, not too far from Laussane. I just know you'll love it. Long walks, riding paths. Charming village taverns…I might join you. God knows I could do with a holiday myself.' Mikki looked at her thoughtfully before saying, 'Amy, it sounds great, but so much is happening right here. Besides, I don't even know what the matter is with me. And I'm tired of being tired…if you know what I mean.' Amy nodded sympathetically, 'Darling, I understand perfectly. But you are much too young to be bogged down with so much responsibility. You hardly go out any more. You used to have fun with people your own age. And now—look at you.' Mikki stared into the distance 'And there's Alisha. I'm so worried about her. She doesn't convince me at all with her religious mumbo-jumbo. I fear she might be flipping her lid. If she'd become a true believer, she would've broken off with that doctor. I've nothing against him…but it's a hopeless relationship. And it is an adulterous one—isn't that considered a cardinal sin by the Church?'

Amy nodded before saying, 'Darling, you cannot live her life for her. She is an adult with a strong personality of her own. You can't go on mothering her like this—it's not good for you and it certainly isn't good for her.' Mikki shook her head miserably, 'I feel so old, so protective, so different. I don't know how to explain the change, Amy. It isn't spiritual, but it may well have been just that. There is hardly any difference in our ages, yet I feel as if I'm dealing with a wayward teenager. She seems so troubled. I can see beyond her act, Amy. She isn't a flighty superficial person at all.'

Amy assured her, 'I know all that. I knew her mother vaguely…it was difficult for me to talk about her to your dear mother, as you can well imagine…but we heard enough stories through the reliable ladies' club. She was an insecure, unhappy woman. Your father, God bless his soul, was a demanding man…and he did tire of the two of them eventually.'

'Yes...but it was Alisha, not me, he left all the money to,' Mikki pointed out.

'That was not planned, darling. He was merely doing his duty at the time. What could he do? Just shrug off a child he'd fathered? The trust was one way of dealing with his guilt, that's all. Nobody could've imagined it would grow into what it did. And nobody could've foreseen what befell Hiralal Industries later. Your mother had hinted that your father wasn't all there during his last years. I don't recall her exact words—and she wasn't one for true confessions—but I distinctly remember her anxiety at his failing memory and all those bad business decisions he made in the end, which cost you your inheritance.'

Mikki had hardly touched her cheese cake. Amy watched her as she picked away disinterestedly at the edges of her pastry, before saying, 'But let's concentrate on you, darling. Tell me what you've been doing?' 'I've been putting in long hours at the office...but my old enthusiasm is missing. I can tell it isn't there...but so can the others. They sense my indifference, and that's not good for the business. The fighting spirit is missing. The killer instinct isn't what it used to be. I don't know whom to trust. Shanay—he's always there when I need him, but I'm not sure that what Ramanbhai says hasn't a grain of truth in it—I can't seem to trust him any more—and Ramanbhai, he was the one person I could depend on when I was a child. Today he's aloof, distant—Lucio is wonderful about the other business we got into. It's strange, but I seem to have the Midas touch. So far, everything I've backed has succeeded, without my killing myself for it. The catering thing has really taken off and we are seriously considering a franchising operation. Alisha has that too—look at her business—it's booming. And it's not as if she's slogging away at it either.' Amy laughed, 'You lucky girls. It's all in the genes, isn't it? Your father in his time, had uncanny business sense. All his early ventures took off spectacularly. He could smell out a business opportunity. Both of you have got that from him. Your mother was a shrewd old girl herself. Did you know she played the stock market secretly? And did very well for herself too! Your father never interfered. It was her money she was playing with, after all. Forget her stocks and shares—she even beat us at bridge. Or rummy when she chose to play it. She was a real gambler, that one. She'd bet on anything—even the colour of someone's sari. You girls are bound to succeed at anything you undertake. What the two of you need are husbands. Good, solid husbands to manage you and your money.' Mikki looked at her watch and jumped up guiltily, 'Good Lord! It's past three. Amy, why is it that I always lose track of time when we meet? I've got to run.' Amy asked for the cheque. 'So do I, darling, so do I. The ladies must be waiting. And I forgot my manicure appointment.'

The two of them rushed out of the Taj and summoned their cars. Mikki noticed someone waving to her from a taxi. She craned her neck to see who it was. 'Alisha!' she called out. Amy turned around to look, 'It's her, darling. But what on earth is she doing running around town in a cab? Where are the cars? Doesn't she know it isn't safe at all?'

Mikki instructed her driver, 'Follow the cab! Hurry!' There was something about the way Alisha was waving that had alerted her. It wasn't her normal, jaunty, defiant wave. She'd caught just a glimpse of her face, and it had looked strained. Mikki hadn't been able to observe whether Alisha was alone in the cab, but it had surprised her to see her in one, in the first place. Where was her own car? Or the doctor's? Assuming that both the cars were unavailable, why couldn't she have taken one of Mikki's? She knew perfectly well that she could use any of them at any time.

Alisha's cab was about to cross a traffic light and disappear into a tiny bylane in Colaba. Mikki urged the driver to jump the lights and follow her as closely as possible. Something was amiss and Mikki had to find out. The cab stopped outside a seedy hotel in the back lanes of the busy Causeway. What on earth was Alisha doing in this locality? It was full of shady characters and small hooch joints patronized by all kinds of undesirables. Nobody dared to venture there, and certainly not a single woman. In the Sixties and Seventies, these bylanes had been taken over by hippies en route to Goa or Kathmandu. In the Eighties they'd been converted into Arab ghettos. And now they were controlled by suspicious characters trading in anything and everything. What was Alisha looking for?

Mikki got out of her car and started following Alisha after instructing the driver to wait. He looked at her strangely and started to say something. Seeing Mikki's determined expression he decided to keep quiet. Amy had tried to keep up with her car and had finally given up. Mikki saw Alisha disappearing down a side street and followed swiftly. Alisha seemed in a frantic hurry and was half-way up the narrow spiral staircase at the back of a decrepit building. Mikki called out to her but Alisha didn't hear. She darted into a half-open door while Mikki ran up the stairs, stumbling in her haste to get to Alisha. The dirty door she'd seen her sister walk through was shut when Mikki got to the top of the stairs. Hesitantly, she knocked on it, reading the graffiti scratched into its grime-laden surface. 'Rocky loves Margot' followed by 'Rocky fucks Margot' followed by 'Margot fucks anybody'. Somebody had drawn male and female genitals in graphic detail next to this with the usual, arrow-pierced heart alongside. Mikki knocked again. The door opened two inches and instinctively Mikki stuck her foot into the space and said, 'I want to see Alisha—my sister. I know she's here.' It was far too dark for her to see anything, beyond the one eye that was staring back at her from behind the door. 'Get out,' a gruff voice commanded before cursing her. 'Please,' Mikki pleaded. 'Let me in. I have to see her.' She felt a heavy foot descend on her toes and was about to withdraw the foot wedged between the door, wincing in pain, but she bit her lip and kept it there, insisting, 'I want my sister. Please, call Alisha—she's the girl who just came in. I saw her. I just want to meet her, that's all.' Silence. Suddenly, she heard Alisha's voice softly telling someone, 'It's O.K., *yaar*. Open the door. She's clean. Harmless.'

The next minute Mikki was inside a dimly lit room. One corner was ablaze with dozens of lit candles in front of a crude altar. It took a while for Mikki's eyes to adjust to the darkness. She spotted Alisha, who was dressed in some sort of a black robe. She ran towards her and grabbed her sister's slim shoulders. 'What are you doing here? Are you crazy? Let's get out!' Then she looked around and noticed about a dozen, similarly-robed people. They were all staring at Mikki silently. 'Who are they?' Mikki demanded, still holding Alisha. 'Friends,' Alisha replied shortly. 'What sort of friends?' Mikki asked, taking in more details now. There was a man with large, luminous eyes at the centre of the group, who was obviously their leader. Alisha shrugged in his direction, 'The master is here. We do as he says.' Mikki stared incredulously at her sister and cried, 'Have you gone crazy—completely crazy? What master? What are you talking about?' Alisha placed a finger on her lips and said, 'Please…we were about to celebrate mass. Praise the Lord.' The others echoed the words and chorused back, 'Praise the Lord.' Mikki smelt the slightly sickening smell of incense, as the leader began passing a plate around. Alisha took Mikki to one side and whispered, 'Look—I can't explain anything just now. Get out of here and fast. This isn't your scene.' Mikki replied, 'It isn't yours either. What the hell are you up to in these clothes and with these hoodlums?' 'Please speak with respect about my friends,' Alisha said, repeating, 'I told you—this isn't for you. It's for the believers.'

The leader came up to Alisha and held out his hand. She took it and floated away as if in a trance. Mikki couldn't believe the change in her. She stood in the shadows, watching as Alisha joined the group and all of them formed a circle around the man with the hypnotic eyes. 'Let us pray,' he said, rolling his words and starting to sway. He set up a chant that Mikki couldn't understand, but she watched fascinatedly as Alisha shut her eyes and joined the others as they sang along. The ritual was brief and before Mikki knew it, a red light was switched on and everybody kneeled in front of the leader, who took some black powder and drew a crude cross across their foreheads. Next, he picked up a small broom and beat the person kneeling before him across the back. The strokes were light enough not to make the person bleed, but firm enough to cause temporary welts. She could hear Alisha's moans as she bowed her head and accepted the lashing. This was followed by a rhythmic dance as the group linked hands and went around in an anticlockwise direction while the leader repeated what sounded like a prayer. Electronic music followed, as the group stepped up the tempo of their dance and began whirling individually, their arms outstretched, eyes shut. One or two screamed occasionally, while the others groaned and wept. The leader's voice had risen by now and Mikki caught a few stray words, 'Let the forces of evil destroy our enemies,' he boomed as the dance became more frenzied and the volume of the music increased further. At some point the group reached for the candles, picking up two in each hand. The leader picked up the brightly painted altar and raised it above his head. Alisha had stopped dancing, but was swaying vigorously in a corner, the candles casting eerie shadows across her face. 'Speak to us, O mighty One,' the leader intoned. 'Speak! Speak!' A woman's voice filled the room, followed by a man's. A few of the people swooned on hearing them. Alisha collapsed into a crumpled heap without a warning and the candles went out abruptly. She kept her head low and continued to moan. The leader went around the group, picking up heads drooping over limp limbs, and pushed small pellets into receptive mouths. The voices echoed in the room as the leader announced, 'The spirits are with us...Come, let us speak to our loved ones.' Two people crawled to him on all fours and began asking some questions, adopting a childish lisp and baby voices. Mikki watched aghast as she heard Alisha murmuring, 'Papa...Papa...Papa,I know you are here...I know you are listening...Mummy...can you hear me, Mummy....'

Mikki felt sick to the pit of her stomach. She couldn't bear to watch any more. She slid out of the room softly and decided to wait for Alisha at the bottom of the spiral staircase. She hadn't realized till that moment how desperately lonely her sister was. And how infinitely insecure. The dank smell of accumulated urine filled her nostrils as a fat rat jumped out of her way and disappeared into the nearby sewer.

*

'You shouldn't have come here,' Alisha said in a small voice when she found Mikki hugging her knees on the lowest step of the wrought iron ladder. Mikki didn't say anything, as she rose to her feet and hugged her sister. Finally, as they walked silently out of the filthy bylane, towards the main road, Mikki asked, 'Why? You don't have to explain anything, if you don't want to...but....' Alisha seemed not to hear. Mikki looked more closely at her and noticed that her eyes seemed different...her pupils were dilated and her eyes were glazed. She shook her as they approached the car, but Alisha kept walking...oblivious to everything, even the traffic whizzing past them as they crossed the busy street. Mikki raised her voice to make herself audible above the noise of the street—the horns of motorists and the whirr of noisy bus engines as they drove past the two frail figures standing bang in the middle of the road. 'Alisha! Answer me...what's the matter?' She gripped her sister's arm and then chafed her long, sensitive fingers...Alisha's hands were ice-cold and clammy. Somehow, they made it to the other side of the street and into the waiting cab. 'Dr Kurien's Nursing Home,' Mikki instructed the driver.

*

'She's possessed,' Dr Kurien told Mikki calmly, studying Alisha's face. 'Rubbish!' Mikki snorted. 'What the fuck are you talking about. Possessed! What nonsense. How do you expect me to believe such nonsense?'

'Look at her,' he said, 'See…the eyes…no expression…dilated. These are the symptoms. Poor girl. The devil has taken over her body. We can't do anything for her…but pray to the Lord.' Mikki got to her feet angrily and shouted, 'I've had enough. I hold you entirely responsible for wrecking my sister's mind. You! It's you! It's because of your influence that she has started fooling around with all this mumbo-jumbo. I'd told you to leave her alone. You have no right to destroy her life like this.'

The doctor looked around furtively. 'Please calm down. I'll explain everything to you. But keep your voice low…please.' Alisha had been sitting through this exchange wordlessly, her eyes blank, a beatific smile on her lips. Dr Kurien continued, 'We broke off—I don't know whether Alisha told you that. I said to her, "It is finished. We are committing a mortal sin. We will have to pay for it." And I did—I nearly lost my child—it was that night I decided. God was sending me a message…a warning…I had the blood of my own child on my hands that night…it was the final sign. I was with your sister…my flesh too weak to resist the temptation. My child developed a sudden fever…a mysterious one. My wife tried to reach me…nobody knew where I was. The child was slipping into delirium. The fever had shot up the spine and would've got to the brain…while your sister and I enjoyed ourselves…adultery…a sin. When I got home, it was four in the morning. My wife was weeping uncontrollably. A priest had been summoned. Everybody had given up hope. I saw my child lying on the bed helplessly…and I swore to myself that if I managed to save his little life, I would never see your sister again. God was punishing me. It was too much of a price to pay for lust…for desire. I rushed my son into emergency…it was meningitis…and it could've been fatal had it not been diagnosed on time. I stayed by his bedside night and day for twelve long days while Michael hovered between life and death. Alisha tried to see me several times. Please…don't get me wrong. I loved your sister…I still do…but it was wrong. The love was wrong. We were both sinners. That is when she started acting strangely. At first I thought it was only to attract my attention and get me back. But soon I realized that the devil had seized her body…she was no longer herself. I told her to see a priest. I don't know what happened after that. I wanted to keep my oath. My son recovered gradually, but he will never be the same again. Never. You see…I've had to pay a terrible price…terrible.'

Mikki didn't know how to react to what she'd heard. She felt defeated…and immensely tired. But she knew Alisha was the priority…Alisha needed help. Mikki turned to the doctor and said bluntly, 'Look doctor…I'm sorry about your son. But right now I'm concerned about my sister. I have to do something for her. I'm afraid I do not believe in possessions. I suspect what's happening to her is something far worse than the devil entering her body. In fact, the devil has a name. No, it isn't Satan. It's drugs. Alisha is on drugs. And you have been giving them to her. Admit it. Or don't. But you know and I know, Dr Kurien.'

'It is up to you to believe what you want…as I told you…she is out of my life.'

Mikki raised her sister up gently and walked out of the place. She never wanted Alisha to come anywhere near the doctor again. And for the first time Mikki was confident Alisha wouldn't want to. Dr Kurien was finally out of her system. Like the drugs that Mikki was determined to flush out.

*

Alisha's blood test established the presence of smack. Mikki, with Lucio's help, got her admitted into an intensive therapy programme under the supervision of a young doctor who had already become a legend in the field. Mikki knew after the first session itself that Alisha was on the mend. It was now time to worry about herself. She'd lost two more kilos during the last month. She couldn't fit into any of her clothes. She had to have most of her sari blouses taken in. People at the office openly expressed their anxiety over her deteriorating health. Shanay, in particular, repeatedly told her to take time off and have further investigations done. But Mikki was resisting all efforts to get better. She had lost the will to live. The tension of coping with the crises that had started to beset her life seemed to overwhelm her. After Binny died something in her had been killed too. Mikki had started to believe her life was jinxed. That she was blighted forever. But she hadn't dared to voice these thoughts to anybody—not even to Amy. And now with Alisha's present predicament, Mikki felt a rage buliding up within her. A rage that didn't have an outlet. 'Why me?' she asked herself as she fell back on her enormous bed at night. There was no solution in sight. About the only comforting factor in her life was the business side, which was on the upswing once more. Mentally, she thanked Binny for putting all the companies back on the track. As of now, there were no imminent threats looming over her head. No take-over bids, no internal sabotage. And the financial picture looked almost healthy for the first time in five years. Mikki wished she could derive some pleasure, some satisfaction, from those victories. But all she felt was a deep sense of betrayal and loss.

Alisha had withdrawn into a shell. Lucio assured Mikki that it was an expected reaction—one stage in the long drawn out therapy. 'There will be worse reactions, darling,' he warned Mikki without realizing the effect of his words on her. 'Like what?' Mikki asked holding her breath. 'Oh...she'll probably go into withdrawal...shakes and all. Maybe not since she wasn't as far gone as I was when I dried out. But prepare yourself for massive depressions and tantrums, anyway,' Lucio concluded cheerfully before dashing off to supervise another *haute cuisine* dinner menu.

'That's all I need,' Mikki sighed as she got dressed for the office.

*

'You're still not dead,' the voice chuckled over the telephone, 'quite a survivor, aren't you?' he carried on. Mikki clung to the receiver. It had been months since the last call and she'd started to believe the anonymous caller was out of her life permanently. And now, as she pored over a project report with nobody except the office peon in the building, a familiar fear crept over her. 'I would've thought it was easy to get rid of a slip of a girl like you. But no...you've successfully evaded death so far. But for how much longer can you run? Aren't you tired? Don't you feel like giving up? For what are you doing all this—working so hard? You have nobody left. No parents, no husband, no children. Nobody. And don't talk about that sister—she will sell you to a drug peddler tomorrow if the need arises. That girl is a whore. No morals. No scruples. So...why? Ask yourself that...why are you playing this dangerous game? Give up. Give up. And your life will be spared. Remember, you don't stand a chance—no chance at all. Your family is to be wiped out—you hear? *Khatam*, finished. You are just a speck...a fly...an ant. It won't take too much of an effort to blow you away. But first, you have to accept defeat. It is not in your stars to enjoy the fruits of your father's evil efforts. Yes—evil. That's what he was. The people he trampled on will never forgive him or his family.' Click. Once again, Mikki was left hanging on to the receiver, staring intensely at nothing in particular. Concentrating on the voice. She was sure she'd heard it before. But where? When? To whom did it belong? She had to find out...but how? The sharp knock on the door startled her. Mikki jumped out of her skin. It was only the peon wanting to know whether he should fetch her some hot tea and a *dosa* from the Udupi restaurant across the street. 'No, thank you,' Mikki told him, 'I'll be leaving soon.'

She hated to go home. She missed Alisha's carefree laughter and her impish jokes. The house was like a tomb with wraith-like servants inhabiting it. The silence would get her down the moment she entered. She'd rush to her room and put on music just to break the stillness. She'd virtually stopped going out. It was something that bothered Dhondu and Gangubai who were accustomed to waiting on her each evening as she dressed for a party. But Mikki didn't have the energy. Nor the inclination. She'd lost touch with her old crowd. Binny's friends shunned her as much as she shunned them. Her business associates were much too old and much too boring for her. That left Amy. Lucio too had drifted off into his own set and found a secure niche within Bombay's burgeoning gay community. He asked her to several of their dos. But Mikki felt hopelessly out of it all. It was work and home. Home and work. With the constant worry that Alisha would somehow fall back into the dreaded world she'd been pulled out of. The doctor had disappeared without a trace. Mikki found out he'd quit his clinic and home and moved to Quilon where he was waiting it out till his papers from the Gulf were cleared. In a way, Mikki was relieved that he was no longer in Bombay. Getting drugs out of Alisha's system was easier than ridding her of the doctor fixation.

The two sisters never spoke about him, which was just as well. There was nothing further to be said on a particularly painful chapter of their lives that they had just about succeeded in shutting out. Permanently, Mikki prayed. Permanently.

*

'I love my morning walks,' Mikki told Amy enthusiastically. Amy was delighted to hear the enthusiasm back in Mikki's voice. She responded, 'Darling, I'm glad you've found something if not someone to love. Tell me...where do you go...how much do you walk...anyone interesting en route...I want to know it all.' Mikki laughed, 'Always the incorrigible romantic, aren't you? Well, the good news is that I've found a secluded area not far from home. I rise at the crack of dawn and it's deserted at that hour. The bad news is there are just stray dogs and the occasional cat I encounter. No humans. And strictly, no men. Terribly sorry to disappoint you...but then I'm not even looking. It's possible that half a dozen hunks jog by, but I don't see them. Does that answer you?'

Amy sighed, 'What's wrong with beautiful young women these days? Jogging in the dark, not looking at hairy legs running past them...tch! tch! In our time we'd make sure to have our rouge on every minute of the day...just in case!'

Mikki told Amy that these days she didn't bother with the rouge at all, even while going to work. Amy chided her playfully and rang off. Mikki had changed so much during the past two years, Amy mused. Matured, definitely. But it was more than just growing up in a hurry. Mikki seemed weighed down and careworn. Amy's heart went out to her. Mikki was far too young to be saddled with so much tragedy, so much responsibility. But if it was a part of her *kismet*, who could change it? Amy reasoned with herself that Mikki's life had only just begun. Soon the bad *karma* would be behind her. Soon things would sort themselves out. And soon Mikki would emerge victorious and free.

FIFTEEN

It was still dark outside when Mikki awoke. She stretched lazily and immediately felt the stomach cramps that signalled the onset of her periods. As she reached out for her robe she considered skipping her walk. Then she reminded herself sternly that she'd cheated twice last week and stayed in bed. No, Mikki decided, the guilt of skipping her constitutional was not worth the small effort it took to get out of bed, dress and leave. It was still so dark outside. She'd come to love this time of the day—when the birds were just beginning to stir and start their dawn chorus.

She went into the bathroom and splashed hot and cold water on her face. Mikki had discovered it braced her and got her wide awake in seconds. She looked at her face closely. Yes—the tell-tale pimple had sprouted in the night. This time it was on her chin. Mikki touched it gingerly with her finger tip. It hurt. She brushed her teeth vigorously and looked for a fresh jogging suit. She pulled her hair into a neat pony tail and put on her watch. 4.45. Good. She was on schedule. In time to catch the first few invigorating rays of the sun. She loved it when its gentle warmth touched her skin and cast a soft pink glow over her face. Mikki moved her toes around in her new Nikes. She liked their cushioned, springy comfort. She was all set. She looked for her freshly squeezed orange juice. It was there in a silver glass right outside her door. God bless Gangu and Dhondu, she said to herself as she drank it down.

Suddenly, the early morning stillness was shattered by the shrill ring of her bedside phone. Mikki picked it up distractedly, imagining it to be a wrong number. Nobody ever called her at that hour. 'Hello,' she said absently, adjusting her ankle socks. After a brief pause, she heard an unfamiliar voice. It belonged to a woman, 'Do you want to know who killed Seth Hiralal and his wife?' she asked. Mikki held her breath. The woman repeated the question—slowly and distinctly this time. 'Who is speaking?' Mikki asked, bringing a forced firmness to her voice. 'Say yes or no. If it is yes I have the evidence.' Mikki paused. She thought quickly that it was time she got to the bottom of this…whoever it was, even a crank caller, she had to know the truth. It was important for her to find out why the person had phoned. Mikki replied quickly, 'Yes, I am interested. Why don't you meet me somewhere with it?' The woman said, 'Good. I was hoping you'd say that. All right. Let's say at the race course in an hour's time. After your walk—don't be surprised, I know your route and your routine well. Can you make it by the paddocks? I'll wait for you.' 'Fine,' Mikki said and rang off. Her mind was racing. This woman could be dangerous. It was obviously a set-up. She didn't want to go alone. There was just one person to call. One person who'd be in a position to accompany her and unravel the mystery.

Fortunately, Ramanbhai was already up and enjoying his cup of tea when she phoned his home. He sounded concerned when Mikki told him about the strange call. 'It must be one of Shanay's tricks,' he cautioned. 'Don't go to this meeting. He is the only person who could try such a thing,' Ramanbhai said. Mikki pleaded, 'Please, Ramankaka, why don't you come along with me? There's nobody else I can turn to but you.' After a long silence Ramanbhai said, 'All right. But there's no time to waste now. In ten minutes time, a car will pick you up from outside your house—just down the road from the bungalow—make sure nobody sees you or follows you. Leave the place as usual. Tell them you'll be back in an hour or two from your morning walk. Also, say you might take longer today since you're meeting a friend. Do you understand?' 'Perfectly,' Mikki said, her voice filled with relief. 'Ramankaka, I can't tell you how grateful I am. Thank you so much.

I'll always remember what you've done for me. God bless!' And she rang off. The ten minutes seemed interminable. After a final look at her watch, she shut her room door softly and left.

Mikki set off briskly down the narrow, tree-lined avenue. She heard the distant sound of milk bottles rattling as the first van arrived at the booth down the road. She noticed the car parked twenty yards down the road. 'Damn,' she said aloud as she stubbed her toe against the back wheel. Soundlessly, the front door opened and a man climbed out, blocking her path. 'Your walk is over,' he said gruffly in Hindi, 'get in....' Startled by the familiarity of the voice, Mikki exclaimed, 'It's you! What are you doing here?' The man pushed her roughly into the back seat and asked 'Why? Does this road also belong to your father?' Taken unawares Mikki struggled to prise away his fingers gripping her thin arms tightly. 'Let go, damn you,' she said, as he swiftly bound her hands behind her back and tied them up. A tape went around her mouth next, while he worked quickly to fasten her feet. She was doubled up on the back seat and unable to move at all. He got in behind the wheel and put the car into gear. He rolled the car silently down the hill, as Mikki lay tense and motionless at the back. The car reached the bottom of the incline in no time at all, and the man gunned the engine. Mikki tried to guess which direction he'd taken. He swerved the car to the right and drove off.

Mikki was alert through the long ride, though she'd given up trying to figure out where they were headed. She realized how quickly one could get disoriented after the first four or five minutes when she couldn't recognize the tops of the tall trees as they sped through the deserted streets. She figured it was an hour or so later that the car stopped. The man's face could be seen now. Earlier she hadn't been able to distinguish his features in the dark. She'd recoiled at the sound of his voice. But now she stared at him and gave an involuntary start. So...that's who it was. The name escaped her...but she remembered him. Who was he...Papa's driver? Watchman? Peon? Clerk? Someone from the distant past. She'd seen him last as he stood in the foyer of their home with Papa shouting something angrily at him. She couldn't recall the words. But she knew her mother had been very agitated and had tried to drag Papa into the house. She also remembered the other watchmen running up and starting to beat the man mercilessly while Papa watched...and then laughed. Yes, she'd never forgotten that laugh...and the man's expression as he stood defiantly, spitting at her father, cursing him, kicking at the men who were raining blows on his body and hitting him with sticks. Mikki had watched it all from her window upstairs, till Gangu had come and dragged her away saying, '*Badmash*, serves him right. Seth was too kind to him. Too good to him.' Mikki had been fascinated by the violence of the scene, unable to understand how her father could be a part of it. She'd tried asking her mother who, in her usual manner, had told her to forget the whole thing, go to her room, and play with her dolls.

It came back to her as she saw the man sneering. He pulled her out of the car and untied her legs so she could get to her feet. He gave her a shove and said, 'Walk...or I'll break your legs.' She didn't know where she was. It looked like an outhouse of an abandoned factory, or a textile mill. She couldn't really tell since it was still quite dark. The man pushed her into a dingy shed and came in behind her. He placed her on some sacking in one corner and stood over her, his lips curled, his eyes narrowed. 'Don't worry...I'm not going to rape you. That was your father's speciality. And he paid with his life for it. No, I'm not rapist. But I will not spare you either. You will suffer—like he made my woman suffer. You will die—like she died.'

Mikki was shivering as she tried to make sense of what the crazed man was saying. Her mind switched from terror to complete bafflement. Whose man was this? Could Ramanbhai have set this up? Or were Shanay and he colluding in some way? Who was the woman who'd made that call? Were they all part of the same gang?

Mikki made guttural sounds through the gag over her mouth. He turned to stare at her and then bent over to pull off the tape. 'Look at you...like a tiny sparrow. A *chidiya*. I can snap you into two with one hand. No problem. Rich people. So much food but nobody to eat it. Right?' Mikki touched her raw mouth and then ran her tongue over her dry lips. 'I can't remember your name,' she said to the man. 'What was it? Hukam Singh, Ram Pyare, Hanuman *bhaiya*... what was it? I was very young at the time, I've forgotten. But I remember your face very well.' He looked at her and snapped, 'Don't talk too much, bitch! Remember, I'm not your gurkha any more. You can't speak to me as if I'm your servant.'

Mikki decided to keep quiet for the moment. The man seemed

tense, as if he was waiting for someone. After twenty agonizing minutes, she heard the sound of an approaching car. The man leapt to his feet and grabbed hold of her, covering her mouth with one rough, smelly hand. Mikki thought she was going to suffocate. The rickety door opened slightly and a voice asked, 'Have you got her?' she recognized Ramanbhai's nasal accents immediately. The man said, 'Yes. The bird is in our cage.' Ramanbhai strode in and stood over her. The man released her. Ramanbhai clicked his fingers and asked him to wait outside.

Mikki stared at Ramanbhai. 'So, it was you all along. I should have known.' Ramanbhai didn't seem to be in a particular hurry. He surveyed her calmly and said, 'Tch! Tch! What a state you've been reduced to!' Mikki cut him short by saying, 'Tell me what you want. I know you're going to kill me...but let's get on with it fast.' Ramanbhai shook his head slowly. 'Still the same arrogant little girl. You've learnt nothing. It was this arrogance that killed your father. And now it's going to kill you. What fools the rich can be! Fools! They really think they can buy the world with their money. But look what happened to your dear family! Dead. And you? What did money get you? A widow before your twenty-third birthday. And dead before the twenty-fifth.' Mikki tried to interrupt him. But he silenced her rudely with a sharp, 'Shut your mouth,' and carried on saying, 'What easy targets you people make. Phut! Phut! Phut! I had you all killed like flies. And nobody found out. Nobody will now either. After I'm through with you, I will kill that animal outside. Bahadur Singh. Remember him? You were just a child then. Sweet child. I used to like you. Bahadur...good man. Useful. If your father had not raped his beautiful wife, he would have still been working for you...protecting you. These hill fellows are like that. Loyal. But if you cross them— finished. There can be nobody worse. It was I who stopped him from murdering your father that time. Why? Because I knew I would need Bahadur Singh's services later. For myself. For all these years, I supported him. Kept him out of jail. The poor man is mad. A maniac. He lost his mind when his wife died getting an abortion—throwing out your father's seed. He kills for money. Anybody can hire him. For a price, of course. I had to pay him a huge *supari* for you. A lakh. That's a lot of money, you'll agree. But he has been useful to me. These people never forget favours. He owes me everything. If I call him in now and order him to kill you with his bare hands, he will do so without asking a single question. I've trained him well. See how he fixed the plane's engine? People talk of security. *Arrey* there is no such thing as fool-proof security. Want to know how he did it?' Mikki put her hands to her ears and pleaded with him, 'Please, Ramankaka, I don't want to hear any more. Just finish me off, that's all I ask of you.' But Ramanbhai wasn't listening, his eyes gleamed wildly as he continued: 'It was easy, any fool could have done it. All it needed was a plan, a simple one. He wore a mechanic's overalls and walked into the hangar to "service" the place and check the engines before take-off. The rest was child's play. And your husband's so-called accident: that was even easier; there are hundreds of hit-and-run cases every year. His was one of them. Bahadur Singh behind a truck is a death machine. Good, clean job that was. I told you, he's an efficient fellow. Picking you up was no problem. I could've done it earlier, but the time wasn't right then. I didn't want to be saddled with companies that had no assets, only liabilities. The picture is different today. You agree? I've spoken too much. I like you, Mikki. I've nothing personal against you. If only you had cooperated, none of this would've been necessary. I was hoping you'd be a good, little puppet...I would've pulled the strings smoothly. But no. You tried to become a tycoon like your father. Even that would've been easy enough to handle. After all, I'd managed to manipulate him very well. But you spoilt it all by marrying that man Malhotra and giving away all the companies—my companies—to him. How long did you expect me to wait? And then, just when I thought it was going to be smooth sailing after Malhotra's death, this Shanay business came up. Whatever I did after that, I was forced to do...you understand—forced. I wanted to put the fear of God in you. And I succeeded. Mercara must've been a little boring, no? You came back to Bombay sooner than I expected.'

Mikki wanted to throw up. But there was nothing in her stomach to eject. She thought she was going to faint. Ramanbhai carried on relentlessly, watching her all the time, pausing to see the effect of his revelations, meandering from time to time to talk about the past, meetings with her father, fights in the office, the emptiness of his own life—a life he had surrendered to her father when he joined his office and devoted himself to looking after his affairs.

Mikki felt intensely sorry for the desperately frustrated man strutting in front of her. She knew she should've been feeling sorry for herself. But her focus remained on Ramanbhai as images from the past flashed in front of her eyes. Ramanbhai dandling her on his knees, taking her shopping for her first big doll, turning up late for a birthday party carrying a huge box with a doll's house inside, rushing her father to the airport an umpteen number of times, escorting her mother to the races when Papa was out of town…and here he was now, staring at her with wild eyes. Somehow Mikki found it hard to believe he'd actually kill her. Then she reminded herself, of course he wouldn't. He'd get the animal lurking outside to do the job. But what puzzled Mikki was the wait. Ramanbhai wanted something from her and her mind raced to anticipate his demand. Of course. It was so obvious and so simple. He needed her signature. Maybe he had prepared a fake will. Mikki wanted to tell him he was wasting his time and energy. He'd never get away with anything so blatant. The police would pick him up in hours. Why would an heiress foresee her murder and sign everything over to a stranger?

Ramanbhai interrupted her thoughts. Maybe he'd guessed what she was thinking. Mikki knew she shouldn't underestimate the man, but he did take her off guard when he chuckled, 'You are wondering what I'm waiting for—right? Actually, it's nothing. You're imagining I'm going to pull out a sheaf of papers for you to sign, right? Oh Mikki—do you take me for a such a fool? Do you really think I'd be stupid enough to get your signature on my own death warrant? No. You will go quietly and violently. It will appear like a crime of passion—vendetta, revenge, just like in the movies. As for Bahadur's death, it will look like a suicide. The man is a known monster. All the *zopadpattiwallas* from his locality will testify to that. They'll tell the police about his history of mental disturbance, his horrible past. They'll tell them how he had been boasting about killing his wife's murderer for years. Nobody paid any attention to him—he was ignored as a drunkard and a madman. For all these years he has lived on the fringes, raving and ranting against your father. Nobody knows about me, or his connection with me. They'll never be able to link all this up. Impossible. The police will close their files after some bogus investigations saying it was a revenge killing, that's all. You'll have no one interested enough to find out the truth. Your so-called sister, Alisha, will be back with her many boyfriends, ruining her life with liquor, sex…and even drugs. Oh yes—I know all her secrets too. I've had her followed as well.

Drugs. Sooner or later she'll kill herself—mark my words. And then? All of you will be finished. Gone. I will have to do nothing but wait for the right moment to move in and take over Hiralal Industries. I have the money. I have everything. While your father foolishly trusted me with all financial matters, I made sure my pockets got filled. Why not? If a man cannot look after his own money there is no harm in helping yourself to some of it. How do you think your father made his fortune in the beginning? By lying and cheating and stealing. That's how. Don't look so shocked, my dear. Seth Hiralal was no saint…he was a *haraami*. An absolute bastard.' Ramanbhai paused and looked out as he pushed the door ajar. 'Good,' he said, 'Bahadur Singh has got the *maal*.'

Mikki closed her eyes and thought of her parents fervently. She tried to think of their last moments, imagining the terror her mother must have gone through as the small aircraft nose-dived and plummeted to the earth. She thought of her father and wondered whether he felt anything, realized something was amiss, as he met his end in so gruesome a manner. She squeezed her eyes and prayed to a God she couldn't believe in any more, 'Make it quick and make it as painless as possible.' She heard the two men talking at the door. Bahadur Singh's voice was barely audible as he croaked, '*Daaru*, give me some *daaru*. I can't do it otherwise. *Daaru*….' She heard Ramanbhai saying something sharply and then she heard a dull thud, as something blunt hit something hard. She opened her eyes to find out what had happened, and was surprised to see Ramanbhai lying prone on the filthy floor with Bahadur Singh staring at him.

'*Badmaash, saala*… Bahadur Singh said, looking stupidly at Mikki. She didn't move. She didn't open her mouth. She waited. After what seemed like an hour but was more likely no more than a few minutes, she saw Bahadur Singh move away. She noticed the crowbar in his hands. He dropped it heavily as he went towards the car. So…he'd killed Ramankaka, she thought staring in horror at his still body lying on the filthy ground. She thought of calling out to Bahadur Singh but stopped herself. She inched her way quietly to the door and saw him open the dicky of the car and remove a jerry can and some cleaning rags from it. His movements were leisurely as he shut the dicky and strolled back to the shed swinging the plastic container and humming absently under his breath. He came up to her, his eyes registering nothing. She watched in horror as he opened the stopper and smelt the contents. He towered over Ramanbhai's body and was about to douse him with the liquid. Before she knew it, a sharp cry escaped from her lips, 'Bahadur Singh—don't,' she said. His eyes seemed to focus all of a sudden as he looked straight at her, the can hanging in mid-air with kerosene dripping from it. Mikki said to him, 'Come on…let's get out of here. I'll give you *daaru*. I have lots of *daaru* at home. Why do you want to waste time on him? I'll give you two bottles to drink…all for yourself. And some to take home with you. All right? Come with me.' Bahadur Singh shook his head, 'No…no. I can never go back to that house. Never. That was where my *biwi*'s honour was looted. Yes…in one of the garages there. No! It's a trick! You want to trap me! But I'm not a fool. I won't come.' Mikki continued to talk, her voice barely above a whisper. 'Bahadur Singh—listen to me. No harm will come to you. I promise you that. I will give you liquor and send you home. Nobody will know what happened. I won't tell anyone you killed Ramankaka or anybody else. Promise.' He shook his head again, 'Rich people's promises don't mean anything. Your father promised many things. To me. To my wife. He didn't keep a single promise. Ramanbhai did the same thing. And now you. No. I'm not going anywhere. I'm tired and thirsty. I just want a drink…a drink…just one more drink….'

Mikki heard the sound of the approaching jeep before Bahadur Singh did. She turned swiftly to see who it was and without another word Bahadur Singh dropped the jerry can and started running blindly across the empty lot. There was far too much dust flying around for Mikki to make out what was going on. In her state she imagined the jeep was full of some more goondas hired by Ramanbhai to take care of Bahadur Singh. She tried to crawl back into the outhouse to hide. While she was dragging herself to a corner behind a large bin, she noticed Ramanbhai stirring. So, he wasn't dead after all, Mikki realized. He was grunting noisily and trying to sit up when the car braked within inches of him and someone jumped out. Shanay! Mikki didn't know whether to shout with relief and joy or to shrink further back into the shadows. She kept very still as Shanay strode up to Ramanbhai and roughly hauled him to his feet. 'Where is she?' he demanded gruffly. Mikki noticed he had a gun in his hands. Oh God! So, he had come there to kill her himself! She wound her body into a tight ball and huddled behind a heap of rags. She could hear the conversation clearly. Ramanbhai slurred, 'I don't know, maybe Bahadur Singh kidnapped her...she isn't here.' Shanay put the gun to his temple, 'The game is over, Ramanbhai...the days of your lying to me and to everybody else are also over. Just tell me where you are hiding her.' Ramanbhai shook his head, 'I don't know anything. She's not here. He took her with him. You are wasting your time.' Mikki cowered inside. Either way she was dead. What did it matter which one of them killed her? She heard Shanay's voice, sharper now: 'The police will be here any minute. I've alerted them. We've found out everything. The car which carried Mikki off was followed by one of my men. You are such a fool. You thought you'd get away with this, didn't you? But no... Mikki is mine. She has always been mine. Right from our childhood.' Mikki heard Ramanbhai's hollow laugh. 'What a pity she's gone. Gone! She must be dead by now. Why waste time with me?' Shanay cocked his pistol and said, 'I'm counting to three. Either you tell me or I kill you. One... two....' Mikki heard Ramanbhai's hoarse voice shouting, 'Hold on...I'll tell you, I'll tell you!' 'She's inside...hiding behind that bin,' he said, pointing to where Mikki was concealed. Without taking his eyes off Ramanbhai, or lowering the gun, Shanay yanked him up by the shoulder and said, 'Walk! Let's go and find her.'

The two of them were silhouetted against the enormous door with the early rays of the sun behind them. Mikki knew her time was up and she crawled out slowly on all fours crying, 'Don't kill me! Please don't kill me!' She heard Shanay's voice saying, 'Mikki! Oh my darling! I'm so glad you are alive!' Startled, she looked up at his face and saw him looking visibly shaken. Seizing the chance Ramanbhai tried to grab the gun out of Shanay's hand but not before Mikki had flung herself at him with all the strength she had left in her frail body. The gun went off at a crazy angle and the bullet hit the tin ceiling noisily. Nobody had heard the police car approach. And nobody noticed the inspector standing a few feet away, his gun at the ready. 'Stop!' he ordered, just as the gun fell from Shanay's hands. Another policeman grabbed hold of Ramanbhai while he tried to make a run for it. Within seconds Shanay was holding Mikki tightly in his arms saying, 'Thank God, it's all over and you are safe.' 'I don't understand...will someone explain...what's going on...please...I don't understand anything....' said Mikki before she passed out.

*

'Mikki…it's me!' Alisha's anxious face came into focus gradually. Mikki wasn't sure where she was or how long it had been since she had lost consciousness. She stared blankly at her sister. Alisha clutched both her hands and repeated, 'Mikki…look at me…open your eyes. I'm here. You are all right. We have been waiting for you to wake up. Look…it's such a beautiful morning. Just look outside the window. See the flowers—your favourites…touch them.' Mikki tried to smile. Alisha smothered her with kisses, her face wet with tears. Gradually, Mikki looked around the room…yes, she was in a hospital…how she hated hospitals. And yes—everything around her was white. Her clothes, the walls, the furniture, the bedsheets—white. Feebly, she whispered, 'I hate white, Alisha, can't they change the colours?' Alisha laughed and cried and hugged her saying, 'Of course they can! Tell me which colour you want and you'll get it. Or we'll get you the rainbow—every colour under the sun. Oh Mikki! I'm so glad to see you're fine—yes, you are!'

Mikki spotted a nurse standing quietly next to the bed observing the scene between the two sisters. 'She hasn't left your side even for a minute since she brought you here three days ago. Look at her…I told Miss Alisha…go home and get some rest. But she wouldn't listen to any of us. "No," she said, "I'll stay by my sister's side. She needs me." No sleep, no food, nothing.' Mikki turned to look at Alisha, and she had tears streaming down her face, 'What happened?' she asked as Alisha shushed her. 'Not now. There's all the time in the world to find out all that later. The important thing is that you're alive. And you're well. I want to see you get strong…you aren't moving from here till I'm satisfied. I don't care what you say. You're staying in hospital till I'm convinced you are well enough to come home. That's an order.' Mikki nodded her head. Alisha chattered on excitedly, 'There's a wonderful doctor here…' and Mikki groaned, 'God, Alisha, not another one.' Alisha laughed happily and assured her sister, 'Don't worry. . .it's not what you're thinking. This one is female. A terrific woman. You'll meet her now. And you'll love her. Dr Shirodkar is the best…and it's thanks to her that…that…never mind the gory details. Let's just say, I owe her a lot. I owe her the life of the person I love the best in the world…' Alisha paused mischievously before adding, 'three tries for guessing correctly who that is...!' Mikki closed her eyes and lay back on her pillow, a smile playing on her pale lips. Three guesses. Three tries. Darling Alisha. Impossible, lovable, incorrigible Alisha. How she adored this crazy sister of hers.

*

'Don't you want to hear everything?' Alisha teased. It's pretty exciting—just like a Hindi film.' Mikki shook her head and said, 'Sure...except that I didn't have a stuntwoman standing in for me. Big difference.' Alisha held Mikki's hand, 'Anyway...this is what happened—that morning I woke up late and found you hadn't returned from your walk so I asked the watchman if he'd seen you leave, and he said no. By the way, I've fired him for that, if you don't mind. And the police picked him up for questioning. He's probably cooling his heels in some rotten *thana* right now. Around seven-thirty, I phoned Lucio. He said he'd spoken to you the previous night and that was it. I called Shanay—and he was missing as well. Now we know why....'

Alisha pointed to an enormous bouquet of roses in one corner of Mikki's room. 'These are from the hero of the story,' she said. Seeing Mikki's puzzled expression she added, 'Don't tell me you don't know who I'm talking about?' Mikki shook her head dumbly. 'Shanay, you nut! Who else?' Alisha exclaimed. 'How is he a hero?' Mikki asked, 'I thought he wanted to kill me.' Alisha stared at her wide-eyed, 'Kill you? Are you crazy? He is the one who saved your life. Ramanbhai was the person out for your blood, not poor Shanay. For heaven's sake, it was his plan that finally exposed Ramanbhai. Don't you see?' Once again, Mikki looked puzzled. 'Let me get this straight,' she said. 'Are you telling me Shanay wasn't after our companies and our money? He wasn't going to kill me? I was so sure he was acting when he saw the police. Pretending he was glad to see me alive when actually he'd have preferred to see me dead. I really thought he'd planned it all so as to make it look like Ramanbhai's crime. What about the last call I received—that woman who phoned? Who was she?'

Alisha smiled and stroked Mikki's forehead smoothening out the frown-lines. 'Calm down, calm down,' she said, 'there's enough time for all the nasty details. The police picked up Bahadur Singh. He didn't get too far. And Ramanbhai of course is in the clink. The woman who called you is the wife of Shanay's friend in the telecommunications office. With his help, they'd had your phone tapped. It was the only way. Shanay was sure you'd phone Ramanbhai. He was taking a chance, he said. But even if you hadn't phoned him and turned up at the race course instead, he was prepared with irrefutable evidence that would've nailed Ramanbhai. His phone was being tapped as well, see? Pretty clever of our Shanay, what?' Mikki's eyes were faraway. She asked Alisha to pluck out one rose from the bouquet and bring it to her. 'Thank God Shanay didn't send yellow ones,' she said. Alisha gave her a gorgeous bloom. Gently, she told Mikki the rest of the story. About how the car was followed by Shanay's friend while Shanay went to the police. 'It was important to unmask Ramanbhai in your presence, Shanay felt, because you never seemed to believe him,' Alisha added. Mikki looked wistfully at the flower in her hands, 'Well, you'd better get yourself psyched up. Shanay will be here any minute.' Mikki said, 'Quick, give me the mirror, I must be looking such a mess.' While she was busy running a brush through her hair Shanay walked in quietly. Mikki stared at him wordlessly. He came up to the bed and asked tenderly, 'Did you like my flowers?' Mikki dissolved into tears while he stood close to her, patting her hair gently and whispering 'It's all over now. It's going to be all right. Everything is just fine.' Alisha slipped out of the room noiselessly, leaving the two of them to make fresh beginnings. It was going to take time. A very long time. But they knew that was one thing there was no shortage of any more.

*

Two weeks later at home, Alisha came in with a big pitcher of orange juice. 'It must have been so terrible for you...so terrible...you poor thing,' she said. Mikki couldn't find any words for a while. Unconsciously, she reached for her pack of cigarettes. Alisha wagged a finger at her, 'No way. No more ciggies. I have some more news for you. While you were in hospital being treated for shock and all those bruises, they ran some more tests on you—yes—my favourite doctor, Dr Shirodkar—she was the one who zeroed in on your condition. And guess what...you've got T.B.'

Mikki collapsed on the bed, saying, 'God! That is all I need to hear. T.B.? As in tuberculosis? How the hell did I get that? Don't be ridiculous. People don't get T.B. these days…not people like us. Are you sure?' Alisha said, 'Yes, I'm sure. But you'd better get it from the doctor herself. Let her tell you.' Mikki picked up a bedside make-up mirror and stared at her face, 'Help! I look awful! You're talking about my hooking guys during innocent walks…who do you think is going to look at me? Shit! I need to fix my face.' Alisha took away the mirror and said, 'No, my darling. You need to fix much more than just that…you need a complete body job. Not my words. The doctor's. The infection isn't as bad as all of us had feared…you'll be fine provided you get enough R and R. You know what that stands for, don't you? Rest and Recreation. Got that?'

Mikki was looking utterly downcast, 'Oh, Alisha, I'm just so tired and fed up.' Alisha put her head into Mikki's lap and said softly, 'That makes the two of us. But we can't take everything like this…lying down. Come on. I refuse to be licked by small things like…like, you know, drugs, kidnaps, attempted murders, thefts, rapes, robberies, frauds…and I know you won't too. We don't need all this junk in our lives, do we? I have this wonderful idea…you're going to love it. Listen….' Mikki barely heard her sister as she chattered on and on. But Alisha's enthusiastic words were like sweet music to her ears…she felt herself wanting to get better…stronger. The sunlight came pouring into the room through the enormous bay windows of Mikki's—and Alisha's—beautiful home, bathing the two sisters in its golden glow. Mikki surrendered to its warm embrace as her fingers played tenderly with the silken tresses of her sister's hair, and she drifted off into a light sleep full of dreams…the future shimmered tantalizingly before her half-closed eyes…and Mikki reached out her hand to touch it.

EPILOGUE

The first class lounge was all but deserted as Mikki looked at her watch. Alisha and she were due to board their short flight to London. Geneva, at this time of the year was always wonderful. Crisp and fresh, with dazzlingly blue skies and bright sunshine. Mikki had finished flipping through all the magazines and she couldn't stand the thought of another complimentary cookie or offer of a drink. Alisha was fast asleep on a comfortable, upholstered sofa. Mikki took in her slim figure lying next to the enormous potted palm and tried to see her sister through a stranger's eyes. How beautiful she looked. Both of them had picked up swanky new wardrobes. Alisha's Hermes shirt worn with simple linen pants was discreetly stylish. She'd flung her co-ordinated handbag and overcoat carelessly across the adjoining settee. Mikki studied the polished brass buckle of Alisha's shoes, took in the scarf and bracelets, plus the new Audemars Piguet she'd splurged on recklessly on their last day at the chic mountain resort. Yes, Mikki concluded, Alisha was looking smashing. Her hair was pouring over her face. All that sun had given it a naturally burnished sheen. Both of them had also acquired an attractive, copper-toned tan. Mikki went into the ladies to freshen up and took a long, critical look at herself. Not bad, she concluded, happily. They'd been away from Bombay for three long months. For the first six weeks Mikki had stayed put in the plush sanatorium, taking supervised walks in the well-kept grounds, but otherwise spending restful hours just eating, reading, watching movies and sleeping. Alisha had sworn at the start of their trip that she'd stay by Mikki's side every minute of the day...but had promptly forgotten her vow after the first week and on Mikki's urging had loafed around to her heart's content. It seemed ridiculous for her to also behave like a convalescent, when she was bursting with energy. Mikki chased her out of the sanatorium and told her to go and have fun. Alisha didn't really need much persuasion and happily pushed off to explore the ski slopes and wine bars around the small village where she'd checked into a friendly, family-run inn. She visited Mikki twice a day and kept her entertained with wild tales of all her discoveries. Mikki preferred it that way. She didn't think it fair to have Alisha hanging around the place—grand as it was. Besides, Mikki was enjoying her solitude—catching up with herself. Getting back in touch with all the areas of her life she'd kept on hold.

And now as she surveyed herself in the full length mirror of the airport dressing room, she was far from displeased. Mikki was looking great. And, more importantly, feeling great. Alisha had talked her into going for one final buying binge before heading back. She'd dragged her from one trendy boutique to the next, making her try on pricey outfits that at other times might have made Mikki recoil in horror. 'Go on...you deserve it all,' Alisha had said as Mikki timidly settled for sensuous silk shirts, well-tailored skirts, smart jackets and sexy dresses. Right now, she was wearing her favourite Japanese designer. She loved his textures and the muted colours he used. It wasn't the usual classic she generally opted for, but it wasn't outrageous either. Eye catching—yes—that was the word for her bamboo-coloured three piece ensemble. Mikki had combined it with bone and wooden accessories that blended very well with her jute bag and soft leather Navajo moccasins. Her cheeks had a naturally high colour that didn't need any blusher to accentuate their fine structure, and her lips were lightly touched with gloss. She'd had her hair restyled and it did wonderful things for her face which was fuller than she'd ever known it to be. The Italian at the salon had gone into raptures over the quality of her tresses saying he'd never touched an Indian woman's crowning glory before, 'So silky...so healthy...so sexy,' he'd said as he snipped expertly at stray strands.

The two sisters had attracted attention each time they stepped out together, to go anywhere—shopping, eating, discoing. They'd been interviewed by a local TV network and made it to the resort's glossy society magazine. Mikki would've preferred a quieter sojourn, but she knew Alisha revelled in the adulation. Surprisingly, neither had met an interesting man. Mikki hadn't expected to. But Alisha had been banking on it. After the first few dates, she'd reported disappointedly to Mikki that most of the gorgeous Latin lovers cruising the bars, dazzling unwary heiresses with their permanent, even tans and hair the colour of bleached wheat, were, in fact, fortune-hunting gigolos. Once they'd discovered that Alisha was not flinging cash in their direction, they'd vanished and spread the word—the lady doesn't bite. After that Alisha had been left alone to entertain herself. She confessed to Mikki that what was worrying her was that she'd actually started enjoying her own company. 'Isn't that too terrible for words?' she'd demanded, clearly alarmed. Mikki had replied, 'I don't know. I seem to have survived the ordeal pretty well myself.'

*

Mikki went across the lounge to wake up her sleeping sister. Their flight had been announced and the receptionist at the counter had walked over to remind Mikki to collect all their packages before she left. Alisha stirred groggily and then suddenly sat up—very awake now. Mikki immediately discerned the new gleam in her sleepy eyes and turned around to check what had attracted her sister's attention. Two men. Two good-looking men. And what's more, they seemed to be Indian. Alisha exchanged a quick conspiratorial glance with Mikki. 'Do you see what I see?' she asked in a whisper. Mikki dragged her to her feet and said, 'Forget it...let's go. We'll miss our flight.' Alisha refused to budge, 'Who cares?' she said, 'I'm in a reckless mood. Come on...let's find out who they are....' Before Mikki could stop her, Alisha was half way across the lounge, shamelessly eavesdropping on their conversation, as they spoke to the receptionist. 'Your flight is boarding, sir,' the receptionist said to one of them after checking her computer. The man she addressed looked at his watch—a slim gold Vacheron,

Alisha noticed, and said to his companion, 'Good! We'll make it just in time for dinner. I know this wonderful little bistro in Kensington.' Alisha ran back to Mikki and exulted, 'Guess what? They're on our flight! Let's go. And I swear I'll behave myself…no passes, no naughty remarks, nothing.' Mikki shoved Alisha's bags into her hands and said, 'Unless we hurry we'll miss them…and the flight. So move it, sister!' Alisha was out of the door before Mikki could finish her sentence.

*

Besides the four young and attractive people, the only other occupant of the first class section was a doddering Englishman, complete with bowler hat, pinstripes, brolly and a copy of the *Financial Times*. The moment he was shown to his seat, he put on his eye mask and promptly fell asleep. Alisha's attention was on the two men as they handed over their jackets and Burberrys and looked around for something to read. 'I don't believe it,' Alisha whispered to Mikki, 'they haven't noticed us.' 'They will, they will,' Mikki reassured her as she adjusted her seat-belt. 'But when?' Alisha moaned, 'before we know it, we'll be on the other side.' Mikki said, 'Calm down. Get yourself a drink and wait.' Alisha squirmed impatiently in her seat. 'Dishy, huh?' she observed, watching them through the corners of her eyes. 'Which one do you fancy?' Mikki teased. 'Both…I can't decide, the one with the mole is more my type.' Mikki nearly whirled around to check before asking, 'When did you notice his mole?' 'The moment I saw him…don't tell me you didn't.' Mikki shook her head, 'Of course, I didn't. I wasn't staring.' Alisha countered, 'Neither was I…what do you think…I'm not that obvious.' Mikki persisted, 'Then how did you see the mole?' 'Because the bloody thing covers half of his face—that's how.' 'Then it's not a mole. It's a disease. Probably infectious.' 'Shut up. I bet he heard that,' Alisha hissed.

Mikki went on, 'Trust you to go for someone with a weird something—like a map spread across his mug.' Alisha sounded irritated, 'You're being awful. I think he's very sexy and very macho. The other one is more your sort.' Mikki was amused, 'What is "my sort?"' Alisha shot back, 'Oh…you know…someone stiff and formal and boring…' Mikki smiled and said, 'Like Shanay?' Alisha looked at her with surprise and said, 'Yes…come to think

of it…like Shanay. Mikki, you mean you are seriously considering…?' Mikki interrupted her by shaking her head, 'Don't push
me, lil sis. I don't know…Shanay is not really my type. He is a bit
scruffy. He needs a better hair cut. And a new tailor—a complete
make-over as a matter of fact…but…all that can be fixed, can't it?'

'It sure can,' Alisha agreed.

Just then the stewardess came up with a friendly grin, carrying
a silver tray with two glasses of champagne and two of orange
juice. 'Drink?' she asked, flashing them a wide, switched-on smile.
'Why not?' Mikki said, picking up the champagne. She handed
Alisha a glass and then raised hers. 'To us,' Mikki toasted her sister.
Alisha clinked her flute and echoed Mikki's words. 'To us,' she
said, adding wickedly, 'and to a great future—with or without
men.' Mikki corrected her promptly, 'No, no. Make that with.'
Alisha laughed, 'You mean that?' 'Of course, I do.' 'But…all the
way?' Alisha went on. 'Yes, all the way,' Mikki responded. 'I had
marriage in mind,' Alisha added. Mikki replied, 'So did I.' Alisha
let out her breath and exclaimed, 'I don't believe this. Why would
any sane woman want to ruin her life that way?' 'Don't knock it
till you've tried it,' Mikki laughed, taking a generous sip from her
glass. 'That's just my point,' Alisha continued, 'you *have* tried it.'
Mikki nodded, adding, 'Yes. And I'm willing to stick my neck out
again.' 'But why?' Alisha wailed. 'Because I like it,' Mikki answered
simply. 'I happen to like being married.'

Alisha shook her head in exasperation and turned around to
stare pointedly at the two men; softly, very softly, she said, almost
to herself, 'One of you guys had better watch out. Your bachelor
days are numbered. It's all over for you now. Alluring Alisha is on
the prowl.' Next to her, Mikki smiled and looked out of the window
at the twilit sky outside. She spotted the lone evening star. Mikki
quickly made a wish. A wish she knew was going to come true.
Finally.